Praise for

'Donald has taken the legen... ..., those frothing-at-the-mouth shield-biters, and made them human, which once again proves that Donald is a writer not only at the top of *his* game, but of *the* game ... It is a wonderful, rich and violent brew. A tale worthy of the skalds'

Giles Kristian, author of the Raven series

'With *The Last Berserker*, Donald has given us the first cut of some serious Dark Age beef. By turns heart-racing, intriguing and touching, this is not a book for the faint-hearted – I can't wait for more'

Theodore Brun, author of *A Burning Sea*

'*The Last Berserker* strikes with the thundering power of Thor's hammer. The tale of young Bjarki Bloodhand finding his calling as a fabled berserker is rich with the earthy depth, historical detail, intrigue, violence and adventure that we expect from Donald. But it is the likeable duo at the heart of the novel, Bjarki and Tor, that makes *The Last Berserker* stand out. Donald's masterful creations will live on in the imagination long after the final page'

Matthew Harffy, author of the Bernicia Chronicles

'A wonderful, blood-soaked tale of redemption and revenge, set amidst the eighth century clash of civilisations between Pagan Vikings and Christian Franks, by a master of the genre'

Saul David, author of *Zulu Hart*

'Well researched detail and stunning battle scenes make *The Last Berserker* a white knuckle ride. A thrilling, up-all-night read'

C. R. May, author of *The Day of the Wolf*

The Loki Sword

Angus Donald is the author of the bestselling Outlaw Chronicles, a series of ten novels set in the 12th/13th centuries and featuring a gangster-ish Robin Hood. Angus has also published the Holcroft Blood trilogy about a mildly autistic 17th-century English artillery officer, son of notorious Crown Jewels thief Colonel Thomas Blood. Before becoming an author, Angus worked as a fruit-picker in Greece, a waiter in New York City and as an anthropologist studying magic and witchcraft in Indonesia. For fifteen years he was a journalist working in Hong Kong, India, Afghanistan and London. He now writes full time from a medieval farmhouse in Kent.

www.angusdonaldbooks.com

Also by Angus Donald

Fire Born

The Last Berserker
The Saxon Wolf
The Loki Sword

THE LOKI SWORD

ANGUS DONALD

CANELO

First published in the United Kingdom in 2022 by

Canelo
Unit 9, 5th Floor
Cargo Works, 1–2 Hatfields
London, SE1 9PG
United Kingdom

Print ISBN 978 1 80032 191 5
Ebook ISBN 978 1 80032 190 8

Cover design by kid-ethic

Cover images © Shutterstock

Look for more great books at www.canelo.co

Printed and bound in Great Britain by Clays Ltd, Elcograf S.p.A.

1

Prologue

The taste of Death

Tor watched her brother Bjarki leap over the barricade of mud, shields and ancient stones in a single bound, and hurtle down the hill towards the foe. His comrades were slower getting past the obstacles – but not much.

They were not many more than a score of fighters by then but they all streamed down the slope in a tight, howling pack, heading straight for the Black Cloak camping ground. The warriors were screaming their war cries as they charged but Bjarki now had fallen silent, and was racing away ahead of the field, with his lofted sword seeming to glow blood-red in the dying light of the day. Tor was roughly in the middle of the swarm, toting shield and spear. She knew that skinny old Valtyr, also armed with a spear, was stumbling along disjointedly only a few paces behind her.

Now they were only two hundred yards from the Christian lines. And she heard the trumpets of the Black Cloaks sounding the alarm, and saw the first unit of troops, half a *cunei* at least, who had been that night's sentries, forming up calmly to block their path. These *Scholares* were the best troops in Francia, perhaps in the whole Middle-Realm. And they could not be caught napping – even by this most unorthodox of attacks.

A hundred paces away now, and the dismounted Black Cloaks had formed a fine, solid wall, a double line of troopers, forty of them, shields locked, helmeted heads tucked in tight, bristling with steel spear points.

And Bjarki was charging heedlessly towards the centre of them.

I

Seventy paces away now.

'Archers,' yelled Tor. 'Archers halt. Thin their middle, thin it now.'

She skidded to a stop and was glad to see her four bowmen, too, halt beside her. All panting hard from the run.

They drew out arrows, nocked, pulled back the string and loosed at the fat line of Black Cloaks, aiming for the very centre of the shield wall. One of the men shot too long, his shaft sailing high over the heads of the enemy. Another shot wide, his arrow smacking into the shield of the Frank on the centre-left of the line. But the third drew, loosed and shot true, and so did the fourth. Their twin arrows hissed lethally into the centre of the enemy shield wall, and caused a ripple of displacement as a Frank fell.

'The middle, target the very centre of the shield wall,' yelled Tor.

All four archers plucked up a second arrow, and loosed again.

And struck. Just a shaved heartbeat before Bjarki's huge charging form smashed into the middle of the thick line of dark-clad enemy troops.

The light shower of arrows had done little damage – one man killed, perhaps, another skewered in the shoulder – and these experienced troops were quick to coalesce again, closing up their ranks instinctively. But the shower of lethal shafts gave them all just enough pause for Bjarki to get his hurtling body inside the middle of the shield wall, to bullock wildly, massively, left and right, and begin laying about himself with his sword.

The blade, wielded by an immensely strong, battle-crazed warrior, seemed to cut through shield, helm and armour, flesh and bone with ease.

As Bjarki shoved the Franks back with his own shield and sliced at limbs and faces with his sword, a widening bloody gap was created in the previously tight-knit line of Black Cloaks, and the rest of his warriors piled in behind him, screaming their hatred, opening up the hole that the *berserkr* had created in the enemy shield wall, and ripping the Franks' formation open. They shredded it, dismembered it, split it wide apart.

In half a dozen heartbeats, the shield wall was no more; dazed Black Cloaks were reeling back on all sides. And Bjarki was still roaring and stamping, hacking and stomping, and slaughtering any man within range of his bloody sword, any man who had the courage to stand before him. His comrades were hard on his heels, howling, shoving the now terrified Franks in all directions, spears flickering out to rip away Christian lives.

Tor's four bowmen, still fifty yards away, loosed two more volleys, and two more, after which they ran eagerly down the hill to join the fray.

'Ward Bjarki Bloodhand; ward the *berserkr*!' Tor yelled as she ran.

A group of three Black Cloaks on foot saw Tor and her comrades pelting towards them, shouted a challenge, and stood so as to bar their careening path. While he was *still running* – to Tor's astonishment – one of the bowmen plucked a shaft, nocked and loosed, and sunk it into the leading Black Cloak's neck. Tor took a heavy chop on her shield from the second man, threw the sword off its painted leather face and buried her own in the man's belly. He made a whooshing sound like a punctured pig's bladder and collapsed. The third man took to his heels and ran away.

Bjarki was still running, Tor saw, screaming, slathered and dripping.

It was clear the *berserkr* was heading towards the black tent – yes, and there, throwing open the flap and striding out, Tor recognised the tall Black Cloak captain. Bjarki saw him too, howled at him like a mad dog, changed direction, and began to bound towards the astonished enemy officer, whirling his red-glistening sword in great loops as he charged.

There was a thunder of hooves and before Bjarki could get within a dozen yards of the captain of the Franks, a score of cavalry surged round from behind the huge tent and crashed straight into the *berserkr*'s massive form, bowling him over like a kicked ball of rags, the iron-shod hooves of the horses knocking him this way and that. The Black Cloak riders, thundering over his body, jabbed down with their javelins at Bjarki's rolling, jerking, thrashing body, plunging their steel points into his flesh. They reined in, turned quickly, and rode over her brother all over again.

Tor shouted: 'No!' And lost sight of the *berserkr* in the dust cloud.

A huge Black Cloak officer on foot popped up in front of Tor and she was obliged to exchange a series of cuts with this warrior, his helmet plume nodding like a fighting cock's wattle – before an archer put a yard of ash through the man's chest from a dozen paces and ended the bout.

When Tor looked again towards the black tent, she saw all her comrades swarming over the Frankish riders, leaping up at the men in their saddles, hauling them down to earth, where they savaged them with swords and knives. Others were duelling with the mounted men, lunging up at them with spears, or cowering beneath the hacking swords and the pawing hooves of their trained horses. There was no sign of Bjarki at all.

Where was he? Where was her big bad Rekkr brother?

Tor stared about her wildly. Bjarki was gone, disappeared – dead, no doubt at all. Trampled under the plunging hooves of the cavalry. That knowledge struck her like a kick to the heart. Bjarki's plan had failed.

Her brother was dead.

Part One

Five months earlier...

Chapter One

The top of the world

Bjarki Bloodhand squinted against the whipping flurries of snow that constantly assaulted his eyes. He wiped a mittened hand across his brow, his face now numb with cold, and thought he saw it again. Something moving out there, on the dim horizon to his right. A dark mass, shifting across the whiteness of the ice fields. In an hour or two, it would be dark again, the days pitifully short up here on this rim of the world, only a brief few hours of light at this time of year. There, yes, movement for sure.

He stumbled forwards eagerly, his deerskin-wrapped legs punching through the snow crust and into a foot of airy powder before finding the frozen earth, a wading action more than a walk, and utterly exhausting. He had run out of food the day before and already his belly was gnawing at the back of his spine, all his limbs feeble and jelly-like. He had been walking for many weeks now, northward, ever northwards. A pulse throbbed in his forehead, and everything ached where it was not numb.

The mass grew slowly closer and he could see at last that it was indeed what he had hoped. A stream of dun and cream animals, a herd, moving eastwards, seemingly endless, grunting softly as they moved. And figures, bundled against the cold but some sporting caps of sky blue and blood red, bold, even jaunty, in the whiteness of the frozen landscape, in and among the mass of the reindeer herd. Five or six of them visible now.

He called out to the riders, who were perched on the backs of their reindeer, and drumming their heels to keep their animals moving forwards into the very teeth of the storm. But his voice was weak from disuse, the words whipped away by the snow-filled wind. He called again and waved his arms and one of the riders, now a hundred paces away, turned in the saddle to look at him. Bjarki waved his arms again, crossing them over his head. An invisible dog barked somewhere in the whirling white. The rider kicked his beast out of the herd and came trotting towards him.

A few moments later the two stared at each other, the big scarred Danish warrior, his long blond hair crusted with ice where it peeked out from under a shapeless woollen cap, and the diminutive Sami rider, his wide face and slanting eyes below the flash of bright colours from his cap, all framed by a deep hood trimmed with dense white fox fur. Now he was asking something that Bjarki did not understand – repeating it, even shouting it. But Bjarki had only a few hard-gathered words of the Sami tongue in his head, which he now shook to signal his incomprehension.

'Clan of the White Bear?' Bjarki said, trying to pronounce the difficult foreign words clearly despite the howling of the wind. The rider shrugged and signalled a clear negative, a waved glove across his chest.

'Where?' said Bjarki. 'The White Bear Clan. Where are they?'

The man extended an arm westwards, and turned his reindeer to go.

'Wait!' yelled Bjarki, now in his own Norse tongue. 'Food, I need food.' He made childish eating motions with his own mittened hands.

The man nodded and burrowed in the breast of his heavy sealskin robe. He fished out a grubby linen bag which he threw towards Bjarki.

'Dying sun,' he said, in passable Norse. 'White Bear Clan towards the dying sun. One day. Maybe two.' And he gestured westwards again.

The bag held three sticks of leather-tough dried reindeer meat, which Bjarki chewed as he turned to face the bloody spill of the early sunset and began to walk. The storm was blowing from behind him now, and seemed to push him towards his destination. One day, maybe two. He would find the clan; he would find his mother's people, with the gods' help. And perhaps her people would be able to help him. Help rid him of this curse under which he suffered. He held an image of Yoni in his mind, her sweet face, her violet eyes, as he walked: a girl he had loved, a beautiful young girl that he had horribly slain. The shame and pain of his past actions drove him onwards into this snow-whipped wasteland.

One day, maybe two. He willed himself forward, gnawing on the dry stick of meat and gulping down the salty, gamy juice as he struggled on.

–

They found him in a snowdrift, half-dead, in a deep and unhealthy sleep, three days later, and erected their *kota* on that spot so that they could bring him inside the shelter. Bjarki woke to find himself on a pallet of thick furs and blankets with a small boy crouching at his bedside staring in silent fascination at one huge, pink, horribly scarred left arm that was poking out of the thick furs. He looked around the tent, a large pyramidal-shaped structure of hides and long ash poles, with a central stone-ringed hearth where a large blackened pot was bubbling over a small dung fire.

A young woman came to sit beside him, bringing him a hot drink, some kind of meat broth, and when he sat up to take it, he found he was naked. He asked them about the clan, trotting out one of his few Sami phrases, and the young woman smiled at him charmingly, showing two missing front teeth, and touched a small tattoo on her neck that depicted a crude image of a standing polar bear. She asked him some questions but he had no idea what she was saying and they subsided into a series of nods and smiles. Then she went away and a moment later a much older woman took her place, folding herself cross-legged beside his pallet.

'I am called Fire Dancer,' she said in good Norse. 'And you, my big Southron friend, look very much like a man I knew well in years gone by, a strong man like you, a warrior from the Land of Lakes and Forests. But an older one. A man in pain, troubled by a wild spirit living in his body.'

'My father's name was Hildar Torfinnsson – if that is who you mean – and he spent some time with your people, with the White Bear Clan.'

'Hildar, yes, that was his Southron name. Your father, eh? We called him Wolf Heart in this *kota*. And he and my daughter... they mingled their essence in love and made... uh, you. I can see it now. You have the resemblance of my daughter Mist-in-the-Morning all around your eyes.'

'You are my... my grandmother?'

The old woman took Bjarki's big left paw in both her hands and smiled at him. Her round face was a mass of wrinkles and lines, the skin yellow and leathery, toughened by many years of snow and sun and wind, the eyes washed out, almost colourless. But he saw that she was beautiful.

He dressed himself in his own clothes and drank some more of the reindeer meat broth and came to sit beside the hearth with the other two dozen members of the household, listening to the rhythm of the talk without comprehending but enjoying the sense of communion and belonging. They ate a hot stew, after a little while, and his grandmother Fire Dancer came to sit beside him and asked him in Norse about his life in the south, and the reasons for his wanderings in the snow, alone, without food or proper clothing, on the traditional pathway of the clan's migrating herds.

'I was seeking you out – you, the White Bear Clan,' Bjarki said. 'My mother's people. My father told me that you had helped him, for a while, to control the wild spirit inside him, a *gandr*, we call it, which gave him so much anguish and, in the end, was the cause of his death.'

He did not add that he and his sister Tor had killed their own father. Driven mad by the *gandr*, Hildar had begun indiscriminately slaughtering people in the small village where Bjarki had grown up, on a tiny island in the Dane-Mark. He did not lie, and he would do the same again, but that did not lessen the shame he felt at father-killing, the worst crime of all.

'Galálar,' said Fire Dancer, 'that was the word your father used for his own sickness. Do you know the meaning of this word, my grandson?'

Bjarki nodded: 'It means that the *gandr* inside you, the spirit that gives you the power and ferocity of a *berserkr* in battle, has taken control of you, taken complete command of your heart, and you are its thrall. A man who is Galálar will kill and kill until he is stopped. Until he is dead.'

Fire Dancer peered at him, silent for a long moment. 'This is what *you* fear, grandson, is it not? I see that you, too, have a beast inside you.'

Her glance was so piercing that Bjarki felt it had bored right into the very core of him. The smoke from the hearth wafted past him and he felt his eyes blur and burn. He wiped away a trickle with the back of his hand.

'My *gandr* is a bear,' he said. 'But, yes, she occupies my heart now. And that is what I fear most – to become Galálar. There was a girl…'

He stopped. He did not know this old woman, nor her people, at all. He had been with them in this northern wilderness only a few hours, and yet he felt the urge to reveal all the terrible things there were in his heart.

'Your mother, my beloved daughter, now lives in the Spirit-Realm with all our ancestors,' said Fire Dancer. 'She passed out of this world in pain and blood, giving up her own life so that you might begin yours.'

'I did not ask her to…'

'It was not for you to decide. This is what we do for our kin, for those we love. And all the folk around this hearth tonight are your kin. You are part of us, and we are part of you. That fellow over there,' she jerked her chin at a middle-aged man who was whittling a piece of antler into a sharp point on the far side of the fire, 'he is called Black Hoof, and he is your uncle. The young girl there, Sunlight-on-Snow,' she pointed at the gap-toothed girl who had brought the broth to his bedside earlier, 'she is your mother's sister's daughter, what you would call your cousin.'

'You are kind to welcome me into your home,' said Bjarki. 'When you do not know me – and I was the cause of your daughter's death.'

'Mist-in-the-Morning is happy in the Spirit-Realm. I *know* this. Death is nothing but a journey from this realm to another. We all must die; even you, one day. Death has value; it can grant life to the living. In the old days, the Sami had a supreme leader of all the clans, the *konagas*, who was chosen by all the elders. A little like your Southron kings, I think. But not a great warrior. He or she ruled over the clans, guided them, made the decisions for them all – but also served the people. And from time to time, when great misfortune arose and the Sami people were dying, the *konogas* would speak with the spirits, and offer his life to them for the well-being of the nation. He would say farewell to his folk and walk out into the snows, never to be seen again – except in the Spirit-Realm. His willing sacrifice always placated the spirits – and made his people well.'

'Did my mother wish to die – to give me life?' said Bjarki.

'No, but she was content, at the end. I was beside her when she went. She had given our clan another member – you. So never forget, my strong grandson: we are your people and always will be. So speak of your troubles or do not, Little Bear, just as you wish. You are with your own.'

Bjarki stretched out his long legs and thought for a moment.

'There was a girl,' he said. 'We were together. And it was good. Her name was Yoni, and I think now that I could have loved her for my whole life. But I killed her when… when the *gandr* was strong in me. In a battle when she stood with the enemy. I did not hesitate, I just slew her.'

'That is a heavy burden to bear,' said Fire Dancer. 'You were in that special state – Galálar – the way your father became at the end of his life?'

'Yes.'

'And you wish us to help you ease your pain, your guilt from that?'

'I want you to help me with the bear *gandr* that lives inside me. To stop it taking control of my body; I want you to curb its power over me. My father said to me once that your people greatly helped him, he said that Mist-in-the-Morning went into the Spirit-Realm and tamed his Wolf spirit, calmed its bloodthirsty ravening, and this soothed him for a time.'

His grandmother did not reply. She knelt by the hearth, reached into a cloth bag and added a few lumps of dried dung to the smouldering fire.

Then she sat back on her haunches. 'Do you understand what it truly means to go into the Spirit-Realm and meet your totem animal?' she said.

'No,' he said, with complete honesty. 'But I know not what else to do. If I do not tame my *gandr*, or expel her from my heart, or kill her – if I don't do something – she will end me, soon; she will cause my death.'

'The Spirit-Realm is the domain of Death,' said Fire Dancer. 'Few have the courage to visit that place, as my brave daughter did, and even fewer have the strength to go there and return to the Middle-Realm after.'

'I believe that I do have enough…' began Bjarki.

Fire Dancer held up a hand to stop him. 'We will sleep on this, my child,' she said. 'You ask a great deal of your kin. Rest now and sleep, my daughter's son, and we shall see what wisdom the morning brings.'

–

The storm eased during the long, long night and when Bjarki emerged from the *kota* to tend to his bodily needs he saw that the world had been transformed into an endless glittering expanse of painfully dazzling whiteness. The reindeer were still scattered all about them, grunting softly to each other, some drifting very slowly eastwards, others with their heads down, grazing, scraping at the snow with their hooves to find the layer of nutritious moss and lichen buried several feet underneath the white crust.

'I will help you, if you still wish it,' said his grandmother, poking her grey head from out of the *kota* flap. 'I am old and tired and my life is nearly over. It has been a good one and I would very much like to see my daughter and my ancestors again. I am prepared to visit the Spirit-Realm for my grandson. But you are young and must be certain of your mind. Think on this matter, Little Bear, and be sure you wish to take this path.'

But Bjarki had already made up his mind. And he willingly helped the White Bear Clan to build a small shelter in the snow outside the *kota*, made from reindeer hides and all covered in snow. The whole group, a dozen folk, came out to admire the 'medicine hut' as Fire Dancer called the small den they had built. Some were holding drums, Bjarki noticed, very strange items – large, flat discs of reindeer skin stretched over a round frame, the surface of the thin leather covered with tiny drawings of animals, bears and deer, hares and snakes, and symbols, waving lines, triangles, and circles within circles.

Bjarki's grandmother went round every one of the clan members hugging them and saying a few words to each one. Some of the band members had tears in their eyes as they spoke to the old woman – as if she were about to embark on a long journey. And Bjarki saw that his uncle Black Hoof was angry. He said things to Fire Dancer that Bjarki did not understand, and jabbed a stubby red finger in his direction several times. But his grandmother talked gently to him, soothed him, kissed him, and, when she was done, the old woman and the warrior both crawled into the tiny tent and sat facing each other, cross-legged, knee to knee.

It was dark in there and very cold. Bjarki could only dimly see the old woman's face in the gloom, from chinks of light that came in through the door-flap. Outside the clan were still gathered around the medicine hut, and Bjarki began to hear the sound of their drumming, softly at first. Complicated patterns of sound, the taps and thumps intertwining, the beats covering each other, layer upon layer of insistent percussive noise.

The drumming grew louder and seemed to enter his body and vibrate inside his lungs, louder still, and then suddenly the weird music resolved itself into a pattern that he recognised: the rhythm of the sacred humming he had learnt in his training at the Fyr Skola to become Fire Born, the hum that summoned the *gandr*, which would turn him a Rekkr, a battle-crazed *berserkr*. A simple four-note tune, repetitive, ancient and familiar.

He felt fear then, not of Death, but of what he might do to these gentle people, if the *gandr* came into him, and if its fury were unleashed.

The door-flap of the medicine hut flipped open in a glare of white and a male hand thrust a small clay pot inside, which Fire Dancer accepted. Bjarki had time to see that there was something dark smouldering inside the earthenware before the flap closed and all was dark once more. He smelled it then, the rank, vegetable stink of the smoke, with notes of dusty sweetness. His nose began to itch, his throat becoming dry.

His grandmother put a steadying hand on his shoulder. 'Do not cough,' she said. 'Take in the essence of the spirit-smoke as deeply as you can. Hold it within your body. Allow the smoke to carry you away.'

He sensed the smouldering pot beneath his chin and leaned forwards to breathe the rich smoke deeply down into his lungs. He felt a mild burn in his lungs and a trickle of warmth in his stomach. A wild sense of near suffocation, initially, almost like a drowning, and then, and then… fine tendrils of exquisite softness began to spread through his whole body and he felt a huge, delicious relaxation, a dissolving of all his muscles, tendons and bones, as if he were floating on a warm sea of scented oil.

'Hold it, hold it in,' said his grandmother. Bjarki did as she said.

A lovely, comforting sense of well-being followed, and a warm grey nothingness tucked itself around his body like a thick, doughy blanket.

Chapter Two

Unexpected guests

Tor split the last log with a neat, single blow from her woodsman's axe; the two halves sprang apart with a crack, both cords toppling off the fat chopping stump and releasing the pleasant resinous scent of broken pine.

The young woman bent with a tiny grunt and retrieved the two split pieces of wood and threw them – accurately – towards the large woodpile under the birch bark roof-shelter by the wall of the longhouse. As the final cord of wood clattered into place, she straightened and put a hand in the small of her back, pushing in to ease the ache of her morning labours.

She called out: 'Inge! Inge! Those pigs will not feed themselves – do you want them to starve?' and hearing no response, she swung the axe once more and buried the blade in the stump, then she walked towards the shed where the animal feed was kept, muttering, 'That good-for-nothing thrall, that day-dreaming slug-a-bed girl…' like a grumpy grandmother, though she was a pretty redhead of no more than twenty-two summers.

She filled a pannier with dried peas, scraping the dirt bottom of the hopper to catch up the last few powdery grey pellets. And thinking, *The hogs will need to start foraging for themselves in the woods soon, when the last of the snow is gone.* The peas had been bought by the sackful at the autumn equinox market in Gavle, as had almost everything the hungry household had consumed in the past six months. And there was scant money left to buy more. So the pigs must be put out to forage, and she would soon have to take her bow out and find some spring game, too.

When she and her brother had picked this spot to make their home – Bearstead they had called it – they had thought more about seclusion and safety than suitability of the soil for crops. And farming had proved to be harder than she had ever imagined it would. She had been bred to be a proud warrior, not a plough-pusher. The winter rye she had sown before the harsh weather set in had turned purple and brown and rotted in the small rocky field that Bjarki had cleared and hand-ploughed before he departed. The cabbages she had planted in the plot behind the longhouse had never grown at all. Birds or wild animals had got them all, she suspected.

Her own stomach gave a little gurgle then. The hogs were not the only ones who needed to be fed. Early spring was the hardest time of year for people as well as beasts. The hungry time, they called it. The winter supplies were all eaten up, all the oats and barley she had bought in Gavle were gone. Yes, she would take up her bow, tomorrow, and Inge would, too – the girl was fast becoming a fine shot under her steward Ulli's tutelage – and they would bring home some venison for the pot, maybe a hare or a pigeon or two. The sea was no more than a morning's walk to the east, in any case, and she could look for mussels, whelks and limpets on the rocky shore, if they became truly hungry. It was time to get the kitchen garden dug over, too, before attempting a spring planting. Ulli could do that, although it was a job for a younger man. She wished, then, that her brother would come home from his travels in the far north, in the snow lands of the Sami. She hated to admit it, but she missed the big oaf.

They would survive, no doubt. But it would cost all of the remaining silver she possessed just to buy enough grain to last them till the summer.

'Inge,' she muttered, 'where are you, girl?' She bent to scoop up the last dried peas with the pannier – and froze in mid-motion, now quite still, bent over the hopper, certain that she had heard an unnatural sound.

She left the pannier, half-full of peas, at the bottom of the feed bin, straightened up and casually sauntered back over to the chopping stump, where she levered the axe's blade free of the clinging wood.

She wished more than anything else that she had remembered to strap on her long seax that morning; she felt the absence of that brutal, single-bladed fighting knife hanging over the loins, the smooth bone handle placed *just so* for her right hand. But the habit of arming herself when she woke each day at dawn had fallen off over the snowy months.

And now Tor cursed herself for a lazy, complacent fool.

She stood perfectly still, listening for a long while. Looking round at the perimeter of her steading. Fifty paces away from the longhouse, the woods began, a long curve of dark pine. The trees thinner at first, where they had been culled for timber and firewood, became an impenetrable wall of blackness deeper in the virgin wild. She could hear nothing from the treeline, save the whisper of the wind in their top branches, nor see any movement. Perhaps it had been an animal – a deer. Or perhaps, and her breath caught at this sweet thought, a bear. Her own beloved bear cub.

She missed Garm terribly – an affectionate young creature she had raised since he was a few-months-old cub. She had found him orphaned in a snowy cave in far-off Thuringia and had nurtured, fed and loved him fiercely ever since. But Garm was fully grown now. A massive shaggy black beast. Then, in the autumn, one day, he had not returned as usual to the longhouse after a day of contented browsing for berries and nuts in the woods. At first Tor had not been alarmed, the curious young bear had probably found something interesting, the carcass of a deer, or a glorious cache of wild honey in the bole of an old tree, and Garm was quite big and strong enough not to need to fear anything in this sparse wilderness.

But, after a day or two, she had become more concerned. She had roused Inge and Ulli from their usual duties and they had searched the forest for three days, making wide loops on foot through the dense tree-scape of Norrland, the remote northern part of Svealand which she had called her home these past eight months. They had shouted till their throats were raw but had not seen so much as a paw print of her boy.

'Likely he has found a nice, dry cave,' said Ulli, who was limping and weary, and much scratched about the face and hands by brambles. 'Bears like to sleep a long time in the winter, mistress – you know that.'

'And what is wrong with the cosy shed I built for him, with nice, clean straw every week and warm blankets?' she snapped at the old man.

Ulli had just shrugged. But they had all begun to make their way home before the sun went down, and the next day, no more had been said about the bear's long absence. *He's just having a nice long sleep*, Tor told herself. *Come spring he'll be back home with us – and hungry as a wolf!*

That was more than three months ago. Now the sad remains of the winter snows lay in long dirty grey ribbons on the black earth between the trees.

She took one final glance along the treeline of the perimeter – nothing there – hung the axe blade over her left shoulder and walked back to the feed bins by the storage sheds to retrieve her pannier of dried peas.

Tor cast the grey peas in a wide arc into the churned mud of the pig pen, and watched the excited snuffling of the three surviving hogs as they burrowed for their breakfast. Two of their brothers had been slaughtered in the late autumn and their flesh had been salted and hung in the smoky rafters of the longhouse. That cured meat was all gone now. One poor hog had grown sick and died of an infected leg wound around Jul-tide. And she knew that they might well have to butcher at least one more of these three lean beasts in the days ahead… *What was that?* She heard the distinct sound of a twig snapping under a foot, turned swiftly from the rootling pigs to see a man, a tall, well-dressed stranger, standing in the treeline.

He wore a red tunic, green hose, boots and a green cap on his head. His features were heavy, his eyes small, dark and close together, his nose thick and prominent. A golden arm ring marked him out as a man of some means. A sword hung at his waist, the pommel inlaid with white bone and polished copper strips that shone *almost* like gold. Not truly rich, then.

Tor took the axe off her shoulder and took a step towards the man.

He turned his head and whistled. And half a dozen more figures stepped out of the gloom of the forest. All men. Tor knew none of them. She thought for a moment about calling for Ulli. The old one had been a warrior and had fought with her in Saxony and he could still use a spear well enough, but he was more proficient with a bow.

She decided not to call out. What was the point? If these men wished to do her harm, to kill her, they could surely achieve it – six against one. But she would not be put down easily and, in the noise of the battle, with all the bellowing and screaming, perhaps Ulli and Inge would have a chance to run off into the woods. If she fought well, she might save them.

She wished once again she had strapped on the seax that morning. She wished Bjarki was here, or even her bear – they would have a decent chance of victory. But then, if wishes were horses, all beggars would ride.

'Who are you?' she said loudly. 'Why do you creep like thieves in the woods behind my house. Name yourselves, if you be honest folk!'

The man in the green cap, the first to appear, blushed angrily. 'We were lost,' he said. 'There is not a road worth the name within five miles of here. We are not thieves! We're the jarl's men – plain, honest Svear.'

'There is a path – yonder,' said Tor, jerking her chin at a gap in the trees, 'which leads to the village of Bjorke. Feel free to make use of it.'

She watched as the companions of the man in the green cap, all armed with swords, seaxes or spears, began filing into the large beaten earth yard in front of the longhouse, blinking after the

20

gloom of the forest and looking about like bumpkins, noting the moderate-sized hay barn, the various grain sheds and huts, the chicken house, the kitchen and the open-fronted unlit forge, also taking in the small stable block with its one unkempt, whiskery dun horse, munching placidly on a net of hay.

'So you men serve Viggo the White, Jarl of Norrland,' she asked, 'King Harald's oath-man, who built his great hall by the river at Gavle?'

'Viggo is dead,' said Green Cap. 'He died in his bed of the bloody flux in the month before Jul. We serve his eldest son Starki – who will surely be our next jarl. We are members of Jarl Starki's *hird*, sent abroad to gather up a spring tribute from all the free landholders of Norrland.'

One of the newcomers, a smooth-faced and much younger fellow, quite handsome, in fact, strolled towards the pig pen, leaned on the wooden wall and peered over, making a friendly clicking sound at the three mud-slathered pigs inside. He leaned in and scratched a piggy brow.

'I have already paid a sum in tribute to Viggo,' said Tor, 'more than half a year ago, when I took these acres of wild forest to make my own.'

'In silver,' said Green Cap, smirking. A deeply unpleasant look.

'It was indeed in silver,' said Tor, frowning at him. 'What of it?'

'You are Torfinna Hildarsdottir, who killed the traitor Jarl Snorri Hare-Lip in a battle down in Saxony and took his head. You claimed the reward – a whole cart load of treasure – from the rich king of the Danes.'

It wasn't a cart load, thought Tor. *I wish it had been*. She'd received less than a bucketful of assorted bits of hacksilver, in truth. The weight of a human head. It had not lasted long. It had, however, allowed her to give Viggo his price – in full – for this patch of his northern wilderness.

At least, until now, she *thought* she had paid him in full for it.

'So you live here now, eh?' said Green Cap. 'In this fine place – Bearstead, I heard it called. They say you live up here quietly with your famous Fire Born brother, Bjarki the Bloodhand. And keep yourselves to yourselves. So then, where is your renowned protector this day?'

'Oh, he's around here somewhere. I couldn't say. Unless he has taken on his bear form and is prowling the woods looking for a snack.'

Tor was pleased to see that her lie had given the man in the green cap a twitch of fear. He glanced quickly over his shoulder at the dark wall of trees. 'I heard he had gone off north somewhere far away,' he said.

'Say what you have to say to me, then be on your way. First, tell me, what is your name? You think you know all about us. Who are you?'

'I am Hafnar the Silent. As I have said, I am from the jarl's *hird*, its chosen captain, and I also serve Jarl Starki as his champion. I have come to your steading to collect the rightful tribute you owe to your new jarl.'

'You don't seem silent to me,' said Tor. 'A little too loud, in truth.'

Hafnar smirked again, more broadly this time, but said nothing.

'And, as you have admitted, I have already paid a tribute this year.'

'You paid a small amount to Jarl Viggo. But Viggo is dead. I am now ordering you to make a fresh payment to your new jarl. Five marks.'

'You're *ordering* me?'

'Yes. Five marks. We require a similar payment from all of the free Norrland folk. I shall be happy to wait here while you fetch the silver.'

'And if I don't pay?'

'If you do not pay, I shall be forced, as the jarl's representative, to take it by force. And if you don't pay you will be deemed by the jarl to be outside his protection. You'll be deemed an outlaw. You understand?'

'What if I cannot pay?'

'Oh, I'm sure you could find the silver, if you dug hard enough. You will have buried it, I suspect. Perhaps somewhere in this very courtyard.'

Tor looked at him for a long while, her head cocked on one side.

'Is it farts?' she said.

'What?'

'The Silent part of your name. Are you famous for silent farts?'

Hafnar's jaw fell open. But Tor heard the smooth-faced youngster lounging against the wall of the pig pen give a tiny snort of amusement.

She looked over. 'Enjoying yourself, sonny?' The youth shrugged.

'I am a silent *killer.*' Hafnar drew himself up to his full height. 'I am the chill terror in the depths of the night. My victims hear nothing before the cold sting of my blade – and then nothing more ever again.'

'Are you sure? It's just that I thought I could smell something foul, something really nasty, but heard no sound. Naturally, I just assumed…'

'You mock me? The jarl's champion?' Hafnar's face was bright red.

'Are you telling me that you *always* smell like rancid pig-shit…'

Hafnar reached for his hilt. Tor took a fast pace back, hefted her axe.

There was a low, warning whistle. The beardless young man spoke up just then: 'Best look yonder, Father, before you do anything too rash!'

The youngster was pointing at the corner of the log-built longhouse, twenty paces to Tor's right. She snatched a look over her shoulder. Ulli was standing by the end of the hall: he had a strung bow in his hands, and an arrow nocked to the cord, which was already drawn halfway to his ear.

'And over there,' said the young man, pointing now at the open door of the thrall's hut, to where a lovely girl, with long hair the colour of flax, was also standing with a bow and arrow in her hands, ready to loose.

There was a moment of rigid silence. Then Tor said: 'You'd best be on your way. That path will take you to the road. But don't linger, my brother is out there somewhere, and he's always on the hunt for a meal.'

Hafnar was actually grinding his teeth in his fury.

'This is not settled,' he grated. 'You'll pay me the silver or else…'

Tor sniffed theatrically, wrinkling her small nose.

'Is that another one? Gods, that's worse than the first. Something is very badly wrong with your guts. Sure you don't need to use the latrine pit before you go? Really? Well, off you trot. Keep an eye out for bears!'

—

They came in the dawn, as Tor knew they would. She had humiliated the man in the green cap, this Hafnar the Silent, in a most childish manner – calling him evil smelling. What was she? Six years old? And worse, she had done it in front of his fully grown son and his men. His honour would demand that he take revenge for the insult, and that he do it soon. So she knew he would come and she prepared Bearstead for the attack. The one thing she did not know was whether he was truly acting for this new jarl, Starki, or whether he was trying to work something for himself, extorting silver from folk on remote farms to line his own pockets. It did not matter in truth, he would come back, and she would be forced to defend herself.

He really was not all that bad – perhaps even deserving his by-name the Silent, Tor thought, as she nocked an arrow to her bow in the gloom of the open forge, standing half out of sight behind the big stone chimney.

He came gliding out of the treeline with his six men behind him like a pack of ghosts in the drifting mists of the early morning twilight. And, if Tor had not been ready for him, he and his men would have been inside the hall and causing bloody mayhem before any of them were awake.

She kept that thought in her mind as she drew back the cord, loosed and put a shaft through his right eye, smacking him over backwards to thump down on the earth of the courtyard. He twitched once and lay still. That killing stopped them all in their tracks. One huge warrior gave a yell and hurried forwards, but before he could reach the corpse of his leader, Ulli and Inge both loosed their own arrows from the stables, where they were hidden. Ulli missed by an inch but Inge's shaft slammed home and knocked the big fellow staggering sideways, the wooden bolt jutting from his ribs. Tor nocked, drew put another arrow into the upper arm of a third man – but by then they were all haring back into the trees as fast as their pumping legs could carry them, leaving Hafnar dead on the ground and his big friend, moaning, bleeding and sitting two yards away from him.

Ulli finished off the second man with an arrow through his fat neck, which laid him out flat. And then they all waited to see what the enemy would do next. After a little while, Inge poked her head out of the stable door, and looked towards Tor in the forge. She gave a calling whistle.

'Get back inside there, girl, they may come at us again,' Tor yelled across at her. She noticed the pretty thrall was as white as fresh milk.

They waited a little longer and the sun climbed slowly over the tops of the trees. And then Tor came out, with a shaft nocked to her bow, and walked over to the two dead men. She prodded the big warrior with her boot but he was as silent as Hafnar. Ulli and Inge came cautiously out at the same time. They all stood looking down at the men they had slain.

'I killed a man,' said Inge, she was snivelling a little. 'I actually killed a living man, I shot my arrow into his chest and now he is dead.'

'What shall we do with them, mistress?' asked Ulli. 'Bury them?'

'No,' she said. 'Take their purses from them. And anything else of value. Spoils of war. Then just drag them both into the forest and let the wolves feast.'

Chapter Three

In the Spirit-Realm

Bjarki Bloodhand opened his eyes. He found himself in a pain-bright wasteland, a crisp white wilderness that stretched for miles in all directions. Across from him sat his grandmother, who was peering closely at him. 'Hold the smoke in, if you can, just a little longer,' she said.

The hide walls of the medicine hut were gone and they were all alone, just the two of them in that vast emptiness. The only feature was a massive pillar of ice, far wider than a man could encompass with his spread arms, soaring upwards, translucent, shining, magnificent. The ice pillar was a tree trunk, he now saw, the frozen surface ridged and rutted like bark. He knew immediately what it was – the Irminsul. The One Tree that was the axle of all the Nine Realms. Destroyed in the Middle-Realm of men but, evidently, still fully intact here in this world of snow and ice.

His lungs were a-fire but he obeyed her and held his air. He could still hear the sound of the drumming, the familiar beat of the Rekkr hum.

Fire Dancer put a flat palm on the centre of his chest and she began to sing a little tune of her own, quite different from the drum rhythm but perfectly complementary. Bjarki's lungs were burning now; he longed to release the smoke-laden breath held tight inside him. He looked upwards, throwing his big blond head back, struggling not to exhale. And above him he saw that the sky was filled with rippling shapes and colours, blues and purples and greens, flowing like swift tides across the heavens – the Northern Lights, they were called – he had seen them many times before.

Some said it was light reflecting off the polished armour of the Valkyries, Odin's shield-maidens, others that it was a glimpse of the Bifrost Bridge that linked the Middle-Realm to Asgard, home of the gods.

Fire Dancer was still singing. Her song had changed, become more strident. 'Come forth, *gandr*, I command it! Quit the body of this man.'

Bjarki felt as if he might burst at any moment. His massive chest was labouring, quivering, vibrating with the forbidden urge to breathe.

'Come out of him now, *gandr*,' said his grandmother. She struck Bjarki lightly with her palm in the centre of his chest, right over his heart.

Bjarki could hold no longer. He opened his mouth and a huge flood of black vapour came spewing out of him, a thick torrent. But not smoke, more solid and granular than smoke, like a thousand tiny flies, pellets of blackness, which formed a cloud. A small dark ball hovering in the air between his body and that of his grandmother, a little to the side.

Suddenly the ball dropped to the pure white crust of the snow, and became more solid yet. It chittered and whined, a tiny wordless voice, but one the warrior knew well. It was the voice of his *gandr*, the high voice that had urged him to kill so many times before. A screeching, pain-filled voice. The ball of blackness was changing shape now – and growing. He saw two orange eyes form and seem to peer malevolently at him. The ball was now recognisable as a cub, furry, curled tight and dark as midnight. It was still growing. It swelled and unfurled like a fern – and rolled away.

A young bear now; no, still growing, transforming into a full-sized black She-Bear, which coalesced on the snowfield a dozen yards away from him. She sat up on her haunches and raised her huge triangular head into the cold air and sniffed deeply, noisily, taking the scent of her new incarnation. She looked about herself too, at the snow field and the huge tree, then pointed her black snout directly at Bjarki and his grandmother.

'*Volva!*' she said, and her voice was no longer the chittering of the blood-mad *gandr*, but a rich, oaky timbre, a voice of rumbling power. 'Why do you wield your foul sorcery against me, witch? This is my man-child. I possess him. He is mine. Why do you interfere between us!'

'He is my grandson, he was my blood kin before he was yours!'

'He summoned me – he yearned for me; he invited me to come into his heart. He sought me out in the Forest and the Fire. And I accepted him as worthy. I gave him my strength. He was made Fire Born by my will.'

'Like all your kind, *gandr*, you used him only to slake your lust for blood. Do not pretend you favour him, by making your den in his heart!'

The She-Bear growled, a horrible sound like the grinding of rocks: 'I made him. And I need him. Give back the man-child to me, O witch! Or I shall destroy you both!' The Beast rose up on her massive furry hind legs. She was huge, a vast black shape against the dazzling white.

The She-Bear opened her jaws, showing rows of long, dagger-like yellow teeth, glistening ropes of drool hanging from her black lips. Then she lifted one threatening paw, fringed with claws, and released another thunderous growl, a sound that vibrated the depths of Bjarki's chest. He tensed his body to fight. Her eyes, he saw, were the hue of campfire coals.

'Give him to me, witch, and be gone from this realm, or I shall…'

Fire Dancer reached into the air, her fingers spread wide, stretching towards the rippling sky. 'Have a care what you say, *gandr*!' she said.

'Do you think I fear you – mortal! You are old. Your days in the Middle-Realm are nearly done. When you return here – to *my* realm – I will make you my plaything for all of time – till Ragnarok and beyond.'

29

His grandmother uttered a yip of command. And before Bjarki's eyes, the Northern Lights seemed to rush down from their heavens and flood into her outstretched fingers, filling them, soaking them with their dancing colours. Her hand seemed to bulge. It shone silver with the rippling power of the heavens. The old woman clenched her hand into a fist, then lowered it and extended a single finger towards the She-Bear.

She barked out one word. A word of deep *seithr* and ancient power.

From the tip of her extended index finger, light flashed out in a thick pulsing jet, all the colours of the sky and none of them, rainbow hues, then an impossibly clear and blinding whiteness. The jet of sheer force struck the She-Bear in her furry black throat, a thick white line snaking around the animal's neck like a hangman's noose or a collar, but of light.

Fire Dancer swept the pulsing finger across towards the massive ice-tree, the Spirit-Realm Irminsul, and gave the digit a little sideways flick. The streak of energy instantly connected the Bear and the One Tree with a line of shimmering white, which swelled and then solidified.

Bjarki looked between the She-Bear and the round translucent trunk of the Irminsul, and looked again in awe. A chain of ice, blue-white, opaque and gently steaming, connected the mighty trunk of the One Tree and a thick ice collar around the *gandr*'s massive neck. The fat ice chain slumped into a low arc, and tinkled prettily as it settled. Bjarki saw the links were secured to a large staple sunk into the ice of the tree's flesh.

'Make no more threats to me,' said Fire Dancer. 'You will comport yourself with all dignity in my presence. For if you do so we will speak together calmly, reasonably.' She spoke as if to a naughty child. 'Behave or else I will dissolve you back into smoke and disperse you for eternity on the winds of time. My *seithr* commands you. I see you understand this now. So, *gandr*, comport yourself and speak. Tell us what is your name.'

The She-Bear made an odd mewling noise, some kind of whining complaint. To Bjarki's surprise, she sat down heavily on her haunches. Her big head drooped; she sniffed at the ice chain that fell from her neck.

'Your name, *gandr*,' ordered the old woman.

The She-Bear shook her ice-collared head, chain tinkling, her spittle flying, spattering the snow. She growled, deep and low. Fire Dancer raised a single finger, and shook it in warning. The She-Bear subsided.

'You chain me like a disobedient cur. Why do I deserve this fate?'

'You think you are the first *gandr* I have met – and mastered? You are not. I know your kind too well – and I know the murderous games you play with the children of men. I know that you feed on the blood that they shed for you; that you revel in the terror of the folk they slay, and I know the agony you cause the ones on whom you bestow your favours.'

'What does it matter?' the Bear growled. 'All men are born to die.'

'Maybe so, but they are *men*, beloved of the gods, not animals for you to herd or cull on a whim. They should not bleed for your pleasure.'

'You do not understand the true nature of men, nor the nature of *gandir*. Nor do you comprehend the bond between warrior and my kind.'

'I understand enough. I know that bond is very old. Perhaps it has even existed since the first man grew angry and picked up a stone to slay his brother. I know that your kind will e'er be drawn to the warrior who willingly lets you into his heart. As, likewise, they are drawn to you.'

'I would do this man-child no great harm,' mumbled the She-Bear.

'So you now say – now you are chained. You *cannot* harm him.'

'What is your name?' Bjarki asked the Bear. 'You lived in my heart for an age, you directed my feet and limbs in battle, yet I never knew it.'

The creature looked coldly at him. 'I am Mockta, Mother of Bears.'

31

'I am called Bjarki Bloodhand.'

'Bjarki – you are the Little Bear. And I am the *Mother* of Bears. Free me of this chain, man-child, and I shall be a loving mother to you.'

'Do not listen to the *gandr*, Bjarki,' said his grandmother. 'She is a thousand-year-old liar and she seeks only to trick and confuse you.'

'The man-child and I are joined for ever. Do not come between us!'

'True. I cannot sever the bond between you. It was forged in sacred fire. Only Death can unmake it. But I *shall* warn my grandchild. Hear me, Bjarki. This *gandr* does not wish to be your mother – only your master.'

'All men are weak, witch, even this one. I have inhabited many a man, and women too. And I know this to be true. The Little Bear shall return to me in time. And one day soon, old woman, I shall repay you for this!' The Bear tapped the ice-chain with her paw, and set it swinging. 'And dread word of my vengeance shall echo around the Nine Realms.'

Fire Dancer ignored the Bear and turned to look directly at Bjarki for the first time, and he saw that her colourless eyes, buried in a nest of soft wrinkled skin, were now reflecting the waves of Northern Lights above them, all the colours shifting and flowing beneath her sparse brows.

'Heed me well, my grandchild,' she said. 'You may return here to this same place in your dreams again. But – remember – dreams are just as real in all of the Nine Realms. Do not let this *gandr* loose – or she will come back into your heart. This mistake your poor father made. He returned here and embraced the Wolf once again. And you know well what he became.'

'I hear you, grandmother. And I shall not forget your words.'

'I have done what I came to do,' said Fire Dancer. 'I shall get up now and go away and seek out my ancestors. Farewell, my grandchild.'

Bjarki looked at her, utterly appalled. 'Will you not return with me to the Middle-Realm?' he said. 'You must go back to your people.'

'I have lived my span – and more. And I was fortunate to have a chance to put my eyes on you, my grandchild, and to help you in your struggle. It is enough. But you, Bjarki, you must now return to the *kota*.'

And Fire Dancer pointed her finger at Bjarki and the light pulsed from it in a flashing, multihued flame, until all the world became white.

Chapter Four

An expected guest

Two days after the attack by Hafnar and his men on Bearstead, Bjarki walked into the courtyard on a sunny spring afternoon as Tor was butchering one of the smaller pigs. She had hung it from a pine tree and was in the act of slicing open its belly and tugging out its massive bloody intestines. She had rushed over to him, thrown her arms around him and hugged him tight. She was slathered in pig's blood, and half-digested pig stomach contents, but he didn't seem to mind at all.

Bjarki was very lean, she saw, his face longer, his cheekbones sharp and mouth drawn. He told her that he had walked more than two hundred miles in the past seven days, coming south through the endless Svealand forest after his strange encounter with his *gandr* in the Spirit-Realm.

She had fed him a big chunk of roasted pork that evening and some elderly apple jam, a small flatbread made from the last of the barley dust in the barrel and a jug of watery ale. And he had eaten and drunk it all, mostly in silence, chewing with an exhausted air but iron determination.

Then, sitting by the hearth, after Inge and Ulli had gone to bed, she told him all about the doings of Bearstead over the past few months, how Garm had gone missing and she feared for his safety; and about Hafnar the Silent's attempt to extort the silver from her, and its lethal results.

'You weren't here, oaf – I swear you would have ripped him apart, if you had been. He ordered me – *ordered* me – to pay him five marks simply for holding this steading. Which, as you know, we just don't have. Not that I'd have willingly given that bastard the skin off one of my turds.'

'Still, killing the jarl's man. There will surely be repercussions.'

'What could I do? They came in the dawn to murder us in our beds.'

Bjarki nodded. Tor had done the only thing possible in the circumstances.

'I will go and see the new jarl at his father's hall in Gavle in a day or so. You say this Hafnar had his grown-up son with him?'

'There was a youth with him who called him Father. He ran off.'

'He might be a problem. If he's the feuding sort. And I recall Viggo had at one time more than two hundred men in his *hird*. The new lord will have inherited them. So we cannot hope to fight them all and live. And if the jarl decides that we must pay the grieving son *weregild*, I don't...'

'We don't have the money. I've had to buy grain and supplies all winter long. We'll be living on seaweed, whelks and rotten acorns soon.'

'Maybe we could appeal to the king for justice? Maybe old Harald Fox-Beard might hear our plea, if we could get the word to Uppsala...'

'The jarl is the law in Norrland,' said Tor. 'Why would a tired old grandfather in Uppsala be interested in the killing of a few spearmen up here in the back of beyond? Harald would just tell his jarl to deal with it.'

'The king is supposed to defend the little man, protect the weak from the strong,' said Bjarki. 'He should be the champion of his people.'

'I sometimes wonder about you, Bjarki. You have eyes in your head and ears, too – do you not understand how the world truly works? Kings only look to their own interests. They're not protectors of common folk.'

'Well, they should be! Otherwise – what is the point of a king?'

Tor laughed. 'Good question! When you become a king you can run around saving thralls from their cruel masters, and personally righting all the world's wrongs. Until then, we cannot expect help from Uppsala. The king would pay us no heed. You're no longer Jarl of the Three Rivers and Warden of the First Forest, Bjarki, with the ear of powerful men. We're nobodies in Svealand, with no silver, no kin, no *hird* of spearmen either.'

'I'm too tired to talk about it now,' said Bjarki, a little sulkily.

'Go to bed then,' said Tor, poking the fire with a stick. 'But here is one last thought before you go. The new jarl of Norrland has not yet been appointed by the king. Viggo the White may be dead but his son Starki has not yet been confirmed as jarl. I think that Hafnar was acting on his own when he came up here. I think he heard of all the silver I won for Snorri's head, and reckoned he might seize a few handfuls for himself.'

'I truly can't think any more. I'm for bed,' said Bjarki. 'We can talk about this in the morning. But don't feel the need to wake me too early.'

'I'll keep watch for a while,' Tor said. 'Hafnar may be truly silent now but I don't think we'll resolve the matter without a deal more noise.'

'Oh,' said Bjarki. 'I forgot to tell you. I ran into Valtyr on the road just outside Bjorke. He is heading for Gavle on some business of his, then he has invited himself to stay with us for a day or two. I couldn't say no.'

'What does that meddlesome old goat want up here in Norrland?'

'He says he's helping a friend of his, a trader, to buy animal pelts.'

'What does he *really* want?' said Tor.

Bjarki yawned, stretched his arms, then shrugged. 'You'll have to ask him,' he said and wandered away into the gloom of the longhouse.

–

'It's a gift, I suppose,' said Valtyr Far-Traveller, who was lounging by their hearth in the centre of the longhouse, grinning and swigging a mug of good ale. 'You make enemies even when you stay at home, Torfinna!'

Tor made a scoffing noise.

'The jarl will have to come after you now,' Valtyr said. He seemed to be vastly enjoying their discomfort. 'With all his two hundred spears!'

Tor was also sipping a cup of ale, which she poured from a leather sack Valtyr had brought when he arrived at Bearstead just before dusk.

She had told Valtyr all about Hafnar over supper and the skinny, one-eyed greybeard, an old and mostly trusted friend of theirs, had agreed that it had been a blatant attempt by Hafnar to bilk her out of her silver.

'But the problem is that this new jarl Starki must be seen to back his man – his champion, you said, the leader of his *hird*. He can't let it go – he would look weak. And a man who is trying to prove himself as a jarl, and attract new followers to his banner, cannot afford to look weak.'

'So what do we do? Bjarki wants to go to Gavle and speak to Starki, explain what happened.'

Valtyr looked across at the big, blond warrior on the far side of the hearth. 'I think that would be a very bad idea indeed,' he said. 'They would seize you, bind you and cut off your head. No, don't go to Gavle.'

'What is your counsel then?' said Bjarki.

'You should buy your way out of this. Pay Jarl Starki compensation for slaughtering his *hird* captain, throw the son a few marks of *weregild*.'

'I don't have any silver left,' said Tor. She was angry now. 'Why does everyone seem to think I have the riches of Njord under my bed?'

'Who?' said Bjarki.

'Njord,' said Valtyr. 'One of the Vanir, the god of wealth-bestowal, as well as god of the sea and wind. Beloved by all the Svear merchants.'

'Oh,' said Bjarki. '*That* Njord.'

'Had you not heard of him?' said Valtyr. 'I've shamefully neglected your education, my boy. Njord was the father of Freya and Freyja…'

'Now is not the time, Valtyr,' said Tor. 'The point is I cannot pay *weregild* to the son – nor can I bribe this new jarl, so what do we do?'

'It somehow always comes down to only two choices in the end – fight or flee,' said Bjarki. And Tor silently nodded her agreement.

'Speaking of fighting, of battling against impossible odds,' said Valtyr, with a cheery wink at Tor, 'how did your trip to Sami-land go?'

Bjarki just shrugged.

'Come on, tell us,' the old man said. 'Did you find your mother's people? Did you banish your *gandr*? I know you wanted to. Did it work?'

Tor looked expectantly at Bjarki. She, too, had been longing to ask him for more details about his adventures with the Sami but he had avoided telling her about it, dodging her questions. She understood he was bone weary and that something terrible had happened in the snows.

'Are you still a Rekkr, still one of the Fire Born?' said Valtyr, with a bluntness bordering on rudeness, only acceptable from a very old friend.

Bjarki gave him a sour look, and took a long swig from his ale cup.

'Will you not tell me the story of your experiences in Sami-land, Bjarki?' said Valtyr. 'Come on. Be fair. I helped to make you into a Rekkr – so I deserve to know if you have successfully unmade yourself.'

'I found my mother's clan,' said Bjarki. 'Eventually.'

'Go on,' said Valtyr, leaning towards him to swipe the ale sack.

'It was all very odd,' Bjarki said. 'I breathed in the sacred smoke, and the clan were all gathered around us drumming up their weird Sami *seithr*. I found myself in the Spirit-Realm with my grandmother and...'

Bjarki stopped, he saw that Tor and Valtyr were watching him intently, and beyond them Inge and Ulli had gathered to hear his tale.

'She made me cough up the *gandr* – in the Spirit-Realm – cough it out of my lungs, as a black... as sort of smoke. Which became a small bear cub and then grew into a massive she-bear. It looked exactly like that huge wounded animal I killed in Thuringia, Tor, do you remember her? The dying mother of our own cub Garm?'

'So the *gandr* had a solid form – like an actual bear?' said Valtyr.

'As real as you or me,' Bjarki said. 'But the Spirit-Realm was completely unreal – it was just a vast empty space, with the Irminsul, the One Tree that the Franks destroyed, still growing there, but made of ice.'

'It sounds like you *were* in a dream,' said Tor. 'Or perhaps that smoke made you a bit brain-addled – like taking Red Spot mushrooms.'

'That's what it felt like – like I was dreaming or drunk. That none of it was real. And Fire Dancer, my granny, was a witch with great powers, and she chained the She-Bear to the Irminsul to stop her getting back inside me. There was a lot of talk between them and the *gandr* became angry. And then I came back into the medicine tent, and my grandmother was...' He stopped again. 'Fire Dancer was dead and cold. Just sitting there opposite me. She died to help *me*. She sacrificed her life – for me.'

Neither Tor not Valtyr spoke for some time.

Tor said: 'She must have been a fine woman. To do that for her kin.'

'And how do you feel now?' said Valtyr. 'Do you feel that the Bear is gone for good? Do you feel as you did before you became Fire Born?'

'No. She is still in there. And she speaks to me still. When I was walking in the woods, coming home from Sami-land, I was alone day after day and I heard the *gandr* inside me speaking, cursing, threatening terrible things she will do to me, if she is ever freed from the ice chain.'

There was a long silence. Then Valtyr said: 'And your power? Have you lost your *berserkr* power too? The bear-like ferocity you had before.'

'The power is gone, I think. But *she* is still there, inside me.'

Tor sucked her teeth loudly. 'That sounds like a bad bargain,' she said slowly. 'It's like inviting a war band into your hall, feeding all the hungry warriors, giving them all your best ale, then they refuse to fight your enemies. Your brave granny did not get a good bargain for her life.'

'At least I won't go Galálar – and start slaughtering my friends.'

'There is that,' said Tor, and they exchanged a look.

'That is a dismal tale,' said Valtyr. 'I was hoping for a joyful yarn.'

'I'm not a storyteller,' said Bjarki. 'That's more your line, isn't it?'

'Yes,' said Tor. 'Tell us a story, Valtyr. Tell us one of the old ones.'

Inge and Ulli loudly echoed the sentiment, coming forwards to sit down nearer the warm hearth. Ulli helped himself to a cup of Valtyr's ale.

'Well then,' said the old man, 'since you ask so nicely: there is one tale that has been on my mind. Do you know the saga of Loki's sword?'

At exactly the same time, Bjarki said 'No,' and Tor said 'Yes.'

Valtyr looked over at Tor. 'Will you hear it again, my girl?'

'If you insist, old man,' she said, smiling, and reached behind her to pull a blanket from the darkness, and wrap it around her thin shoulders.

'And you, Bjarki, are shamefully ignorant of far too many things. So you must pay particular attention to my tale. You may learn something.'

'Whatever you say, old man. Just sling over that ale sack to me.'

And so Valtyr began.

Chapter Five

The Loki Sword

'Once, when the world was still fresh,' Valtyr said, reciting the familiar, traditional opening words like a soothing *seithr* charm, 'the mischievous god Loki left his home in Asgard and set out on a long, long journey. The god, the embodiment of all trickery, liked to disguise himself and wander the Middle-Realm visiting the halls of mortal men. It amused him to play little pranks on his hosts but, also, he liked to drink their mead, eat their meat, and listen to their songs and stories during the winter nights.

'One day he came to the Groves of Eresburg, and stayed for a time in the Wolf Lodge as a guest of the old Mikelgothi, claiming to be the son of a great king of a faraway land and demanding suitable hospitality for his high rank. The Mikelgothi of the Fyr Skola suspected this stranger was not who he said he was, but he was a generous man and, perhaps, he sensed Loki's magical power – and was wary of it. Anyway, he allowed the trickster god to remain for many days in the great shadow of the Irminsul, the Mother of Trees, as an honoured guest of the Fyr Skola.'

Bjarki yawned and reached for his bearskin cloak, pulling it around his shoulders. He glanced over at Inge and saw that she had her eyes half-closed now, drooping with tiredness even as she listened to the old tale. He, too, was enjoying the lulling sound of Valtyr's voice and his word-skill but he was determined not to doze. He hated being called ignorant.

'The kindly Mikelgothi feasted Loki lavishly that winter, seating him at his right hand at the high table in the Wolf Lodge and giving him the best cuts from all the various roasted meats, and filling his horn to the very brim with mead. And Loki enjoyed the attention, eating his fill and drinking deeply, long into the night, every night the last to sleep. But each morning he paid the price for his excesses – made worse by the crowing at dawn of the great rooster that lived then at the very top of the Irminsul.'

'Vithnofnir,' murmured Tor.

'Yes, Vithnofnir was the giant rooster's name – a mighty bird, a magical bird, who had summoned the dawn on the very first day that the Middle-Realm was formed. Vithnofnir was a creature the size of a full-grown ox, or bigger, whose feathers were a thick, shining armour of polished bronze and blue enamel. Impregnable to any blade, it was said.

'The first time that Loki was awakened in this way at dawn, he ignored the blaring cries of Vithnofnir and shook his poor, aching head, drank some water and rose like all the other inhabitants of the Groves.

'On the second day, when Loki's stupor was once again abruptly ended, he got up, cursing, and went down to the forge of the Fyr Skola, which was in one of the caves below the surface of the Groves, where the Dwarf-Master Dwalin, the lord of all his kind, and his sons, laboured in the red-tinged darkness to fashion fine weapons worthy of the Fire Born.

'In their hot, dwarfish lair, the god asked the great ironsmith to create for him a special sword. "It must be a magical weapon," Loki said, "a blade that will cut through anything, no matter what; a sword that will slice through iron and stone as if they were no more than curds." And the Dwarf-Master sucked his teeth, scratched his bald head, but finally he nodded and said he could make such a blade. "It must be completed in a single day," said Loki. And once more Dwalin scratched his head and sucked his teeth, and said that it might be done. But the dwarf-lord then demanded a high price in gold for his cunning work, done at such speed, which Loki grudgingly agreed, although, in truth, he had no gold to give.

'The Dwarf-Master and his sons sweated over the forge all that day and long into the black winter night, heating the iron, hammering and quenching, again, and again, polishing and sharpening it with all their cunning skill, and at last, just before dawn, the new blade was finally made. So they summoned Loki to view his marvellous prize and to pay for the beautiful weapon that Dwalin and his sons had forged. And Loki, who had once again been wrenched from his slumbers by the crowing of Vithnofnir, accepted into his hand this finest of all swords – which was indeed magnificent, with a broad shining steel blade, engraved with magical runes, the hilt wrapped in fine silver, with a great blue jewel set in the pommel. It was sheathed in tooled leather. He named the sword Tyrfingr and promised payment in full to the Dwarf-Master by nightfall.

'Loki came back to the surface of the Groves and standing below the mighty Irminsul he squinted upwards at the very highest branches, where he could just glimpse the glint of bronze and shine of blue enamel that revealed the great cockerel's roost.

'Then Loki hung the sheathed sword from his belt and began to climb.

'It took the god the whole day to reach the high nest of Vith-nofnir, for, as you all know, the Irminsul was the tallest tree in the world. But in the last rays of the setting sun, the god Loki reached the branch near the top where Vithnofnir made his home. As darkness fell upon the Middle-Realm, Vithnofnir tucked his head under his wing and went to sleep. And Loki sprang forwards and, with one mighty blow of Tyrfingr, he slew the cockerel, the magical sword cutting through the polished bronze and hard enamel, as if Vithnofnir were protected by no more than mere feathers.'

'I've never understood why so many people like Loki,' murmured Bjarki. 'Some worship him. But he always seems to behave like an arse.'

'He's a god,' said Tor. 'And gods can do whatever they like, oaf. You know that. Everyone knows that. Carry on Valtyr, go on with your story.'

'So Loki came down from the tree in triumph, carrying the corpse of the giant cockerel, and waiting for him at the base was Dwalin, the Dwarf-Master who was expecting his payment, and the Mikelgothi, who was furious with the guest who had desecrated the Irminsul with murder.

'Loki snapped off a single shiny bronze tail feather from the dead cockerel and threw it down at Dwalin's feet: "That's all the bright metal you shall receive from me, my greedy little friend," said the god. Then he turned to the Mikelgothi and said: "And here is another fat capon to roast, as recompense for all those I have enjoyed at your table." Then he shed his disguise and was revealed at last as the trickster god Loki, father of Queen Hel of the dead, and blood-brother of Odin, the All-Father himself.

'"Farewell to you all!" shouted Loki. And before either the Dwarf-Master or the Mikelgothi could react, Loki transformed himself into a giant eagle and, clutching the magic sword in his talons, he flapped away into the dark night. And Loki never again returned to the Groves of Eresburg, and no one there ever saw the marvellous sword Tyrfingr again.'

'I told you so,' exclaimed Bjarki, 'that Loki is a selfish prick.'

'Hush now, oaf, or you will spoil our story. Finish it, Valtyr.'

Valtyr cleared his throat, and polished off the ale in his cup. 'The Mikelgothi stroked his long white beard,' he continued, 'standing silently for a time under the Irminsul, contemplating all his own actions and weighing them. Then he shrugged, finding no fault in himself, and went about his duties. But the rage of Dwalin, the Dwarf-Master, knew no limits. From the corpse of Vithnofnir, he plucked out the cockerel's heart, which had been cut nearly in two by the sword Tyrfingr, and clutching the huge, still-warm and bleeding lump, he summoned his sons and went back down to his cave workshop deep beneath the roots of the One Tree.

'Deep in his dwarfish lair, Dwalin used the half-severed heart of the rooster and his own dark *seithr* to place a curse on the perfect sword he had created. "The sword shall indeed cut through iron and stone as easily as curds," pronounced the Dwarf-Master, "that magic is too powerful to be undone. And he who wields the sword shall surely have victory over his enemies – yet when he wields it he too shall taste of Death itself. This is my curse on Loki and his blade. May all gods witness my words.'"

Valtyr stopped talking, and got up to put another log on the hearth. Then he poured himself another cup of ale, and drank it all down in one.

'So what happened to the sword, then?' ask Bjarki. 'Did the curse come true? You said it was never seen again? The tale is half-finished.'

'I said it was never seen again *at the Groves of Eresburg*. Loki had many, many adventures all across the Middle-Realm, too many to recount in this one night – and the Dwarf-Master's curse did indeed come true. When Loki drew the sword in battle against a ferocious frost giant, he killed him. But the giant's body fell on Loki and squashed his bones to mush. The trickster god wielded the accursed sword and tasted Death.'

'But…' said Bjarki. 'Surely the god Loki did not *actually* die?'

'He was restored to life later by his daughter Hel – but she made him promise he'd never use the sword again. So he gave it to Angantyr, king of the Goths, in payment for a service Angantyr had rendered him.'

'Typical Loki: to pay off his debt with a cursed sword,' said Bjarki. 'Did the Loki Sword go on to kill this unlucky king of the Goths then?'

'That is a story for another night,' said Valtyr. 'But you know who the Goths are now, don't you, Bjarki? We call them Geats these days.'

'Of course, I know who the Geats are. I'm not as ignorant as you try to make out. They live not far to the south of here, in the lake-lands and on the west coast between the Svear and Danes. Everybody knows that.'

'Just so,' said Valtyr. 'But did you also know they originally came from even further south than that? Hundreds of years ago the Goths lived beyond the southern shore of the Austmarr, the Eastern Lake, beyond the Wends, in the lands of the Slavs. That I wager, Bjarki, you did *not* know.'

'I'm too sleepy, old man, to hear you lecture me on ancient history.'

'Then perhaps this information will enliven you. I believe I know where Loki's sword Tyrfingr is *today*. Not hundreds of years ago. Now.'

And Valtyr's surprising words did have a marked effect.

Bjarki sat up straighter on his bench. 'What are you saying?' he said. 'I thought this was a yarn, a tale to amuse friends round the hearth.'

'How much of that ale have you drunk?' said Tor.

'You complained that my tale was only half-finished,' said Valtyr, 'and so it is.' He fixed the astonished young man with his one bright blue eye. 'But we can remedy that fault together. I told you this particular yarn for a reason. It was not chosen by chance. And I now invite you two, you, Bjarki Bloodhand, and you, Torfinna Hildarsdottir, to come with me and create a fitting conclusion to this most excellent story, just for ourselves.'

'What *are* you talking about?' said Bjarki.

'I invite you to come with me over the seas and far away to retrieve the sword of Angantyr, king of the Goths, from its resting place; to come with me to unearth the very blade of Loki, the weapon that the god named Tyrfingr; and bring the sword back home to the North where it belongs.'

'If you are not drunk, you must be quite mad,' said Tor. 'Magic swords? Odin's hairy balls, what pile of steaming horse-shit is this? Do you truly believe Tyrfingr exists: a sword that can cut through *anything*?'

'Magic?' said Valtyr. 'Honestly, I could not say. But old King Angantyr was a real flesh-and-blood man – there are enough folk around who claim he was their ancestor. You remember our friend Angantyr, Bjarki, Father of the Bear Lodge when you came to the Fyr Skola? He claimed the king of the Goths was his great-great-something grandfather. He said his *berserkr* blood came down from him. Your own father Hildar believed the same thing, he boasted he too was descended from the king. Although, I could not swear it was true. Anyway, the point is that old Angantyr possessed a fine sword that his people *believed* to be magical.'

'So where is it now?' said Bjarki.

'Ah! *That* knowledge I believe I shall keep to myself for the time being,' said Valtyr. 'I would not care for my secret to reach the ears of our enemies. The Franks have many spies in the North, even up here in Norrland. Or so I have heard. They say Bishop Livinus, Karolus's cunning chancellor, has been recruiting agents among our folk. Paying them handsomely, too, I've heard. The traitor Snorri, whom you killed, Tor, was paid by Livinus. Now, of course, I trust you folk, absolutely, and I will, naturally, inform you and the others about the location of the sword as we near journey's end. But I don't want this knowledge to spread too soon.'

'Did you say *others*?' said Bjarki.

'You really are mad,' said Tor, 'if you think we're going to drop everything and run off on some absurd quest to find a rusty old sword.'

'Yes, others. I cannot do this with just you and Tor, you know,' said Valtyr. 'There are great distances to cross, and some not inconsiderable dangers. We'll need a full ship's crew, most likely a score of warriors, all fully equipped and provisioned – but there will be lavish rewards, too, a great treasure to be unearthed, vast amounts of rich booty for everyone.'

'No,' said Tor. 'It's completely out of the question. Bjarki has just got back from a long, gruelling journey in the North, he needs to rest and recover at home. And my bear cub Garm is lost somewhere in the woods near our steading. The spring planting needs to be done, and some of the shingles on the roof need replacing... and a hundred other things. So the answer, Valtyr, must be no. Thank you, no. We cannot come with you.'

'Are you forgetting about Hafnar the Silent? Are you forgetting about his vengeful son, and Jarl Starki and his two hundred shields?'

'What are you saying?' said Bjarki.

'I am offering you a way out of your troubles. Come on this journey with me, leave Norrland for a time, and come back with riches to spare.'

'The silver could be useful, sis,' said Bjarki.

'No, it's insane. The whole idea is as mad as a sackful of badgers.'

'Would it change your mind, Tor,' said Valtyr, 'and convince you to come along, if I told you that I planned to hand the Loki Sword, when we have it, over to Widukind, to help him in his struggle against the Franks?'

There was a long and awkward silence then. Widukind of Saxony was fighting a stubborn resistance against Karolus and his Christian legions, who had overrun most of his lands, fighting in the thick woods, waging a campaign of ambush and retreat into the densest parts of the forest. Tor had been his bed-mate, briefly, and had even thought she loved him, and he loved her. He had preferred, instead, to remain with his wife.

'As bad as that, is it?' sneered Tor. 'The Saxon Wolf is putting his faith in ancient legends now, is he? Wagering all his hopes on a *magic* sword? Come on! Even Bjarki isn't stupid enough to believe such a vast pile of arse-fresh, piping hot pig-manure. I'm surprised at you, Valtyr!'

'Hey,' said Bjarki.

'The Loki Sword is a powerful symbol of the North,' said Valtyr angrily. 'It's a sacred totem of our people, of our shared history and our beliefs. I do not expect – and neither does Widukind – that the sword will *actually* summon a real god's aid, nor slice through solid iron and stone like curds. But it *will* gladden the hearts of his poor, beleaguered people.'

'But if he used the sword, wouldn't he die?' said Bjarki.

'He's not going to *wield* it,' snapped Valtyr. 'It's hundreds of years old. It's more like an old tattered battle flag – or a talisman

– to give his Saxons something to rally around. It might even turn the tide of the war.'

'Well, I shall not be rallying,' said Tor. 'And neither will Bjarki.'

Valtyr, clearly irritated by Tor's refusal, was getting stiffly to his feet, collecting up his wooden staff, bag and his nearly empty ale skin.

'I hear you, Tor,' he said. 'Clearly. And I will not try to persuade you further. But know this. I am gathering my people down in Birka – only a few days walk south of here. We will leave from that port by ship in less than half a month's time, once I've made all the preparations. So, if you do change your minds; if you do decide that, rather than looking for lost bears in the woods, or mending your leaky roof, or slowly starving to death while you wait for an angry jarl and his two hundred warriors to come and slaughter you... if you decide that you would rather take a chance and earn fame and renown and wagon-loads of booty, well, Birka is where you will find me. I shall be leaving before dawn to catch a ship from Gavle. So I bid you thanks and farewell. Now, I'm going to my bed.'

Chapter Six

A thing of beauty to behold

'I want you to leave his shed door open all the time, Ulli. Even in a storm – particularly in a storm,' said Tor. 'And always keep one eye on it too. If my boy returns home, and I am sure he will, that is where he will go. And make sure you feed Garm properly, meat, of course, and honey. Buy some in Gavle, if you can get it. Here.' Tor handed the old steward a very slim purse of silver. 'You'll need to go in for supplies. Get honey just in case.'

'Yes, mistress,' said Ulli.

'And make sure you tell them all in Gavle that we have gone south,' said Bjarki. 'Tell everyone you meet. There is an ale-house there. Have a drink and spread the word. You are not to even think of fighting them if they come here to Bearstead to look for us. Run into the forest and hide.'

'I don't think they will bother me,' said Ulli, 'if they know you are both gone. Who is to say whose arrows killed Hafnar and that other one?'

'You are sure you do not want to come with us?' said Bjarki. 'I expect Valtyr would not object to one more seasoned warrior joining his crew.'

'I'm too old to row,' said the steward, 'and the sea always makes me vomit. I'll stay and tend the steading while you're gone. Return rich!'

'You should be staying with him here as well,' said Tor, looking at Inge, who was pink-cheeked with suppressed excitement at being included in the adventure. 'You're too weak to pull an oar,

51

and a ship full of hairy warriors is no place for a young girl. You should stay with Ulli.'

'Bjarki… *tell her*!' the girl wailed. 'You *promised* me, Bjarki.'

'I did say she could come,' Tor's brother admitted, shame-facedly. 'She said she wanted to see something of the world. You've done your share of travelling, Tor – Inge should be allowed a chance too. Don't fret. I'll look after her. I won't let anything bad happen to her. I promise you.'

Inge was a thrall. She was not a free woman. Usually, the life of a thrall was one of unrelenting drudgery, worked to exhaustion and then, when they were too old to work, put out of their misery like a broken-down mule. It was legal, in fact, for a master to beat his thrall to death, if he chose, so long as he did it in public. But decent folk frowned upon it.

And while Inge was certainly expected to work hard every day for the upkeep of the steading, in truth, both Tor and Bjarki treated her more like a foolish younger sister than a slave; as a full person, not a chattel.

'Just try to keep up in the march, that's all I ask,' said Tor. 'And don't shake your arse and tits at any of the crew when we get to Birka. If you have a problem with anyone, it's *your* problem – understand me?'

–

Six days later, footsore, grimy and hungry, they found themselves in the vicinity of the small port of Birka. The long, exhausting march from their home at Bearstead had been uneventful. They had mostly avoided any settlements, staying on back roads and forest tracks, and heading more or less due south all the way. Once or twice Inge had been sent into a remote village to buy fresh bread and keep an ear out for word of Jarl Starki and any sign he sought vengeance. But apart from her short encounters, they had seen few people in the dense pine forest through which they marched.

Tor and Inge had hunted wild game when they saw it, squirrels, pigeons and deer, mainly, sometimes successfully, sometimes not, but most of the time they trudged through the gloomy forest, hour after hour, their feet making little sound in the thick carpet of pine needles, rarely speaking to each other but making good time.

Inge's enthusiasm swiftly waned when she encountered the reality of so many hard miles on foot. 'We should have gone with Valtyr by ship from Gavle,' she said at camp on the third night, as she sat on a pack of her belongings and poked at a huge, yellow blister on her right heel. 'We would already be in Birka by now, not stuck in these boring old woods in the middle of nowhere.'

'If you've had enough of this little jaunt already, girl,' said Tor, 'I suggest you stir your lazy bones and walk ten miles in that direction.'

Tor pointed east through the tall, close-growing pines. 'After about half a day's walk you'd find yourself at Uppsala, where King Harald Fox-Beard has his great hall. Knock on his royal door and ask for a hot meal and bed for the night. I'm sure Harald will be delighted to accommodate you. If you ask nicely he might also give you a box of gold and jewels.'

Bjarki frowned at his sister. 'I'd have taken a ship from Gavle, too, if we could have done so safely, and could afford the price of passage.'

'I wouldn't mind a king giving me a box of jewels,' said Inge.

'She's teasing you, Inge, just ignore your cross-grained mistress.'

'What would *you* do with all that expensive jewellery?' asked Tor.

'I'd wear my lovely jewels all day, every day when we got back home – milking the goats, weeding the leeks, even feeding our pigs. I'd be known by all as the fanciest, prettiest girl in the whole of Norrland!'

Bjarki laughed so hard the ale he was drinking came out his nose.

'And when I went to market-day in Bjorke, all the boys would see me and say, "Who is this beautiful queen, this marvellous goddess, who walks among us?" I'd smile at the handsome boys, and allow them to...'

'Rob you?' said Tor. 'Or rape you? Most of the lads I knew when I was growing up would have done one, then the other, in short order – and the foolish girl who smiled at them would end up poor *and* pregnant.'

Inge pouted prettily. 'I'd allow them to woo me, if they were kind and sweet and worthy of my love; then I'd marry the best-looking boy and have my own fine house and lands – and I'd buy lots more jewels!'

'At least one of us would be rich then,' said Bjarki, wiping his face.

And this time they all laughed.

–

'Jarl Starki has declared you an outlaw, Tor,' said Valtyr. 'You too, Bjarki – even though you never laid a finger on Hafnar. The jarl figures that if Tor is outlawed, you ought to be too. And Hafnar's son Rorik, the tall lad you saw at Bearstead, has sworn an oath to seek vengeance on you both. Your killing of Hafnar and fleeing to the south was the talk of all Gavle when I set sail from there only three days ago,' he added.

'Am I supposed to be scared of that lanky stripling?' said Tor.

'I'm quite sure you could slaughter him, one on one, in a fair fight,' said Valtyr. 'But he has Jarl Starki's support – and all the men of the jarl's *hird*, too. So have a care, Tor! However, there is some good news, too.'

'Yes?' said Bjarki. They were sitting at a table in a small house in the busy port of Birka, not far from the water's edge. They had slipped into Birka only the night before, at dusk, ferried across Lake Malaren by a kindly fisherman returning home with his catch. They had swiftly found Valtyr by asking for him by name at the busiest ale-house on the harbour.

'So what's the good news then?' asked Bjarki, picking up the last crust of barley bread from his empty platter, and swiping up some gravy.

'I never heard Ulli's name mentioned at all,' said Valtyr. 'There were a few blowhards in the ale-house who wanted to come south after you – youngsters, the jarl's riders, looking to make a name by killing you outlaws. But no one spoke of going to Bearstead and troubling old Ulli.'

'That's good,' said Bjarki.

'Ulli can look after himself well enough, anyway,' said Tor. And then she said: 'Are you enjoying this, old man? Do you like it that we are now outlawed, and forced to come to you with our begging bowls out?'

'No. Of course not,' said Valtyr. 'I have known you since you were a little child, Torfinna. I feel almost like a *fostri* father to you. But…'

'But you're happy that we are coming with you on your ridiculous sword-hunt in the lands beyond the Austmarr?' finished Tor. 'Is that it?'

'More or less – and this will be good for you, Tor, I swear it. And good for you, Bjarki. It's better than throwing away your lives in the deep woods, seeing nobody new day after day, going mad from boredom. If we find the Loki Sword, your names will be spoken with awe for a hundred years. And there'll be treasure – lots of treasure. Not just the sword…'

'Gold and silver is not everything…' said Tor.

'Listen, Tor, at the moment you can *never* go back to Norrland. But with your share of the hoard you could pay *weregild* to that lad Rorik, as the price for killing his father, and you can give Jarl Starki his five marks, too! To garner his favour. Silver will set all things a-right in Norrland.'

Tor said nothing for a while. She hated the logic of Valtyr's words.

Bjarki said: 'We shall go with you, Valtyr. We have both already decided. And Inge wishes to come along with us too. If you will allow it.'

'We cannot take passengers, Bjarki. Everyone must have a role.'

'She can cook well enough, and she shoots a bow better than Tor.'

'All right, she can cook for us, but I hope she won't cause problems with the men. She might be a bit, uh… distracting for some of the crew.'

'I'll watch over her, old man. So… who else is coming with us?'

'Oh, you will meet them all in a couple of days. Indeed, some you may already know. We plan to sail at dawn the morning after tomorrow. Till then, I suggest you stay here safely out of sight. Jarl Starki has many relatives and friends – perhaps even some down here in Birka – and many folk here would like to earn the gratitude of the new jarl of Norrland.'

–

For Bjarki, it was a thing of beauty to behold: a low, sleek, clinker-built, single-masted vessel, obviously fast through the water, recently painted a gleaming black with fresh pine tar and with enough room for eight pairs of rowers – sixteen warriors. It was tied up to a jetty that pronged out into the placid, shallow harbour of the port of Birka. Her prow and stern both swooped up into spiral decorations, the front depicting the head of a snake, the rear its coiled tail, as befitted her bold name: the *Wave Serpent*.

'I know this ship!' he said to Valtyr, who had just indicated the fine vessel, which would bear them all south, with a flourish of his right hand.

'Bjarki Bloodhand – the mighty Rekkr,' said a voice, and a middle-aged man stood up in the stern of the vessel, a familiar beaming red face.

'Captain Lars,' said Bjarki, and smiled, but stiffly, in return. His stomach had just given a sudden lurch as the memories of this very ship dropped into his mind. This jolly seafarer had once taken Tor and him from Rerik in Wendland to Hedeby, a fast-growing port in the Dane-Mark, in a trading vessel, and they had been attacked on the way by this ship – *Wave Serpent* – and its crew of Norse pirates, a type commonly known as vikings. They had fought them off and Bjarki had summoned his *gandr*, made a slaughter of all the vikings and given the ship to Lars.

'I prayed to Njord that our paths would cross again, Rekkr,' said the captain. 'The sea god heard me! It's an honour to behold you once more.'

Bjarki clasped his right hand dutifully, walked up the gangplank and was treated to a pride-filled tour of his small ship. 'These cleats here are freshly installed,' said Lars. 'And we have a new mast – good straight Sandviken pine! And you will notice the old tiller-arm's been replaced.'

Bjarki nodded and mumbled approval. He saw that there were a number of sea chests already on board, which would serve as seats for the rowers. Bjarki had brought his weapons, armour and some spare clothes with him from Bearstead, but not much else, and he had lacked a chest until Valtyr provided him with a strong, capacious, elm-wood one, from his Birka stores, with a B rune burnt on the lid to identify it as his own.

Lined all along the centre of the deck were a series of big, bulky, shapeless parcels, tightly wrapped in rope and waxed linen, and perched on the nearest bundle was a man in a fine blue woollen cloak, which was trimmed with what looked like real gold thread. He had black curly hair, jet eyes and a deep tan. Bjarki merely nodded at him. He had indulged in a quantity of ale the night before at Valtyr's house with a few of the other members of the crew and was in no mood for chit-chat at this early hour.

'May I present to you Aistulf the Lombard,' said Lars, indicating the seated man. 'He is the owner of the goods we shall carry to Truso.'

The stranger did not smile but, instead, he nodded politely to Bjarki, who managed to say: 'Greetings, friend… what's the cargo in there?'

'Furs,' Aistulf replied. 'The finest pelts in all Norrland – wolf, fox, otter, mink, lynx, rabbit and red squirrel – something for every taste and every weight of purse. And I would even give you a good price for that fine bearskin on your back, my good fellow, if you would part with it.'

'Not for sale,' said Bjarki, turning away. The fine bearskin was a personal treasure – a heavy, thick, glossy garment that came from the huge bear he had killed in Thuringia some years ago when he discovered his *gandr*. The skin had been stripped from the animal and fashioned into a warm fur cloak by his sister, a rare gift from her – and he saw now that she was coming on board the *Wave Serpent*, carrying her own elm-wood chest, with Inge on her heels. Bjarki observed several other folk behind his two women, men stalking up the pinewood gangplank, talking quietly, some suffering as much as he from the after-effects of last night's ale.

One of them, a man with whom Bjarki had drunk especially deeply the night before, had been a surprise to encounter: he was an old friend from his time in Francia as a captive of King Karolus, a dark-haired Danish man called Brandt, who was a most accomplished swordsman.

As they all found places for their sea chests, and themselves, Tor seating herself behind Bjarki in the end spot nearest the long tiller on the steerboard side of the ship, there was a general murmur of anticipation and excitement on the cramped deck, and a little confusion, with several crew members squabbling about the positions they wished to occupy.

Once that was settled, there was the business of finding the right oars for each rowing place. Each oar was between eight and ten foot long, but cut to a slightly different length depending on the curvature of the ship's side, the oars in the middle of the ship shorter, those at the ends longer, so that all the blades of the oars might be aligned in a straight line when in the water. Lars oversaw that complicated affair, handing out the long, unwieldy rowing blades with minimum fuss, and only one oar-bumped head. They fitted each length of smoothed pine into the slanting slot cut in the side of the ship, and into the round rowlock at the bottom.

Finally everything was in place.

'Mark well the individual runes carved on your particular oar,' said Lars, his voice carrying the length of the ship. 'It shows which side and in which place in the row of eight it should be used. Mark this well: each oar has been cut specially for your position, so don't take another rower's oar when we board the ship in the mornings or we will all be in disarray.

'And if you are clumsy enough to break yours,' he continued, 'you will anger not only me, but our esteemed passenger Aistulf, and all the rest of the crew as well: since we will have to interrupt our journey, find a convenient pine forest near a suitable beach and cut another oar just for you. So have a care with them, people. Treat your own particular blade like a cherished heirloom.'

The captain paused then for a moment to let this sink in.

'Now, you will also need to listen to, and commit to memory, all of the traditional commands that I shall give: this one is the most important – it means 'oars out', which means lift all your blades clear of the water.'

Captain Lars seized a small ram's horn that was hanging from a leather thong around his neck and blew two notes. 'That sound I just made is "oars out" – does everybody hear it? Yes? Now remember it.'

Valtyr, who was spared the hard labour of rowing because of his advanced age, stood on the prow under the curling dragon's head and together with Lars they untied the ropes and used slender elm poles to shove the ship away from the jetty, the vessel slipping smoothly out into the harbour of Birka with barely a whisper of noise. Inge was crouched beside Valtyr, looking nervously out at the grey water, and at the few other craft in the bay – mostly fishing smacks, which were scudding easily across the surface like huge water insects. The only other person who had no oar, out of the ship's complement of twenty, was Aistulf.

Bjarki had heard Valtyr refer to him admiringly the night before as their own personal 'silver mine' – and it appeared that he had paid for this entire expedition from his purse. Valtyr had sat down with Bjarki two nights ago and explained their mission to him. At the time it had seemed straightforward enough: they were to transport the Italian merchant three hundred miles south across the Austmarr, or the Eastern Lake, to Truso, a Slav port on the southern coast near the mouth of the great River Wiessel.

There the Lombard trader would exchange his fat bales of northern furs for hundreds of small pieces of amber, valuable jewel-like glowing nuggets that could be found on the southern coasts of the Eastern Lake. These chunks of amber were small, light, beautiful and much prized for jewellery-making across the whole of the Middle-Realm, but particularly in north Italy. And, on the shores of the Austmarr near Truso and further north into the lands of the Balts, they could simply be picked up by any casual walker on the beach. Over many generations, the local Slav tribes had built whole towns and created much wealth from this lucrative trade.

Once all the trading was done in Truso, which Valtyr said would only take a day or so, they were to provide continued protection of the merchant Aistulf as he travelled on farther south. They would take the valuable amber consignment a hundred miles down the River Wiessel in the *Wave Serpent*, and then finally the merchant would set out on a well-worn overland route that would lead, ultimately, to the sunny lands of the Mediterranean. Though the ship's crew would not be going that far south, Valtyr admitted.

After safely delivering Aistulf and his cargo to a meeting at an agreed trading place where the River Donau and the River March met, an ancient Roman town called Carnuntum, they would leave the merchant with his new-met friends and set out on their own quest to find the Loki Sword. While Valtyr explained their itinerary, Bjarki became quite dizzy with unfamiliarity of all these faraway places. There was a good reason, he thought, why the old man was by-named Far-Traveller. But when he asked about their ultimate destination, and the location of the tomb of Angantyr, legendary king of the Goths, Valtyr suddenly became more closed-mouthed. 'All in good time, my boy,' he said, 'all in good time.'

Their departure from Birka was neither swift nor dignified. Not all sixteen rowers of the *Wave Serpent* were equally skilled or experienced; some had never rowed before and others were more at home in a skiff in their placid home waters, and so it took a while for the crew to find their unity. The stroke was ragged, to say the least. At one point, to Captain Lars's fury and embarrassment, one of the middle rowers on the larboard side, a young man called Lief, caught his flailing oar on the stern pole of a passing fishing smack, prompting an angry bellow of: 'Mind your oars, you plough-pushing dunderheads!' from the furious, red-faced fisherman.

To which Lief, quick as a flash, replied: 'Talking of 'ores, give my love to your sister!' And that set the whole of the *Wave Serpent* a-roar.

But if their initial progress was jerky and erratic, it was not long before they left behind the curve of Birka Harbour and its rows of small houses, workshops and warehouses, and found their true tempo. Soon they were skimming along towards the eastern end of Lake Malaren, and heading into the series of narrow channels there that would take them out to sea.

Tor pulled her heavy pine oar, trying to keep in time with the rhythmic sea-chant started by Captain Lars, and already feeling the strain in her shoulder muscles. She watched the broad back of Bjarki, for whom this all came far more naturally, moving forwards and back on his sea chest, his back muscles writhing like fat snakes under his linen shirt. The thought of watching this for the next ten days was not appealing – she was already bored – but, presumably, when they reached the open sea, they would raise the sail and she could rest. She hoped this was true, but had not asked anyone to confirm it. Tor's ignorance of nautical matters was profound, but it was something she preferred to keep to herself.

She looked to her left at the man on the larboard side of the ship, a small middle-aged fellow, roughly her size, balding with dark, sunken eyes. His name was Halvar, she had gathered, and he was a Svear like her and she felt sure she had seen him somewhere before. She knew she would probably have to associate with him over the next few weeks and perhaps months – he was sitting right next to her, just a few feet away, and would be there day after day. But something stopped her from making an overture – she would discover if he were worthy of her company soon enough. She concentrated on her oar and the timing of the stroke. And thought about Garm – she wondered if he had returned to the steading and if Ulli was feeding him up after his long winter sleep.

Something caught her eye, some movement, and she looked over to the coast of Uppland, a low, marshy expanse of grassland that slid by on the right side of the ship. Horsemen, a whole squadron of them. They were galloping along the coast in the same direction they were travelling in, the man in front spurred his horse on to a knoll of land a little ahead of the *Wave Serpent*'s dragon prow, and there he reined his mount in.

They were no more than a long bowshot away from the ship and Tor could clearly see the face of the leading rider. He was a youthful man, sitting in his saddle, patting his horse's neck, as his companions caught up with him, about thirty warriors, all mounted. The young man gazed out over the lake at the *Wave Serpent* as it passed by. His expression was bleak, angry. He said something to the nearest horseman and pointed directly at the ship. She recognised him them. It was the tall lad who had visited Bearstead with Hafnar the Silent. It was the dead man's son, Rorik, the one who had sworn vengeance. And the thirty young horsemen all about him were no doubt members of Jarl Starki's powerful *hird*.

Tor turned her head and spoke over her shoulder to Lars, who was at the tiller. 'Best if we camp on the south side tonight, Captain,' she said.

The ship's commander looked over at the crowd of horsemen and, after surveying them for a moment, said: 'Those your enemies, then?'

Tor grunted an affirmation.

'Better if we leave them far behind,' said Lars. He raised his voice: 'Listen, everyone: this command is called "double time" – you all need to follow the lead of the First Oar; that is that strapping ginger fellow, up there, who is called Svein the Horse. If you can't guess why he's called that, I'm sure he would be delighted to drop his breeches at camp and show you. So, now, on my command, we go to "double time" and…'

He blew three escalating notes on his little ram's horn, and the rowers increased their speed, following the tempo of the big red-headed man in the first position at the prow on the steerboard side. The *Wave Serpent* shot forwards, a surprising increase in their speed. The rowing was brutal, the motion twice the pace of the previous beat. But in spite of the burning in her arms and shoulder muscles, Tor was pleased to see the horsemen rapidly fading into the distance as the ship surged towards the eastern end of the lake. Within moments Rorik and his men were out of sight and the *Wave Serpent* was entering one of the many sea channels.

As the flat landscape closed in around them – the thick reed beds were only a dozen oars' lengths away on either side – Tor wondered if she would see Rorik again. It seemed unlikely. They were going far, far away and the lad could not possibly know where they were heading. But if they had stayed in Birka one more night, it might have been a different story.

–

They drove the ship up on to a flat muddy beach on the south bank of one of the many salt-water channels they had threaded that day, stacked their oars between a pair of Y-shaped stands before the mast, and disembarked.

It was late afternoon – and Tor had never been so glad to stop doing anything in her life. Her hands were both rubbed red-raw from contact with the rough wooden oar and her whole body was thrumming from the unaccustomed and repetitive exercise. It had been a long and often lazy winter. Yet she refused to show her weakness in front of her comrades. She got Inge to come over and massage her neck and back muscles with sweet oil, while the evening stew was cooking on the big communal fire, then dressed her hands herself with a goose fat and herb concoction and wrapped them in clean linen. They would surely grow calloused in time.

Bjarki was in high spirits. In just a few quiet days at Valtyr's house, he seemed to have completely recovered from the gruelling walk south from the Sami lands and six days of travelling through the Svear forest.

He was singing to himself – some weird old Sami tune he had picked up on his travels – as he laid out his bed roll, then sat down and began cleaning his weapons and kit: a fine steel sword in a leather sheath, a good byrnie of iron links, a plain steel cap with a nasal guard and round, lime-wood shield with a big iron boss in the centre, leather faced and painted with a simple bear design. Bjarki sat comfortably on his blankets and carefully, methodically began sharpening his blades, sword, axe and seax, then oiling them and putting them away again. Tor knew that she must soon attend to her own weapons – the sea air, as everyone and their grandmother knew, was utterly poisonous to all un-oiled iron implements.

She sat for a few moments longer, resting, watching her brother at his work. Her whole body ached from her neck to her ankles, and her fingers were stiff as sticks of kindling. He was happy, she could see that. It was not just the soft singing, his whole body signalled his contentment.

She realised that, aching bones and blistered palms aside, she too was contented. She was still worried about Garm – but he could take care of himself in the woods, and Ulli was there at the steading to feed him if necessary. The threat from Rorik – and Jarl Starki – had never bothered her much, and it was receding with every mile they rowed from Norrland.

Yet this fine feeling was the result of much more than all that.

After a long winter – a dull period of several cold inactive months – she was taking action. She was heading off on a fresh voyage, a bold adventure, heading south to experience new lands and new people, with the prospect of a great heap of glittering treasure at the end of it. She felt like a warrior once again, not a... what did that rude fisherman say? A plough-pushing dunderhead. And that fiery knowledge kindled her spirit.

She hated to acknowledge it, but old Valtyr had been right: she needed this. A lifetime spent in Bearstead would have been one of slow, unrelenting torment. And she suddenly found that she too was humming along, just under her breath, to Bjarki's jaunty Sami folk tune.

She sat a little longer, happy, humming with her brother, avoiding her weapon-cleaning duties and looking at the new faces around the big central bonfire: twenty adventurers, a good many of them strangers to her.

There was Aistulf the Lombard, a rich man, she had heard, talking to old Valtyr on the far side of the fire, both men sharing an elaborate silver drinking horn. The trader looked a little foreign to her eyes, like a Frank; he was a fellow from the far south, that was for sure. Untrustworthy? She did not know. Merchants were often famously devious by their nature. Yet Valtyr seemed to trust him, and she trusted Valtyr – up to a point.

Aistulf the Merchant was the only reason they were able to go off on this mad voyage to find the Loki Sword – if it even existed, which she seriously doubted. Still, an abundance of treasure had been promised, and having her coffers at Bearstead filled with silver and gold was a very fine thought indeed. She could buy Inge a shiny bauble or two, even some jewels, perhaps, and get her some decent clothes to wear in Bjorke at festivals, maybe enough even to be able to pay a bride-price for her when the time came to marry her off. And Tor would not resent acquiring a few new clothes herself, and maybe a fine new horse for riding – the dun they had was getting old; and now it was more of a plough horse than a mount.

The young warrior Lief was joking with the mean-eyed little fellow who sat across from her in the rear of the ship; the little man was rebinding the hand-grip on his bow. Lief seemed to be telling a funny story and Halvar, that was his name, was grimacing at his comic words. Beyond them, Inge was filling soup bowls from a cauldron suspended over an extremity of the bonfire, a peninsula of flames that jutted out like a limb to allow food to be prepared without the cook scorching her hands.

Inge handed over a brimming bowl to a fellow called Rangvar, a tall, rangy warrior, almost as big as Bjarki, but older, whose few remaining teeth were yellow-grey and rotting in his mouth. He was a Geat, she had heard, from the vicinity of the town of Gothenburg on the west coast near the Dane-Mark. This Rangvar, who rowed on the steerboard side, five places up from Tor, was now sitting on his own, drinking ale, and as Inge passed the bowl over to him Tor saw him slide his right hand up her bare leg and further on up inside the simple woollen shift dress she wore.

She saw Inge flinch at his touch, the too-full bowl of scalding soup spilled and boiling liquid splashed over the big warrior's arm.

Rangvar jumped to his feet with a yell. He swung his open palm and swung a hard slap at Inge, aimed at her cheek. Inge dodged away in time but soup splashed everywhere. Rangvar, cursing and shaking his scalded left arm, now cocked his right fist and drew it back for a powerful punch. But before Tor was even half up, Bjarki was there, standing in between Rangvar and Inge, one palm out in a universal command that meant: stop!

'Get a hold of yourself, man,' Bjarki said.

'That stupid thrall bitch burned my arm!' snarled Rangvar.

Tor was up, too, by now. 'That's because you grabbed her arse!' she yelled. 'You horny old goat. A good scalding's no less than you deserve.'

'Everybody stay calm,' said Bjarki. He was looking around the circle of faces by the fire. 'This seems as good a time as any to say this: Inge is my thrall. She is under my protection. Treat her with due respect!'

'Or what?' said Rangvar, still bristling with anger, fists clenched.

Bjarki slowly turned to face him. He looked at the man for a long, long moment, then he struck. His head surged forwards as fast as an adder, swinging around slightly for extra momentum, and his forehead crashed into the bridge of Rangvar's big nose. There was a popping noise like a stone crushing a grape. Rangvar immediately dropped to the ground, boneless, knocked cold by the massive head butt, and lay there completely still. Bjarki stooped over him, noted that he was still breathing – noisily, now blowing blood-bubbles through his smashed-in nose – then he stood tall and looked round the fire circle again, holding all their eyes.

'Or that!' he said, into the astonished silence.

Bjarki stalked back to his blanket, sat down, picked up his sword and resumed sharpening its blade with deliberate strokes of a whetstone.

Valtyr was now crouched next to Rangvar, who was conscious again, more or less, tending to him, mopping at his big, flat, bleeding nose and whispering in his ear. The injured man glared angrily over at Bjarki – but he made no move to approach him. Tor went to sit next to her brother.

'Seems I'm not the only one with a gift for making enemies,' she said.

Chapter Seven

Beyond all the rules

The north wind was chilly and held a bite of salt, but Bjarki relished it. It played with his thick, shoulder-length blond hair, and pleasantly ruffled his beard. He pulled the bearskin tighter round his shoulders, and smiled.

A mere hour after they had rowed out of The Throat, as the narrow entrance to the major inland waterways of Svealand was called, the sixteen oars had been drawn in and stacked long-ways in their Y-frames, and the sail lashed to the yard and hauled up. Now the big black square of woollen cloth was taut and curved like an old man's belly, and swiftly powering the *Wave Serpent* south, down towards the island of Gotland.

They had embarked before dawn and Captain Lars seemed to think they could make the journey to Visby Harbour in a day's good sailing and would, if the wind held true, be arriving sometime this evening, with luck before nightfall. Till then, all Bjarki need do was sit back on his sea chest, with his spine braced against the gunwale, legs out in the middle of the ship, and enjoy the breeze and the warmth of spring sunshine on his face.

There had been no repercussions from the brief fracas the evening before. As they were breaking camp, Bjarki had deliberately faced and stared at Rangvar, to give him the chance to challenge him, if he wished to, but the big man had avoided his gaze and meekly continued packing his gear. Bjarki was quietly pleased by this. He was not afraid of the big man. A stupid fellow in his estimation. But the last thing he wanted was to fight seriously and perhaps kill a fellow crew member.

He suspected that Valtyr had been spreading the word about his fabled status as a Rekkr and, while both he and the old man knew it was no longer true, Bjarki did not mind the misapprehension. That lie had probably saved Rangvar's life. Bjarki was a skilled warrior, even without his *berserkr* fury. If he and Rangvar had fought, Bjarki was confident he would have triumphed. Even if he'd lost, and been killed by Rangvar by some slip or lucky blow, he knew with stone-cold certainty that Tor would have soon avenged him.

The thought of vengeance naturally took his mind to Rorik. That whole unfortunate business had been brought about because Hafnar the Silent feared neither him nor Tor. They had thought he and his sister were weak – vulnerable. And Hafnar's belief that he could take advantage of them had led to a confrontation, which led to Hafnar's death and Rorik's oath of vengeance. So, although Bjarki disliked dishonesty, on balance, it seemed a good idea to continue the pretence to the ship's crew members, fostered by Valtyr, that he was still a wild *berserkr*. It might well preserve him and Tor from any aggravation. No ordinary warrior would challenge a Rekkr to a fight. It would be considered a form of suicide.

The sea was calm, a deep blue, the surface barely rippled by the breeze, and off to his left, beyond Captain Lars's shoulder, Bjarki could see three smooth shapes rising from the water. They were ten times the length of a man, mottled grey and brown, with one sharp fin towards the rear of their long smooth bodies. These magnificent creatures plumed, one after the other, spraying jets in the air, high above their glossy backs.

All along the ship's length there was a general stir of interest and the traditional shout of 'Whale, ho!' and some fool on the larboard side was yelling something about spearing one and dragging it to land. Before this nonsense could be taken any further – the *Wave Serpent* was far too fragile a vessel to engage in whale-hunting – the pod of three leviathans sank back gracefully beneath the silky surface, never to be seen again. Bjarki leaned back against the hard gunwale, closed his eyed, and smiled.

The north wind died with the daylight, and they had to row the last dozen miles along the rocky, pine-fringed coast of Gotland and into Visby's cliff-lined harbour. It was a clearly wealthy place with many large, well-built houses on the quayside, some as many as two or even three storeys high, and most freshly painted with lime wash. The external wooden structures of the houses, the crossed end beams and gutters, were all intricately decorated with carved dragons, monsters and gods – and also with more homely images of goats, deer and swine. When the ship slid into the bay, a good hour after nightfall, the entire harbour front was lit with flaming pine torches. It was a pleasant welcoming gesture, which the tired *Wave Serpent* rowers appreciated, even though they knew it was not laid on entirely for their benefit.

The inhabitants of Visby made their living from sea trade, and Gotland stood at the centre of several lucrative routes – whale roads, as they were sometimes called – which ran from the eastern lands of the Finns across the Austmarr south and west to the Dane-Mark. But these ancient sea routes also ran from Svealand, and the far north, all the way south to the lands of the Prussians and the Wends.

With trade came silver, and with much silver came the predations of young men possessed with the urge to sail off a-viking and fill their own coffers by piracy. So Visby was not only a rich town but perforce an alert, well-defended one. The harbour torches were both a welcome to peaceful sailors and a means of casting light upon the ships of predators.

The town was also walled all the way around on the landward side, and there was a high watchtower at the north end of the harbour to keep a look-out for approaching ships, and a fortress at the south end, where the famously wealthy Jarl of Visby kept his great hall and a lavish table.

The *Wave Serpent* was greeted by a force of forty well-armed, hard-eyed local warriors, the moment their ship touched the greasy wooden planks of the crowded jetty. And the *hersir* in command, a gruff Geat, with his head shaved in parts and his remaining grey locks plaited into many warlike ropes, demanded to know their business. After a brief conversation between Valtyr, the *hersir* and Aistulf – the merchant was apparently well known and liked here – they were all conducted to the south end of the harbour where they were told that the jarl was feasting that night and they were cordially invited to join in the festivities. This was welcome news for Bjarki, who had eaten nothing but a slice or two of rye bread, a piece of cheese and a curl of pickled herring all that day.

Jarl Olaf was a generous host. The crew of the *Wave Serpent* were seated at one of his long tables and a succession of platters and trays of food and drink were brought out for the hungry voyagers. And when they had all eaten their fill, jugs of warmed mead fragranced with herbs were brought out. In due course, a skinny skald with a golden torc around his neck placed himself on a stool by the high table – where Valtyr and Aistulf were seated with Jarl Olaf, his closest retainers and family – struck his lyre strings in a bold, stirring opening chord and began to sing.

After a little while, Brandt, the dark Danish warrior, who was sitting opposite Bjarki, leaned forwards and said: 'That is a sweet melody, is it not, Bjarki? I've not heard music of this quality since leaving Aachen.'

Bjarki nodded. 'You never told me why you left the Auxilla,' he said. 'Did you grow tired of serving Karolus and his Christian priests?'

He and Tor had once been a part of this small Frankish unit, which was made up of foreign fighters. They had been forced to join after being captured in battle and had eventually fled from it – and last summer they had faced it in pitched battle, during which Bjarki, driven to fury by his *gandr*, had slaughtered his Auxilla lover Yoni. That thought still burned.

'The Auxilla is no more,' said Brandt. 'Did you not know that? After the battle at Lubbecke when Tor slew our captain Count Simon, and *you* shattered our ranks in your wild Rekkr rage, Karolus disbanded us.'

Bjarki looked closely at him. He was trying to decide if Brandt held still any trace of animosity towards him. He had, after all, been indirectly responsible for destroying the Danish warrior's livelihood as a mercenary.

'I've been up in the far North,' Bjarki said, 'out of touch with the doings of Francia. So the Auxilla is all gone? The people now scattered?'

'Best thing that could have happened to it,' said Brandt, taking a swig of his herb-flavoured mead. 'The company was rotten right through. Count Simon – or Snorri Hare-Lip – liked to play favourites with his warriors, promoting lickspittle toadies, ignoring the true fighters. I hated that puffed up pig's bladder, as I think you may recall. Many of us did. I praised Odin the day I heard he'd died. And when Karolus kicked us all out of the Auxilla compound at Aachen, I realised I had wasted too many years serving the Christians. I was *glad* to quit Francia and return north.'

Bjarki remembered a conversation in Aachen in which Brandt had seemed to be encouraging him to try to murder the Auxilla captain Snorri Hare-Lip. 'You did not fight with the rest of them at Lubbecke, then?'

'No – lucky for me, eh?' Brandt grinned at him. 'I would have had to face you and Tor across the shield wall – who can say what might have happened then. I broke my toe in camp at Buraburg, and remained with the garrison there for the whole campaign. And when it was over, I went back to Aachen, just in time to be told that the Auxilla was disbanded.'

'I'm sorry. That must have been hard. To be tossed aside like that.'

'Some of the very best Auxilla fighters were invited to join the Black Cloaks,' said Brandt, referring to the Frankish king's elite guards. 'In fact, they asked me. But I felt the call of my homeland. I wanted to get back to the Dane-Mark. So I took my pay and packed up my things.'

'You were fleeing some unpleasantness up there, if I recall.'

'I killed a boy my age over a girl we both liked up in Viborg – a stupid brawl that got out of hand – and his father and uncles wanted my head on a spike. But they were all killed in another feud a few years later. No one is seeking my head now,' Brandt chuckled. 'So far as I know!'

'But you didn't want to stay in Viborg?' asked Bjarki.

'I ran through my Frankish *deniers* faster than I thought possible. Then Valtyr came recruiting for this little expedition – and I thought: why not? I should very much like to be a rich man, and one of the warriors who found the Loki Sword. I'd like to be a man of renown in the North.'

Bjarki grunted. Brandt's story seemed to hold together well enough.

'You believe in this magic sword then?'

'I've never seen an enchanted blade myself – but I have heard enough stories about them to think there must be something in them. I wager if we asked that skald, he could spin us more than a few old tales.'

They stopped talking and listened to the lyre-player then, and drank their warm mead. And, although he sang later of a magic ring, also forged by the dwarves, there were no swords in the skald's repertoire that night.

When the evening was over, and the warriors were finding their places on the benches for sleep, Bjarki sought out Valtyr and spoke with him about the dark warrior, who had once been in the ranks of their foes.

'I'm su-sure we can trust him,' said Valtyr, who had taken in quite a lot of mead. 'What he says about the Auxilla is all tr-true. And it is your fault, and Tor's. You smashed them all apart at Lubbecke, and they all ran away. Ha-ha-ha! Bishop Livinus accused them of cowardice and King Karolus disbanded them sometime last autumn. When I found Brandt he was penniless, doing fancy sword-fighting demonstrations for his bread at local fairs right across Jutland. He's very skilled with a blade, you know.'

'I know,' said Bjarki. 'And I like the man and trust him. It's just that it seems a little odd he once served our greatest enemy – Karolus.'

'So did you – so did Tor,' said Valtyr, leering drunkenly. 'No one mistrusts you. And you're both wicked outlaws on the run from a jarl.'

As Bjarki was preparing for sleep, wrapped in his warm bearskin in a dark corner of the Visby hall, he pondered what Valtyr had said – and it made him feel a little uncomfortable. An outlaw was someone who could be killed out of hand by any passerby, with no penalty in law. The killing was even encouraged. Outlaws, by definition, lived beyond all the rules.

He wondered if Starki had also placed a fat price in silver on Tor's head, and on his as well. It would not surprise him and it would surely make any murderous passerby even more likely to attempt to kill them.

Chapter Eight

Asa's Landing

They were back in their rowing places on the water the next day, a little after dawn, and to Bjarki – who had been enjoying a dream in Jarl Olaf's hall about Yoni, in which she kissed him and forgave him for killing her – there seemed to be an unnecessary degree of haste in their departure from Visby. It felt as if they were fleeing. He signalled to Valtyr as the old man made his way up the centre of the ship, clambering over all the bulky parcels and packages. He crouched down by Bjarki's side as he plied his long oar.

'What's all the hurry?' Bjarki asked. 'I hoped to see a bit of Visby.'

'We have appointments to keep,' said Valtyr. 'We need to deliver Aistulf and his goods to his meeting place by a certain time of the month. And, as well as that, we have to be at...' The old man suddenly stopped.

'The tomb of Angantyr?' said Bjarki. 'I thought that had been lost for generations. Are we meeting someone? Is that what you're saying?'

Valtyr said nothing but shook his head and set his lips in a grim line.

'So other people *do* actually know where the tomb is?'

Again Valtyr shook his head.

'You promised you would tell us more in due course, old man.'

'And I will – but not just now. And I'm not going to be badgered by you into revealing anything more at this point in our long journey.'

'But we *do* have an appointment at Angantyr's tomb, yes?'

'I'll tell you closer to the time,' said Valtyr crossly. 'Don't pester me. Mind your business and pull that oar. Set an example for the others!'

Once clear of the cliff-lined harbour, the *Wave Serpent* caught a sweet, blustery, north-western breeze that filled their sail admirably. Soon they were spinning effortlessly southwards, driven by the wind, with the dark shape of the island of Gotland sinking into the ocean at their backs.

The breeze held and they sailed steadily south all that day – and all that night, too, with Bjarki and most of the crew dozing in the bilges after nightfall, with little to disturb them but the occasional murmured order from Lars to his First Oar Svein, the soft creak of the wooden bones of the ship, the thrum of ropes and the slap of the waves against the sides.

In the first pink streaks of dawn, Bjarki sat up and rubbed his eyes, and looking forwards he saw that the southern coast was now visible in the half-light as a black line beyond the curling serpent prow of the ship.

All that morning the line of the land grew thicker, filling out with beaches, marsh banks and ragged treelines. Birds wheeled and called above their heads in great flocks and the salt air now smelled of mud and vegetable rot. At about mid-morning a leggy crane flapped slowly across the salt marshes, east to west, paying them no mind at all. By high noon they were nosing into a wide-mouthed bay, with sandbanks on either side and beyond them scrubby woods as far as the eye could see. There was little sign of human habitation, just a few lonely fishermen's huts, some with slime-covered skiffs pulled on to the mud banks beside them.

Yet it was clear that Captain Lars knew this drab coast well, and was pleased to have made safe landfall here, for he was in a jovial mood all morning, laughing and cracking jokes. And as the sun passed the high meridian, he ordered the big sail to be pulled down and stowed, the oars unshipped, and all the rowers to go back to their places on the sea chests.

Then they all began to laboriously pull the *Wave Serpent* upstream, rowing hard against the slow current in the centre of the River Wiessel.

The woods on either bank gave way to farmlands and small kitchen gardens of leeks and cabbages and it was not long before they began to see the first permanent habitations of the local Slav folk: low, dark longhouses not too dissimilar to those found in villages in the North, but also smaller round huts, thatched with brown reeds. There were people here too, in smocks and loose trews and shapeless caps, staring from the banks as they passed, and occasionally grubby children waved at them or ran along in packs cheering their progress in some game of their own. Once, a clinker-built fishing boat, driven by a large red triangular sail, came round a bend in the river and whipped past them a dozen paces away on the steerboard side. The man sat at the tiller, an elderly fellow with a lined, leathery face, called out some words of greeting in a harsh tongue Bjarki did not understand. The merchant shouted something back in the same language, and the fellow waved a genial hand and was gone.

By mid-afternoon, they were able to lessen their hard labour considerably, as Lars steered the *Wave Serpent* off the wide river and into a narrower tributary, an offshoot that ran north-east. This waterway was a bowshot across here but the current was now running in the direction they wished to travel, so only light strokes were necessary to keep the ship moving.

A little before dusk, they moored the *Wave Serpent* at a long, slime-covered, rotting jetty on the eastern bank of the river – one of half a dozen such landing places – and cautiously began to disembark. There were no other ships there but only a sad-looking hamlet of sorts, a muddy, run-down place with a dozen slumped, mouldering huts and warehouses, and a few dazed or drunk-looking natives, slouching by on the bank, all filthy, ragged and mostly incurious about the newcomers and their ship.

A gibbet had been set up not far from the jetty and Bjarki saw that it was adorned with the hanged corpses of three men. Their faces were dark and beginning to rot. They had evidently been dangling there for a time.

There was a large ale-house in the centre of the village – a barn-like building with big open doors at each end, and smoke trickling out of the wind-eyes under the apex of the thatched roof. As they approached in a loose gang, Bjarki, Tor and Inge clustered together with the others behind them, a tall man, broad shouldered and very pale-faced, and with a mass of fiery red hair, stepped out. He wore a thick leather jerkin, studded with iron rivets but with no shirt underneath, exposing his huge, white, well-muscled arms. Below the jerkin he sported baggy, red-and-white striped woollen trews, stuffed into leather boots that came almost up to his knees. He had a brutal-looking seax slung across his loins. And it came as no surprise to Bjarki when the man addressed the arrivals in perfect Svear.

'Welcome to Asa's lodging-house,' he said, smiling at them. 'The ale is fresh-brewed and sweet, there is a hot leek pottage in the cauldron over the hearth, and any fleas you find in our beds were brought by you.'

'What is the name of this place?' asked Bjarki.

'It doesn't have a name, except my own – I am Asa, from Uppsala, originally. This is my landing place on the River Nogat. I offer food and drink and a bed for the night at very reasonable rates. And you will find whatever else you may desire in the town of Truso by the big sea lagoon – trade goods, ships' stores, sail cloth, clean whores – even trouble, if that's what you seek – whatever you may require, is two miles that way.'

He jerked his head east.

–

They rested in Asa's lodging-house and ate. And despite the lateness of the hour, the merchant, Valtyr and two well-armed crew members, one named Baldur and the other Fiske, set off on the muddy track towards Truso. Bjarki understood that Aistulf would be looking to sell his entire cargo of furs to the merchants of Truso, Slav folk who called themselves Prussians, and to buy a quantity of amber from them at the same time. But he knew nothing of such dealings and, if he was honest with himself, he was not much interested. He disliked haggling: if someone offered a price for some item, he either accepted the deal or simply walked away.

He sat on a stool of the lodging-house, with his belongings spread out all around him, and began to clean and oil all his war gear. Tor, sitting a little way away, began to do the same. Inge, strangely, was speaking animatedly to one of the old women who tended the lodge hearth.

'I understand this grandmother,' she said. 'Bjarki, pay attention, I understand her tongue! It is similar to the words I used to speak before.'

'This is your homeland, then?' Bjarki asked, looking up from the straps of his shield, which he was gently massaging with some pork fat.

'I don't think so. These people who live here are Prussians. And not my folk. But she is not from here but from the south. She is a thrall, too.'

'So where is she from?' said Bjarki.

'She said the name of her village but I do not know it. She was captured a very long time ago. But I think my people come from near her homeland. Her village. Wherever that place is. Is this not very exciting?'

Bjarki and Tor had acquired Inge as a thrall after the bloody sea fight with some vikings three years ago, the one in which they had captured the *Wave Serpent*. She had been a terrified girl of only eleven summers then – now she was a confident, sweet-blooming woman. Bjarki realised that he had never spoken to her about her life before she came into their household.

'Do you miss your family?'

Inge frowned. 'You and Tor and Garm *are* my family,' she said.

'I meant your real family. From the time before you belonged to us.'

'I used to miss them. I used to think about them all the time. I wept for them for a long time. But, now… now their faces are not very clear in my mind… My father was killed. Bad men came to our village with red fire and bright swords. I will never forget *that* day. Father tried to fight them but they killed him very quickly, cut him down without mercy – my uncles, also, were slain. My grandfather – he was a big man, a great chief of warriors, I think, but he was away somewhere on some errand when the bad men came to our house. And my mother was captured and… and they lay with her; they forced her. Many men. They hurt her very badly. And took her away with them. I think she must be dead now, too. She was bleeding a great deal when they dragged her away. Weeping as well.'

'Did they hurt you too?'

Inge just nodded. 'I was passed from one band of men to another. I forget how many. We went to the coast and they sold me on to the men in the ship, our ship, the *Wave Serpent*. Then *you* came and killed them all.'

Bjarki looked at her bunched-up little face and said: 'While I have strength in my bones, no man shall hurt you like that again. I swear it.'

–

The arrow missed Bjarki by less than an inch. It was long past nightfall, nearly midnight, by his reckoning, and he had awoken for some reason and left the lodging-house to piss. A lattice screen had been erected behind the building, set up behind a stinking latrine trench, with a stout rail to hold on to, and Bjarki stood there, swaying pleasantly, expelling his evening's intake of ale. He saw something glint by his feet in the starlight – there was no moon – a silver coin, he thought, and bent to pick it up.

At that very moment, the arrow sliced over his bending shoulder and thwacked into the wooden lattice screen. The hissing shaft passed so close to his bare head he felt the rough brush of its fletchings on his scalp.

He whirled round, drawing his seax and tucking his parts away in almost the same movement, and saw a figure – a man, he thought – much darker than his surroundings, and recognised the long curved line of a strung bow in his hands. The man was twenty paces away in the lee of a hut. Bjarki did not hesitate: he charged straight at the figure, pounding across the muddy yard with the blade in his hand and a snarl on his lips.

The man immediately disappeared around the side of the hut. And Bjarki only just stopped himself in time from rounding the corner at full speed. He slammed into the side of the hut, his weight making the whole structure vibrate, peeked round the corner and saw the man in the act of loosing another shaft. The fellow was hooded and his face was in shadow, a tall-ish man, he thought, but perhaps fear had grown his enemy. Bjarki only caught a glimpse of him. He paused with his right shoulder pressed against the corner of the hut, listening. He could hear the owner of the hut inside swearing in his foreign tongue through the flimsy wattle-and-daub at the disturbance but nothing else. So Bjarki snatched another glance around the corner of the hut but there was no one there. The archer was gone.

For a mad moment, Bjarki thought that it must be Hafnar the Silent who had attacked him. But then he recalled that the jarl's man, whom he had never laid eyes on, was lying dead in a forest in Svealand, food for the wolves. Then he thought of the son, Rorik, the lanky boy who had sworn vengeance and ridden along the banks of the lake in Uppland with the jarl's cavalry. But that was madder still. Rorik and his men were many hundreds of miles away. A whole expanse of salt water separated them.

He went back to the latrine. And since he had not finished pissing, he resumed the task. The arrow was still there, embedded firmly in the lattice work, and so he pulled it out and went back to the lodging-house.

The longhouse was dark but for a faint glow from the banked hearth. Everyone seemed to be fast asleep – the sound of gentle snoring could be heard vibrating on all sides. He sat up for a while, beside Tor's sleeping form, rolling the arrow between his fingers.

He had no urge to sleep. But neither did it seem worth waking everyone to tell his tale. What could he even say? 'Someone shot an arrow at me; it was a man, I think, but I have no idea know who it was. I didn't recognise him in the darkness.'

He waited to see if someone entered the longhouse that night – the hooded archer, perhaps, returning stealthily to his sleeping place. For one thing was clear to Bjarki: he knew no one in Asa's Landing and had done nothing that could possibly have offended a local. The man who had tried to kill him was, without doubt, one of the *Wave Serpent* crew. A friend.

Chapter Nine

Snake-tongued liars

'Whoever it was,' said Asa, his big hands planted belligerently on his hips, 'it was *not* one of my Prussian folk here who tried to murder you.'

Bjarki had felt slightly embarrassed telling their Svear host about the attempt to skewer him the night before. But Tor had persuaded him that it was a good idea to have it all out in the open. They had nothing to hide, she said, and the murderer might try again. It was better that folk knew.

'See them over there,' said Asa, pointing to the three rotting corpses hanging from the gibbet by the jetty. 'That's how we deal with miscreants at Asa's Landing. Everyone round these parts knows it well enough. Tell me who your assassin is, and I'll gladly string him up right next to them.'

'Who are they? What did they do?' asked Tor, looking up at the sad dangling shapes. She fancied she could smell the rot coming off them.

'Thieves,' said Asa. 'A trio of cunning Polans. Up from their filthy mud villages on banks of the Oder. Called themselves merchants but they were just snake-tongued liars. Most Polans men are warriors, and the best can make very fine soldiers, under the right leader, but a lot of them are lawless bandits. These three so-called merchants thought they could cheat my guests in a dice game. With a pair of their own dice. I was on to their tricks from the first and they paid the price. That is how we treat cheats and thieves here. This place is honest. And must be shown to be honest.'

At about noon, Valtyr returned to Asa's Landing from their visit to Truso with the merchant Aistulf, who was looking pleased with himself. They were accompanied by a large four-wheeled cart pulled by a pair of oxen and by half a dozen burly Prussian men, who immediately began unloading the *Wave Serpent's* bulky cargo and stacking the bales of furs into the ox cart-bed. There was a Truso merchant along with them, Tor noticed, a sad-looking, sallow, elderly fellow, almost completely bald but with a few strands of yellow-white hair brushed over the top of his pink liver-spotted scalp to make him appear to be younger and more virile.

The local merchant poked and prodded in to the bundles of furs, ordering one of the big packages to be opened. But after he had examined the glossy furs, fingered the silky pelts, he seemed very satisfied. Then Aistulf and he retired to the ale-house to discuss business over a drink.

Tor and Bjarki took the opportunity to stretch out their spines and practise their swordplay. In a patch of bare ground near the riverbank, they exchanged a few half-hearted cuts and parries, practising their familiar routines at no more than half speed – more for the exercise and to pass the time than to hone their already considerable skills. After one such lacklustre bout, Tor noticed that Brandt was silently watching them, waved, and invited him to join them. The Danish warrior readily agreed.

He faced off against Tor, with one sword each, and the left hand tucked into their belts at the small of the back. After two loud clashes, Tor found herself flat on her back in the mud, looking up along the length of Brandt's blade, the tip of which was now gently pressed to the hollow base of her throat. Bjarki was grinning, and applauding like a simpleton.

She got to her feet – angry now, despite herself. This was supposed to be a friendly bout. She faced the former Auxilla swordsman again.

This time she was more cautious. She probed with the point. And he retreated. She swept at his legs. He stepped back once again. She attacked very swiftly down the left side, forcing Brandt to block, then switched the angle of attack to come at him later-ally. And he ducked, stepped in and laid his sword, gently, across her left side. A killing blow – if this had been a real fight. And Bjarki was clapping away like an idiot once more.

She gritted her teeth in fury. And attacked with all her speed and strength. Her sword flashed at his head, their steel clanged, and she swept it low at his right arm – a blow that would have severed it, had he not twisted his limb out of the way at the last instant, stepped smartly in and shoulder-barged her off her feet, laying the tip of his sword this time softly on her belly button, as she gasped on her back on the ground again.

'Enough,' spat Tor. 'That's quite enough humiliation for one day.'

'Don't feel humiliated,' said Brandt. 'I beg you, Tor. I have spent years and years practising the arts of combat. I rarely do anything else.'

'I meant enough humiliation for *you*!'

'Oh, right. Yes, of course,' said Brandt, and he laughed with her.

'I'll give you a match,' said Bjarki, drawing his own long sword.

'No, your sister's right. I've had quite enough humiliation today already without being carved into bloody chunks by a famous Rekkr.'

Bjarki bit his lip, on the edge of telling Brandt he was no Rekkr, that his grandmother had tamed his *gandr*. But, at the very last instant, he refrained. He wasn't sure why. He liked Brandt but still held his tongue.

Captain Lars was blowing his ram's horn and Aistulf was coming out of the ale-house with the little merchant. Svein the Horse was walking beside them both and carrying a huge leather satchel in one hand.

Valtyr appeared beside Tor. 'We're leaving,' he said. 'Aistulf has completed his business with the Truso people and it is time to move on.'

'What's the hurry?' asked Tor.

'It's wise to be fast-moving,' Valtyr replied, not quite meeting her eyes. 'Before word of our affairs – and what we carry – spreads too far.'

It was Asa who made the point more specifically, when they were all aboard and poling the *Wave Serpent* away from the slimy wooden jetty.

'Better keep a good look-out down river,' he bellowed, as the ship slipped out into the middle of the stream. 'Every Polans horse-bandit within a hundred miles will be looking to make himself rich. But you'll always find a safe haven at Asa's Landing. Smooth sailing and farewell!'

They camped that night where the River Nogat met the mighty River Wiessel, and Aistulf insisted that Valtyr set sentries who would watch throughout the night. They piled the fire high with logs and all slept with their weapons to hand. Aistulf, Tor noticed with wry amusement, curled up in his blankets with the big satchel cuddled tight in his arms.

'How much amber is in that bag?' she asked Valtyr, as they sipped their soup together later and watched the fire. 'It doesn't look that much.'

'I think he bought some three or four hundred pieces of varying size. So that satchel is worth three or four times its weight in hacksilver. And it will increase in value every mile further south we carry it. They pick up good-sized pieces on the shore of the lagoon, just pluck them from the sand, did you know that? They've been doing it here for centuries. But the amber only starts to get truly valuable when it gets to Carnuntum, a town on the River Donau, which is where we part company with Aistulf.'

'We are leaving him there with a satchel full of amber?' said Tor.

'He won't be alone. He will be met in Carnuntum by a well-armed band of his compatriots, who will escort him home to Lombardy. Our task is to get him down there safely; if we do that, we will have more than earned our pay – and struck a blow against our Frankish enemies to boot!'

86

'What's this, old man? I thought we were after an ancient sword.'

'There are many different advantages to making this long, arduous journey – apart from shaking you and Bjarki out of your sluggish torpor!'

'I think you'd better tell me,' said Tor, glaring at him suspiciously.

Valtyr looked about. Inge was bent forwards, scrubbing the cauldron clean with river sand, her thin dress pulled tight about her haunches. But no man even dared to look at her shapely rump now. Bjarki's message to Rangvar had been taken seriously by the crew. Her brother was curled up in his bear robe, fast asleep, he was due to take the midnight watch and had eaten and immediately dropped off. There was no one close enough to overhear. Even so, Valtyr leant in very close to Tor and spoke quietly.

'Aistulf is not only a merchant. He is also a patriot. He is part of a conspiracy in Lombardy, led by Hrodgaud, Duke of Fruili, who plans to raise a rebellion against the Franks – this spring, any day now, in truth.'

'Is that so?' said Tor, frowning. 'And what has that to do with us?'

'If Lombardy rebels, it will force Karolus to go south again with his troops to deal with it, which allows Widukind freedom to act in Saxony.'

Tor pretended to yawn. She'd had quite enough of the Saxon conflict.

'But Duke Hrodgaud badly needs silver for his rebellion. For troops, but he also needs plenty of money to bribe their Pope to support his rebel cause. The Pope is like a sort of Mikelgothi, the highest priest in the…'

'I know what a Pope is,' snapped Tor.

'The amber we are carrying will be sold in Venice and will gather money for the duke. He will be able to raise his personal standard and keep an army in the field all summer, which helps our folk in the North.'

'You're not inviting Bjarki and me to fight for this duke, are you?'

'Would you do it?'

'No.'

'Then it's just as well that that is *not* my plan. All you and Bjarki and the rest need do is act as guards for Aistulf and his precious amber. That will be enough. Once we have safely delivered the merchant and his amber to Carnuntum, we are free to go and find the tomb of Angantyr, king of the Goths, and unearth its many treasures. If we're successful, the Saxon Wolf will owe us all – you and Bjarki, too – a great debt, and if, say, you found you could not go back to Norrrland, or chose not to, then…'

'I'm not getting pulled back into the Saxon nonsense, old man.'

Valtyr shrugged expansively, as if to say, 'We shall see about that.'

Tor thought for a moment. 'Carnuntum – this trading place is on the River Donau, yes? The great waterway that runs right through Francia? Bjarki and I sailed down that river on the way to Regensburg. So you're taking us into Karolus's territory. Do you know how dangerous that is?'

'We won't be plunging deep into Francia – calm yourself, my dear.'

'I am perfectly calm. I am *always* calm.'

'The Donau runs from the highest Alps all the way to the Greek Sea north of Miklagard, far to the east. Regensburg is in the duchy of Bavaria, more than two hundred miles *west* of Carnuntum. We will be beyond the furthest edge of the territory directly controlled by Francia – in the Avar March, as they call it. It is a wild land with no one in authority. Neither the Avars nor the Franks have tamed it. It is a twilight world, you might say. The agreed border runs north–south down the River March that joins the Donau at Carnuntum, but we'll remain safely on the east bank in the borderlands the whole time. We should be well beyond Karolus's grasp.'

'A lawless and dangerous place, then?'

'There may possibly be a few unsavoury types about. No one our lot cannot handle – I selected this crew with great care. Not scared, are you?'

Tor did not deign to answer him.

—

They saw the horsemen the next day around mid-morning – about forty riders in fur-trimmed felt hats and boiled leather armour. They were trotting their little ponies along the western bank of the Wiessel, and all of them were staring at the *Wave Serpent* as they pulled the ship along the middle of the river, heading south and west. The strange riders had javelins in small leather buckets on their ponies' withers, and most had long knives or axes in their belts. Some had war hammers, others bows and arrows. They were small men, mostly – and all were men – some as fair as Norse but others with rounder, grey-stubbled heads and ruddier cheeks and long beards. But the designs on their shields were alien to Tor's eye: images of terrible winged or horned gods, crude criss-cross designs.

Tor kicked Bjarki in his straining back and when he turned round crossly to look at her, she jerked her chin towards the riders on the bank.

'I see them, sis,' he said. 'What do you want me to do about it?'

They pulled over to the far bank at noon, to eat bread and pickled herring, and watched the riders on the other side of the river, a hundred paces away, stop and do nearly the same thing. There was no doubt the warriors were following them. Bandits seemed the most obvious guess.

Halvar, the stumpy fellow who sat across from Tor, stood on the bank and shouted out a rude question to the knot of horsemen on the far side. The horsemen shouted something back in their Slav tongue. Halvar made an insulting sign at the strangers, poking one finger in to his other curled hand to imitate a male–female coupling, then picked up his bow and was about to shoot an arrow across the water, but Valtyr stopped him.

'Save your shafts, Halvar,' the old man said, 'of both wit and wood, till we have decided what to do about our importunate new friends.'

Then Valtyr, Captain Lars, Svein the Horse and Aistulf formed a huddle to discuss the matter of these Polans bandits. Tor was too far away to hear them and was too proud to move closer and reveal her curiosity.

Run or fight. Those were the options. Those were *always* the only options, as Bjarki had pointed out in Bearstead. In truth, she did not care much which they decided on. A good fight might be what she needed. Her bout with Brandt had shown her how dull her fighting edge had become. And, though the bandits had twice their numbers, she reckoned this hand-picked ship's crew would have a good chance of beating them.

They ran.

Svein the Horse came sauntering round the various groups of *Wave Serpent* crew sitting on the riverbank and eating their meal and spread the word. A few moments later, Captain Lars gave one short blast on his little ram's horn and, forewarned, the crew all immediately scrambled for the ship. They found their places, shipped their oars all with exemplary dexterity and speed, and when the last oar clunked into its rowlock, Lars immediately blew his ram's horn, three sharp escalating notes. The call for 'double time' – and the crew of the *Wave Serpent* put their backs into their work. The ship shot away from the bank and surged up the brown river, leaving a thick, creamy wake behind them. Their sleek viking ship was built for speed – and that afternoon she proudly demonstrated it.

Their abrupt departure seemed to take the horsemen on the other bank by surprise. Many of them were dismounted, lying down, chewing their midday meal; some were even sleeping. But they all sat up in alarm when they saw the Northerners jump aboard and cast off the mooring ropes. The Polans reacted well, leaping up as their leaders shouted the call to arms, and soon they had swung up into their little ponies' saddles and were pounding down the track beside the Wiessel in tight formation.

What the bandits hoped to achieve, Tor had no idea. The *Wave Serpent* forged ahead of the horsemen with every powerful stroke of the oars, and by the time they had finally rounded the first gentle bend in the great river, their pursuers were almost completely out of sight. Yet Lars allowed them no respite. He and Svein the Horse drove them at maximum speed for more than two solid – and for Tor, at least – agonising hours, their oars thrashing the waters of the Wiessel to froth, until all were spent.

They came eventually to a wide place where the river was bisected by a long, narrow island, thickly wooded with alder and ash and clothed in long grasses. There, at last, Captain Lars called a halt to the back-breaking work of powering the ship onwards against the strong current.

Yet, though they had stopped rowing, their labours were far from over. On the furthest tip of the island, they moored the *Wave Serpent* to a pair of alders, and set to cutting branches and collecting fallen boughs to cover the obvious outlines of the vessel from all but the sharpest eyes.

Then they hid in the trees, twenty folk, all prone, looking out at the far bank and waiting to see if the Polans horseman would appear. The vegetation was dense, and Valtyr commanded them to keep silent, and they all lay in thick, waist-high grass and peered through the foliage, to see what their swift-riding enemies might do when they reached this spot.

They waited for an hour, and then another. And the sun was low in the sky when Valtyr proclaimed that they were no longer being followed.

They remained on the island that night, resting after their arduous day. An air of merry deliverance infected the whole crew. Jests were called out, there was singing to be heard. Even Aistulf was seen to crack a smile and accept a cup of mead with his mutton stew and twice-baked bread.

Although, of course, he never once let go of his big leather satchel.

The next day, they carried on up the wide river, at a much more leisurely pace. Tor was pleased to find that, while she had been stiff at dawn, when she rose and helped to clear the ship of branches, by the time she was back on her sea chest, and rhythmically pulling on her oar, she was feeling much better. Moving smoothly. Her body becoming hard.

As she watched the vast, straining, linen-shirted back of Bjarki in the rowing place in front of her, her mind went back to the mystery of the archer-assassin. She had discussed it briefly with her older brother and he seemed to believe that the would-be killer was someone among the crew.

The more she thought about it, the more that seemed likely. As far as she knew, Bjarki had angered no one at Asa's Landing. So it seemed unlikely one of the locals had taken it into his head to murder a visitor. Therefore, it had to be one of their crew – someone who was good with a bow. That meant herself, Inge or Halvar – those were the only ones that she knew of who would shoot a bow with any great skill in darkness. No, Lief, too, she now remembered, had admitted at camp one night that he used to shoot a bow as a youth. Or maybe it was someone whose bow skill she was not aware of. It was not her or Inge, that was certain, and as far as she knew, Halvar held no animosity towards Bjarki. Lief seemed quite harmless. The obvious choice was Rangvar – he had reason to hold a grudge. He had been humiliated by Bjarki. But could he shoot a bow?

She looked up the line of the ship's wall at his large form, bent over the long oar, four places up from Bjarki. He had made no further trouble for her brother since the episode with Inge – indeed, he now seemed subdued, even meek around her brother – but who could know what a man felt inside his secret heart. She considered confronting him, accusing him of the murder attempt, before witnesses, but if he denied it, she had no proof to the contrary – and worse, it would alert him to her suspicions.

She would watch him closely, she decided. Indeed, she would watch them all. Her eye ran over the rowers on the larboard side of the ship. And stopped on Brandt. He had surprised her with his superb sword-skill in their practice bout, and she still felt the burn of shame at his having bested her. But she felt something else stirring too. He was a handsome man – the way that pitch-dark hair fell in a raven's wing over his bright blue eyes. His square jawline hinted at a strong personality; and his body was clearly in fine condition. She wondered what he would look like with his shirt off… and stopped herself. This was no time for such thoughts.

–

They rowed all morning and, in the afternoon, after a short break to eat, Captain Lars took advantage of a breeze, blowing across the river from the north-west, to raise the black sail and allow them to rest for an hour.

They saw no more of the Polans horsemen, and passed by several settlements on the riverbanks without being molested – and with only a few dirty children shouting questions at them from the banks, demanding food or gifts, she thought. Nevertheless, when they stopped for the night, although they made their fire on land and Inge cooked their usual soup on the bank, Valtyr, after conferring with Lars, insisted they sleep in the ship.

'We may need to make another speedy departure,' he said, in response to the loud groans of complaint from the *Wave Serpent*'s crew.

Around noon the next day they stopped at a slightly larger village than the ones they had passed – a place that reeked of rotten fish, habitual squalor and back-country ignorance, and as they tied up at a long wooden jetty, alongside several smaller craft, Captain Lars stood on the planking and said: 'This place is called Byd, and this is as far as the *Wave Serpent* is going on this leg. This is where we part company with you, my friends.'

'What does he mean by that?' Tor asked Valtyr, who was in the act of clambering over the ship's side on to the jetty, exposing the skinny white legs he usually kept mercifully hidden under his long black robe.

'Exactly what he says,' said Valtyr. 'Captain Lars, Svein the Horse and two members of his usual crew will remain right here with the *Wave Serpent*. The Wiessel takes a sharp turn to the south-*east* here at Byd, and we are going south-*west*. We'll board this ship again – but only when we return triumphant from our mission in the south. They shall wait here.'

'But how will we get all the way to Carnuntum and the Donau?' Tor found she was oddly upset that they were leaving the vessel behind them.

'We'll get there the way that the gods intended us to travel,' said Valtyr, slapping one of his pale, stick-like shanks, 'on our own two feet!'

Chapter Ten

The Amber Road

They did not bid farewell to Captain Lars, Svein and the two *Wave Serpent* sailors immediately. Instead, they held a feast that night, in the small, fish-and-mould smelling house that Valtyr had secured from the Byd village chieftain – Svarog – a sullen little man who had lost his nose in some recent conflict, and now breathed, or rather snuffled, out of two raw, painful-looking, snot-crusted holes in his round, squashed-in face.

He didn't look much like a chieftain. But then it was not much of a village to be chieftain of, Bjarki reckoned. It resembled the hamlet on the fly-speck Danish island of Bago where he had grown up, with one muddy street lined with reed-thatched cottages and one hall where the *hersir* lived, in this case the swinish Svarog. There were even the same piles of damp fishing nets beside each sagging dwelling, and racks of copper-hued fish being smoked over sullen fires, though the sea-tang was absent.

Aistulf had been persuaded to spend a little of his silver for the benefit of the company and had procured a small, rather elderly horse from Svarog to roast for the festivities, which would take place in and around their borrowed house that night. Since a whole horse, even a small one, was beyond Inge's capabilities, Bjarki took charge of the cooking.

He dug a wide trench behind their house, filled it with firewood, and erected an oak pole spit above the cooking pit. It took him most of the afternoon and part of the evening to cook the animal, turning the carcass slowly and often, and brushing the blistered flesh with a lard-smeared cloth, but he was not sure that he had done justice to the huge slab of meat by the time they sat down at the long table – all twenty of them – to eat the chewy, badly charred and in some parts distressingly bloody flesh.

Inge had quietly prepared a mass of vegetable pottage with leeks and beans and baked loaves of rye bread, and unwrapped a large salted cheese from its nettle-leaf covering, and Svarog had grudgingly allowed them to carry in a vat of their local and, they soon found, very strong ale.

They ate and drank and Valtyr urged them to fill their bellies since the fare on the road would likely be poor – even worse than this filth, he joked. They told stories, sang songs and Lief got up, towards the end of the feast, and related a comic saga about a fox who fell in love with a dove.

The locals, a pack of grubby wretches who stared rudely but offered no words of welcome to the strangers, mostly stayed away from the house while they feasted that night. Although through an open door Bjarki glimpsed Slavs from time to time, peering in on the Northmen at table.

He ate a great deal of the half-raw horse meat, and drank a large quantity of strong ale, and as a result he had no difficulty at all in falling asleep on the benches at the side of the hall wrapped up in his bearskin.

And he found himself once more in the great, white wilderness.

'I smell fresh horse meat on you, man-child,' said Mockta, Mother of Bears. 'I smell it on your breath, on your skin. All over your fingers.'

'You are just a dream, *gandr*,' said Bjarki. 'I'm not afraid of you.'

'In dream or life – I am real to you, man-child. And you fear me. That's why you had the witch fetter me to the One Tree with this chain.'

Bjarki looked at the ice links that ran from the blue-grey collar round the bear's neck to the soaring majesty of the translucent Irminsul. The Spirit-Realm did not seem to have changed in the slightest: empty snowfields led away into the grey distance as far as the eye could see.

'What do you want?' he asked. 'Why do you haunt my dreams?'

'You know what I desire.'

'I do not.'

'I wish to be freed from the One Tree, untethered from this chain.'

'My grandmother warned me not to do this. So I shall not. I think you would try to control me, as before, if I were to free you. I believe you would try to drive me to madness – once more. It was *you*, after all, who made me kill my lover Yoni. A sweet girl who did not deserve to perish.'

'She was your enemy, man-child. She stood in the battle line against you. My task is to slay your foes. I would do so again, if you would but trust me. I would be a friend. I'd not seek to master you. Unchain me!'

'I shall not do that.'

'You *must* free me,' said the Bear. 'Break the chain. Let me loose.'

'I will not.'

Mockta let out a roar, a vast, deafening wave of frustration and fury.

–

Bjarki awoke. Captain Lars was yelling something. The air was thick with smoke. There was the sound of screaming but Bjarki could see little by the dim glow of the hearth fire. Folk were fighting, that was for sure. A patch of the reed-thatch above his head was smouldering. There was a flash of steel and someone cursed and fell heavily across him. He rolled off the bench, and reached under it to pull out his axe and the scabbarded seax. He shoved the knife into the waistband of his trews, hefted the axe.

'They are all over the ship,' Lars was screaming. 'Looting, burning her…' The sea captain was outlined in the open doorway, a dark but recognisable shape against the reddish glow from the exterior. Then two more figures loomed up in front of him, Bjarki saw the swing of swords, a gleam of reflected firelight, a meaty thud and Lars fell. Something was crunching, cracking, away to his left, a hacking sound of iron blades on wood or wattle. He heard Tor cursing foully, and another man, Brandt, he thought, yelling angrily, 'Pull out the whole fucking section, woman!'

There was a tearing sound and a large part of the lower wall of the house was ripped free. A pinkish light flooded in and Bjarki could see two men struggling on the floor near him, knives in their hands, wrestling and rolling. One was the warrior Lief, the other a stranger, who seemed to have the upper hand. He flipped over on top of Lief, knife hand drawn back and ready to strike, and Bjarki stepped forwards and swung the axe – just once. Hard. The blade *chunked* into the back of the stranger's skull.

Bjarki tugged the blade free, turned and surged out of the door, the long bearskin flapping out behind him. He leapt over the collapsed form of Captain Lars and landed in the street outside the house, skidding in the mud. He collided almost instantly with the squat form of the chieftain Svarog. The man staggered back, his pig-face demonic in the firelight. The little man leapt forwards and slashed at Bjarki's belly with a knife.

Bjarki swerved out of the path of the swinging blade, punched the blunt end of the axe in Svarog's face, then kicked the Slav with all his strength in the fork of his legs. The man howled and folded at the waist, and Bjarki stepped in to finish him, lofting the axe above his hunched...

Someone was screaming at him in a strange language, a big fellow with a war hammer. He swung the weapon at Bjarki, who shot out his left hand in a desperately late block and caught the swinging wooden shaft of the hammer in his meaty palm. He felt the savage blow jolt all the way up his left arm, but ignored the pain, and swung his own axe, weakly, one-handed, in a low diagonal arc across his own body, whacking the blade in behind the man's braced left thigh. He fell, shouting, and Bjarki stepped towards him and sheared off half of his face with a down-swoop of the axe.

Bjarki took a breath. There were knots of struggling people all over the muddy street outside their guest house, and fifty yards away, by the riverbank, he could see the outline of *Wave Serpent* now burning merrily, casting a dancing, bloody light over the whole village. He saw Halvar with his bow, shooting a shaft into a screaming warrior's contorted face at a distance of only three paces. The arrow entered his mouth, and burst right through, exploding from the back of the man's neck in a shower of gore. Bjarki snatched a look back at their house and saw that it, too, was aflame. There was Tor, unwounded, he thought, with Brandt behind her emerging from a ragged hole they had hacked in the side of the house; now Inge's little blonde head was poking out from the gap behind them.

A high, chittering little voice inside his heart, a familiar voice, was saying: 'You want my help, man-child? Free me. Cut the foul ice chain!'

Bjarki shouted: 'No!' But part of him wanted to say the opposite.

A wide, shaven-headed man loomed up before him, curved sword and spiked shield in his thick hands. He screamed a challenge and drew back his curved blade, ready to slice. Bjarki surged forwards and barged straight into him, crashing his own huge bulk into his shield-side, just missing the sharp central spike, but still knocking the squat warrior back a couple of steps. Tor was there now, dipping in to slash at his booted ankle with her seax, tumbling him in the mud. Brandt lunged in from the right-hand side with a spear and neatly ripped out the fallen man's throat.

'Morning,' he said amiably to Bjarki. 'Sleep well?'

Bjarki laughed. Then the three of them advanced, in a line, heading towards the ship. Killing as they went. Wiping foemen from the world.

They overwhelmed a pair of charging warriors, cutting them down mid-stride in a few neat, efficient strokes. Svarog came stumbling back into their path, screaming, and Tor's sword hacked his right arm off at the shoulder then immediately opened his belly with a lateral stroke that was almost part of the same movement. Bjarki spotted Rangvar and Svein the Horse fighting, back to back, a dozen yards from the burning ship, with a crowd of warriors boiling and surging around them, many swords swinging, slicing, spears jabbing, the enemy adorned with fur-trimmed caps and boiled leather cuirasses. These were clearly the Polans river-bandits who had pursued them on the banks, now dismounted to fight.

Bjarki, Tor and Brandt fell on the mass of enemies around their two shipmates from behind, hacking mercilessly into their unguarded backs. Bjarki lopped off a fur-hatted head; Brandt drove his spear deep into a man's kidneys through his leather armour. The enemy shrieked now with surprise or fear – some ran off into the darkness. The crowd dispersed, melted away under the combined assault from Bjarki, Tor and Brandt.

Rangvar, holding a sword and seax, grinned at the three of them, showing his bloody teeth in the flickering firelight. More of the enemy were running away now, scurrying like rats exposed by lamplight, some of the Polans swinging up on their little ponies and thundering off.

Bjarki saw Aistulf huddled in a ball on the ground in the churned-up space where Rangvar and Svein had made their bold stand; the merchant was curled around his leather satchel, horror etched on his face. Svein the Horse was down, badly wounded, his belly gleaming black with blood.

Yet the fight was not over. The foe was regrouping, over to their right, further down the single village street, a crowd was coalescing, perhaps a dozen Byd villagers and half a dozen of the remaining fur-capped Polans, too, in a collection of men, rather than a formation. But they were advancing, more or less together, towards the burning ship, determined. Bjarki wondered what had united them against the *Wave Serpent*'s crew – then cursed his stupidity. The amber, of course. They had conspired to murder the foreigners and rob them of their cargo. A story as old as time.

An arrow arced into the advancing Slavs from the left, piercing a man's cheek and dropping him immediately, and Bjarki turned to look and saw Inge, by the wall of the burning house, bow in hand, full quiver on her hip, already nocking another shaft. She must have gone back into the burning house simply to fetch her war gear. *Brave girl*, he thought.

Halvar was now also loosing arrows at the advancing Slav company.

'Come on, Rekkr, let's just smash them,' shouted Brandt cheerily. 'They won't stand! I know it – they cannot hold against the likes of us!'

Bjarki looked at the man – he was grinning madly, his face spattered with blood. A gory spear in one hand and now a spiked shield in the other.

For a cold, hard moment, he missed his *gandr*. He missed the surging *berserkr* fury pouring from his heart, the feeling of being lighter than air, stronger than a mountain, faster than a swooping falcon. 'No!' he said aloud. Brandt shot him a look. 'No, they'll not stand!' he added.

'*Wave Serpent*, on me,' Bjarki bellowed. 'On my command, we are going to charge the enemy ranks. We're going to hurl these dirty little back-stabbers into the next life.' He hefted his axe, and drew the seax.

'Everybody ready?' he looked round in the red-tinged darkness, and saw nearly a dozen familiar faces looking to him. 'Right then – *charge*!'

–

It shouldn't have worked. By all the laws of war, they should have died swiftly on the enemy spears. A handful of warriors, some even wounded, charging a mass of foemen three times their number – it was impossible!

And yet.

Bjarki sprinted twenty yards towards the enemy mass at full pelt, with Tor hard on his right shoulder and Brandt on his left, a crude arrow-shaped formation, with all the survivors of the *Wave Serpent* piling in behind him in a loose but swift-running pack. Bjarki was very lucky, admittedly. The man he targeted in the centre-right of the loosely formed Slav crowd was a simple fisherman, who instinctively flinched and tried to shrink back as the enormous, screaming Norseman came charging straight towards him. The Slav fisherman cringed away from Bjarki – who simply hurled himself right into the centre of the gaggle of enemy.

A lunging spear tip reached out and tore through Bjarki's beard, miraculously missing his skin, but now he was in the thick of the enemy mass, stabbing with the seax, jabbing at enemy faces with the blunt end of the big axe. Brandt then burst into the crowd of foes only a yard to his left, a heartbeat behind Bjarki, his long spear doing terrible work in the Slav ranks, darting in, striking, coming back bloody, and on his right Tor was cursing and shoving and cutting her bloody way through the press.

All Slav cohesion disintegrated. The whole *Wave Serpent* crew were in and among them now, screaming and stabbing, slashing and slaying, wreaking vengeance for the base treachery they had suffered at the hands of their hosts. They were indeed a fearsome crew. Valtyr had picked them each for their battle skill and their savagery. And they slaughtered the enemy, they ripped and cut, they slew and maimed the Byd folk.

The *Wave Serpent* company destroyed the Slavs; they tore them apart. In moments, any surviving foes were tossing aside broken shields and spears and running for their lives, back into the depths of the village, or howling in terror and fleeing in panic into the safety of dark woods.

One lone warrior stood his ground.

A young man, trembling with fear, but glaring at them over the rim of his spiked round shield, his spear drawn back ready to stab forwards.

Bjarki stood before him, panting, slathered in fresh blood, filth-grimed axe in one hand, gory seax in the other. Dripping into the mud. Tor circled around behind the warrior, her sword also smeared with gore. Her expression grim. Brandt stood, spear cocked, ready for a kill thrust.

Bjarki, who spoke a little Wendish, said in that tongue: 'Surrender!'

The man, desperation carved into his face, looked at the surrounding northern warriors, at the ring of grim faces. He nodded slightly. And lowered his spiked shield a fraction. His spear drooped. He repeated the Wendish word 'Surrender?' but strangely, in the accent of that region.

Bjarki said, in his awful Wendish: 'We look answers. We make questions. You answer. No kill you. You surrender. We no kill. No hurt.'

The Slav nodded. The spiked shield came down a little further.

And Halvar stepped forwards and put an arrow through his throat.

–

Valtyr was alive. And what was even more extraordinary, for an unarmed man, he was more or less unhurt except for a large bruise on his forehead. He explained to Bjarki a few hours later what he thought had happened.

'Their initial night-attack, it seems, was very badly organised,' said Valtyr, rubbing his sore brow. 'Not clever at all. Which is probably why it failed. I spoke to one of the wounded village men before he died. It seems the two factions – the bandit horsemen, who had followed us here along the river, and Svarog's people – were both Polans but from different clans. And crucially they did not fully trust each other.

'I'm guessing that the bandits proposed the robbery to the villagers, who agreed, then invited the horsemen into the village. It was the Polans horsemen who got inside our guest house and started murdering our folk – Fiske was slain while he slept, did you know? So were poor Orm and Baldur – and we might all have been killed, had not the villagers, on their own initiative, set fire to the roof from the outside. As I said, not clever.

'The fighting woke me up; someone trod on my leg in the darkness and then when I stumbled upright I took a bad smash on the brow from someone, which knocked me out for a time. By the time I woke, the house was roaring with flames – and I just managed to crawl out alive.'

As he spoke, Bjarki looked over at the house, which was still a vast pyre. And since the *Wave Serpent* had already burnt itself out, the burning building shed was the primary light on the single street, firelight gleaming in the puddles of mud and blood. It was clear this had been a battlefield. There were dozens of dead Polans, villagers and bandits, scattered about on the ground. The wounded, those who had not run away into the dark, had been sent into the next world by the *Wave Serpent* folk. It seemed the Svear warriors – Valtyr's hand-picked crew – had given a good account of themselves, very good, considering they'd been attacked while asleep.

But they had also paid a heavy price: Fiske, Orm and Baldur, and Svein the Horse were dead, and Captain Lars was only just in the land of the living with a badly bashed-in skull. Valtyr did not think he would live to see another dawn. And young Lief had been stabbed deep in the right shoulder and could not use that arm. Bjarki and Tor had a few minor cuts and bruises, but the ever-skilful Brandt was untouched by the hand of war.

The Lombard merchant Aistulf, although very badly shaken by the experience, also survived completely unhurt – and had even preserved his precious satchel – but he was extremely vocal in his desire to leave the battle-torn village and get away and back on the road as soon as possible.

'What should we do now, Valtyr?' Bjarki asked the old man.

'I think the Lombard is right,' he replied. 'We can't stay here – they could return any time with reinforcements, with friends, family, or just another band of thieves. We can't go back to Asa's Landing, where we might get help, since the *Wave Serpent* is now at the bottom of the river. There is nothing for it – but to go on. We follow the plan. Let us pack our belongings and move out as soon as we can. Let us take the Amber Road!'

Part Two

Chapter Eleven

Basic precautions

Captain Lars died in the grey, watery light before dawn and he and the other dead of the company were laid in the still-smouldering house and covered with fresh kindling and firewood. Then the surviving members of the *Wave Serpent* crew – thirteen men and two women – took the road south, heading out of the abandoned village of Byd as the sun rose, pink and vengeful over the wide river on their left-hand side.

Valtyr insisted they carry only what they deemed essential, their own weapons and kit, sleeping gear and spare clothes, but since they had rounded up three of the dead Polans' ponies, they loaded them up with all the food stores and cooking equipment. They searched the village for valuables and found a pot half full of silver and copper coins in Svarog's hall, a sack of onions, a few bunches of dried herbs and a side of bacon.

They left the drab settlement with Valtyr and Tor in the lead, the laden ponies and crew in the middle and Bjarki taking up the rear, and hanging back from time to time, crouched in deep foliage, to watch for pursuit. Although they did not expect the defeated villagers to regroup and attack them again, and the horsemen had left a good quarter of their number lying dead in the street, it seemed wise to take basic precautions.

'Word will have spread all along the Amber Road by now,' Valtyr told Tor. 'But that is not entirely a bad thing. Other predators along the route will know we carry a valuable package of the stones, but also that we can defend ourselves pretty well. Only the strongest bandits will be tempted to try anything and gangs like them are few and far between.'

'So this Amber Road you speak of,' asked Tor, 'is this the one that goes all the way to Italy, to the Middle Sea of the old Roman Empire?'

'We are only travelling part of that road,' said the old man. 'It's less than four hundred miles to Carnuntum – three weeks' march, if we keep up this pace – and there are, in truth, several routes. But I have chosen the one least populated with the human wolves who might lie in wait for us.'

'Four hundred miles?' said Tor. She had taken a shallow cut to her left calf muscle during the fight in the village street and even after only a morning's stroll, she already found it almost too painful to put weight on.

The land was flattish but thickly forested with firs and birch on the higher ground and criss-crossed with many streams in the lower places, even though, by mid-morning, they had left the River Wiessel far behind. Yet the Amber Road here was a clearly marked, well-worn and muddy track, which cut through the dense trees as straight as an arrow – and it was not a difficult terrain to traverse so long as you did not mind wet feet.

On the first night they made camp in late afternoon in a wood by a reed-fringed marshy mere and Rangvar went out with his lines and hooks and some of the bacon rind, and came back an hour later with a dozen eels. They cut their snake-like catch into thick chunks and roasted the pieces on long, nodding stripped-willow sticks over the campfire, picking the succulent, fatty flesh from the fishes' many hairlike bones with relish.

That evening, Tor found her calf was swollen to an angry purple and, when she examined it, she worried that the warrior who had given the wound to her might have poisoned his blade – something the Slavs were rumoured to do. Whether this was true or not, the injury was extremely painful and Valtyr fussed over her calf for some time, cleaning the cut and dressing it with a pungent herby ointment of his own concoction. At last he bound the leg up in clean linen and told her to rest – someone else could be found to do her sentry turn that night. He made her drink a bitter draft of henbane and warm ale, from a small supply of the drug that he carried in his pouch, and she very swiftly fell asleep by the campfire.

The next morning, the wound site was still very hot to the touch, and he decreed she must ride one of the captured ponies for a day or two and that animal's load of kit was distributed among the unhurt marchers of the company. Tor protested only a very little at the old man's emphatic ruling.

Perhaps oddly, they saw few people as they travelled this ancient trade route, occasionally a lone peasant, weeding a small field of rye or oats, or clearing out a clogged drainage ditch. When they did so, the mud-slathered man or woman would almost always look up and stare at them silently in amazement – or fear – as they passed, as if they saw a *draugr* or some other terrifying ghostly creature walking around in full daylight.

Sometimes they would glimpse a local huntsman in a gap through the dense trees, a man, usually, clad in fur and leathers, standing with bow or boar spear in hand. Yet no one they met offered any violence, not even a harsh word, and they plodded on, hour after hour, day after day, without incident to break the monotony. On the afternoon of the third day after quitting Byd, Tor found Brandt tramping beside her Polans pony.

It seemed that he had something on his mind.

'Do you mind if I ask you something about your brother?' he began.

'Ask away,' she said, tucking a loose tendril of her red hair behind her left ear, and wishing she had washed her face a little more thoroughly that morning. 'There's not much more to the big oaf than meets the eye.'

'I know he is Fire Born,' Brandt said, 'everyone says so. But I noticed that in the battle at Byd he did not… change his form. I have heard that *berserkir* transform into bears in the heat of battle. He did not seem any different to his usual self. Did the Bear spirit not come to him?'

Tor was now regretting her earlier dismissive quip about Bjarki. 'It's complicated. His relationship with his *gandr* is… unusual.'

'So *is* he Fire Born – or not? He wouldn't pretend to be, would he?'

Tor felt a flare of anger at this impertinent question. 'My brother Bjarki Bloodhand is a fine warrior. And he has been hailed as a true Fire Born by *gothi* and jarl alike. A terrible Rekkr. Valtyr himself has vouched for his true status as a *berserkr* – and *I* have seen the Bear come into him many times, transforming him into a creature of incredible raging power. Do you call me a liar – as well as suspecting my brother is an impostor?'

'No, no, of course not. But… why then did he not… transform himself… in the battle at Byd? It would have made our victory easier.'

'Perhaps he did not feel the need. Perhaps he knew that we could triumph without invoking a *gandr*. You'll have to ask him that yourself.'

Tor felt uncomfortable lying to Brandt. She liked him, and admired his battle skills and his lean, dark looks, and she very much wanted him to like her in return. But after discussing the chaining of the *gandr* in the Spirit-Realm with Bjarki, she too had come to the conclusion that it was far better to let their companions believe he still had his Rekkr powers.

'I would not dare ask your brother,' said Brandt, with a disarming grin. 'I wouldn't take the chance that he would turn *berserkr* on me!'

And there they left it. Instead, they talked about Francia – did he miss the Auxilla? she asked. Not at all, he assured her. And then Brandt asked her to tell him about her various adventures in Saxony, and her meetings with Karolus himself. She obliged him – happy to talk about anything rather than discuss her brother and his struggle with his *gandr*.

–

They crossed a mighty river the next day, a slow, green, three-bowshot-wide body of water, the well-trodden road leading them directly to the old fording place, which was marked with oak posts driven deep into the bed.

It still took them most of that day to get the whole company and the three Polans ponies and baggage across and, in the centre of the stream, they were all obliged to swim a few strokes. Those who could not do so with any confidence, young Lief, for example, gripped tightly to a pony's mane as the pack animal struggled and splashed across the short distance.

Bjarki ploughed across the deepest part of the river first, swimming strongly, even dragging a heavy, sealed bag of his belongings behind him. Then he stood up to his broad chest in the swift, freezing water, and urged the others to follow him across. Tor, who was by no means as natural a water-creature as her brother, kept close to her swimming mount for the twenty yards or so when her feet could not touch the stony river bed.

However, she abruptly waved off Bjarki's reaching arm on the other side and made it to the muddy beach without mishap on her own. Indeed, they all got across safely – no one drowned, no one was swept away downstream by the powerful current. Valtyr said that Rán, the goddess of watery places, must have warded them all as they crossed.

Tor scoffed: 'Gods don't care if we live or die!'

'They may not care if *you* live,' Valtyr retorted. 'But they've always looked after me very nicely! Perhaps if you showed a little respect…'

–

Two days later at evening camp, Halvar came into the circle round the fire, and reported to Valtyr that they were being followed by a large force of horsemen. It had been his turn to take the position of the rearguard all that day and he claimed he had watched their back trail with the utmost care.

'I hauled myself up into the fork of a big old ash,' he said. 'To get a better look at the trail behind. And I saw them, clear as day, several score or more perhaps, horsemen, armed with lances, crossing that big old river behind us. Last I saw, they were setting out southwards on this road.'

'Polans bandits, you think?' said Bjarki. 'Are they following us?'

'I cannot say,' said Halvar. 'But they are on this very same road as us, and only half a day's ride behind.'

'That doesn't mean they're following,' said Lief. 'They could be innocent travellers, traders – you said this was a well-trodden route, Valtyr, used by hundreds of folk every year. Maybe they are transporting a hoard of amber down to the River Donau just like us.'

'They might also be a patrol from Poznan, the hall of the Duke of Polans, which is about two days' ride to the west of here,' said Valtyr.

'We cannot take that chance,' said Aistulf. 'We must flee – now.'

Bjarki was on his feet by then, and Valtyr, too. Tor stayed where she was, lying on her bedding. Inge was retying the bandage on her wounded leg, which was noticeably less swollen, and seemed to be knitting nicely. She had taken another draught of powdered henbane and ale, from Valtyr, and was feeling pleasantly woozy. Perhaps the Polans blade that cut her calf had not been poisoned after all. She certainly felt a good deal better.

'Aistulf is right,' said Valtyr. 'It would be better, I think, not to cross paths with them. You said several score, Halvar – that many, yes? – then they are far stronger than us. And some of our people are wounded.'

He jerked his chin over towards Tor's relaxed, lounging form in the blanket, and young Lief, too, who had his hurt arm supported in a dirty sling. Tor fought the urge to giggle like a girl – for no good reason at all.

'You want to run?' said Bjarki.

'No,' said Valtyr, 'hide – we'll lie up and watch them from cover.'

There were a good few under-the-breath grumbles at this decision of Valtyr's – growls of 'I hide from no man' and 'Are we cowards now?' But no one was *too* vociferous in their objections to this sensible course.

There was nothing to be done that night but post extra sentries and, in the chilly dawn, they left their camping place by rutted road and in growing daylight Valtyr led them all away to the west into the thickly forested, hilly countryside. The walked in single file for about a mile before Valtyr pointed to a low hill, treeless on top, with the half-rotted remains of a wooden perimeter wall. It had evidently once been a fortress of some kind, perhaps held by an old warlord, now abandoned. That was where they settled, waiting for the horsemen to either attack or pass by.

They rested and slept and, although Valtyr said that she must not tire herself or unnecessarily irritate her leg wound, Tor took her stint like all the others, watching the back trail. She found herself around noon, with Halvar, hidden in a stand of alders, twenty paces from the Amber Road. Once again she was struck with the notion that she had seen the little man before, and recently. She was about to ask him if that was the case when she heard a great mass of horsemen splashing and clattering beyond sight.

They were Polans, that was clear from their fur-trimmed felt caps, the angry-looking horned god painted on their shields, and the needle-point lances they carried in the leather buckets on their horses' withers. About fifty of them, young, well disciplined and in something of a hurry.

But Tor did not know if they were the same folk who had attacked them in the village of Byd or some different band. But they looked like a well-seasoned, dangerous company. She recognised none of their faces, although it had been dark in the street during the battle. Yet this group of horsemen did not seem to be tracking their crew – or anyone. They rode fast, with no regard at all for the marks left in the mud by other travellers.

She reported all this back to the rest of the company, and saw the smiles of relief on more than a few faces. Valtyr said: 'We should rest here for the day, anyway – and put a little distance between us and them.'

No one complained about the prospect of a full day spent loafing about in the old fort, mending kit, sleeping or resting. They had been on the Amber Road for nearly a week now and a respite was more than welcome.

Even Tor relaxed, taking her ease and getting outside a bowl filled with fresh bread and hot, fried slices of bacon that Inge had cooked. As she lazed, her eye happened to fall on Halvar, her sentry companion, who was sitting beside Valtyr offering a slice of crispy fat to the old man.

And she remembered.

She remembered where she had seen Halvar – at Gavle on market-day last autumn. Halvar had been drinking with a group of warriors in the ale-house, and one of them had bumped into her and she had nearly come to blows with him. Nothing had come of it but she remembered Halvar had jeered at the idea of a woman warrior and she had hated him for it.

Did that mean anything? She wasn't sure.

If he was from Norrland – then he probably knew about the killing of Hafnar the Silent. The group of warriors he had been with in Gavle were not Viggo the White's men. But that did not mean he now did not want to gain favour with the new jarl, perhaps by killing her and Bjarki.

No. Just because he was from Norrland did not necessarily make him the assassin in Asa's Landing, though he *was* a fine bowman. She considered confronting him. But what could she say if he denied her accusation?

Instead, she decided to keep a closer watch on Halvar and over Bjarki, too. To ward her brother from another potentially lethal attack.

So that night, having slept deeply all afternoon, she stayed awake long after sundown, lying wrapped in her blankets and pretending to be asleep, but keeping her half-open eyes constantly on her older brother's enormous fur-wrapped bulk on the far side of the dying campfire.

She did fall asleep, eventually, she could not help it – the henbane swept her away – but not for very many hours and, as dawn broke, she found to her relief that Bjarki was alive, already washed and dressed and adding a bundle of kindling wood to the fire to build it up for their breakfast.

–

They went at it hard for the next two days, marching till it was full dark then making a dry, fireless camp off the road and rising before dawn to push on into the chill, misty morning. Valtyr was strangely insistent that they speed their pace – although he could not be persuaded to reveal the reason why. They saw no sign of the company of Polans horsemen, which pleased Tor, since she had been the one to conclude that the swift-riding Slavs were not, in fact, chasing after them.

And Tor decided that her wound was now healed enough to march on. She soon grew tired, however, of Bjarki walking along beside her at her slow pace and peering down anxiously every second stride at her left leg and, when she finally lost patience and dismissed him, she noticed that Inge immediately took up his place by her side and burbled on about foolish things, while also covertly watching Tor's hobbled step like a hawk.

In the end, she got back on one of the ponies after the midday meal break, to everyone's silent relief – including, secretly, her own. And there she stayed for the next two full days, lolling in the saddle while they passed through a low, flat country with large, well-tended fields, placidly grazing sheep and cows and even occasionally a decent-sized village, where they were able to buy bread and ale with Aistulf's store of silver coins. On the afternoon of the fourth day after their day of rest in the old fortress, when the whole company were footsore and snappish, except Tor, who was feeling bad about her horse-borne idleness, they found the banks of the Oder – and with it a town, occupied by thousands of people.

It was a humid place, warm, marshy, with reed-covered margins, with a wide landing place for trading vessels. There were a few old warehouses, a dozen dwellings, an ale-house, a pen full of bleating goats and a stable in which she could see three or four fine horses. However, the true town was not on this east bank of the Oder but on an island in the middle of the stream – a far grander place, connected by a narrow bridge.

'This is what they call *gord*,' said Valtyr. 'It belongs to the Silesia tribe, who are the power in these parts. They are, I believe, related by blood to the Polans, distant cousins or some such, but they all hold themselves apart from those horse folk – they're much richer, for a start.'

Tor surveyed the big island in the middle of the wide river, which was filled almost entirely by a huge timber-walled fortress with several tall wooden watchtowers. She could see scores of alert spearmen on the walkway above the gate at the end of the bridge, and strolling in pairs along the crenellated fortress wall, clad in leather armour and iron helms.

'What do they grow rich on in this backwater?' asked Tor.

'This is no backwater but an important market. A thriving bazaar that has sprung up here at the crossing place of three roads,' said Valtyr. 'This is where all the amber trade coming down from the Austmarr, via the town of Truso, meets the precious metals trade that flows up the Oder from the south-east, from the mountains of Moravia, called the Western Harvaths, where there are rich silver mines. Goods and chattels flow from this town, along the River Oder, all the way up to Wendland and from there by sea to the Dane-Mark, Skane and even Svealand. Timber, slaves, grain, furs, wax and honey all travel down from the North through this *gord* to the warm lands further south. There is even an old trackway, I am told, that heads directly west from here all the way, hundreds of miles, to our own First Forest in south Saxony and beyond into the Christian realm of Francia. Wine and pottery comes flowing up from Italy; amber, salt, slaves and furs come down from our own Eastern Lake; silver, tin and iron come up from the mines in Moravia… and the Silesian folk of this *gord* grow rich from all the trade that passes through their sticky hands!'

'So they're just money-grubbing merchants then?' said Tor.

Aistulf, who was standing behind her, gave a furious snort. 'The Silesians could buy the services of a hundred common warriors like you!'

Tor gave him a look. But she felt too tired to teach him a proper lesson in manners. And Valtyr had impressed on her on the journey that she must always treat the Lombard merchant with extravagant respect.

'They might be able to purchase *common* warriors…' she began.

Valtyr shut her down. 'Look there, Tor,' he said. 'They're opening the gates. Welcoming us to the *gord*. How would you feel about a nice hot meal – and afterwards a steam bath? It's a famous Silesian specialty. These folk may be money-grubbers but they know a great deal about pleasure. No? You should try it. It will sweat the ill-humour out of you.'

Chapter Twelve

'I shall honour my promise'

Bjarki had never experienced anything like it. He was sitting quite still and completely naked on a bench in a small, cramped, windowless log hut – a bath-house – near the south wall of the enormous, roughly circular *gord*, and the sweat was running freely down his huge body in a hundred tiny rivulets. It was the day after their arrival and Bjarki and a few of the other *Wave Serpent* crew had decided to try out this unusual local bathing custom – which Valtyr most heartily recommended – for themselves.

So Lief, Halvar, Valtyr and he had tramped across the *gord* to one of the town's many bath-houses and had taken their places in this bizarre little wooden box filled with near-scalding steam. They were in there with several local merchants and two grim warriors, strangers to Bjarki but men who bore such a close resemblance to each other that they must have been brothers. Both warriors were squat, hairy brutes, much given to crude tattoos and livid scars. However, as Bjarki looked down at his own battered, stitched and burnt naked torso, he realised it was just as much a landscape of hurt and pain as the hides on these two brutal-looking men.

No women were allowed in this bath-house – there was a separate one for the ladies of the town, he had been told, next door, where he guessed Tor would now be having an uncomfortable time with the wives of the local merchants – and talking was, apparently, also frowned upon in here, which was a relief to Bjarki. He did not much like being naked in front of strangers and he liked the idea of making conversation even less.

One of the warriors got to his feet and walked to the centre of the steam-filled space, where a small hearth was filled with heated rocks. He grunted something in his own guttural tongue, a request or demand for permission from his fellow bathers, and when nobody answered him, he dipped a big ladle in a wooden bucket and poured cold water all over the hot stones. There was a loud crack, as one of the rocks split apart, and the small room suddenly filled with a blinding, skin-tingling cloud of steam.

It was actually very pleasurable, Bjarki realised, when he got over the strangeness of the experience. He could feel all the grime of the road, the old ale and stale mutton grease, oozing from his battered skin with the streams of sweat. He closed his eyes, leaned his back against the rough log wall and felt his mind drift off to a strange place, too. And when he opened his eyes again, he found he was in the Spirit-Realm once more.

However, the snowy wastes were gone and the winter landscape had been replaced by a bright featureless expanse of white sand, as if he were standing on an enormous, endless beach, but with no sea or lake in sight.

'You do not trust me,' his *gandr* said, in her deep, dark voice. Quite different to the voice she used in battle – that horrible chittering shriek. 'You do not trust me – but I would be a good friend to you, if you did.'

'Why would I trust you?' Bjarki replied, looking at the She-Bear, big, black and monstrous, sitting on the pure white sand only a few yards away. She was still chained by the neck to the One Tree, but the Irminsul had transformed into a vast sandy rock column, ridged with crumbling sandstone bark. Bjarki saw that the chain links were no longer fashioned from pale blue ice, they had become thick hoops of grey iron. 'You are not my friend. You do nothing to help; you but only beg me, endlessly, to slaughter more folk – and risk my own life again and again in battle.'

'Life is a battle, man-child. And I grant you my strength and ferocity in the endless wars of mankind. I preserve you from the blades of all your foes. You should trust me – I am worthy of trust, after all we have done.'

'I don't think so,' Bjarki said. 'My short life means nothing to you.'

The She–Bear laughed, a low, fruity, rolling rumble.

'Short it may be – and your doom is very near. But your life has value to me. Shall I tell you why? Because you feed me – you allow me to feast on the life blood of the men you slay. You are useful to me – and if you will trust me, then I will strive to prolong your short life, in any way I can. Do you know what happens if I do not have a man-child to nourish me? If I do not have a Rekkr to urge to the slaughter? I die, man-child, I will fade away and eventually perish. That is my doom as a *gandr*. I need you, man-child, without the blood you provide, I will be no more.'

'The ones I kill serve only to feed you?' Bjarki was shocked. 'You gorged on the blood of my Yoni, then? And now ask for my friendship?'

'The ones you kill are a sacrifice to me. Do you not slaughter a lamb or goat for Odin, from time to time? Even a captive thrall? I know men do. Besides, the dead are dead. You will soon be dead. So, one day, will I. Do you resent the worm for feeding on the corpse? Or the raven for feasting after the battle is won? Death is life – and all life ends in death.'

'You do not persuade, *gandr*. I shall never put my trust in you.'

'Then free me, anyway – cut the chain and let me find another man-child. I'll make another Rekkr to reap a corpse-crop for my sustenance!'

–

Bjarki sat up with a jerk. There were far fewer people now in the steam room. Valtyr was opening the door to leave. 'Do not stay in here too long, son,' he said. 'This heat will boil the remaining brains inside your head.'

Bjarki mumbled his agreement. A moment later, he too got to his feet. He felt light-headed, dizzy, in truth, and not only because of his dream.

He stepped outside of the little log chamber, into clear, cool air, and into a much larger room where a long rectangular pit had been dug in the earth floor and filled with murky grey water. Several men were paddling in the pool, including Valtyr and Lief, and some other naked folk that he did not know, and Bjarki took two quick steps and plunged straight in.

The chill shocked his whole body like a gigantic slap. He surfaced noisily, surging to the top and blowing out air and water-spray like a fin whale. Then he felt the delicious creamy shiver all across his bare skin as the rosy heat from the steam room was quenched by the cold pool water.

'The wise men of Serkland say these steam-baths serve to expel any noxious humours in your blood,' said a voice with a strong Svealand accent. 'They're supposed to clean you thoroughly, both inside and out.'

Bjarki wiped the water from his face and looked over at the speaker. It was a man of about middle years, clean-shaven, with a huge floating cloud of long black and grey hair spread out all around him in the water.

Bjarki frowned at this fellow. And something stirred in his memory. He knew this man; he was sure of it. But where had he seen him before?

'Although why our blood should contain any "noxious humours", or what these humours might be, I could not say,' said the long-haired man. He was a lithe fellow and now he hauled himself effortlessly out of the pool and strode over to a pile of linen cloths on a long bench nearby.

Bjarki followed him out of the pool, and over to the bench. He picked up a clean towel and began drying himself beside the stranger.

'Your name is Goran,' Bjarki said, after a little while, flicking back his own blond hair and tying the damp cloth around his waist like a kilt. 'I've been looking for you, all over the Middle-Realm, for a long time.'

The man, who was rubbing vigorously at his very long hair, stopped drying it at his words and gave Bjarki a keen glance, laced with more than a little nervousness. 'Have I offended you in some way, Northman?'

'You were in Brenna five years ago – at the spring market, yes?'

Goran nodded slowly. He peered beyond Bjarki's huge, scarred naked shoulder, as if looking out for a friend in the pool room. Preferably several large and well-armed friends. But they were now entirely alone.

'You serve the Duke of the Polans, do you not?'

'Why don't you tell me something I *don't* know,' muttered Goran, but cautiously. He was fumbling at a pile of his own clothes; there was a sheathed dagger tangled in there, and Goran took a grip on its bone hilt.

'You don't remember me?'

'My apologies, but no. I do not recall you. We had some business?'

'In Brenna, you showed me a picture of a lovely farm, with a pig and a garden and a fishing boat, by the sea, it was... very beautiful. You said your master the Duke of Polans would give away the land, for free, to any decent warrior who would take an oath and faithfully serve him.'

'Right, yes. That picture always had them drooling. I signed up dozens with that pretty board. I received a bounty in silver for each one I sent off to the duke. Now I recall you. You didn't want to take the oath.'

'I had made too many oaths, then, to too many different people.'

Goran allowed himself to relax a little.

'But you liked the idea of free land. Of course, you did. Everybody does. And is the offer still available? That'll be your next question. So... have you changed your mind about serving the Duke of Leszko? With my help, friend, I could easily secure you a place among his *druzyna*, his elite warrior band, if you chose to serve him. And the free land too, naturally. Are you ready at last to make the ancient oath of fealty to my duke?'

That stopped Bjarki. He had been so caught up in the unexpected triumph of finding this elusive man, this Goran, the long-haired man he had sought for so many years, over so many miles, that he was suddenly at a loss when the man himself popped up in this strange steam-room building and repeated his proposal for land in exchange for oath-service.

'I… um… I don't know.'

'Five years of searching for me – and you *still* don't know?'

'I did not expect to meet you here. In truth, I did not expect ever to see you again. And I have something else I must do first. A task… a mission…'

Goran already had a light linen shift on and was now slipping a wool tunic over his wet head, and belting it at the waist, arranging the sheathed dagger and his purse in their correct positions directly over his right hip.

'A mission, eh?' he said. 'That sounds interesting. Tell me more.'

'Your duke – is he leader of all the Polans? Because we had trouble in the north with some Polans horse-bandits, at a little place called Byd on the Wiessel, a fight, lots of bloodshed. Were they the duke's men?'

'The wild lands between the Wiessel and the Oder are not all completely tamed yet. Duke Leszko claims overlordship of them all from his hall up at Poznan, and he is the most powerful man in these parts, but the truth is… well, I must not be disloyal to my master. But… the truth is the various Polans tribes are divided. They squabble and fight with each other. Not all have seen the wisdom of bending the knee to my good duke and accepting his overlordship. He needs more brave warriors – strong men like you! – to give him the power to unify all the different tribes of Polans under his one banner. But whoever you fought, and killed – I am sure it will not be a problem if you wished to join us. Be easy, friend: I'd have heard if you had slain any Leszko oath-men. I'd be surprised too. Now, tell me a little more about your most intriguing *mission*…'

The man was tugging on knee-high boots, stamping them in place.

'I can't talk about it. It is a… I think it's supposed to be a secret.'

'A secret mission – that's even more exciting. Well, if you want to join us, I can easily be found out and about in the *gord* – I live here most of the year; I keep an eye on business affairs for my master up in Poznan. The *druzyna* here, that's the duke's man who is in charge of this *gord*, is an old fellow called Piast, a clever man, but greedy as a magpie. Slip him a silver coin and he'll tell you where I am on any day. Give him a bag of gold and he'd probably sell you his own daughter. Find me, if you want.'

The man paused and looked hard at Bjarki. 'But do not waste my time, or my master's. Decide. Duke Leszko *will* require an oath of you.'

With a wave of his hand the long-haired man turned and walked out of the bath-house, leaving Bjarki bemused, alone and starting to feel cold.

–

When he was dressed and armed again, with the heavy seax slung across his loins, next to his purse – which, unusually, now jingled with the few coins that Aistulf had grudgingly handed out for expenses to the members of the *Wave Serpent* crew – Bjarki too left the bath-house and began to stroll back to the lodging-house where Valtyr had arranged for them to stay. He did not yet know the Silesian *gord* well but he had a general sense of direction and knew that the lodging-house was towards the west.

It was nearly dusk and he was feeling pleasantly clean and refreshed by the bath-house experience. And a little hungry. Yet his mind was oddly divided: one part was prodding at the old idea, the long-cherished dream of taking an oath and serving this Duke of Polans and receiving a stretch of land by the sea for his pains. Could he do that? It sounded wonderful – but he was also aware that Goran's true profession was artful persuasion.

Did he trust him? No. The long-haired man might say anything to get him to take the oath. And, even if Goran lied, Bjarki would still feel bound by his promise. Furthermore, would serving Duke Leszco be any better, or any less dangerous, or more rewarding, than this quest he was already on? If they found the magic blade, and there was indeed a hoard of treasure, he would be rich and, more importantly, a fellow of renown. The hero who found the Loki Sword – the skalds would sing about *him*.

He wasn't sure he *could* take the oath. He couldn't leave Tor in the middle of nowhere, nor Inge, that was for sure. So, not now. One day.

The other part of his mind was taken up with observing the most interesting comings and goings of this strange island town, this oddly situated Silesian *gord*. This fortress in the middle of the River Oder.

The *gord* was three bowshots wide from side to side, and criss-crossed with broad streets, which had been strewn with fresh straw and bark to keep down the mud, and which were lined with timber-and-thatch houses, ale-shops, warehouses and workshops.

The town also contained more different types of people than he had ever seen in any one location before.

There were the local, well-fed merchant types, older men mostly, with braided hair, silver or gold chains at their fat necks and fine rings adorning their stubby fingers, and they strutted about the streets in their rich robes trimmed with sable and mink. They were followed by their slaves, iron-collared men, usually, who were laden with heavy goods.

He saw more than a few Polans, too, in their fur-trimmed felt hats, walking the streets in small groups with the slightly bow-legged gait that resulted from life in the saddle; and, here and there, were some more familiar Northern folk – blond, bearded men, with red-flushed cheeks and hard, watchful eyes the colour of a Norrland lake in winter – Svears, Geats, even a Dane or two. There were Wends, as well; he recognised their tongue: curly-haired ogres with big bellies and booming laughs.

He spotted Avars, slight, sun-tanned men, but proud as robins, with narrow eyes and tall iron helmets made even taller by horse-hair plumes. There were even a few lean, much darker-skinned men in long robes and turbans, with veils covering their faces except for their glossy black eyes. Men of Serkland, he suspected – who, according to Goran, believed that your living blood contained poisons that must be pushed out by sweating in steam-baths. They had big, broad daggers thrust into their embroidered belts, the sheath curling impossibly upwards like a ram's horn, and these leather-tough men looked no one in the eye, nor stepped aside for anyone.

There were women too – merchants' wives, big and bustling, talking too loudly to their friends and maid-servants as they visited the fruit-sellers, or eyed the fripperies on display at market stalls, fingering the finer cloths, and cooing with pleasure. They bought little packets of honeyed sweetmeats from street vendors to nibble and share with their friends. And there were many whores, too, of all sizes, dressed in flimsy, revealing gauzes, with big, jewel-like eyes lined with kohl, beckoning slyly to Bjarki from a doorway, or inviting him to join them in an alley.

He beamed at all the harlots, but refused their blandishments, just sauntering onwards, heading vaguely west, and stopping here and there to peer at the unusual trade goods on display on the shelves outside the fronts of the many, many shops – pottery, glazed and plain, in all shapes and sizes, bolts of all kinds of cloth from felted wool to fine silks, gleaming steel knives and swords outside the roaring smithies, food in abundance, from glittering river fish to pale cheeses made from ewes' milk.

He stopped at a stand in a street full of shops displaying freshly butchered meat where a man with a brazier was grilling coils of sausage over the coals, and bought a good length of the garlicky pork, which the vendor wrapped in a round flat bread for him to eat as he strolled along.

As he took a squelching bite of the hot meat and bread, chewed and swallowed the delicious mouthful down, wishing he had some fresh ale, he happened to glance up the street behind him and saw the two men, the brutish warrior brothers, who had been in the steam-house with him that afternoon. He would have thought no more of it – called it a coincidence, nothing more, this being a bustling town – except that, when they saw him looking at them, they dropped their gaze and dodged into a doorway.

All the fine hairs on Bjarki's neck stood erect at once.

He walked away from the sausage-seller slowly, chewing, thinking hard. Then he licked his greasy fingers clean, and wiped them dry on his tunic. He did not want his grip to slip. The crowds were thinning now, as the light began to fade; most people headed for their homes at the end of the trading day. He walked on for a little while, slowly, then turned into the first suitable side-street he came across, an alley, narrow and boggy underfoot. It was dim in there, with houses close together above him and blocking out the light. He pulled the seax from its sheath, holding it down by his right leg, hidden, and he waited.

And waited.

Nobody entered the alley. A little blonde girl ran past the entrance, laughing at some childish amusement. The daylight slowly died. He heard a bell ringing somewhere to indicate the closing of the town gates, the time for all decent *gord* folk to head back to their hearths. Still he waited.

Had he been mistaken? Was it simply a coincidence? Why should he *not* see those same two warriors walking about the streets of their town?

Bjarki stepped out of the alley. He looked left, in the direction the two men had been coming from. There was no one there. And the street was much less crowded now. He looked right. Saw two dark shapes loom up and – *bam!* – something crashed into his face with a shocking force.

A club, a fist, a sword butt... Bjarki could not tell. The blow rocked him right back, and he staggered away drunkenly; he'd heard the crunch of cartilage and felt a hot spurting from his nose, his knees sagged down. Everything swam, the world swooped and slipped left, yet he did not fall.

Bjarki sensed rather than saw the warrior rushing towards him in the gloom, a dark shape, hissing with rage, and he had just enough remaining consciousness to sidestep, and swivel his whole body round to the right.

The sword blow, a downward chop, missed him by only half a foot. Bjarki snapped back into the world. He reversed the direction of his turn, coming round fast on the same tight arc, his right hand flickering out, fast, punching forwards, still gripping the vicious foot-long seax blade.

He plunged the seax into the belly of the first attacker. The sharp blade slid through his skin and muscle easily enough, cutting through the ropes of the man's intestines, the point coming to an abrupt halt on the inside of the man's left ribs. Bjarki felt the bone-jar all the way up his right arm. He screamed 'Odin!' and shoved the ruined man off his slick blade with his left hand, a hard shove, and propelled him straight into the path of his brother, who was now surging forwards, his own sword raised.

The brothers tangled with each other like a pair of clumsy dancers.

Bjarki slipped past the slumping, mortally wounded first attacker, and hooked his seax towards the other man, a high, wide – and obvious – sweeping cut with the knife, which the warrior simply ducked beneath.

Which Bjarki had been expecting.

He booted his enemy hard in the chest with a fast swinging left foot. The kick bowled the heavy man over backwards, to splash arse-down in the muddy street. The man gasped, yet recovered very fast. He jumped up and came forwards again, the sword scything out towards Bjarki's head.

Bjarki leaned back out of reach of the swinging sword, and snatched at the man's arm as the steel flashed past his face. His fingers found a grip on a woollen sleeve and Bjarki hauled – and the man shot forwards, off balance, and Bjarki met his uncontrolled movement with his hard forehead, head-butting him savagely, knocking him into the mud again.

He leapt on the prone man, landing on his knees, his seax punching down hard. He hacked at the man's neck, but the fellow rolled his head to one side at the last moment and Bjarki's blade only scored deeply along his stubbled jaw. The attacker fought to bring up his sword, but Bjarki pinned his right arm with his chest, his weight pressed down, and gripped his enemy's bloody jaw with his left hand and sliced down again with the seax. The heavy iron blade ripped through the flesh, tendons and veins of the man's exposed neck. And Bjarki tore the knife free, pulling it back towards himself, slicing across his whole open throat. The man coughed massively, still struggling to free the trapped sword, a red gout shooting from below his chin. He gargled, moaned, huffed out a meaty mist, his eyes jerked and fluttered, darting here, there; then rolled inside his skull.

Bjarki pushed off the gore-drenched, dying man and got to his feet.

The first attacker was writhing and moaning, rolling side to side. Bjarki kicked away his sword, and dropped a heavy knee on his sternum.

'Why?' he said in bad Wendish. 'Why you do this killing me?'

Through his terrible pain the warrior muttered something, a filthy insult, in his own Slav tongue. Something to do with Bjarki's mother.

He set the point of the seax into a groove in the man's ribs, just to the left of his own knee, and pressed. 'Tell me why you attacked me – why?' In his anger and shock, Bjarki spoke in his own tongue – Norse.

The man moaned, the street beside him was puddled with his blood.

'For silver – why else take such a… risk with a famous Rekkr?' To Bjarki's surprise, the man had replied in his own language. But he was now panting in his pain like a deer at bay, clutching his ripped-up belly. His face was sickly pale in the twilight. Bjarki glanced about the street: it was nearly empty, but fifty yards further up there was the light of several moving torches and a group of men, spears and shields, fast approaching.

'Who paid you to kill me?' he asked. 'Tell me – or you die.'

But the fellow weakly shook his head. 'A Northman… like you.'

'What is his name? Tell me and I'll get help for your belly wound.'

'No, I am dead... and I shall hon... honour my promise to him.'

Bjarki put weight behind the seax point and was about to drive the blade down when a new voice shouted out something in the local tongue.

He looked up from the stricken man on the muddy street, both his hands still on the handle of the seax, and saw a short, wide warrior with a bow, a dozen yards away, the cord drawn back, an arrow ready nocked and aimed at him, and more men, a full squad of soldiers, behind him.

The bowman yelled again: it was clearly an order of some kind.

Chapter Thirteen

A terrible grief assuaged

It was clear to Tor that the local watchmen who had captured him in the street had had their fun with poor Bjarki. His face was a swollen mass of purple, black and red bruises and welts. His arms were bound tightly and awkwardly by the elbows behind his back and he was sitting on the rush-strewn floor of the *druzyna's* hall looking very sorry for himself indeed.

Tor caught his eye across the space, and rolled her own. Bjarki tried to grin in return but, instead, grimaced from the pain of his battered face.

The great hall was in the northern part of the *gord*, a high, airy stone building with a great wedge-shaped hearth in the corner nearest the door, a square sacred pillar in the opposite corner, which Valtyr had explained was carved with the images of their local four-faced god – four weird and ugly witch-like visages, to Tor's scornful eye. And, at the base of this bizarre pillar-altar, offerings of eggs, bread, ale and flowers had been laid.

Along the northern wall of the hall, a long trestle-table had been set out, beside which sat the *druzyna* of the Silesian *gord*, a straight-backed, white-haired, twig-thin old aristocrat who was known as Piast the Wise.

Valtyr, Aistulf and Tor had formed a small delegation to pay a visit to the hall and its ruler that morning, after they had discovered that Bjarki had been seized, bound and imprisoned by the town watch the day before.

They waited in silence while the *druzyna* ran a chilly eye over them.

'My watchmen say they caught this big Danish lump in the act of murdering two of my warriors, my good and loyal men Bolrog and Kust, in the Street of the Butchers yesterday evening. What do you say to that?'

Piast the Wise spoke very good Norse, with only a slight accent. And Valtyr replied to the lord of the town in that same fine, homely language.

'He was defending himself, your excellency – those same two warriors followed him from the Dreszky bath-house and attacked him in the street with swords, for no good reason at all, as he was walking home. They were clearly robbers, trying to relieve Bjarki Bloodhand, a plain and honest traveller, of his purse. And they paid the price for their greed and stupidity with their own lives. My friend is innocent of any wrongdoing.'

Bjarki opened his mouth – it seemed to Tor that he was about to speak, to deny the robbery story. She glared at him and shook her head.

'Well, they are certainly dead,' said Piast. 'Which puts a heavy thumb on the scales in your favour – for we now have only your Danish brute's version of the story. And, since he knows he now faces certain death for his crime, if I do find him guilty, we can also presume that he might say anything, anything at all, in an attempt to preserve his life!'

'He is no liar, your excellency,' said Valtyr. 'And neither am I.'

Piast the Wise lifted his chin. 'My dusk patrol saw all three of them fighting desperately in the street, swords and knives, gore everywhere, and immediately ran to intervene. By the time they arrived, both my men had been cut to ribbons. This fellow Bloodhand is well named, it seems.'

'Bjarki is indeed a fine warrior,' said Valtyr, 'and very terrible when roused to anger but, surely, he cannot be blamed for defending himself?'

Piast sniffed disbelievingly. 'You story seems unlikely. My warriors Bolrog and Kust have never been suspected of theft before, nor accused of anything similar – and those who knew them well say they had a fine sense of honour. There is more to this affair than meets the eye. We must put this Bloodhand to the question to see what answers can be extracted.'

'You've already hurt him enough,' snapped Tor, stepping forwards, bristling like an angry she-wolf. 'You beat him most cruelly when he was bound and helpless. Now, you speak of torture. I warn you, I'll not...'

Tor was brandishing her left index finger at the Silesian lord, but her right hand was tightly gripped on the worn handle of her seax.

'Peace, Tor, I beg you,' whispered Valtyr, putting a restraining hand on her thin shoulder. 'Your excellency, if I might offer an elegant and simple solution to this vexing problem: I can see you have suffered a sad loss in the deaths of these two warriors from your loyal retinue, what did you call them – Bolrog and Kust? A tragic and unfortunate loss. And even though Bjarki is innocent – he did slay them. So I think it only right that we make a small gesture of compensation, to assuage your terrible grief.'

'A *very* small gesture,' muttered Aistulf.

'I was thinking five silver Frankish *deniers*, would be an appropriate level of compensation for these poor dead heroes,' said Valtyr smoothly.

Piast the Wise stared hard at the one-eyed man for a long moment.

'I believe that ten silver *deniers* would be rather *more* appropriate,' he said. 'To assuage the agony of my sorrow and grief at their deaths.'

'*Ten?*' said Aistulf, in a kind of low, muffled squeak.

'Each,' said the *druzyna*.

–

They left the *gord* very early the next morning, the whole company including the three pack-ponies being ferried across the River Oder in the *druzyna*'s personal barge and set down on the bank near the Amber Road. Piast the Wise, after graciously accepting his *weregild*, seemed keen to get these dangerous, lethally efficient Northmen out of his nice *gord* just as quickly as it was possible. And so out they were – and safely across the River Oder before the sun was a hand's breadth above the horizon.

They set off on the wide road, heading south at a brisk pace, with Valtyr assuring Tor that they should be at the famous market at the old town of Carnuntum in only six days, five if the weather was kind. Which it was: a fine, sunny day with scarcely a cloud in the enormous blue sky.

Tor was pleased to find that her wounded calf, after only a couple of days' rest in the *gord*, and perhaps as a result of Valtyr's attentions, was almost completely healed, hardly painful to walk on, once the muscle was well stretched and warmed up. So she refused Valtyr's offer of a ride on one of the ponies and stumped along the track beside the one-eyed man.

'We need to find who is trying to kill Bjarki,' she said, after a mile or so. 'And soon. Those two Slav bastards he put down had been hired to murder him. And this is the second time – remember the archer in Asa's Landing? If we don't find out who is responsible, then one day soon, we will wake up to find Bjarki cold in his bearskin with a blade in his back.'

She then told Valtyr what Bjarki had revealed to her the night before about the Silesian assassin's dying words in the Street of the Butchers.

'He spoke Norse?' said Valtyr. 'Are you sure? That *is* interesting. And this fellow had also been informed that Bjarki is – was – a Rekkr?'

'It is not *that* interesting,' said Tor. 'These two incompetents were hired by someone in the *Wave Serpent* crew – all of whom speak Norse. The fellow admitted he was hired by a Northman before he died. If the would-be killers did *not* understand our tongue, then we could narrow it down a bit. But we can't. If that were the case, only someone who spoke Silesian – or another Slav language – could have given them the orders.'

'These languages are all similar,' said Valtyr. 'I have no great word-skill but I can make a Silesian understand my Polans – and vice versa.'

'My point is that this knowledge does not really help us,' said Tor.

'I think I know how to proceed with this,' said Valtyr.

That night at camp, in a sparse copse of birch a little off the Amber Road, Valtyr gathered the whole company around the bonfire.

'Some of you know this already – one of you certainly does. But someone in our midst, one of you, is trying to murder our friend Bjarki.'

There was a shocked silence. Inge, who was as usual bent over the bubbling cauldron of soup, suddenly burst into tears. Tor beckoned her over, put an arm around her and brought her into a tight embrace.

Valtyr continued: 'Whoever this person is, he has twice tried to kill Bjarki. Once at Asa's Landing he shot an arrow at him from the darkness; then at the *gord*, two days ago, he hired two locals to attack him in town.'

As Valtyr spoke, Tor closely watched the faces of the assembled company in the red flickering firelight. She was looking for a reaction, some expression of guilt or hatred. Her eye lingered on Rangvar, the man whose nose had been so savagely broken by Bjarki, but his bovine expression revealed nothing. She glanced at Halvar, who was ignoring Valtyr's speech and rubbing wax into the bow that always seemed to be in his hands. She caught Brandt's eyes, and he grinned at her, like a naughty child, then winked. And she found herself looking away hurriedly, feeling a pleasant warmth in her lower belly. She looked over the other crew members, skimming over Aistulf's puzzled frown, and her eye fell on Lief, who was open-mouthed, gawping with sheer astonishment on the far side of the fire – or was he overreacting, pretending to know nothing of this?

'These attacks must end,' said Valtyr. 'We have a hard road ahead and must all pull together. We *must* be able to trust each other. The unity of our company cannot be weakened by any suspicion. Stand up, Bjarki.'

Tor watched as her brother got to his feet, moving stiffly and with some difficulty, obviously in pain. He had his sword belted at his waist and his long Dane axe in his hand. His face was hideous, swollen and bruised, both eyes nearly closed. Yet he looked calm, too. And resolute.

'I issue this challenge,' said Bjarki, 'to the person who has been trying to kill me. Come out of the shadows and face me in the *holmgang*. I am hurt, as you can see – and weakened by the injuries taken during my imprisonment. But I will fight you now, man to man, in the hazel square. And there will be no penalty, nor any vengeance taken by my friends and family if I fall. Come forwards, face me in a duel – let us end this tonight.'

There was a long silence, broken only by the crackle of the campfire and a huge wet sob from Inge.

Bjarki turned towards his sister: 'Tor, tell them all that you will forgo revenge, if my foe reveals himself and fights me fair and square.'

'Bjarki, I... I don't think this is very wise...'

'Tell them, Tor, swear that you won't seek vengeance! Do it for me.'

Tor stood up: 'I... I swear I will not pursue my vengeance against any man who fights and kills my brother in the *holmgang* this night.'

But after *this night*, she told herself privately, *I'll hunt you to the ends of the earth. I will rip all the flesh from your bones and piss on it.*

Tor looked around the circle of faces once again. Nobody moved, nobody spoke. Bjarki actually stamped his right foot in his frustration.

'Will you not come forth, even now, and fight me fairly? You seek my death. Make it so! If you will not come forward, you are a coward, a *nithing* – and I spit on you and all your line. Come forward and accept my challenge. Odin watches us, Thor hears us, Tiw, the one-handed god of war, laughs at your shame. Come out, and reveal yourself. Fight me!'

Nothing.

Valtyr sighed and said: 'If the murderer will not face Bjarki in the hazel square, in hallowed combat, then we must all of us, each and every one, watch out for him. Keep an eye on your neighbour, observe your shield-mate, we must all ward our friend Bjarki's life. Do not let this sneaking dog achieve his ends. He has had his chance. If Bjarki dies now, by foul means, I shall use every skill I possess to hunt down and revenge myself on his chicken-livered killer. Mark my words, if Bjarki is slain by a skulker in the shadows, I shall not rest till I am revenged on him.'

'I, too, swear this same oath tonight,' said Tor. 'Furthermore, I promise the coward's end shall be neither swift nor clean. He'll suffer as long as I can keep him alive. I will take my vengeance in full measure.'

She sat down. Inge went back to her cauldron. Valtyr went to speak privately with Aistulf, and Bjarki came hobbling over to sit beside her.

'That,' he said, twitching his face into a painful grin, 'should do it!'

—

After two days, the land began to rise and Tor could see the high, jagged shapes of the Western Harvaths in the distance. After the long miles of muggy flatlands in the river basins of the Wiessel and Oder, Tor relished the cold smell of mountain air, even if the going was harder underfoot and the land more barren and sparsely forested. There seemed to be no cosy farms and villages up here, it was a wild land, untamed country.

They came across a band of a dozen men one morning, on a bright cold late spring day. They came swaggering round a bend in the road in a pack as if they owned the world. Both groups immediately stopped still and stared at each other. Nothing was said. The strangers were all men, all armed, but not well – rusty knives shoved in their belts, a spear or two, only one had a sword, and one rascally baldy simply had a wooden club.

Tor knew they were bandits – she also knew that the *Wave Serpent* crew was more than a match for them. Halvar strung his bow and nocked an arrow, Inge did too, while Bjarki just stood in the middle of the road, his hands on his hips, allowing them to get a look at his size and his scars.

Valtyr strode forwards, pushing past Bjarki, while the company all readied themselves for a fight. The one-eyed old man said something in Polans, which Tor took to mean 'Stand aside, lads'. And the bandits muttered to each other for a moment, and then the big man in the middle bowed in a fancy, comical fashion, and led his men off to the side of the road. They watched from the pines as the *Wave Serpent* crew filed past.

And that was it.

They did not scale the peaks of the Western Harvaths, which were always on their left, to the east of the Amber Road, but kept to the passes and valleys between the heights, always following the well-marked track southwards. Now, most nights in their cold, uncomfortable camp, they heard the music of the grey ones, which made all their hearts beat faster.

As Tor curled up in her blankets, close to Bjarki and with a naked blade tight in her right hand – she still took the threat against her brother's life very seriously – her mind drifted back, as she listened to the weird harmonies of wolf-kind, to the time when she too had tried to become Fire Born, a *gandr*-ridden Rekkr like Bjarki, and had willingly undergone a terrible lonely ordeal known as Voyaging.

She had lived rough in the First Forest, far to the west of here, naked with only a wolfskin and a knife to her name; trying to connect with the Wolf spirit, and entice that strange being into her heart. It had not worked, not even a sniff of a *gandr* did she get in those weeks, but it was now the yardstick of fear and pain against which she had since measured hardship.

This march was nothing compared with that cruel season. She had the big, comforting bulk of her brother against her back, food in her belly, and two warm blankets. They were going on an adventure into unknown lands to find a great talisman, a magical sword she only half believed in. And a hoard of gold, silver and jewels in which she had much more faith.

The next day they began to descend from the mountain passes and all of a sudden Tor found herself walking next to Brandt and Halvar. The tall, dark Danish warrior was obviously in an ebullient mood that day.

'A few days, three, four, and we'll be in Carnuntum,' Brandt said. 'We can get some decent food and drink – when Aistulf has filled our pouches with his silver. That's something rather fine to think about, eh?'

'And maybe a willing woman,' said Halvar with a filthy chuckle. 'Nothing like a pouch full of silver to make a girl suddenly friendly.'

Tor gave him a scornful look. 'You would need a shipload of gold, two shiploads, to entice anyone half-human into your stinking blankets!'

Halvar scowled at her. 'I hear you won't bed anyone of lesser rank than a Saxon duke,' he said. 'But not all of us are quite as prissy as you.'

Tor rounded on him, her fist cocked, pulled right back ready to strike. Brandt stepped in front of her. 'Go on up ahead, Halvar, and scout the road. It's your turn to take vanguard. Be a good fellow. Go on now.'

A muttering Halvar did as he was bid, and stomped off towards the head of the column. Tor and Brandt marched on together in stony silence.

'You didn't actually think you were protecting me from that mutton-brained prick, did you?' Tor said. 'I could kick his dirty arse from Hel's Realm to the halls of Valhalla any day, with no difficulty whatsoever.'

'I'm sure you could,' said Brandt, sweeping the raven's wing of hair from out of his lively blue eyes with his hand: a gesture Tor knew well.

Then he said: 'Mind if I ask you something, Tor?' And, before she could reply, he said: 'Is it true you were the Saxon duke's lover during the rebellion last year? That's what old Halvar was poking at, wasn't it?'

'What's it to you?'

'Nothing. I just wondered. Why are you not still with him?'

Tor said nothing for a long time.

Brandt said: 'I am sorry. I've obviously overstepped the boundary mark of our comradeship. I beg you will forgive me, Tor.'

'No, no, it's not that, I just find it hard to speak about Widu-kind...'

Brandt nodded but said nothing. They walked in silence for a while.

'It just didn't work out with us – with Widukind and me,' said Tor, who found to her fury that she was blushing. 'We had different ideas about love.' She was not sure why she was talking about this with Brandt – she had only ever spoken about it to Bjarki before, and even he knew not to probe too deeply. But she liked this dark, handsome man – she liked him a great deal, and she realised that she wanted to open her heart to him.

'Have you ever loved?' she asked him. 'Truly loved someone?'

'Yes. Well, not successfully. There was a girl in Viborg that I bedded enthusiastically, and often, and thought I loved her. But I didn't, in truth; I just enjoyed her. And there was a girl in the Auxilla, who would never have me, but I loved her fiercely. I still do, even though she is now dead.'

'Why would she not have you? You seem a, uh... a suitable man.'

'She did not like something that I had done in the past. A killing. I had killed someone. And she said she could never love a murderer.'

'I'm sorry for you,' said Tor.

'Life is strange, isn't it? And love is by far the strangest part of life.'

—

They came to a dirt-poor Slav hamlet that evening, where, since it was raining hard, the water falling like enemy spears, Aistulf stumped up for their miserable lodgings with a coin or two. They bunked down in a filthy hovel, also occupied by several pigs, on mounds of pig-urine-smelling straw and, at dawn, all were itching and covered with tiny red bite marks.

'Makes you long for the clean, scalding steam of the *gord* bath-house,' said Bjarki cheerily, as they trooped out of the hamlet – which was now gleaming in the rain-washed sunshine – early next morning. All of them tired, cross and irritable, except apparently for him. His big face was healing now but it was still a rainbow of hues, from sickly yellow to angry red to a greenish purple. Yet he never complained of his hurts and volunteered that morning to take vanguard duty and scout the road ahead.

They came to the River March two days later, and Valtyr took Tor by the elbow and said quietly: 'See over there?' nodding towards the furthest bank, a long bowshot away. Tor looked at him questioningly. 'That's Francia on that side. Thuringia. The river marks the boundary line. Those are Karolus's lands. Well, you would still have to ride a good fifty miles west to meet a Red Cloak trooper, but you know what I mean.'

'And on this side?' she said.

'Borderlands. The Avar Kingdom but, in truth, a no man's land!'

The land across the river – enemy territory – appeared no different at all to the rough ground on this side, at least to Tor's eyes – sparse trees, sandy soil, a few dusty shrubs, grasses and bushes, but not a person or dwelling in sight. The only sign of life was a doe watching from the treeline.

'The Great Plain is five days' march that way.' Valtyr pointed south-west. 'Beyond the Harvaths. An ocean of grassland, forest and swamp.'

The road they followed was joined by another and became wider and more rutted and ran due south along the eastern bank of the March. And Tor had a sense that they were emerging from the wild and coming into more civilised lands. They began to see the detritus of other travellers. Campfire ashes smouldering, broken egg shells, mutton bones, an old boot strap. A cracked leather bottle abandoned by the side of the road.

'Several different routes down the Amber Road all converge here,' said Valtyr. 'We may meet other folk, so be prepared for company. The day after tomorrow, we should be in sight of the market at Carnuntum.' He waggled his eyebrows. 'And that's when the *real* adventure begins!'

'Are you going to tell us at last where the Loki Sword has been hidden all these years?' asked Tor. Despite herself, she felt a jolt of raw excitement at the idea of the ancient blade, even if it wasn't truly magic.

'I'll tell you tonight, after supper. I'll give you the saga of the battle between the Goths and the Huns, when the Loki Sword was last wielded.'

Chapter Fourteen

Goths versus Huns

'In the days of our grandfathers' grandfathers,' began Valtyr. 'When the ancestors of those Geats who now live in the North were still living in their southern heartland, not so far from this spot *here* where we make our camp...' The old man patted the turf beside his rolled-out blankets.

'In those glorious days of old, there lived a venerable king of the Goths called Heidrikr who had two sons by two of his many wives. One son, the eldest, was named Angantyr, and he was a mighty warrior, tall and strong – whom some believe was the first *berserkr* – and he was destined to rule over all the tribes of the Goths when his father had gone to the Hall of the Slain, to feast with Odin. The second son was called Hlod, a smaller, weaker man but crafty – as cunning as Loki, folk said.'

Bjarki settled back comfortably on his thick bearskin cloak. His bruises were more or less healed from the savage beating he had taken from the watch-soldiers in the *gord*; he had a belly full of hot venison stew, made from a young fallow doe expertly brought down by Halvar's bow right across the River March, the carcass collected by Bjarki – as the best swimmer of the company – and beautifully cooked with ale and wild onions by Inge over the campfire, and he felt a warm sense of well-being.

Since his public challenge to the unknown assassin – which had been ignored in such a cowardly fashion – he had felt a good deal safer. The would-be murderer had been shamed. And even if he did manage to kill Bjarki, he would for ever afterwards be known as the *nithing* who ducked the challenge to fight his enemy in an honourable manner. It felt very much like a victory, to Bjarki. And he was aware his friends were now constantly looking out for him. The other morning, when he had gone out to empty his bowels after breakfast, he had seen Brandt, with a naked sword in his hands, watching over him from a nearby bush while he did his business; and Tor too, walking not far behind Brandt. His sister had apparently decided to take a stroll with a spear as her walking staff.

He felt guarded, well protected. It was a good, comforting feeling.

'Hlod the Sly grew ever more jealous, day by day, of his mighty half-brother Angantyr – whom he believed was unfairly favoured by their father,' said Valtyr. His story had swiftly entranced the entire camp; every face in the dancing firelight was now fixed on the old man's.

'Angantyr had been married the year before to a beautiful young princess of the Prussian folk, and Hlod demanded that he, too, be given a bride of equally high status and fine looks. He asked his father to secure for him a great lady of the Hunnish people, a hardy horse-folk who had recently come from the east, over the high peaks of the Eastern Harvaths in their thousands, and who were living in the most distant, most easterly part of the Great Plain. To Hlod's astonishment, his father readily agreed to this demand. The Huns had long been the mortal enemies of the Goths, since the days when these fierce interlopers had first invaded their lands. The Goths had fought many a fine, bloody battle with them but had been pushed back and back into the west of their territory by the newcomers.'

'The king of the Goths said…' here Valtyr changed his voice, sounding like a frail old man in his death bed: '"Your marriage, my son, will achieve a lasting peace between our two peoples, a peace that will hold long after I am gone. Go to the Huns, with my blessing, marry your princess, let our people live in amity." So Hlod took his horse and rode.'

Bjarki got up and went over to the wood stack. He selected a dead fir branch and tossed it on the fire, which blazed, making Valtyr's face seem even more lean and shadowy, his one blue eye gleaming in the firelight.

'Years passed – and to the surprise of many folk peace and harmony prevailed between the nations of the Huns and the Goths. For the first time in an age, the pastures of the Great Plain were unwatered by blood.

'The old king of the Goths died quietly in his bed and his eldest son Angantyr was duly acclaimed the ruler of the nation in his stead – yet, strangely, his half-brother Hlod did not reply to the invitation to come to witness the funeral rites of their father; nor did Hlod attend the formal acclamation of Angantyr by all the Goth people; nor even did he participate in the ceremony of blood sacrifice, the dispatch of a dozen thralls, when the royal helm-crown was placed on Angantyr's brow and he took his seat on the Throne of Arnheimer, the ancient chair that had supported the Goth kings for so many generations.

'The first the Goths heard of Hlod's activities came a month after Angantyr's coronation feast. The peace was shattered when his Hunnish armies erupted out of the eastern part of the Great Plain and began to burn the farms along the River Tisza, killing the honest Goth husbandmen who tilled their fields there, taking many slaves and vast piles of booty.

'Therefore Angantyr roused himself and girded for war. "Fetch me the blade of my father, and of his father before him, fetch me the Loki Sword," he thundered to his Royal Companions, "bring me Tyrfingr!"

'He rode out with his Companions, a hundred of the bravest and mightiest horse-warriors of the Goths, each a champion who had sworn to die rather than allow the slightest dishonour to stain their king, Angantyr, or his royal line for ever. With the mounted Companions came the massed ranks of the famous Goth infantry: hundreds of iron-tough hillmen from the Harvath Mountains; doughty shield-men from the villages along the Donau; stout-hearted farmers from the Great Plain with their long axes and even longer memories – all came when the king summoned them, and marched proudly under the banners marked with his Bear symbol.'

Inge was coming round now with the heavy ale sack, pouring out cups for the listeners. Bjarki sank a cup and, before the thrall left, he asked for another. Inge poured it for him and they shared a smile before she moved on. *She should have a man*, Bjarki thought, *a good man to stand beside her – one whom I can trust to treat her well all her life.*

And, just as he thought this, he saw that she had stopped in front of Lief, and was smiling and blushing as she poured a nut-brown stream of ale, lingering, while the handsome youngster made some joking remark.

Bjarki scowled. *Not him. That young man is clearly a capering fool.*

'Five thousand strong was the army of Angantyr,' Valtyr spoke with a fine heroic ring to his voice, like a well-trained skald. 'And they met the Hun host in fair and open battle, without flinching, forming one great line of massed warriors on foot. Shields high, hearts higher. And behind them, the disciplined ranks of the noble Companions, with King Angantyr in the centre, under his royal banners, seated on his great white stallion.

'They met the enemy forces at a village called Dunheidr, on the Great Plain a little to the west of the Lake of Tears, as that great body of water later became known. Hlod himself was in personal command of all the teeming Hunnish battalions – his beautiful princess now the queen of the Hun nation, and he her loving consort, a king himself in all but name.

'The Huns charged, shouting their battle cries, and galloping their little steppe ponies at the bristling battle line of the Goths, who stood firm as troll stones, brave as badgers, as the Hun arrows fell on them all in a black killing rain. They endured, they sheltered under their shields and endured the terrible onslaught. And the Huns, seeing that, would not move from their position, and fearing to engage them honourably, even from the backs of their mounts, turned their ponies and fled in abject terror.

'So the Goths cheered their victory, five thousand throats roared out their scorn and derision for the fleeing, cowardly foemen. And followed after them, the Royal Companions leading the charge, seeking to catch up with the lightly armed Huns and slaughter all these *nithings* to a man.

'The swift-running hillmen charged with the Companions' cavalry, bounding along beside their warhorses, holding their stirrups, and all the axe and the shield-men broke out of their tight ranks and came rushing forwards, too, haring across the open field of war, five thousand brave men, eager for the slaughter of the hated Hun and calling on Odin to witness their mighty deeds. And then… And then…' Valtyr's voice cracked and broke; he wiped a single teardrop from his withered cheek.

'And then disaster struck. The Huns, schooled in deep cunning and low tricks by their new general Hlod, turned their nimble horses round and fell on the pursuing Goths, who were now strung out all across the battlefield, all their cohesion lost. The eastern horsemen massacred them, shooting them with their arrows from afar, then chopping them down at close range with sword and axe. The Huns' retreat had been a clever trap all along, a cunning stratagem – more Huns appeared from the north, and south too, and Angantyr's mighty army was encircled and overwhelmed.

'The Goths fought like heroes, of course, and sold their lives as dearly as they could, and many a Hun horseman met his demise on the blood-drenched fields by the Lake of Tears. But a handful of the Royal Companions, a few dozen men only, so the legend tells, saw the danger of the Huns' trap early and forced King Angantyr to withdraw before he too was surrounded and slaughtered. And so they did. Yet the Battle of the Lake of Tears is still remembered as a terrible day, a black day for the whole Goth nation, and they never again regained their homelands in the Great Plain. Never! And subsequent generations of Goths would move ever westwards and northwards, until, eventually, in time, the ancestors of our own Northern folk, the Geats, crossed the salty Austmarr and made a home for themselves in the endless pine forests beyond the northern sea. But our people have never forgotten the catastrophe of the great battle at the Lake of Tears, nor the terrible events that happened just after it…'

Valtyr stopped speaking and drained his cup of ale with a flourish. He beckoned Inge to refill it, looking slowly round the circle of faces.

'Nobody ask him,' said Tor. 'Nobody do it! He always does this same silly little trick when he's telling us a story – he stops right before the very best bit. Stay quiet. Don't indulge his stupid skald's tricks.'

'But I have to know,' said Bjarki. 'Come on, Valtyr! I know you want to tell us. What happened? Where did the king go? Did he escape?'

'Well, since you ask so courteously, Bjarki, I shall tell you.'

Valtyr cleared his throat.

'Angantyr and a few dozen of his most loyal Companions galloped due west, the king weeping scalding tears and cursing the Fate-Spinners, and his brother Hlod the Sly, who had deceived him so artfully, with his remaining men trying in vain to comfort the king. He had not even drawn his ancestral blade at the battle of the Lake of Tears, Tyrfingr remained sheathed the whole time – perhaps because he was mindful of the curse that Loki had placed on the blade, that any man who wielded it would taste Death. Yet Angantyr was also consumed with a great shame at the loss of the lives of so many of his men, who had been sacrificed in vain – so he wept as he rode, inconsolable, salty tears running down his cheeks.

'West, he rode, ever westwards. Yet he could not escape the foe. He was pursued, harried, mile after mile, by his half-brother Hlod with a strong force of Huns. For Hlod hated his older brother, and coveted their father's kingdom to add to his own wide lands. And he had vowed, long ago, long before he even left the Goth kingdom, that Angantyr must die.

'Hlod hounded Angantyr, his tireless Hunnish riders always in sight behind the fleeing king and his retinue. They fled west all the way to the banks of the mighty River Donau, then northwards, and still his brother came after him. And, eventually, their poor horses failing beneath them, and in the shadow of the Western Harvaths, Angantyr was brought to bay.

'He and his last remaining men formed a tight ring of shields at an ancient fort on a small hill, a castle built by the trolls long before the Age of Man. And there they stood in brotherhood and waited for their end.'

Valtyr took a swig of his ale. Bjarki found he was so absorbed by the tale he was holding his breath as he imagined this heroic last stand, the doughty Companions, gathered around their king, ready to die with him.

'What happened next? Go on, Valtyr, don't leave us hanging.'

'The Huns completely surrounded the hill on which the troll ring stood, ensuring there could be no escape for Angantyr. And Hlod himself came forwards to the bottom of the hill. "Surrender to me, O my brother," he said. "Renounce for ever your claim to the Throne of Arnheimer. Kneel before me in the mud and beg my forgiveness – then, perhaps, I shall spare your miserable life. But first of all you must render to me the sword of Loki, the blade known as Tyrfingr, which is the symbol of our House."

'Angantyr stepped out of the ranks of his men and faced Hlod on the slope. "This sword?" he said, drawing the Loki blade from its sheath. "If you want *this* sword, brother, you'd better come up and take it from me."

'Hlod the Sly smiled, and shook his head, and went back down the hill to his waiting men. He gave orders for the assault on the fort to begin.

'The Huns unleashed a storm of arrows on the handful of brave men on the top of the slope, and so thick was the cloud of black shafts, the skalds say, that although it was noon, it blotted the light of the sun...'

Tor made a scoffing noise. 'The skalds always spout that sort of stupid horse-shit,' she said. 'It's impossible, you know, you would need thousands upon thousands of arrows all in the air at the same…'

'Shut up, Tor,' snapped Bjarki, 'you're spoiling Valtyr's story.'

'Shall I go on?' enquired Valtyr and a chorus of eager voices begged him to do so. 'Well, then… Angantyr and his Companions endured that first terrible arrow onslaught, although almost a fifth of their number succumbed·to the deadly hail. The king said to his remaining warriors, "If we stand here, we shall die like sheep in a slaughter yard. Let us take the fight to the enemy. Let us go down from this hill and fall on our foes – we may perish, no doubt we *shall* perish, but we shall make such an ending that men will speak of it with awe and wonder for a thousand years!"'

Valtyr mopped again at his teary cheek. 'And that is exactly what they did. King Angantyr, wielding the Loki Sword, the heirloom of his House, charged down the hill and attacked the Huns – and although they were greatly outnumbered, they slaughtered their enemies, and set the more cowardly Huns to flight. The Companions fought like the heroes of old, each man with the strength of ten. And Angantyr surged into the very centre of the Hun ranks, filled with a wild *berserkr* fury, and calling out to his brother to face him in combat. Nothing could stand in the path of his frenzy, nor could any withstand the power of his sword – no armour, no blade, not even the stoutest shield could survive a blow from Tyrfingr.

'Angantyr slew his enemies: he reaped them like corn, he left them lying in their scores in bloody swathes across the field of battle and when, at last, he came face to face with his brother, he paused, and lowered his dripping blade. "Kneel and beg for your life, Hlod – and I shall spare it."

'The Huns were all in full flight by now. After seeing their leader, a foreigner, a Goth, prove to be a weakling and coward, at the mercy of the mighty Angantyr and his magic sword, they vaulted on to their ponies and galloped away east. And Angantyr and Hlod were left, facing each other on the gore-enriched field, alone but for a few of the Companions, most now grievously, or fatally wounded, who had survived the awful carnage.

'Hlod threw down his sword, and knelt on the earth, hot tears of shame streaming down his face. "Forgive me, O my brother," he said. "I have been rash and foolish and full of envy. Spare me, I beg, and I shall honour you as my king and serve you faithfully till the end of my days."

'Angantyr was filled with pity for Hlod, whom he had loved in their childhood, and took mercy on him. He opened his arms and embraced his half-brother, weeping for all the blood that had been so needlessly shed.'

Valtyr paused again, and looked round the circle of faces once more.

'But Hlod was cunning and cruel, and even as his older half-brother embraced him in a spirit of love and forgiveness, he pulled an assassin's dagger from the back of his sword-belt, a hidden blade, a slim and deadly knife, and wielding it well he treacherously pierced his brother's belly.

'Angantyr staggered back, hurt, surprised, oozing gore – and looked over, astonished at Hlod the Sly's expression of triumph, and at the bloody knife in his brother's right fist. Angantyr screamed a war-cry, part pain, part fury, and swung the sword Tyrfingr, one last time, and sliced the head of Hlod clean from his neck with one mighty blow. Hlod fell dead, but Angantyr, too, alas, was mortally wounded, and sank to his knees, as his Companions rushed to his aid, spilling his life's blood on to the turf.'

There were gasps of shock all round the fire.

'And that is where Angantyr fell, and that is where he is buried, in a warrior's tomb, interred by his grieving Companions. He had wielded the Loki Sword – and he had tasted Death. The curse had been fulfilled. And in Angantyr's final resting place, in his tomb, they deposited the treasures of his realm beside his body: his war axe, his helm-crown, and his Bear banner. They sacrificed his white stallion and laid it beside his body, so that he might ride him in the Spirit-Realm and, lastly, they placed the hilt of his sword into his hand. And that,' said Valtyr, 'was the last time that Tyrfingr, the Loki Sword, the wondrous blade fashioned by Dwalin, the Dwarf-Master, and cursed by him too, was ever seen by mortal eyes.'

There was a long shocked silence. Somebody sniffed wetly.

'So where is this tomb?' said Bjarki. 'Where exactly, I mean?'

Valtyr was silent for a time. Then he said: 'All I have is a witch's vision and two scraps of verse. But it should be enough. This poem is old, and was made by Hirdstein Silver-Tongue, greatest of Geat skalds.'

He intoned:

''Neath a troll-wrought rock where the blackbird sings in silence,
The last gleam of Loki's Day lights a doorway to Hel's own realm,
And the resting place of Angantyr, lord of Goths, shall be revealed,
Where felled by brother's spite, our king lies ever in his splendour.'

Valtyr took a breath. 'This next one is a bit simpler,' he said. 'I've heard a more elaborate version of the poem performed in Uppsala at King Harald's court. But I like this one – I heard some children singing it at a cattle market at Vestmar in the Little Kingdoms, west of the Dane-Mark:

'Where the Duna turns south to face the noon sun,
The king he fled north, a full day at the run.
He found his last fortress, a troll circle of stones,
And there he did battle, and there lie his bones.'

'And what is all that mystical babbling supposed to mean?' said Tor.

Valtyr smiled at her. 'I'm sure we'll work it out in time,' he said.

Bjarki was frowning and counting on his sausage-like fingers. 'I recall Loki's Day,' he said. 'Big party. The first day of summer, isn't it?'

'It is celebrated every year on the first day of the month of Harpa.'

Bjarki was still ticking off his fingers. 'Unless I have this utterly wrong, that's in only six days' time. Isn't that right, Valtyr?'

The old man did not reply – he just winked slyly at the younger one.

Chapter Fifteen

An enemy of Karolus

The ancient town of Carnuntum was once home to a powerful fleet of military galleys, which patrolled the eastern part of the River Donau in the name of Rome in days gone by. Now, it was little more than a few weedy mounds of tumbled brick, broken marble columns, deformed statues, rubble and mud on the far bank of the river, from what Tor could see.

However, the location that the Roman town had occupied all those years ago was still populated by a large section of humanity – but instead of grand temples and red brick villas, the inhabitants lived in tents and wooden shacks and other make-shift shelters set between the piles of broken stone. Carnuntum might no longer be a city of gilded bronze and polished marble, but it was still a hive of activity, a thriving marketplace.

They had arrived at the northern bank of the River Donau in a heavy thunderstorm, with veils of water sweeping across the choppy surface of the wide river, and had to wait for two full hours, sheltering under their shields, until a boat could be induced to take them across to Carnuntum.

Tor observed the sprawling tent town half a mile away on the south bank of the river. It was not at all what she had been expecting – it seemed far less permanent than in her imaginings, but also far more busy. Valtyr had told her that huge amounts of trade came into the town along the River Donau, from the rich lands of Francia, even from distant Frisia, too; and from the other direction, hundreds of folk sailed upstream from the scattered Avar farms and settlements on the Great Plain, bringing wheat, wine and fruit to sell to the Franks and others. As well as that, it was an important stopping place on the Amber Road, with folk coming down, as they had, from the Slav lands in the north, bringing precious cargoes with them; and others coming up from the sunny Mediterranean to exchange goods at this convenient locale. All required food, drink and shelter.

When they finally attracted the attention of a small timber barge, and induced its Wendish owner to ferry them across, everyone in their party was soaked and snappish, Tor most of all. Only Bjarki maintained his sunny outlook, making jokes in the captain's tongue with real merriment.

Once they had disembarked, the rain eased and Tor discovered as they shouldered their way through the busy streets that Carnuntum was overflowing with hundreds of different peoples speaking the tongues of many nations: slight Avars discussing with hulking Prussians, fur-capped Polans drinking ale with hardy, mountain-dwelling Moravians, bluff, fair-skinned Northern folk like themselves swapping gossip and goods with tanned, sloe-eyed Italians, as well as a horde of Serbs and Sorbs and other Slavs. But the ones who gave her most cause for concern were the Black Cloaks – the elite troops of Francia, the vast Christian kingdom that stretched from this muddy tent town all the way to the Western Ocean. For the Black Cloaks, Karolus's household troops, were here in force.

These soldiers were formally called *Scholares* and their primary task was to safeguard the sacred person of the king of the Franks. However, quite often, Tor knew, they also undertook special, even secret missions for their royal master or senior members of his court in distant Aachen. Furthermore, they were even sometimes used as glorified watchmen in the more unruly parts of Karolus's realm, places like this frontier town, for keeping the peace and hunting down malefactors. And, while Tor knew this, and also recognised it was inevitable that Black Cloaks would be found on the Frankish border, she found their presence discomforting.

She and Bjarki had had several run-ins with the Black Cloaks over the years, which had usually ended in bloody violence. However, on that day she had no sense that they represented a threat – they paid the *Wave Serpent* crew no particular heed, as far as she could tell. And when Tor accidentally bumped into a Frankish officer with a fine black plume nodding on his polished iron helmet, the man actually apologised to her for his clumsiness. The ordinary Black Cloak troopers flocked around the tightly packed goods stalls just as eagerly as any of the other travellers; they visited the food carts, made tantalising with the smell of frying onions; they eyed the wares on the covered tables, fingering the goods and making admiring sounds; and when they made their purchases they brought out purses packed with glinting silver coins. They behaved no worse than any other traveller – in fact, they had rather better manners than most. No matter. Tor hated them anyway, from the core of her being.

As the rain began to patter again, Aistulf led them to a huge wooden shed in the south of the make-shift settlement, a hastily constructed and draughty space, which served as a lodging-house for travellers. The merchant soon secured them a corner of the shed and a glowing brazier, where they could wring out their clothes and dry them near the red coals.

Almost immediately, Aistulf went out again into the drizzle to search for his friends and kinsmen, all fellow Lombards, with whom he wished to make the arrangements for a discreet handover of their valuable cargo.

Valtyr gathered the whole company around the glowing brazier. He leaned in, as if conspiring with them in some desperate scheme.

'Listen, all of you: this is the last and most perilous part of our service with Aistulf,' he said. 'The merchant will deliver the satchel over to his friends, and will take possession of their silver coin. Then we shall all be paid our share of the profits. When we have divided up the money fairly, and everyone is happy, we will take leave of our friend. He will go south into Italy; we go east in search of Angantyr's tomb and the Loki Sword.'

There was a good deal of excited merriment at this news. But Halvar said: 'You still don't know exactly where the sword is, do you, old man.'

'Not exactly, but if you trust me, I shall find it. *We* shall find it.'

'You said something about a witch's vision,' said Tor. 'What is all that about? Along with all those weird verses, a vision. Who's the witch?'

'I'll explain later. Just trust me. For the moment, we need to keep our thoughts fixed on Aistulf and the safe delivery of his amber satchel.'

They ate wooden skewers of grilled pork, purchased from a man with a tray of them, and drank some ale and dried off a little in the shed; then Bjarki wandered off to speak to some other travellers sheltering inside. Eventually, Aistulf came back, wetter than ever, and reported that the meeting for the handover had been set: that evening at moonrise.

'There's no need for any concern,' he said, 'we shall be among my friends. I trust them completely. But since there is a large amount of cold hard silver and some valuable goods involved, I should like all of you to accompany me, armed and alert. Though I'm sure there'll be no trouble.'

Tor slept a little.

Valtyr had gone out to seek a shipmaster who might be willing to take them on the next part of their journey, eastwards along the Donau.

Bjarki roused her in the early evening with a cup of warm ale and honey and they both began to dress and arm themselves. She put on her iron-mail byrnie and slung a round shield over her back, and strapped her long sword at her side. It felt odd to be dressing for a battle in the middle of a big draughty shed full of damp merchants, but she saw that Bjarki was also donning his byrnie and bearskin and picking up his long Dane axe. She was just strapping on her own war helm, a fine piece with cheek-flaps and a nasal guard, when Bjarki said: 'Did you know – there's been some sort of rebellion against Karolus in Italy? I was talking to this fellow just up from Carinthia who says a Lombard duke called Hrodgaud has risen up, butchered all the local Red Cloaks, and declared his duchy of Fruili independent from Francia. Should I tell Valtyr, do you think?'

'He knows about that,' said Tor. 'So do I. That's the point of...'

'Gather round, everyone,' said Valtyr. 'It is time to watch over our good friend Aistulf for the last time on this journey. The rain has finally stopped, you will be glad to hear. So let us depart now. Bjarki, would you be good enough to do the honours and carry that heavy satchel for him?'

Bjarki slung the bulky leather bag over his shoulder, picked up his axe and shield and they trooped out into the grey twilight, with Aistulf in the middle of the pack in his finest clothes, and Valtyr leading the way.

Carnuntum had come alive that evening. Every small group of tents had a bonfire blazing outside and men and women were gathering around the flames, rubbing their hands against the chill, drinking hot ale and telling tales of their homelands. They skirted a huge pile of weed-covered bricks and walked past a large canvas tent, brightly lit inside, from which issued the raucous sounds of women's laughter, the music of a lute, and loud singing. One fellow, clearly drunk, reeled suddenly through the tent flap, arm in arm with a slatternly woman with hair dyed scarlet, and her large, sagging grey breasts half exposed by her open shift. She flashed a gap-toothed smile and a wink at Rangvar, who immediately growled a friendly greeting in response. Then, as the drunken couple staggered away into the darkness, Tor heard him mutter to Halvar: 'When this business is done, and our pouches are full of Lombard silver, I shall come back and pay a visit to that tent – you'll come with me, won't you, Hal?'

'Aye,' said Halvar, throwing Tor a sour look. 'That I will, Rang, and gladly. It's been a long, lonely road. We deserve a little jollity tonight.'

Inge, who was walking beside Tor, with her light bow slung across her back, said: 'That place *does* look like it might be fun to visit – that woman who passed us just now seemed happy. Could we go there later?'

'Over my cold corpse,' said Tor. 'They would gobble you down like a fresh oyster in there, girl. You'll stay by my side all night in *this* town.'

The tracks between the clumps of tents were glutinous with deep mud, and strewn with big white stones, and they had to pick their way carefully. Here and there they saw the prone bodies of travellers. Men, usually, who were either actually dead or had drunk so much ale or wine they had fallen dead asleep on the swampy ground. Some had obvious fresh wounds; some had been robbed of their boots. They ignored them all. This town was lawless. Despite being inside the Frankish realm, there was no sense of an overarching authority. The *Scholares* had all vanished.

Away to their right, Tor could just glimpse the wide black waters of the Donau, and the bare tree-like masts of several ships moored on the bank. She wondered if Valtyr had managed to make an arrangement with a kindly ship's captain. The sooner they quit this horrible place the better.

They came to a grand circular tent, made of light and dark striped material, a fine pavilion, and Tor could see a pair of large mailed warriors standing under the long awning that jutted out from the tent's flap entrance. They were clearly tent guards, experienced men with long swords at their belts and spears. They snapped erect and bristled when they saw the crew of the *Wave Serpent* – fifteen of them – approaching them.

'Name yourselves,' said the guard on the right, levelling his spear. He spoke in Frankish, a tongue that Tor could understand, but with a strange foreign accent, perhaps the dialect they spoke down in Lombardy.

'I'm Aistulf of Pavia,' said the merchant. 'I'm here at the invitation of Stephen of Ravenna for an appointment. Stand aside, my good man!'

To Tor's satisfaction, both the guards instantly dropped their spears, bowed very politely, and even held back the flaps to allow them to enter.

Once inside, it was clear that the Lombard merchants who had arranged to meet Aistulf here were even richer than he was. The interior of the tent was draped with many expensive cloths of velvet and silk, purples and scarlets, black and green. There was a beautiful tapestry hung all along one wall, depicting elegant hunting scenes, picked out in silver and gold thread. There was a pinewood table in the centre of the room, covered with a blue silk cloth, the hanging border embroidered with gold.

A merchant, a fat, middle-aged fellow with thinning black hair, stood behind the long table, a warm smile of welcome on his chubby lips. He seemed hot, possibly even a little feverish, with beads of sweat on his wobbling jowls. Before him on the table were some sheets of parchment, and a set of large brass scales, along with various small weights. Beside him, actually very close beside him, stood a thin man dressed all in black, with a large crucifix hanging over his chest. The glossy brown hair on his young head was cut into a ring, showing a pink, freshly shaven bald spot over his crown. Tor recoiled in surprise – she had not expected to find a priest at this meeting. She knew Aistulf was a Christian – Valtyr had mentioned it – as were almost all his Lombard countrymen, but he had never made a show of it on the road. He never prayed or wore a cross.

The priest had one hand resting on a big wooden box, which was bound with iron bands, which looked very solid indeed. He seemed very nervous, and Tor noticed his hand quivering as it rested on the dark wood.

The fat merchant came around the table and bustled forwards.

'Aistulf, my good cousin, you are well met,' said the big man, reaching forwards a sweaty hand for the other to clasp. They gripped each other's forearms, smiling into each other's eyes. 'A pleasant journey, I trust,' said the fat man. 'Not too much trouble on the northern roads?'

'Nothing my bold comrades and I could not handle, Stephen,' Aistulf replied. 'A few bandits gave us a fright in Byd – but little else.'

'I am happy for you,' said his cousin. 'So, you have our amber?'

'You have my silver?'

The Lombard merchant flicked a fat finger towards the strong box.

'Well then, let us get to it,' said Aistulf. 'No time to waste, Stephen. My dear Bjarki, if you wouldn't mind bringing my satchel to the table.'

As Bjarki came striding forwards with the heavy leather bag, Tor had a good look round the tent for the first time since she had entered it: there were a dozen guards in there, she saw, standing around the circular walls, these men built on the same general design as the two outside the door – tall, mail-clad fellows, with swords and spears, iron helms but no shields.

The interior guards observed the *Wave Serpent* crew with a stony glare. That didn't surprise her; they were paid to look hard. But there *was* something odd about them. It took her a while to realise what.

None of them had beards. Not one. No luxuriant moustaches either. The fat merchant Stephen, now back behind the long table, had a square bushy hedge below his bulbous nose. Their own friend Aistulf, too, was handsomely provided with a well-trimmed, sandy-coloured jaw-warmer. But the guards inside the tent were all clean-shaven, recently barbered. Perhaps it was the fashion for Lombard soldiers. How should she know?

Her attention was distracted by Bjarki, who was carefully bringing out the various packets of amber from inside the open leather satchel. He handed them reverently to Aistulf, who opened them with care and spread the contents on the blue silk cloth – and Tor was immediately entranced.

Each nugget of amber was a magical burst of colour and light. The pieces varied greatly in size, from items with the dimensions of a single elderberry to great jagged lumps with the heft of a man's fist. But that was to be expected – Valtyr had described them as coming in a range of shapes. What Tor had not been expecting was the enormous variations in their hues – from the pale yellow of barley straw, through to rich, honey-coloured stones; to golden pieces filled with captured sunlight and all the way down to deep brown knobs the baleful shade of a scabbed wound.

Tor found she couldn't tear her eyes away from them. She watched as each piece was brought out, admired by both Aistulf and Stephen, held up to the candlelight for a brief moment and weighed on the scales; then Stephen would mutter a word to the priest, who would nod agreement, dip his quill in the ink-pot and scratch out a brief note on his parchment.

Tor realised that Bjarki was back at her elbow and whispering something oafish to her about the Lombards. 'Yes,' she said, irritated at being diverted from the rhythm of the amber inventory, 'these people are all Lombards, good Northern stock originally, but now living in Italy.'

'I was only saying that it was strange that this transaction should still be going ahead, now that their rebellion has so swiftly been quelled.'

Tor turned and looked at her brother. She said: 'What?' then, as quietly as she could manage, 'What! What do you mean by that, oaf?'

'I tried to tell you before – but you said you knew all about it.'

'Just tell me!' Tor kept her voice low, but out of the corner of her eye she could see the slender priest watching her, with narrowed eyes.

She drew Bjarki further away from the table, and leaned close into him. 'What do you know about the rebellion in Lombardy?' she said.

'Duke Hrodgaud rebelled a little over a month ago, about the time we were leaving Svealand,' Bjarki instinctively kept his voice low. 'I was told this only today by a trader who had just arrived here from Carinthia. It all went badly wrong. Some of the duke's own people were in the pay of Karolus, or perhaps bought by his chancellor Bishop Livinus, our old enemy, you remember him? The rebellion was betrayed from within by Livinus's spies. Karolus rode south from Aachen, fast as lightning, and the uprising was crushed, almost as soon as the duke raised his standard.'

'Valtyr!' Tor's voice was battle-loud: 'It's a trap. A fucking trap!'

At that very same instant, all the brightly coloured cloth walls of the tent collapsed. Someone, somewhere, had cut the vital ropes. The tent walls all dropped to reveal the outside world of Carnuntum at night and to display a ring of twenty Black Cloaks surrounding the now wall-less tent with their bows in hand and a score of arrows ready nocked to the string.

A black-cloaked officer, his dark plume nodding, stepped forwards.

'Stay exactly where you are, you barbarians! Move – and you die.'

One of the clean-shaven guards, none of whom had shown even the slightest surprise at this development, stepped forwards smartly and drove his spear deep in the Aistulf's lower back. The merchant screamed, and sprawled on the floor, spilling a handful of amber across the beaten earth.

'Remain perfectly still. All of you!' the *Scholares* officer was now shouting. 'Anyone who moves so much as a hair will be instantly slain!'

'You promised me my cousin Aistulf would not be harmed, Clovis,' bellowed Stephen, pointing a pudgy shaking finger at the priest. 'Look at him now – you fucking murderer.' Then the fat man came bustling round the long table and knelt down beside his writhing, blood-soaked relative.

'He is the enemy of Karolus, our noble king, and my master Bishop Livinus,' said Clovis. 'He was a paymaster for the duke's rebellion in Fruili. He deserves death – *at the very least*. As do you, Lombard pig!'

The thin priest made a signal with his hand, and the same spearman stepped forwards again and thrust his point into Stephen's unguarded back.

Chapter Sixteen

A place filled with enemies

At the second brutal spearing of an unarmed man, Lief moved. Out of the corner of his eye, Bjarki saw the young man haul his long sword from its scabbard and take a step forwards, covering Inge with his body. An instant later, three arrows thudded into his chest. He coughed gore and collapsed.

Bjarki moved. He was aware Tor and Valtyr were also in motion.

He hurled his Dane axe – a very unconventional move. The weapon was a broad-bladed wedge of sharp, heavy steel on a five-foot-long pole, and designed for chopping through shields and lopping heads in battle.

Bjarki threw the weapon laterally, the long instrument spinning round and round through the air, flying parallel with the beaten-earth floor. And, astonishingly, the axe struck its intended mark. The steel head thunked hard into the belly of the black-plumed officer just as he was shouting something, some order, to his men gathered outside the tent. The axe cut him off abruptly, the blade burying itself deep in his guts. He was knocked over and, an instant later, the tent was full of arrows.

Bjarki rolled forwards fast, coming up at the left-hand end of the long pinewood counting table. He saw Valtyr there, too, snatching at the big iron-bound strong box, contesting it, briefly, with the young priest Clovis.

The one-eyed old man lashed out with his walking staff, a yard and a half length of ancient knotted blackthorn. He thwacked the priest smartly around the side of his white face with the staff, causing the Christian to stumble blindly backwards and fall. And Tor, he saw, had her shield on her left arm, limb through the leather loops, and she was covering Inge's cowering body as the wicked shafts flew thick and fast around them both. Two arrows were already embedded in the shield's leather-faced surface.

All this Bjarki took in, in the blink of an eye, he also saw that two of the *Wave Serpent* crew were already down, bleeding, cursing, and curled around the arrows that had punctured their bodies.

One of the tent guards was slashing his sword down at little Halvar, who dodged the blow, somehow, and pulled out his seax. The Frankish sword missed the bowman by an inch, and Halvar bobbed up and in return jammed his seax into the outside of the guard's upper thigh.

The Black Cloak howled and Halvar shoved him away hard, then whirled and slashed another *Scholares* right in the face, just as that fellow was coming forwards. Rangvar, too, was wrestling with one of the nearer Black Cloaks, both struggling with the Frank's long spear. He let go one hand, swung his elbow, a tight fast forward arc, cracked the soldier in the nose, then ripped the spear free, flipped it and buried it in the man's belly.

Bjarki took a grip on the end of the wooden counting table and, summoning all his considerable strength, he lifted the heavy slab of pine, twisted his body, wrenching the table up with him, and hurled the whole piece of massive furniture, silk cloth flapping like a flag, across the space and into the wall of Black Cloaks by the northern side of the tent. The table, a massive object the weight of a full-grown cow, tumbled lethally, over and over, smashing into the line of archers, hurling them this way and that like skittles in an alley when struck by an ale-house bowling ball.

'This way!' Bjarki bellowed. 'Come on. Follow me – everyone!' And, whipping out his sword, he charged straight out of the tent into the disordered line of Black Cloaks, smashing down into a fallen man who was trying to rise as he swept past him.

One Black Cloak archer who had miraculously been missed by the flying table was drawing back his cord about to loose a shaft at Bjarki from a yard away. Bjarki lashed out with his sharp sword, his long arm at full stretch, crunching through the wood of the bow, collapsing it all into a mess of string and sticks in the man's astonished hands. Then Bjarki jammed the long blade into his ribs, jerked it free – and slashed him across the face.

Another Black Cloak lunged at him with a spear, and Bjarki had to jink and parry hurriedly to knock the point out of its lethal line. The spear slid past him. He allowed his own momentum to carry him on, crashing into the Frank, knocking him down with his huge hurtling weight alone.

Bjarki snatched a glance behind him, and with relief saw Tor and Inge there, Tor's shield high, the round face now decorated with half a dozen more shafts, but both seemingly unharmed. And there was Valtyr, too, the strongbox cradled in his arms. Behind the three of them was Rangvar, the spear hefted in his hand; and Halvar, snarling, seax bloody, hunched as if moving in a storm, and coming up fast behind Rangvar.

They all pelted out into the fire-lit darkness, blindly following Bjarki – who, in truth, had no idea at all where he was leading them. They were going away from the Black Cloaks, that was good enough for now.

They dodged behind a brightly lit tent, cut through behind another dark one, Bjarki tripping over guy-ropes invisible in the night, sprawling and nearly cutting himself on his own sword. A man shouted from inside the collapsing tent. A torch flared somewhere on the left. And Rangvar reached out a big hand and hefted Bjarki up on to his feet. On they ran.

They crept between a line of empty market carts – Bjarki treading on a sleeping man's belly, who moaned, rolled, and puked wine in the mud.

They ran again. And found themselves, breathing like hound-hunted deer, on the south bank of the Donau, crouching behind a dark and silent tent, some sort of spice emporium. There, they paused and took stock.

They listened intently. There was no sound of immediate pursuit but in the distance they could hear the soldierly barking of an officer, a Frank, it seemed by his language, who was trying to gather troops for the chase.

'This is their territory,' panted Valtyr. 'This town is inside Francia – the Black Cloaks will do as they please. They will not stop hunting us.'

'Is everyone all right?' said Bjarki, looking round the depleted group of *Wave Serpent* folk, those who had somehow survived the Black Cloak's ambush. Rangvar had a nasty cut all across his right cheek, above his beard, where a passing arrow had sliced his skin, and which was bleeding profusely. Halvar had a shallow sword gash on his left forearm, which Tor was busy bandaging with a bit of her own torn woollen tunic. Bjarki had two waggling arrows embedded in the back of his bearskin, but they had not penetrated the good, iron byrnie he wore underneath. Inge had twisted her ankle running in the dark, and it was swollen and hot, but she could still put weight on it. She was weeping, but quietly, almost silently, and Bjarki was not sure if it was because of her ankle or the death of young Lief. And yet, all things considered, this small remaining group had escaped the trap in the tent remarkably unscathed.

'What about the others?' said Rangvar. 'Should we wait for them?'

'All the others are either dead, wounded or prisoners now,' said Valtyr grimly. Bjarki noticed that he was still hugging the iron-bound box in his arms. 'And whatever their condition, we can do nothing to aid them. If we go back we will be in the same state as them. We must flee.'

'Should we not at least *try* to rescue them?' said Halvar.

They stared at each other in silence – just the six of them in the dark, on the edge of the Frankish realm, in a town filled with their enemies.

No one had anything practical to offer.

'I say we go – and go now,' said Valtyr. 'If any of you wish to remain, to attempt a rescue, I will not stop you. But I am heading east.'

–

The boat that Valtyr obtained for them was not much bigger than a large fishing smack. But it cost him a small sack of silver coins, just the same. The man who sold it to them claimed it was his livelihood and he did not want to part with it. So Valtyr paid the man from the stolen strongbox, which was filled with half a dozen similar bulging linen bags, and all six of them had scrambled into the vessel, and shoved off into the darkness.

The night remained dry, which was something. But it was bitterly cold on the water with a brisk west wind whipping across the water's surface. Yet Bjarki did not feel the cold; he kept seeing the falling, arrow-stuck body of young Lief in his mind's eye, over and over again. Valtyr gave him a sharp elbow in the ribs and he shook his head and roused himself to attach and hoist the single triangular sail and, with Valtyr at the tiller, they sailed into the middle of the stream, aided by the strong current, and were swept away giddily from the torch lights of Carnuntum.

There seemed to be a sizeable commotion coming from the tent-town, now behind them, much angry shouting and the outlines of soldiers and spears against the torchlight, dozens of folk running here and there. But they were swept speedily down-stream, the black bank whizzing past on their right, the steerboard side, until the lights of the town winked out.

And, so far as they could tell, there was no serious pursuit. Not yet.

'How did you know it was a trap?' Bjarki asked Tor, after a while.

'The guards had no beards – like nearly all the Black Cloaks I have ever had the misfortune to encounter, they were clean-shaven like youths. When you told me that the duke's rebellion had failed, that the amber deal had no point... it all seemed...

off. That fellow Stephen, Aistulf's cousin, he seemed nervous, too. He sweated like a pig the whole time.'

'That traitorous *nithing*!' said Valtyr. 'May he freeze his cock and balls off in Hel's icy home until Ragnarok and the doom of all the gods.'

'Or burn for ever in agony in that Christian place!' said Tor, who was gently levering the stuck arrows out of the leather face of her shield.

'What's your plan now, old one?' she continued, looking at Valtyr.

'It has not changed, girl. Down the river, east. Then we make our way up to Angantyr's tomb. And find the Loki Sword – and the treasure.'

'Will you tell us again what you know about the place where he is buried?' said Bjarki. 'No one can overhear us. You said something about a blackbird and Loki's Day and a troll circle. A witch who had a vision?'

Valtyr nodded: 'The battle between the Goths and the Huns is recounted in an epic poem made by the skald Hirdstein Silver-Tongue. The poem has been passed from skald to skald from that distant time down to this moment. It is a masterpiece that details the catastrophe of the Battle at the Lake of Tears, as well as Angantyr's doom. But this is the only verse – the very last one of the poem – that concerns us right now.'

The old man recited once more:

> '*'Neath a troll-wrought rock where the blackbird sings in silence,*
> *The last gleam of Loki's Day lights a doorway to Hel's own realm,*
> *And the resting place of Angantyr, lord of Goths, shall be revealed,*
> *Where felled by brother's spite, our king lies ever in his splendour.*'

'The second verse I recited is doggerel,' said Valtyr, 'a children's rhyme, but it is very old and I think it holds some truth in its simplicity.'

> '*Where the Duna turns south to face the noon sun,*

169

The king he fled north, a full day at the run.
He found his last fortress, a troll circle of stones,
And there he did battle, and there lie his bones.'

'Very nice,' said Tor. 'But what does all that actually mean?'

'It means that Angantyr lies buried under a troll ring – you know those odd circles of massive old stones that you find in high places? No one knows who built them or why – though I think the trolls constructed them as fortresses of some kind. Or boats. Stone boats on land, maybe.'

'You're maundering, old man. *Where* exactly is this troll ring then?'

The one-eyed man sighed: 'Since we now have a little time on our hands, I shall tell you all I know about the site of the tomb of Angantyr.'

There was little traffic on the river at night, although they could see vessels moored on the banks, and the dotted lights of campfires by them.

'Keep a good look out there, Rangvar,' Valtyr called to the big man at the prow of the boat. 'We don't want to hit a snag or some floating log.'

'Just tell us,' said Bjarki, 'I'm getting tired of your evasions.'

'Very well. Let us start with the second verse: the Duna is an old word for the Donau,' Valtyr began. 'And the place where the river makes a big turn to the south – towards the sun – is eighty miles away or so. That's where we leave this boat. The king rode north for a day at the run – that is clear enough, I think, even for a dull-witted oaf like you, Bjarki. So we go north for about twenty miles, give or take, from the bend in the river until we find an old hill, crowned with a troll stone circle, which is where Angantyr and his Companions made their final stand.'

'That is not exactly precise,' snapped Bjarki, he was feeling irritated at being called a dullard. 'It could be anywhere within a two-day march.'

'Fortunately,' said Valtyr, 'I have the testimony of another wise and far-seeing person to help us. You remember young Katla? The dark-haired girl who was a *gothi* for a short time at the Groves of Eresburg?'

Bjarki did not reply. He cast his mind back to the time he had spent at the Groves – a time of many joys and also great sadness. He had been trained in warcraft at the Fyr Skola in the Groves, where he had met the Fire Born for the first time, and had gradually come to understand his own power. And, some years later, he had been made jarl of south Saxony by Widukind, including the Groves of Eresburg, which had been in his charge, with the Fyr Skola under the shield of his personal protection.

The Fyr Skola had been destroyed, almost casually, by his greatest enemy Karolus. The elite troops of the mighty king of the Franks had effortlessly overrun the Groves of Eresburg, slaughtered all the defenders and the resident *gothi*, and hacked down the One Tree, the totem of the North, the mighty Irminsul, the tree on which Odin had sacrificed his life, the All-Father hanging from its branches for nine days to gain wisdom.

The Franks had simply chopped straight through the enormous girth of the Irminsul's trunk and toppled the Mother of Trees; and, to add insult to injury, they had built a Christian church from its flesh on that very site.

Bjarki's failure to protect the Groves was a bitter memory, one which still burned in his heart, and would smoulder on perhaps for ever.

Valtyr was still speaking: '…and she wrested her knowledge from the waves and sea, and the people of the mountains and forests, and now Katla is a true wise woman, an *alsnotr*, and, some say, a powerful *volva*!'

'What does this witch have to do with Angantyr's grave?' said Tor.

'She saw it,' said Valtyr. 'She saw it in a dream, or a vision, if you like. She saw the place and described it to me. She also saw old Angantyr reborn, and full of youth and strength, and wielding his sword Tyrfingr.'

'This is all nonsense,' said Bjarki suddenly. 'Angantyr has been dead for hundreds of years, and the Loki Sword is likely no more than a rusty pile of flakes in a mouldering sheath. If we even find the place…'

'Katla saw a hoard of treasure, too, gold and silver and fine jewels – and they do not corrupt, even as the ages pass. Think on that, all of you!'

The old man's tone was triumphant, almost gloating. And Bjarki saw by the faint moonlight that Halvar was grinning under his scrappy beard.

Inge was owl-eyed at Valtyr's words; she no longer looked utterly frightened. Tor, too, had a thoughtful expression on her face. Bjarki was about to say something about the gods-cursed crime of grave-robbing, about disturbing the hallowed dead, pillaging their tombs just to put some silver in their pouches, just like a gang of greedy thieves. And then he thought of Aistulf, curled up in agony on the earth floor of the tent, with a Frankish spear deep in his back, and wisely decided to hold his tongue.

'One more thing,' said Valtyr. 'According to the skald Hirdstein Silver-Tongue, the entrance to the tomb will only be revealed by the last gleam of sun on Loki's Day. It will shine on a blackbird singing silently – whatever that is supposed to mean. So we can't afford to waste any time.'

'Is that why you have been in such a hurry all along?' said Bjarki.

Valtyr shrugged, but he did not deny it.

'Is that why you would not wait an hour longer in Carnuntum to try to rescue our poor comrades?' said Halvar.

'No,' said Valtyr. '*That* was because there were a couple of hundred angry Black Cloaks looking to fill my belly full of arrows.'

'How long till Loki's Day?' asked Tor.

'Three days from dawn tomorrow,' said Valtyr.

–

The boat sailed on swiftly under the stiff breeze and the powerful river current, with Bjarki using all his skills to keep the speed of the craft up. The hours drifted by and they saw little sign of local life upon the dark water. They took turns in steering the craft, under Bjarki's instruction, while some dozed, but in truth the wind and river did most of the work.

The Donau was wide here, two full bowshots across, so there was little danger of running aground. And they sped along, all through the night, ever eastwards, towards the slowly lightening sky. Finally, when the red rim appeared beyond the boat's prow, Bjarki steered them expertly towards the northern bank. As they hauled down the triangular sail, and stowed it away in its locker, and climbed stiffly out of the craft, Valtyr guided them through a forest of bullrushes, to the marshy bank beyond.

Bjarki splashed ashore, the last to leave the boat, stretching his sore, cramped limbs and yawning. He looked out over the wide grey waters, now tinged with a bloody pink from the rising sun. He could see that the Donau was indeed beginning its great curve south over the next mile, and silently admitted that, perhaps, Valtyr did know what he was on about.

A hissed warning: 'Get down, now, everybody on your bellies.'

It was Tor's voice. And as Bjarki crouched in the reeds, he saw where she was pointing. West and south across the wide waters, to where the stark outline of a ship could now be easily seen in the growing light.

It was a galley, a long, lean, fighting vessel, painted black, with sixty black oars on each side, and a single fat, black-painted main mast. No sail was hoisted that morning, but the oars worked the water to the beat of a deep, slow, majestic drum. At the rear of the ship was an awning, a tent-like shelter, and Bjarki could see that the decks forward of this awning were packed with fighting men, helmed in polished iron, armed with spears, and wearing the distinctive garb of their enemies: Black Cloaks.

Chapter Seventeen

In no mood for a massacre

The fishing smack was hidden in the bullrushes. And the six surviving members of the company hugged the damp ground, peeping out through the dense brown reeds as the ship slipped past their refuge. The only sound was the dull throb of the drums that drove the oarsmen onwards, and the faint, rippling splash of the banks of oars as they churned the water white.

It took until the sun was a hand's breadth above the horizon before the galley made the turn around the long bend of the river and began its slow journey south. Tor watched it dwindle and disappear with her heart on her mouth and a sense of cold dread in her belly. She heard a rustling beside her and turned her head to see Valtyr crouched at her shoulder.

'I think one of our people must have survived the ambush in the tent,' he said softly, 'and, whoever it was, has been forced to talk.'

'You think they are seeking us?'

'Without a doubt. A fine Frankish warship, filled with hundreds of Black Cloaks, would not normally venture into the near-hostile Kingdom of the Avars. Into these unclaimed wastelands north of the great river, yes, maybe. But southwards down that big bend of the Donau is true Avar territory. There is a large town down there called Buda. A big armed incursion would be seen by their Khagan, their king, as a gross act of war. They are here to find us, I'm sure of it – and they're prepared to risk the wrath of the Avar Khagan and all his horse-warriors to achieve their aim.

'You think they want the Loki Sword? Why? A rusty old blade.'

'The Franks understand – as you do *not*, it seems, Tor – the potency of that symbol in the hands of the North. Bishop Livinus is behind this. I know it. I can smell his foul Christian touch all over this affair. He clearly arranged the amber-ambush in Carnuntum, via his agents, for sure, but he himself gave the order to kill. That bastard bishop isn't done with us yet.'

They collected their war gear from the little boat and knocked a hole in its bottom, sinking it in the reeds, where with a little luck it would remain undetected for some days. Then they headed north at a fast trot.

Valtyr seemed to know where he was going, but Tor wondered whether this was merely his usual bluster. They soon came across a road of sorts, and a collection of wooden huts, thatched with rye straw, at a crossroads. It was a homestead, raising a rye crop, kitchen vegetables and pigs, Tor reckoned, but the women and children all immediately fled at their approach. A middle-aged man came out to greet them, an axe in one hand and a brave-but-terrified look on his face, shaken at the unexpected arrival of half a dozen gaunt strangers, dirty, damp and all heavily armed.

They could not make themselves understood to this dull fellow, who had the dress and facial appearance of an Avar – even when Inge piped up in her own faltering Slav tongue – but with crude mimicry, pointing and a good deal of shouting, they made him understand that they needed food.

The situation looked set to turn ugly, the man clutching at his wood axe with both hands, and Halvar with an arrow ready-strung, when Valtyr produced a silver coin, as if by magic, in his fingers and held it up high, twinkling in the weak sunshine. Then all was smiles and laughter, and good fellowship, and the women and children were summoned back to the house, and the farmer fed them warm rye bread and slices of delicious salty smoked pork, and a kind of thin soup made from cabbage and garlic.

It would have been very pleasant, Tor thought, to bask away the afternoon, sitting with full stomachs on a split-log bench outside the Avar's house in the warm sun, telling tales or just dozing. They were all tired. But Valtyr insisted they get back on the road as soon as possible.

'Loki's Day looms,' he said. 'The Black Cloaks are on our trail. They'll come here. We'd be wise to kill the Avars, to still their tongues.'

Yet, after the generous hospitality they had received, and the recent deaths of so many of their friends, no one in the company was in the mood for a massacre. Bjarki, bristling like an angry mastiff, said he would stop anyone who tried to harm their hosts. So, having purchased a sack of provisions, and two leather bags filled with fresh ale, with a few more of Valtyr's *deniers*, they left the Avar a happy man, waving from the door of his hut, with his wife and his offspring chattering all around him.

They pushed on until the early evening, always heading north-wards, the ground rising under their feet with every step, and made their camp in a patch of woodland a bowshot away from the main road, by a stream.

Ahead of them all that day they had seen the foothills of a mountain range, brown and purple with high, distant white-capped peaks even this late in the spring – the Western Harvaths, Valtyr told them, the same range they had seen on their left flank as they came down the Amber Road, but now they were looking at them from the other, southern side.

Looking south from the camp, through the trees, Tor could see a long stretch of empty road behind them, with only a lone farmer on a mule plodding down towards the great river. Not even a sniff of a Black Cloak, she told herself, as she wrapped her blanket round her shoulders and prepared for sleep. The *Scholares* had either given up the chase or gone on down the river in their galley on some other business entirely.

In the chilly dawn, they washed in the stream and ate a hot breakfast of smoked pork, eggs and bread, and full of good food they were soon on the road again, still heading north towards the distant mountain range.

They saw the dust at noon, a large cloud moving up the road, half a day's march behind them, Tor reckoned. But moving swiftly. Horsemen.

'Run or hide?' said Tor to Valtyr. 'Or should we stand and fight?'

Valtyr goggled at her. 'There are two hundred horsemen behind us! Can't you see? And you talk about a fight. We hide, girl, we hide like trembling hares in a ditch and pray the gods shield us from their view.'

It wasn't quite a ditch, more a shallow fold in the increasingly hilly landscape behind a screen of elm trees, but they took refuge there, and watched hearts in mouths as the cloud of dust approached along the road.

They *were* Black Cloaks, Tor saw, with a sense of sour resignation. Of course they were Black Cloaks. More than two hundred of them, too, maybe two hundred and fifty, even three hundred mounted and well-armed, well-trained soldiers, a *scara*, or regiment, of *Scholares* cavalry.

Their excellent full-length scale mail reflected the sunlight, and she could make out the distinctive two swords at their sides, a long blade and a short one, and the javelins in holders at the horses' withers. They even seemed to slow their approach menacingly as the company watched them come from behind their low ridge, all six of them lying on their bellies, and peering at the enemy through clods of broken earth and long grass.

The horsemen stopped about two hundred paces from their hiding place and, at an order from a plumed officer, they dismounted, seemingly all at once, like a wave. It was too far away to make out the individual faces of the Franks, and they were all helmed in polished iron, with long nasal guards, and cheek pieces as well. But there was something familiar, Tor thought, about the way their leader strode up and down the length of the columns, exchanging a few words, jokes and oaths with his troopers.

Now they were all drinking from their leather water-bottles, gathered together in small groups, and their plumed leader was striding back up to the head of the column. Then some sort of discussion occurred between him and his second-in-command, a very slender, almost waif-like man.

The slim lieutenant took off his helmet and wiped the sweat from his face with a gloved hand. The day had been surprisingly hot, a promise of a fine summer to come hanging in the air. Tor realised, from a glimpse of pink scalp as the man bent his head, that he wore the tonsure, the sign of a priest. Could that be Clovis, the man who had murdered their friends?

Tor would have bet a whole sack of Valtyr's silver coins on it.

–

'I think we need to be a little further east,' said Valtyr, when the dark horsemen had remounted and ridden away north and the road was empty once more. 'Angantyr was coming from the east, and when he hit the Donau, he turned north. We came in from the west. I think the troll circle is likely to be a little further that way,' he pointed at a hilly, rock-strewn landscape beyond the road, where a few thin, stunted sheep were grazing.

'Do you think we are near the treasure now?' said Rangvar.

Tor gave him a little sideways grin.

She had once suspected that Rangvar was the one trying to murder Bjarki – as revenge for his crushed beak. But the nose was healed, if still a little askew, and that idea seemed unthinkable now. All the hardship and dangers of the journey, particularly surviving the ambush in Carnuntum, had forged them into a tight unit, with a bond almost as strong as kinship.

'If I am right, the fortress of troll stones where they made their stand will be in those woodlands yonder. East.' Valtyr pointed. 'I think we have come about as far north from the bend as a man on a horse in a day's run, and from Katla's description, yes… I think we are very close now.'

'Do you think the Black Cloaks know where it is, too?' said Tor.

No one answered that question for half a dozen heartbeats.

'They do not have Katla's vision to guide them,' said Valtyr.

They marched a few miles east and then Valtyr had them searching the foothills, in pairs, in a half-mile long line of hunters, always within sight and call of each other, looking for anything that might resemble a troll stone circle on a hill or the tomb of a long-dead king of the Goths.

Bjarki and Tor formed one pair of searchers. They wandered across bald hills and sparse fields, seeing the occasional empty stone-built sheep fold, but little else. Tor pondered the likelihood of them stumbling over a centuries-old grave site containing a fabulous hoard of treasure. Away on their right they could see Valtyr and Inge investigating the ruins of an old roofless hut or hovel, the circular stone walls tumbled into mossy rubble.

'It feels like the edge of the world up here,' she said to Bjarki, who had stopped walking and was looking up and watching a falcon circling effortlessly in the blue sky. 'Like a place shunned by mankind. Cursed.'

Bjarki looked at her. 'It's the borderlands. Valtyr called it a no man's land. If it was filled with hundreds of people and their farms, villages and towns, I doubt Angantyr's tomb would have remained lost for very long.'

'You think we will find it?' she said. 'Because a witch dreamt it?'

He did not reply but resumed watching the hunting bird. When she had almost given up on getting a response, he said: 'I believe in dreams – I think they reveal truths to us mortals in the Middle-Realm. And if Katla says she's seen the king's tomb in dreams, I'm inclined to believe her.'

'Are you talking about your *gandr*? And the Spirit-Realm she's in?'

'Partly. That place is real and not real at the same time. I go there in my dreams but she – my *gandr* – can affect me in this world, too. You've seen it when the She-Bear comes into my heart. It's as *real* as anything.'

'Do you miss it?' asked Tor. 'Being a Rekkr? I know that I would.'

Bjarki didn't say anything for another long time.

'I feel her absence when we fight,' he said at last. 'It's like a cold hole in my heart. I feel slow and weak, and as if I am fighting knee-deep in a river of honey, with something vital, like a hand or leg, missing...'

She waited for him to resume but he said no more.

'I miss Garm,' she said. 'I wonder what our boy is doing now.'

'He has probably got his nose in a crack in an old tree, licking at an enormous comb of wild honey, and guzzling till he makes himself sick.'

'I hope he's all right,' said Tor. She found her eyes blurring. It wasn't just missing her cub: this journey had cost them so many friends. Captain Lars, Svein the Horse, Lief and Aistulf. But most of all she grieved for Brandt, his handsome smile, the raven-black wing of hair that was for ever flopping down over his lovely blue eyes, his dancing eyes.

Bjarki put his heavy right hand on her shoulder.

'Well, we certainly won't find this fabled treasure,' he said, 'if we don't put any effort into looking for it!' And they resumed their search.

At dusk they all gathered, tired and despondent, in a grove of alder, where they made a fire and Inge began to make the usual evening soup. At least they had not seen any Black Cloaks since noon, Tor thought. Which was a good thing. Or was it? Maybe the Franks knew where the tomb of Angantyr was located and were waiting there for them to find it.

It was a subdued camp that night, the mood testy. Halvar seemed particularly irritated they had failed to discover the tomb and its treasures.

'Tomorrow is Loki's Day, old man, so I hope you are sure about this,' he said. It was almost a snarl. 'I would hate to discover that you were full of piss and wind. I'd make you pay for it, Valtyr Far-Traveller.'

Bjarki looked over at the little man. He wore a warning expression on his tired, drawn face. 'We have spent only one afternoon, a few hours, searching for something hidden, in a land none of us has seen before. Did you think Angantyr's grave, lost for hundreds of years, would have a row of flaming beacons to point the way to its door? No. We will resume our search tomorrow and, until then, unless you have a helpful word to say to us, I strongly advise you, Halvar the Complainer, to shut your fat mouth.'

They all slept uneasily that night, with one of their number always on guard, with orders to wake the whole company at the slightest thing.

A little before midnight, Inge shook Tor awake. She sat up immediately. 'What?' she said. 'I've already taken my turn on watch!'

'I can hear something, Tor. Very faint, when the wind blows from the west. Then it stops. It sounds like… it sounds a bit like singing.'

Tor sat with her a while. But she could hear nothing. 'I don't think there is…' she began. And then she heard it too. A pulse of drums like the beat of a distant heart, and some weird, eldritch noise, singing but as soft as the flapping of butterfly wings. They listened for a while, then it stopped; Tor noted that the breeze was coming in from the north-west.

'I don't think it is dangerous,' Tor said. 'Perhaps a family wedding or some other big celebration. Far away. Maybe a local feast day of some kind. Whatever they have here. You go to sleep, Inge, I will stay alert and wake Rangvar when the moon touches the tops of those trees over there.'

In the morning, over a meagre breakfast of stale rye bread and the very last of their ale, she told Valtyr what she and Inge had heard.

'Hmm, maybe,' said the old man, distractedly. 'But we have seen no signs of life, no occupied farms or settlements since the fellow who sold us the food. The land here is too rocky for proper farming – a few sheep and goats, is all. This is the borderlands; the folk who live here are few and far between. Sure you did not imagine it? Trick of the wind?'

'It was singing,' said Tor flatly. 'Many voices, men's voices, and coming from some miles to the north-west. We should go take a look.'

'We don't have time. And that's the wrong direction,' said Valtyr. He seemed agitated. Almost angry. 'We need to be searching further east.'

'Could it be the Black Cloaks?' Inge said. 'Their camp?'

'Maybe,' said Valtyr, tersely. 'Another reason to avoid the place.'

He gathered everyone together in a circle after breakfast and said: 'Today is Loki's Day. If you cannot find the troll ring, and the hill on which the stone circle stands by sunset today, then… we may never discover the tomb of Angantyr. So I want your best efforts. All of you. No day-dreaming, no slacking. Keep your eyes open, your senses sharp…'

'I've been thinking,' said Bjarki. And, as Valtyr opened his mouth to say something hilarious, Bjarki held up his palm. 'Just let me speak!'

Valtyr closed his mouth.

'King Angantyr came this way a long, long while ago. You said that all this happened in our grandfathers' grandfathers' lifetimes, yes?'

'It's just a figure of speech,' said Valtyr. 'It might be as much as three or even four hundred years ago – nobody knows, no one can reckon that length of time. But a long, long while ago, yes, that is certainly true.'

'And rivers move over time – is that not also true? They can slowly change their course, just a few dozen paces or so in one man's lifetime.'

'True – oh, I see. By all the gods, Bjarki, I think that may be the cleverest thing I have ever heard you say. Yes, the River Donau might well have changed its course considerably over that great length of time.'

Bjarki looked down modestly at his boots.

'The river flows west to east,' said Valtyr, 'and so where it bends southwards the bank would have been worn away the most by the flow of the current, and the bend itself would have moved further east with time. Therefore in Angantyr's time, the bend would have been further west…'

'So we've been looking in the wrong fucking place,' said Halvar.

Chapter Eighteen

A powerful seithr

The circle of troll stones must have been ancient even back in Angantyr's time, thought Bjarki. On the top of a low, grassy hillock, rising perhaps three times the height of a man on the brow of a small hill, stood a dozen broad, squat, grey, lichen-covered boulders, in a rough circle. Bjarki had seen similar groups of these troll stones in the North – some folk said they were the remains of night-dwelling trolls, caught out in daylight, which immediately turned their bodies to stone. Other said they were the remains of houses, or even fortresses, built by giants in days of old. That seemed more likely because they formed a kind of half-palisade, almost a defensive wall, but with wide gaps between the blotchy, grey boulders.

And it was a decent defensive position, too, Bjarki admitted, with the ground falling all round the stone ring, the slope steepest to the north, where the land plunged down towards a small river at the bottom of a narrow grassy valley. An attacker would be quite worn out climbing the steep slope to get up to the troll circle – even Bjarki was a little breathless when he reached the summit – and to come up here in full armour, shield and helm, at the run, under a hail of missiles would be a daunting task. No wonder Angantyr had chosen the spot for his stand against the Huns.

'Was it truly a troll fortress?' he asked Valtyr.

'Some people think these places were temples – something to do with the alignment of the stars and the sun. Nobody really knows,' said the old man. 'But trolls are magical creatures and there is still a powerful *seithr* here, I can tell you that. So maybe you're in the right.'

Bjarki agreed. This place was full of magic. Just looking up at these forbidding, silent stones sent a cold shiver all the way down to his boots.

It had taken them most of the day searching to find this place once they had crossed the main road again and begun combing the hills on the western side of it. Valtyr made regular encouraging noises, saying fatuous things such as 'Ah yes, I'm sure this place was the one described in Katla's vision!' and 'I think we must be very close now!' which, after a while, began to grate on Bjarki's nerves. But it was Rangvar whose keen eyes first spotted the hill and its crown of ancient stones in the distance.

They saw nothing of the Black Cloaks that day, which was cheering, but Bjarki thought he glimpsed a pair of old men in raggedy grey garb watching them from behind a clump of alder bushes. But when he drew Tor's attention to them they had disappeared. 'Probably local shepherds worried we will steal their new lambs,' she said. 'They look dangerous?'

They had not looked dangerous, exactly, but there was something about their watchfulness, and abrupt disappearance, that made him wary.

There was something else that raised his hackles. On top of the hill, in the very centre of the ring of stones, was the remains of a campfire – cold now, but it had clearly been alight as recently as the night before. And there were fresh scuffs and marks on the turf to indicate that a group of people, maybe thirty of them, had bivouacked recently. Tor found a discarded earthenware jug, cracked and dry now, but still containing the faint, sweetish smell of mead. There were a few scraps of bone too. And a place where something, some animal, perhaps, had been butchered. Or sacrificed. The blood had soaked into the earth, staining the green grass.

'Do you think this is where the singing was coming from the other night?' Bjarki asked Tor.

'It is the right direction from where we camped,' she said.

'Probably it's some locals out drinking,' said Valtyr. 'I don't think we've anything to worry about. Perhaps they get drunk at the stones…'

'Sun will be setting soon,' said Bjarki, jerking his head to the west.

'Then we had better get busy – the last gleam of Loki's Day will show us the way. That's what Silver-Tongue's ancient poem promises.'

So the six of them split up and began to examine the flanks of the hill, walking around the small oval shape, a journey that took no more time than it takes to milk a cow. Bjarki walked in a sunwise direction and he met Valtyr coming the other way on the widdershins circuit.

'What kind of blackbird sings silently?' he asked as he passed.

Valtyr shrugged. 'Keep looking: you'll know it when you see it.'

After his second circumnavigation of the small hill, Bjarki sat down on the grass and looked at the empty landscape. Scrubby pastureland dotted with rocky outcrops, patches of thistles. A pair of spindly ash trees.

'This has to be the place,' he said to no one at all. 'How many troll stone rings a day's ride north of the turn of the Donau can there be?'

A pair of swifts flashed past him, heading down the valley to the south towards the distant ribbon of road. Swifts, not blackbirds.

'What in the name of Odin's arsehole are you doing sitting down?' said Tor, coming round the corner of the grassy slope. 'Look at the sun!'

Bjarki glanced westwards, at the red orb already clipped in half by the horizon. Midges hummed around his head. He stayed where he was.

'What happens if we don't find the tomb this evening?' he said.

'We go away and come back next year at the same time,' said Tor.

Bjarki laughed. 'Or we just sit here for a full year on our backsides and hope the Black Cloaks never find us.'

'That works too. Or we could just go home and never stir again.'

'And face outlawry and that angry stripling looking for revenge?'

'Rorik?' said Tor. 'I gave him some thought on the Amber Road, and I don't think he will be a huge problem. He has no reputation as a warrior. Tempers will have cooled by the time we return – and if not...'

'Hey!' shouted a voice. 'Hey! Everybody. Come here. Come now.'

It was Halvar.

–

They found the stocky bowman standing by the eastern flank of the hill, beside a large willow tree that was growing out of the side of the slope.

'Look,' Halvar said, pointing at one of the old stones on the top of the hill, a man's height above his head. 'Does that look like a blackbird?'

Bjarki peered through the gloom of twilight at the ancient rock. There seemed to be a sort of pattern etched into the stone. It had faded and some of it was covered by lichen and wind-blown dirt but it might have been a bird – possibly a blackbird – with its beak open, as if in song.

A shaft of dying sunlight from the west struck the face of the stone obliquely and the shadows caused the bird to spring into sharper relief.

''Neath a troll-wrought rock where the blackbird sings in silence...' said Valtyr. 'Rangvar, pull back the branches of the weeping willow.'

The big man gathered up the long, trailing, delicate fronds of the willow and swept them aside like a curtain. Tor handed him a leather thong and he secured the branches to the trunk, and all six of them found themselves staring at a block of stone set into the side of the hill. It was covered in smears of earth and patches of moss, which made the bare rock look very similar to the ordinary side of the hill, but now that they looked, they could see it had a square shape that couldn't be natural.

Inge busied herself with flint and tinder and soon had the stub of a candle alight and by its flickering glow, they examined the door – for that was what it clearly was – more closely. Brushing away the dirt and debris, they found the edges of the stone, but it took the combined strength of Bjarki and Rangvar to shift the granite slab out of its limestone frame.

There were no bolts or hinges: the weight of the portal was its only defence. When they had finally manoeuvred it out from under the stone lintel, they peered inside the opening to see by dim candlelight a wide, pitch-dark chamber with hard-packed earth walls and little stone shelves set into it on both sides. There were a few empty mead cups, a nub of fat beeswax candle and two round wooden plates, greasy to the touch, on the shelves. But, best of all, they discovered two earthenware lamps, filled with some liquid combination of animal fat and oil. Feeling a cold shiver of anticipation, Bjarki used Inge's candle to light the wicks of both lamps.

He passed one to Valtyr, and together they stepped inside the tomb.

The chamber was small, about half a dozen paces long and four wide, and very low – he could not stand to his full height and had to crouch uncomfortably. The walls on either side were smooth hard-packed earth, which had been painted with white lime to reflect the lamplight, but above his head was hard, painful stone. The roof was made of regular, square slabs of this material, the kind that you might find on the floor of a princely hall. Bjarki had a sudden flash that they might be underneath some great prince's palace, looking up at the floor above their heads. Yet he knew this could not be true. Above their heads, beyond the slabs, there was a mass of earth, some grass, and the ring of troll stones – somewhere.

Rangvar and Halvar crammed into the low space with them, and Tor was at the open square of grey twilight peering inside too. Inge quickly squirmed inside as well, past Tor, and came to stand beside Bjarki.

'What is that over there?' she said, pointing at the far side of the chamber. When Bjarki approached with his lamp, he saw the second door.

This one was made of solid elm-wood, set on iron hinges in a second square limestone doorway at the very back of the first chamber.

'This may be the tomb of the long-dead king of the Goths,' said Bjarki, 'but it's a place looked after by real, living people. That elm is no more than ten years old. And those door hinges have been recently oiled.'

'I was thinking the same myself,' said Valtyr. 'No dust. Oil lamps still half full of oil. You might almost believe someone lives in here.'

He turned to Tor: 'You, Halvar, Inge and Ranvar go out and keep watch. Bjarki and I will go through this door. Call us if you see anyone.'

'I'll go up top with Inge,' she said, 'you can see a light coming for miles from up there.'

The wooden door was not locked, it was not even latched, and Bjarki pulled it open with his left hand holding up the lamp with his right.

He found himself looking into the blackness of a long corridor, earth-walled like the antechamber but not limewashed, with here and there the cut-off stubs of roots. The walls were smooth and flat on both sides, with a low stone ceiling and the passage well-trampled underfoot – but nothing could be seen beyond the yellow spill of the lamplight. The darkness seemed to bore deep into the heart of the hill.

'You think old Angantyr is truly in there?' he whispered to Valtyr. He was, he found, filled with dread, of the kind he had not felt in an age.

'Only one way to find out,' said Valtyr, and he slipped past Bjarki's bulk and plunged fearlessly into the dark passageway.

The corridor had been recently swept, the marks of the twig broom visible in the dirt floor. And there were no cobwebs or drifts of long dead leaves. As they advanced, Bjarki saw that there were cunning designs etched into the stone ceiling along the route: stick-like men with spears and bows, horses and horned beasts that resembled big cows or aurochs.

Colours had been used to bring these images to life, although they were a little faded now, but warm yellows and reds could be made out – a golden sun with waving rays was clearly visible – and the haunches of the massive aurochs were a fine bluey-black. In the flickering lamplight, the tiny figures seemed to be moving, as if taking part in a kind of dance. Or a hunt – it came to Bjarki, all of a sudden. The people were hunting the animals with their spears: here was a deer-like creature, fallen on his side with a spear sticking from its belly, its red tongue lolling. They were the depictions of a famous hunt that had taken place at some time – or were they perhaps using *seithr* to help them to succeed in some future chase?

The feeling that this place was full of a powerful old magic was so strong that Bjarki could almost taste it. Up ahead, Valtyr was making little squawking noises of excitement. The hunting drawings were finished and now the ceiling showed pictures of a huge battle, many small men on horses with bows and arrows and another smaller group of big men, in a circle, with their round shields all linked together in a classic *skjaldborg*.

'It's the final battle between Huns and Goths, do you see it, Bjarki?'

Bjarki did. He was, in truth, lost in wonder. Transported. He felt he was actually inside the *skjaldborg* himself, his round shield locked tight against his neighbours, as the horde of enemies surged up against them, yelling; he felt the crush and shove of the battle, the smell of sweat, open bowels and blood, the ringing of steel, the terrible cries of the wounded…

'Bjarki, look!' Valtyr was pointing at something to the side of the passage. And he collected himself and hurried forwards, the lamp sloshing.

Valtyr was pointing at a space, another chamber that opened off the main passageway. Bjarki shoved his lamp forwards and saw what looked like a pile of powdery old sticks and a small round boulder in the middle and some broken pots. There was plenty of thick dust in here, cobwebs too, and piles of grey material that he could not identify. A horrible smell. Something very nasty indeed. Something dead and rotting. He was about to step inside the room when Valtyr halted him with a hand on his arm.

'Do not disturb them. This is not Angantyr,' he said. 'These bodies are far more recently interred than our king. Perhaps they're his spirit-guardians. But whoever they are, they are *not* hundreds of years old.'

Belatedly, Bjarki saw that the sticks were bones and the boulder an ancient skull. There were more skeletons lurking in the shifting shadows, thigh bones, fingers, and eyeless holes in a crumbling dome. There was something wet and rotten on the floor at the entrance to this chamber: a small animal, a lamb, he suspected. It had died recently, within weeks.

'It is a sacrifice,' said Valtyr, 'to feed the spirits of the men who occupy this chamber. And there's another room on the other side, look!'

Opposite the side-chamber, on the other flank of the narrow earth passageway, was another black open space – the smell was even stronger here and the several clearly human corpses could be made out in the weak lamplight in different stages of decomposition. That one there, at the back – was it ten years old? Twenty? There were still a few rags of clothing on that one over there. Bjarki believed he could make out a rusty spearhead in the floor beside the collapsed skeleton, seated in some kind of chair.

'There are dozens of folk in here,' said Bjarki. 'Who can they be?'

'Oh, I think there are a lot more than a few dozen. Generation after generation, I'd say; generations going back for some hundreds of years.'

'But who are they?'

'Companions. That's my guess. But look, see, this whole tomb has been constructed to resemble the shape of a giant sword. Is that not most encouraging? *The* sword, Bjarki! That long entrance passage with the ceiling pictures is the length of the blade. These two chambers, here and here, make the cross-guard; now we are heading into the sword's hilt.'

Bjarki followed Valtyr further into the stinking darkness. The dim passage narrowed considerably here and became even lower but, even as Bjarki ducked, he had to hurry to catch up with the old man. 'And this,' said Valtyr, with a sweep of his free hand, 'this is the sword's pommel.'

He lifted up his lamp and Bjarki's breath caught in his throat. He could see the glitter of bright metal reflected in the yellow light. He held his own lamp forwards and gazed in astonishment at a small chamber, roughly the same size as the ones they had already examined, but with three curved lobes, three alcoves, and reaching much higher above his head. He was actually able to stand upright for the first time since they had come underground. And this chamber was stuffed with goods, piled shoulder high with hundreds of different shining, glittering objects.

Treasures – a little dusty, perhaps, but a fabulous treasure hoard like the ones in the great stories of old. Cups and candlesticks, goblets and plates, all made of bright silver and warm gold, engraved, or inlaid with ivory, and piled high; jewelled collars winking with little red and green gems, thick golden chains from which precious stones the size of river pebbles dangled, piles of loose nuggets of crystal and blue gemstone, red and green jewels filling silver buckets; beautiful enamelled sword belts, beaten copper shields inlaid with swirling ancient designs in silver, finger-sized ingots of pure gold in little mounds, chests brim-full of old coins, stamped with the faces of long dead Romans, gilded armour, elaborate helmets with ivory cheek panels and animal designs, weapons – daggers, swords, an axe with a ridged horn handle embedded with tiny pearls – fat blood-red rubies spilling out of a huge bowl of solid gold…

'All this hoard needs, really, is a sleeping dragon,' said Valtyr.

Bjarki looked at him and saw that the old man's lined face was beaming with a pure and perfect joy. 'Look there,' he said, 'at the back.'

Valtyr followed the direction of his finger. And saw at the rear of the chamber a large rectangular stone box, a coffin, seven foot in length and four feet wide. He moved towards it, drawn forwards by an invisible force.

Bjarki followed him. In the light of their lamps they saw that a human face had been carved on the slab that formed the top of the receptacle.

It was a man's face, bearded and grave, his features fixed in a stern and noble expression. Underneath was a stick-like inscription in runes.

'What does it say?' said Bjarki, who had never learned to read.

'"Here lies Angantyr the King, Beloved of the Bear; here shall he rest until called forth to do battle once more at the ending of the world."'

'Beloved of the Bear – was he, was he… Fire Born… like me?'

'So some of the legends say. But never mind that now – help me!'

Valtyr was struggling with the stone slab. Bjarki put his shoulder to it and shoved. The slab immediately slid sideways and toppled off the box and the two men held up their lamps and stared inside the grey stone sarcophagus at the mortal remains of Angantyr, last king of the Goths.

Lying on a crimson cloak was a complete, fleshless skeleton, every rib in its correct place. The bones were a brownish colour but clean of all matter and looked as if they had been lovingly polished or lacquered with some substance, oil or wax perhaps, to preserve them. The big brown skull was pillowed on a scarlet cushion, with little tassels of gold at each corner, and a helmet, a shining steel dome topped with a gold crown, embedded with carnelians, had been placed atop his polished skull. The black empty eye-sockets gazed back at Bjarki sternly from under the helmet rim and he felt the old king looking directly into his secret heart.

Lying across the skeleton's pelvis bone was an old-fashioned sword resting on top of its plain leather sheath. The hilt was leather-wrapped wood on an iron tang, covered in gleaming silver wire for a better grip; the round pommel was set with a huge sapphire, the size of a hen's egg.

Valtyr gave out a little cry. And reached forwards, gently lifting the sword in both hands from Angantyr's ancient polished bones. He peered closely at the shining blade, tracing an etched rune word with a fingertip.

'This rune says… Tyrfingr,' he breathed. 'The Loki Sword.'

Valtyr handed the sword to Bjarki, who set his lamp on a nearby ledge, accepted the weapon and stared hard at the runes – they meant nothing to him, a row of slashes and grooves marked into the fullered blade. He felt the weight of the sword. It was light, and shorter than the ones he was used to, and broader, but there was a hum of magic about it, a warmth that he could feel coming through the silver wire-wrapped handle and into the bones of his fingers. He started to raise the sword in the air, as if to make a practice cut, and Valtyr bellowed: 'Stop! No! Do not wield that ancient blade. Put it safely in his sheath. Here!'

Bjarki stared at him.

'Remember the curse. Loki's curse. Any man who wields the sword will gain victory over his enemies – but he himself will taste Death.'

Bjarki looked down at the length of steel in his right hand. It was shiny, impossibly bright and clean for such an ancient weapon. Someone had been cleaning it – regularly – even polishing it. He took the leather sheath from Valtyr and slid the blade safely back into its ancient bed. He offered the sword wordlessly back to Valtyr. The old man shook his head.

'You must be its guardian from now on, Bjarki. Carry this wondrous weapon for our whole company. I'm too old for sword-play these days.'

Bjarki frowned. It was a weighty responsibility. And the reminder of the ancient curse unnerved him a little. But he kept the sheathed sword gripped in his left hand anyway, and reached forwards again with his right, lifting the golden helmet-crown from the age-browned, polished skull.

'No curse on this fancy head-warmer, I trust?' he said, smiling.

'The Crown of Arnheimer,' said the old man, reverently. 'The crown that Angantyr wore during his short reign. Try it on and we shall see.' He helped to place the ornate helmet of steel and gold over Bjarki's head. It fitted him perfectly. And it felt strangely light to the young man.

'In another age, you'd have made a fine king, Bjarki Blood-hand!'

The helmet felt good around his head; indeed, it felt oddly... right.

'We had better get back to the others,' said Valtyr. 'The sooner we can get all these treasures packed up, out of here and away, the better.'

Bjarki agreed. He was thinking of the freshly slaughtered lamb, and the oil that had half-filled the lamps, and the polished sword of the king.

They went down the passage as quickly as they were able, Bjarki holding the lamp high in his right hand, once more having to stoop, and holding his helmet in place with the hand that grasped the Loki Sword.

When they reached the entrance chamber they were a little surprised to see that it was empty. There was no sign at all of Rangvar and Halvar.

'They must have gone up top to check on Tor and Inge,' said Bjarki, blowing out his lamp and setting it back on a shelf fitted in the earth wall.

Valtyr said nothing as he stepped out of the entrance of the tomb... into the bright light of a dozen torches, screwing up his eyes at the glare. Momentarily blinded, Bjarki stumbled after him, on his heels. And froze.

His first impression was of a wall of fire-lit warriors. A score of grey-clad folk, with spears in hand, shields, helms, some with bows and some with blazing torches, all with swords at their waists. They hissed their hatred at Bjarki and Valtyr, who, bewildered by this sudden turn of events, were standing flat-footed in the darkness by a hole in the hillside.

'I'm so sorry, Bjarki, so very, very sorry,' said Tor.

Part Three

Chapter Nineteen

The heir of Angantyr

Tor could feel the bite of cold iron from the blade pressed to her neck. The soft turf under her knees. And she cursed herself for an inattentive fool. The warriors had come hurtling silently out of the night like avenging wraiths and had seized her and Inge without Tor managing to strike a single blow in her own defence. She must be getting old, she thought ruefully, as she felt the trickle of hot blood run down her neck.

She had not been paying full attention on the summit of the hill, that was the real problem, she had kept only a half-hearted watch – she and Inge had been deep in a discussion of the possible whereabouts of Garm – for both women loved that wayward bear, and feared for his safety.

While they talked, she had kept one eye on the dark surrounding slopes, which had been completely empty, and appeared to remain that way – and, in truth, she was expecting, if anything, to see the glow of torches or a line of yellow lamplight, which would give warning of the approach of the Black Cloaks. Instead, their attackers must have crept up on them in the pitch darkness, and in absolute silence. It had been done with impressive skill, Tor acknowledged, and, if it had not been about to cost them all their lives, she might have been awed by their prowess.

They had been knocked down, stripped of weapons and gear, swiftly bound with rope, and pushed down the steep slope to find Rangvar and Halvar had been very similarly ambushed and were trussed, bruised and sullenly awaiting their doom by the tomb's willow branch-covered entrance.

Now they were all in a line, herself, Inge, Rangvar and Halvar, kneeling under the torches, with blades at their throats and listening to hissing orders in a half-recognisible alien tongue to remain silent or die. Behind and around them were more than twenty warriors, all in grey, raggedy, dirty clothes but with impeccably clean weapons and kit, who were now shouting at a dumbfounded Valtyr and Bjarki, who was looking more than usually oafish, with his mouth hanging open and with some kind of fancy helmet – could that be a crown? – on his big fat head.

The warriors were shouting something about Bjarki and Valtyr throwing down their weapons – or they would be immediately skewered. Several of the grey men had bows drawn ready to carry out their threat.

Then Valtyr Far-Traveller did something completely unexpected.

He bellowed: 'Companions! In the name of King Angantyr, Lord of Goths, Beloved of the Bear, I command you all to lower your weapons!'

To Tor's astonishment, all the shouting suddenly stopped, and some of the bowmen even lowered their points. A man, a fellow of an age with Valtyr, but shorter, stockier and grizzled by experience, stepped forwards: 'Who are you, strangers? Who are you to invoke the name of the king! You who have looted his resting place and hold its spoils in your hands!'

'This proud young warrior, who now stands before you,' said Valtyr, gesturing at Bjarki, 'is the true heir of Angantyr the king. He, too, is Beloved of the Bear. His noble line in the Northlands stretches back all the way through the generations to the great king of the Goths himself.'

Noble line? By Odin, thought Tor, *Valtyr's gone too far this time.*

But to her surprise and utter shock, the grey warriors were all now muttering together, each one looking at the other. The grizzled one, their leader, Tor presumed, stepped forwards, sticking his bristled chin out.

'If he is, as you claim, the rightful heir of Angantyr, then why does he creep into the royal tomb like a thief, to steal the treasures of our lord?'

'Fair point,' someone said behind Tor. And somewhat belatedly she realised that these strange grey folk spoke a dialect that was not so very far away from her own tongue. They used older, odder, more ornate versions of the words they all spoke. But there *was* a kinship there.

'Bjarki Bloodhand, son of Hildar, son of Angantyr, is no sneaking thief in the night,' declared Valtyr. 'He does not steal the Crown of Arnheimer, nor purloin the Loki Sword. He *cannot* steal them. They are his, by birthright. He is merely retrieving them for his Royal House. All hail Bjarki Bloodhand, heir of Angantyr, who comes into his own at last!'

There was a good deal more muttering from behind her, and Tor heard someone say: 'Can it be that the prophecy has come true at last?' And someone else said, 'Well, he looks the part... very noble, very bold, even regal!' And a third person said, 'Who would *not* look regal with the king's helm-crown on his head and the royal sword gripped in his right hand?' And a fourth said: 'You wouldn't, Boden! You old nanny-goat!'

That was when Tor knew they were *not* about to die – not just yet.

–

They did not set them free, though. They remained bound, all except Bjarki and Valtyr, whom they surrounded with drawn weapons. They took the Loki Sword and the helmet-crown from Bjarki but they did not make either him or Valtyr submit to the indignity of bound hands. Then all six of them were ushered north, at spear point, down the steep slope on that side of the hill, heading down to the river valley. Tor found it difficult to walk with her arms tied behind her back in the darkness and on several occasions she stumbled and fell hard on the grassy hillside.

The warrior who picked her up and set her back on her feet was younger than the rest, not much more than a boy, but ugly as an ox and about as strong. He had close cropped hair and an awful cast in his left eye, that made him look as if he were staring down the length of his nose.

'Where are you taking us?' Tor asked the boy, when she fell over for the third time, and the warrior again hoisted her effortlessly upright.

'You will all go before the Law-Speaker,' the fellow said. 'He will decide your fate. And if he deems you to be thieves, you will be punished.'

'Punished, eh?' said Tor. 'A small fine, perhaps? A smack on the bum, kicked out of your lands, if we promise never to do it again?'

'Ha!' he said. 'You are funny! Everybody knows the punishment for disturbing the king's tomb and trying to steal his treasures is death. Now, hold your tongue, woman! Or someone will cut it from your mouth.'

Tor held her tongue, but only for a while. 'What is your name then, warrior? Who are you? By what authority do you threaten us with death?'

'My name is Gisli, son of Harknut, a *Felaki* blood-warrior.' His tone held a ring pride. 'We are the Companions. We guard the body of our king and keep him safe from the ravages of time and the predations of wolves and thieves, until he shall come again – as has been prophesied by the Seven Sages of the Plain – to restore our folk to glory once more.'

'Didn't you people all die many years ago in the battle against Hlod and his marauding Huns?'

'You know of the Great Battle?' The boy seemed confused. Then he rallied: 'Of course. Our valour must be famed across the Middle-Realm!'

'Oh yes, indeed,' said Tor, 'we speak of little else in Norrland. But we thought that you Companions had all perished in that glorious fight.'

'It is true that many of our heroes fell in the Great Battle against the eastern hordes – but not all. A few survived to mourn Angantyr the king and to install him up there in his deep tomb. Since that baleful day...'

'That's enough chattering,' snapped the warrior in front of them, a grizzled, scowling creature. 'These folk are vagabond thieves who would steal the inheritance of Angantyr, not new best friends to gossip with in the ale-house. If she persists in asking questions, Gisli, bind her mouth!'

They fell silent. Tor did not relish the thought of being gagged. And anyway, she had plenty to think on.

This muscle-bound boy-warrior might talk glibly of a sentence of death but she could see that the matter was very far from decided by this odd company of warriors. Bjarki, who was walking down the slope a few paces ahead of her, was unbound. But no one had laid a finger on him, nor did they shove him along with spear butts to make him go faster. Valtyr, too, was untouched by these folk as they shepherded them down the hill. Inge, Rangvar and Halvar were tied and surrounded by *Felaki* blood-warriors but they had not been badly treated, given the circumstances.

They came to the *Felaki* village after only half an hour's stumbling down the dark slope from the tomb – a small, homely place. It was not far from the banks of a river that she'd glimpsed in the torchlight on the way down. Tor reckoned a short stroll out of the village along the riverbank in daylight would allow any villager to look up and see the troll circle.

We should have done a better reconnaissance, she thought. *But then we would have missed the last gleam of light that showed us the old tomb.*

They processed through the muddy main street, and all the denizens of the village came out to watch them pass, many holding pine torches or glowing oil-lamps – women with babes in their arms, excited urchins up long past their bedtimes, grand-fathers hobbling forwards to get a better look. Warriors, too, swaggering about, chewing, spitting, or swigging ale.

They looked very much like the kind of people Tor might see in Svealand or the Dane-Mark – or even in Saxony – except fewer of them were tall, fair and pale with bright eyes. Most were a little shorter and more squat, strong but swarthy, and here and there she saw the almond-shaped eyes of Avars, but set in a big, red-cheeked Northern-looking face.

She gauged the size of the village at about two hundred people, which suggested that they might be able to field about fifty fighters in a time of war. Far more than their little band of six could hope to defeat.

She guessed that it was around midnight when the six captives were shoved roughly inside a grain store, and the outer door bolted, and from what she could hear, there were two warriors posted outside the locked door. They were released from their bonds, which was a relief to Tor, and also given several small loaves of rye bread and two leather sacks of ale to drink. A kindness she had also not been expecting. Bjarki and Valtyr were already arguing with each other in whispers in one of the corners.

Tor was only half-listening. She was trying to work some feeling back into her numb forearms after their long, uncomfortable binding.

'…can't be stupid enough to believe that I am really their long-dead king reborn. It is an absurd idea, Valtyr. Foolish. I don't know what you were thinking when you said it. We need to say it was a mistake…'

'And allow them to dispatch us as common grave robbers? How can even *you* be that stupid? We brazen it out. It is the only way we can live through this. Besides, how do you know you are *not* Angantyr reborn?'

'What are you babbling about, old fool?'

'You saw the engraving on his stone coffin – it looks exactly like you, down to the beard and eyes and your big, square chin and that cow-like expression on your face. Yes, that one – the one you have on now.'

'Catch,' said Tor, and she tore off a heel of rye bread and threw it to her brother. He caught it without looking. He was still glaring at Valtyr.

'Listen, Bjarki, I know this is all horse-shit,' the old man said, 'but it is the kind of horse-shit that might just save our lives. My life, your life… Tor's, too. And your mad father did once claim that he was descended from Angantyr – along with about a thousand other folk. Go along with it and we might get out of here with our skins, and even a bit of treasure.'

Bjarki turned away, came over to Inge, snatched up the ale sack, and walked away into the furthest corner, where he sat and began to drink it.

Tor said: 'I thought that was some fine quick-thinking, Valtyr, up on the hill. Whatever the oaf says – you did the right thing. So, what's next?'

'I need your brother to believe it. To act the part, whole-heartedly. But he's so fat-headed. It is the only way to get us out of this mess alive!'

'I'll go talk to him,' Tor said. And she looked over to the far side of the dusty grain store, where Bjarki and Inge were sitting on the ground by Halvar and Rangvar, now eagerly tearing into one of the loaves of bread.

'I'm sure I can soon make him see the sense of it,' she said.

Chapter Twenty

In the hands of Fate

The hall was most unusual, to Bjarki's eye. It was big enough for two hundred folk to meet in, constructed of beams and lime-washed wattle-and-daub and thatched with straw, like many other buildings of its type. But it was round, not rectangular, and that he found rather disconcerting.

What was far *more* troubling – in truth, what made him feel deeply uncomfortable – was that he was pretending to be something he was not.

Tor had chewed his ear half the night before and made it plain that if he did not go along with this silly pretence, and repeat convincingly the insane claim that he was old Angantyr returned to life, or the heir of the Goth king, or whatever nonsense Valtyr was suggesting, then he would be betraying her, his beloved sister, as well as little Inge, and all his friends.

'It's a ruse of war,' Tor had said. 'That's all. To save all our lives – and make all these *Felaki* yokels happy into the bargain.'

'It's a trick to allow us to steal their gold and silver,' he had replied.

Nevertheless, he'd agreed, at last, exhausted by her tenacity, and now he stood before a very old man, with sagging skin and opaque, milky eyes, who he had been told was Leofric, Law-Speaker of the *Felaki* tribe.

'Tell me the na-na-names…' quavered this blind old fool, who was seated on a throne in the centre of the round hall – an intricately carved piece of furniture, old and stained black with time – 'the… na-na-names that you were given as a ch-child.' The old man was looking in the wrong direction. When Bjarki spoke, he jerked his head round to face him.

'I was named Bjorn Hildarsson,' he said, 'but very soon everyone in Bago, the island where I grew up, began calling me Bjarki – little bear – and then, there was an incident, and I was by-named the Bloodhand.'

'Bjarki Bloodhand,' said the Law-Speaker. He mashed his gums for a bit, as if he were tasting the name, as if it were a bit of chewy pork rind.

'An in-incident, you say…' Leofric continued. 'What was this in-in-incident that caused men to grant you the by-na-name Bloodhand.'

Bjarki caught Valtyr's eye. Who frowned, stared hard and shook his head very slightly, as if to say: 'Do not on any account tell him *that*!'

But Bjarki had had enough of being told what to do. He looked round the circle of two score *Felaki* blood-warriors who had come to hear the Law-Speaker's verdict. A ring of stone-hard faces. Not one friendly.

'I fought with three boys in Bago. They insulted my girl, and me, and I lost my temper and slew two of them. My hands were covered in blood when the village men found me standing over the corpses. I've no memory of the incident. But it caused me to be expelled from the island.'

There was a sharp intake of collective breath.

'You freely ad-admit to being a mu-murderer?'

'I killed those boys. But it was not murder. They picked the fight.'

The frail old man was now squirming pathetically in his huge black chair, and gesturing weakly for help. Two big warriors immediately came forwards and helped him slide out of his seat. With the two *Felaki* holding his arms, the Law-Speaker shuffled slowly over towards Bjarki until he was standing directly in front of him, gazing blindly up at his face. Then the old man lifted one trembling blue-veined arm and gently put his hand on Bjarki's face. The chilly fingers running over his cheek, his beard and brow, his lips and his over-large, lumpy nose, were as light as a moth.

Then the old man reached down and grasped Bjarki's heavy right hand in his two feather-light ones. He stroked the battered knuckles of the younger man's paw, feeling the cuts, abrasions and patches of hard skin.

'The Bloodhand,' he said, gripping that massive fist in both of his. 'I see you are well named. Now, warrior of Bago, killer-but-not-murderer, tell me, and speak the truth. Are you, indeed, the true heir of Angantyr?'

Bjarki opened his mouth wide – but nothing came out.

'Speak, Bloodhand, I command you to speak!' said the old man.

Bjarki tried to pull his right hand from the blind man's grasp but it was like a vice. He could not free himself.

'Tell him the truth,' said a dark voice inside his heart, 'or I will.'

Bjarki said: 'I… I… I do not know. It has been… suggested.'

The old man suddenly let go, turned his back and began to shuffle away. Bjarki's right hand seemed to flare up suddenly with extreme heat.

The two *Felaki* blood-warriors guided the Law-Speaker back to his throne, one of the men turning round to give Bjarki a venomous look.

When the old man was once more safely ensconced in the massive black chair, he aimed his milky eyes directly, unerringly, at Bjarki and said, 'You answered well, son. Take comfort in that.' His voice now had firmness, the quaver of before was gone. He spoke like a younger man.

'Yes,' the Law-Speaker said. 'It was a fine answer, Bjarki Bloodhand. And an honest one. I felt the Bear move inside you – indeed, I even heard her voice – you *know* of what I speak. The She-Bear was the spirit of Angantyr, his own personal *gandr*. I believe it is yours, too. Furthermore, you say you do not know if you are the true heir of Angantyr, or not… and, in all truth, neither do I. But I have touched you, and felt your *gandr*. The Bear spirit is strong in you, yet she is… controlled, constrained. I must think on this. I shall dream on it. But until I have a true answer you and your friends are to be as honoured guests in our village. See they are all well treated, Kynwulf! Honoured guests. I will retire to my bed and take the usual potions – and sleep and dream the truth. Tomorrow, yes, tomorrow I shall know it all. May the Bear guard you, while I dream.'

'It has been suggested! It has been *suggested*? Can you not even tell one tiny little fucking lie, oaf, to save all our lives? What is *wrong* with you?'

'I don't think our lives are in danger, Tor,' Bjarki replied. 'Not any more. That old man, he… he looked right inside of me. Some *seithr*, I think. I had to tell the truth. Had to. He would have known if I had lied.'

Bjarki and Tor were still in the hall, seated next to each other at a large round table with their comrades. The air in the hall had changed, immediately, upon the Law-Speaker's pronouncement. All around them were smiles and nods and friendly faces. *Felaki* women and girls were bringing ale jugs and leather cups to their table and platters of rye bread and butter; there was the smell of meat roasting somewhere out of sight.

Valtyr was away at the side of the hall in lively conversation with a group of *Felaki* warriors, who seemed to treat him like a favourite uncle.

The one called Kynwulf, the grizzled captain of the band who had captured them, was now standing before them. He bowed low to Bjarki.

'Bear Warrior,' he said, 'a noon-day meal of roasted mutton and leek pottage will be brought to you for your pleasure and sustenance, and we are preparing a guest hall for your use in the village. Your personal belongings, your bedding, and so on, will be placed there for you. But not your weapons. Those we will retain until the decision is made by the Law-Speaker. Furthermore, we must ask you not to attempt to leave the village, for any reason. Is there anything you require for your comforts? A young lamb or a bird to sacrifice to the gods? A thrall to warm your bed?'

'That's a fine idea!' said Rangvar. 'A couple of pretty thralls…'

'We don't need any of your dirty whores,' snapped Tor.

'Ah, I see now,' said Kynwulf, 'perhaps you, or the lovely young maiden yonder, prefer to tend to the Bloodhand's desires in person.'

'What? No! Euch!' said Tor, jumping furiously to her feet.

Bjarki forestalled her. He got up and stood between them. 'You are most kind, Kynwulf, your generosity is overwhelming, but all we shall require is a dry hall, good food and maybe a tub of hot water to wash in.'

'It shall be done, Beloved of the Bear,' said Kynwulf, bowing again.

–

'They believe themselves to be the descendants of the Companions,' said Valtyr, 'the handful of men of the king's personal bodyguard who fought with Angantyr against the Huns in the great battle at the troll stone circle, all those years ago, and who somehow survived the final slaughter.'

He was addressing the whole group, all six of them, in the small guest hall that they had been given to rest in. He was clarifying the situation for them, as he saw it, after much badgering from Halvar and Rangvar.

'They believe they are the rightful guardians of the Throne of Arnheimer, and they are the ones who have been tending Angantyr's tomb down the generations, burying their own dead in there, too, and often sacrificing newborn lambs for all the spirits of their departed kin.'

They had eaten well, washed in a huge tub of very hot water in the cosy hall, and after an afternoon of much needed rest and desultory talk, were at their ease beside the hall hearth at dusk, where a turf fire glowed.

'I think we had grasped most of that already, old man,' said Tor.

'Indeed, Tor? Did you also know that their wise men, a long-dead group of worthies called the Seven Sages of the Plain, had a prophecy of their king returning in glory, to lead them to victory over their foes?'

'No. Did you?' said Tor. 'If so, you never mentioned it to us.'

'I'd heard whispers of it. Yes. I knew they were expecting someone like Bjarki to turn up one day. They have been waiting for generations. There is also a prophecy about fighting the hordes of darkness under his Bear banner. Defeating a Dark Warrior, who is the incarnation of all evil. The sages prophesied this Dark Warrior would hunt and kill the women and children of the *Felaki*. He is supposed to be an incarnation of Hlod.'

'How did the *Felaki* keep going all these years after Angantyr was dead?' Bjarki was picking shreds of mutton from his teeth with a fingernail. He was pleasantly full, comfortable. He decided not to think about the danger of the Law-Speaker rejecting his claim to be the king reborn and deciding they were robbers. At this very moment, he felt good.

'Apparently, each Companion, when he grew too old to fight, would induct his eldest son into their elite little company – a tradition that went back long before even Angantyr was king. They married local Avar women, I suppose, or carried them off as thralls. The older ones, when they became too decrepit to fight, hung up their swords and lived the rest of their days raising sheep and goats and watching their grandchildren grow. In this remote village, with only a few scrubby fields and pastures, they were beneath the notice of both the Christians of Francia to the west and the Kingdom of the Avars in the south. I'd imagine they gave a little tribute to the Khagan each year and, in return, he left them here in peace.'

'So what is the plan, Valtyr?' asked Halvar. 'We just sit here like ducks on a summer lake until they decide whether to slaughter us or not?'

'We should make a run for it,' said Rangvar. 'There are no guards posted on the door. I looked. We could slip out in the dead of night...'

'And go where, you idiot?' snapped Tor. 'Back up the Donau and over the mountain passes again? Back to the Silesian *gord*? All the way back to Asa's Landing or Svealand? Just the six of us, without weapons?'

'They would hunt us down in less than a day,' said Valtyr. 'And it would be seen as a clear admission of guilt. We must stay here and brazen it out. Once Bjarki is recognised as old King Angantyr returned to...'

'I'm no idiot,' snarled Rangvar. 'The Western Harvaths are due north of us, isn't that right Valtyr? If we went hard and fast, this very night, I think we could get up there and hide from any pursuit. Then we turn bandit in the high places. We'd soon feed and equip ourselves...'

'With no food or shelter, in those freezing mountains, with all these *Felaki* blood-warriors hot on our trail,' said Tor. 'You're stupider...'

Bjarki let it all wash over him. He knew he was not going to run off anywhere this night. The fire was warm, there was food in his belly. Tor was right and Rangvar was wrong – but he felt little urge to add his voice to the argument. He was, in truth, bored by all this squabbling. They were not going anywhere. He leaned back on his bearskin and closed his eyes.

Could I really be Angantyr reborn? he thought. *It's not impossible. If mad Hildar spoke the truth about his own ancestry, then I am indeed of that line. So is Tor.* He mused on that for a while. *But I don't feel like a king*, he thought. *I don't feel even a tiny bit royal. I feel, in fact, like a liar.*

Then he fell asleep.

They came for them in the morning. A dozen warriors with spears and swords at their belts; very stiff and formal. Kynwulf was in command once again. It occurred to Bjarki that he was the most important fellow in the village after the Law-Speaker – the equivalent of a *hersir*, perhaps.

The *Felaki* surrounded them but kept a distance and indicated they should accompany them to the round hall they'd gathered in before.

As they walked through the muddy streets, the people once again came out of their huts and little halls to stare at the strangers, and mutter indistinctly to each other. Did they all know what was about to happen? Bjarki couldn't decide if he were receiving looks of awe at a king reborn, and walking among them, or pity at a shameless liar condemned to die.

'Has the Law-Speaker dreamed the truth?' Bjarki asked Kynwulf.

'I could not say,' the warrior replied.

'Does that mean that you do not know? Or that you *do* know and do not want to tell me?'

'I could not say,' said Kynwulf again.

Bjarki gave a snort of irritation.

'I was told to bring you to the great hall, that is all,' said Kynwulf. He gave Bjarki a look of embarrassment, and also, possibly, of apology.

Leofric the Law-Speaker was in his big black throne in the centre of the hall when the six strangers to the *Felaki* village were ushered in. He looked very much the same as the last time Bjarki had seen him. But his milky eyes were now fixed sightlessly, unerringly on the six newcomers.

The Law-Speaker held up a hand and all chatter in the hall ceased.

'Step forwards, Bjarki Bloodhand – the man whom some here have claimed is our beloved Angantyr now returned to us. Come closer to me.'

Bjarki stepped forwards until he was a mere two paces away from the blind man on the throne.

'I have slept – and I have dreamed,' said the Law-Speaker. 'But before I pronounce on the matter, there are more answers that must be sought. Certain accusations have been made, which must be addressed.'

Then to Bjarki's utter shock, the Law-Speaker said: 'Step forwards, Captain Brandt Haraldsson, of His Majesty's Eighth Scara of *Scholares*.'

And their comrade Brandt, now incongruously dressed in the scale armour and black cloak of their Christian foes, emerged from the crowd.

Chapter Twenty-one

Certain accusations

Tor found herself goggling at the handsome Black Cloak officer, who had just pushed his way through the throng in the round hall into the space before the blind Law-Speaker. The man had the usual two swords at his belt, a tunic of fine scale armour, steel greaves and a polished Frankish helmet with a glossy black horsehair plume held in the crook of his arm.

She gaped at him because his face was that of their old friend and comrade on the long journey south from Svealand – Brandt, formerly of the Auxilla. And she was suddenly torn between the urge to rush over and throw her arms around him and hug him tightly to her breast, and the equally strong desire to punch him repeatedly and very hard in the balls.

In the event, she just stood there with her mouth hanging open like a backwoods simpleton, while the Law-Speaker said: 'You have made certain accusations, Captain Brandt, about this company of strangers who are now among us. I invite you to repeat them openly in their presence.'

Brandt cleared his throat: 'First, your excellency, I must tell you this,' he said. 'I am an officer of His Majesty Karolus, King of Francia and Lombardy, whose near-limitless lands lie only a few days march to the west of here, and stretch all the way to the great western ocean…'

Leofric said drily: 'I know very well where Francia is, Captain. And I know its reach and power. I have lived in its long shadow all my life.'

'Indeed, Excellency, but I must inform you that I have the honour to serve my beloved king as a member of his *Scholares*, his elite personal bodyguard, which gives me certain rights and duties anywhere in his realm – *or out of it* – and that I am now detached on a special duties at the orders of his personal chaplain and chancellor, his strong right hand, a man blessed by God, Livinus, Bishop of Aachen, Archbishop of Saxony.'

'No! You are a traitorous, shit-eating *nithing*, a black-hearted turn-coat, a milk-sop, mother-loving coward: that's what *you* are, pretty-boy!'

Tor felt the words boiling out of her, completely beyond her control. She was aware of Valtyr beside her trying to restrain her furious tirade with a hand tightly gripping her right forearm. She tore her limb away.

'I ought to gut you like a flapping trout right here, right now, you traitorous scum-bubble, you fey, floppy-haired, pig-fucking little...'

She was now groping wildly for the seax handle – forgetting that the weapon had been taken from her when she was captured by the *Felaki*.

Valtyr whispered: 'Get hold of yourself, Tor; or you'll destroy us.'

'Be silent, woman, be silent this instant, or I will have you gagged, and bound and summarily removed from my hall,' said the Law-Speaker. Anger had given his whey face a little colour. It was now a yellowish hue.

With an effort of will Tor clamped her jaw together. She glared at Brandt from across the room, and a small part of her was gratified to see the man in black looked uneasy to be the recipient of her blazing hatred.

'I am no traitor,' Brandt said to her. 'I cannot be. I have always faithfully served my God and king. I have never once deviated from my loyalty to Francia. I joined your miserable gang of tomb robbers at the direct order of my commander-in-chief, Bishop Livinus of Aachen. My deception of you and your rabble of murderous thieves was merely a ruse. You've often said yourself, Tor, that a ruse is perfectly acceptable in war. And we civilised Christian folk are eternally at war with you pagan barbarians, you who persistently rebel against the rightful authority of Karolus's rule, as ordained by God Almighty and His Son Jesus Christ.'

A mewling Christian? thought Tor. *I never suspected* that *of him.*

And, suddenly, a huge chunk of knowledge fell into place in her mind. Brandt must have joined the Black Cloaks when the Auxilla was disbanded. He had obviously lied about his longing to return to the North – he was a Christian, after all. She presumed Livinus had recruited him to… to do what? Kill Bjarki? Was he the man who had tried to kill Bjarki in Asa's Landing and in the *gord*? Why would Livinus care so much about the life of one warrior? She had to force her mind to the present.

'You have made serious accusations about these folk, Captain,' said the Law-Speaker. 'I invite you to repeat them before all in this hall.'

'As you command, your excellency,' said Brandt. He cleared his throat, shot Tor a hot, poisonous look and said: 'I have been informed that one of these shiftless vagabond thieves, that man over there, Bjarki Bloodhand, claims that he is King Angantyr magically returned to life. I know this, for certain, to be absolutely untrue. He's from an insignificant, fly-speck island in the Dane-Mark, a stupid, penniless nobody, and his father Hildar was a blood-crazed killer of women and children. Bjarki too is a killer of women. He slew his own lover, Yoni, a lovely Irish girl…'

Brandt faltered and stopped. 'Bjarki Bloodhand is a habitual liar as well as a traitor damned by God Almighty – he made an oath of service to my king, a few years ago, and broke it without the slightest hesitation, murdering many of Karolus's good men in a despicable plan to facilitate his escape. He claims that he is possessed by a demon, a kind of bear, which gives him the strength of ten men. This is also a lie, like so many others he has told. I've seen him in battle – and he fights like any man.'

'These are grave charges, indeed,' said Leofric.

'And I have more,' said Brandt.

'Might we be allowed to refute them?' said Valtyr. 'It seems only fair to let us reply.'

The Law-Speaker turned his milky eyes upon Valtyr. 'You will speak when Captain Brandt had finished,' he said coldly.

'Thank you, your excellency,' said Brandt. 'Where was I? Oh yes, Bjarki is a habitual liar – and a murderer – and an oath-breaker and black-hearted traitor. He is also a wanted outlaw – condemned in Svealand by the Jarl of Norrland for his many vicious crimes. And I may inform you now that he, his sister, and this band of desperate criminals, came to your lands with one purpose, and one purpose only. They came here with the desire of discovering the ancient tomb of your venerated King Angantyr and making away with its valuable contents for their own personal gain.'

Captain Brandt drew himself up to his full height. 'These Northern scum are thieves, plain and simple. And Bjarki Blood-hand is the worst of them by far. I have discussed this disgraceful robbery with them on many occasions on the journey from Svea-land. And the callousness and naked greed they have displayed, time and again, was in truth quite sickening.'

'That is most interesting, Captain,' said Leofric. 'I must thank you for bringing all this to our attention. Do you have anything else to add?'

'Only this, your excellency. My men and I...' Brandt gestured behind him, and Tor saw that the treacherous bastard was not alone. There were half a dozen armed Black Cloaks standing quietly by the far wall. '...we would be most happy to take charge of the treasures of Angantyr. Even his mortal remains as well, if you would graciously allow it. To keep them safe from any predations in future by thieves such as this band of cut-throats. I would see to it personally that the bones were preserved in respectful splendour in a special chamber in Aachen. Indeed, if you and your people wished it, you might also come to live in Francia – I am sure that King Karolus would welcome you and allow you to make a comfortable home his lands. There would also be a generous sum paid in compensation to you, several chests brimming with silver *deniers*…'

'Thank you, Captain, for your kind offer,' said the Law-Speaker. 'But the treasures of Angantyr, and his hallowed bones, will remain under the wardship of the *Felaki*. We have, after all, guarded them some while.'

Captain Brandt bowed low to the Law-Speaker but said no more.

'Is that it?' said Valtyr. 'Is that all the stinking, watery slime that this lying Christian pig wishes to squirt out of his puckered shit-hole?'

'You wish to refute these serious accusations, or perhaps defend or explain your actions, Valtyr Far-Traveller? Very well, you may speak!'

'Bjarki Bloodhand, son of Hildar, of Bago Island in the Dane-Mark, is *indeed* the true heir of Angantyr! He is your king returned to life!'

Valtyr made this statement with a tone of cold, utter conviction.

'I too can pluck the truth from my dreams,' he continued. 'And I dreamed the truth about Bjarki Bloodhand long before we embarked upon this long and perilous journey to your domain, Excellency. I dreamed of it many years before I even *met* Bjarki. The All-Father, Odin, the mighty Spear-Shaker himself, came to me one night, when I slept on the benches of the royal hall in Uppsala, and he spoke to me like this: "Hear me, Far-Traveller, the true heir of Angantyr is alive this day. The king reborn is to be found on the small island of Bago, a young man, untried, unaware of his power or his heritage. But he is beloved of Odin. And beloved of the Bear. He has been chosen by me. Find this youth, Valtyr, train him and mould him in the ancient ways of the Fire Born! Bring him to understand his destiny." Thus the All-Father spoke in my dream – and I listened.'

Tor was caught up in Valtyr's magical skald-speaking – his words were moving, even though she suspected them of being just as shit-filled as the lying speech made by Brandt. She noticed that Leofric, the Law-Speaker, was leaning forwards in his throne, as if to hear him the better.

'I will also say this,' Valtyr continued. 'This sly, creeping fellow, this Brandt, was once of our company, and joined it as a spy, as a traitor, so that he could earn our trust and friendship only to betray us. He was like a worm in our apple, the weevil squirming inside the loaf, joining us on the secret orders of his devious Frankish masters. He admits this. He admits his lying. His word therefore cannot be trusted. And ask yourself this too: why does he ask to take the treasures of Angantyr back with him to Francia? To better guard them – I think not. This lying worm-weasel plans to steal them – he plots to rob the treasures from you, even now.'

'That is a lie!' Brandt protested. 'This old fool is twisting the truth.'

'Be silent, Captain. You have had your time to speak,' the Law-Speaker's voice was stern. 'Now's the time to listen to your adversary!'

'May I continue?' asked Valtyr.

Leofric gestured vaguely with one pale and stick-like finger.

'It is true that Bjarki has killed many folk – he is a fine warrior. It would be strange, if he had not slain many of his foes in battle. And it is also true that he was outlawed by Jarl Starki of Norrland, with whom he had a quarrel over a little money. And we did, indeed, come here in search of Angantyr's tomb. We do not deny any of that. But we came here so that the Bloodhand might come into his rightful inheritance. For he *is* Angantyr reborn. He is the true heir. The man prophesied to return to you by the Seven Sages of the Plain. And this foul liar, Brandt – this dark-cloaked serpent who stands before you – he is in truth the Dark Warrior, prophesied by the same Seven Sages. Look at his raven hair, at his pitch-black cloak! He is the embodiment of all that is wrong and evil in the Middle-Realm, and he stands before you now, attempting to have you deny the king's true heir. I have one more thing to say to you – good blood-warriors of the *Felaki* tribe, faithful wardens of the tomb of the last king of the Goths and the Throne of Arnheimer. I say this: your king is returned to you – rejoice. Rejoice!'

To Tor's complete surprise almost every man, woman and child in the great hall burst into a roar of approval. There were cheers ringing out from the rafters, where several tiny children were perched. People were surging forwards to slap Bjarki on the back, folk reaching out vainly in an attempt to touch him. Her brother looked more astonished than she felt.

The Law-Speaker was now calling for quiet, and this time it took a while for the tumult to die down. Tor turned to look for Brandt and saw that he was now edging backwards towards his men at the side of the hall.

'I will have *silence* in my hall,' the Law-Speaker was bellowing, a huge volume of sound erupting from such a frail, elderly body.

The crowd eventually settled down.

'I have pondered this, and I have dreamed on it,' he said. 'But I must ask Bjarki Bloodhand one last time before I speak my law to you.'

The Law-Speaker was leaning right forwards now, his wrinkled, wispy head cocked up like a hunting dog scenting its elusive quarry.

'Do you, Bjarki Bloodhand, who was born Bjorn Hildarsson, a native of the island of Bago, in the realm of the Dane-Mark, do you now swear on your honour, on your very life, and from the truth that resides deep in every honest man's heart, that you are indeed the true heir of King Angantyr? That you are indeed the king reborn and returned to us?'

Bjarki stepped forwards, shrugging off the many clutching *Felaki* hands, and the crowds around him slackened in return and gave him the space he required. He opened his mouth to speak, and stopped...

Just fucking lie, oaf. Just fucking tell them what they want to hear.

The moments passed. Tor could hear the beating of her own heart. There wasn't a sound from the hundreds of folk gathered in the great hall.

Come on, brother. You can do this. Do this one small thing for me.

Bjarki took a deep breath – and the words erupted from his throat.

Chapter Twenty-two

The gandr child

In some ways, Bjarki knew the sensations very well. The swelling in his heart, the slowing of the world around him; the red-tinged light that filled the air and the sound of water rushing like a mighty waterfall in his ears. In others, it was a totally new experience, unlike any he had had before.

He felt a great dark presence envelop him, it was *not* inside his pumping heart but all around him, encasing him in warmth and strength; he felt the usual power surge like lightning through his veins but this time it seemed to be coming from outside rather than deep within his body.

He spoke. Rather, he roared like the She-Bear herself, a great meaty blast of sound: 'I am the Bear. I am Angantyr. I am your king reborn!'

The Law-Speaker was staring at him open-mouthed, his unseeing eyes wide with shock, his face as pale and blank as a field of snow. He slid bonelessly off his seat and knelt before Bjarki's feet, his head bowed.

'There can be no doubt,' he said. And, lifting up his right hand, he placed it on the arm of the chair, and slowly levered himself fully upright.

'The Throne of Arnheimer, which we have safeguarded faithfully, generation after generation, since you last graced it, sire, is yours again!'

Leofric the Law-Speaker lifted both his arms in the air: 'Hear me, people of *Felaki*: all hail the heir of Angantyr! Our king has returned!'

The cheering in the hall was like a solid wave of sound that crashed over Bjarki's head. He felt suddenly weak, his legs shaking, and it was only with some difficulty that he tottered over to the great wooden chain and, guided ineptly by the blind man, took his place in its hard embrace.

Yet he had not completely lost his wits in all the public acclamation. After a moment or so, he looked over at the place where Brandt had been standing when he made his accusations before the Law-Speaker. It was in his mind to have him detained, held by the *Felaki* men until they could determine what to do with him and his six Black Cloaks.

But Brandt was no longer there. He and his men had disappeared.

–

Casks of ale were broached, mead flowed like water, and all the servants of the *Felaki* tribe began to prepare a feast of celebration in the great hall. Pretty young women wove wild flowers into delicate chains and came forwards to place them around Bjarki's thick neck, kissing his bearded cheek as they did so. Kynwulf knelt before him, placed his two hands between Bjarki's and pledged his everlasting loyalty, and asked if he might be allowed to retain his position as the War Chief of the *Felaki*, which Bjarki graciously permitted him. He was introduced to several of the more important warriors of the tribe, who offered their sword blades for his touch in homage, and then kneeling swore eternal fidelity to him.

'I think it would be best if we held the ceremony of coronation this very night, your highness,' said the Law-Speaker, who was now standing unsteadily beside the throne. 'There is no advantage in delay.'

Bjarki nodded gravely.

'So it shall begin at dusk up on the hill in the tomb of your great ancestor,' the blind old man said. 'But do not concern yourself about the finer details, I beg you. All will be explained at the ceremony, I shall lead you through it myself, but now, if you do not object to my absence, I shall retire to my home and discuss its conduct with the elders of the *Felaki*.'

'By all means,' said Bjarki, dismissing the old man with what he hoped was a suitably regal flap of his right hand.

'Perhaps now we might be allowed a tiny moment of your valuable time – Your High and Fucking Mightiness!' It was Tor's voice, of course.

Bjarki looked to his left and saw that his sister and Valtyr were standing on that side of the throne. Both were grinning hugely at him.

'You did very well, Bjarki,' said Valtyr, when they had withdrawn to a private chamber off the main circular hall. It had once belonged to the Law-Speaker but now they had it to themselves. 'You seemed to be pulsing with power; I swear you actually glowed a kind of gold colour.'

'It really wasn't me,' said Bjarki, 'it was the Bear. My *gandr*. She spoke the words through me. If it'd been up to me, I'd have probably...'

'...said it has been *suggested*? Doesn't matter, oaf. You did fine!'

'Tor, um, I think,' said Bjarki, 'I think what you meant to say just then was: "Doesn't matter, oaf. You did fine... *your highness*!"'

And they sniggered at each other like a pair of naughty children.

'I think we need to talk about Brandt,' said Valtyr.

Tor and Bjarki stopped laughing.

'A Black Cloak – I would never have believed it,' said Bjarki.

'Do you think he was the one trying to kill you on the road?' asked Valtyr. 'It now seems pretty likely.'

'But why? I don't understand why Bishop Livinus would want to insert Brandt into our company,' said Tor. 'It cannot just have been to take out Bjarki – he's not worth the trouble. No offence, your highness!'

'None taken, my humble subject!'

'It's for the sword,' said Valtyr. 'Neither of you seem able to grasp what the Loki Sword would mean to the North. If Widukind were to display it in battle, it would transform the fighting spirit of the Saxons.'

Neither Bjarki or Tor said anything to this for a while. They hated talk of the war in Saxony. Indeed, the silence became a little awkward.

'So Brandt was sent to spy on us to stop the Loki Sword falling into Saxon hands? Is that what you think, Valtyr?' said Bjarki, eventually.

'More or less. The Franks were also determined to crush Hrodgaud's rebellion in Lombardy, from both ends, and make sure the money from the sale of poor Aistulf's amber didn't get into the rebels' hands in Italy.'

'Have you still got all that money, you know, the packed bags of silver coins that you grabbed from the table in Carnuntum?' asked Tor.

'Uh, no, not much of it. I have a little left,' the old man replied. He looked suddenly rather uncomfortable, even just a little bit shamefaced.

'So what happened to it?' said Tor. 'To hundreds of silver *deniers*.'

'If you must know – I made a very generous gift in coin to the Law-Speaker. I thought it might encourage him to come to the correct decision in respect of Bjarki's claim to be the heir of Angantyr, and rightful king.'

'Oh,' said Bjarki, his shoulders sagging.

'Did you *really* think you were the heir of Angantyr?' said Valtyr.

'Well,' said Tor. 'We won, which is all that matters. But if Brandt is truly after the sword, he is going to come at us with all the Black Cloaks he can muster. This fight is very far from over, oaf. You do realise that?'

'Yes,' said Bjarki. 'So I suppose we'd better continue the charade.'

Bjarki had bathed in hot water, washed and combed his long hair and trimmed his beard, and he had dressed himself in all his finest war gear, including his mail and greaves and the magnificent bearskin cloak, which was draped around his shoulders, clasped at the throat with a gold brooch.

He had led the procession up the hill to the stone circle and the tomb of his ancestor, with the women and girls of the village strewing the hillside path with flowers and the accompanying warriors singing a slow, rather beautiful song. As he listened to the words, Bjarki realised they were singing a saga that told the story of the great battle between the Goths and the Huns, and he felt a cold shiver of *seithr* all along his spine.

Inge, who was walking beside him, very pretty in a newly sewn dress of white linen, said: 'This song! I've heard it before. I heard it the night we camped in the alder grove when we were looking for the tomb.'

The Law-Speaker, who had had to be carried by two strong men, in a kind of sling, up to the summit of the hill, overheard her comment.

'We come up here on the eve of Loki's Day, young lady,' he said. 'Every year, all the living Companions, and tend to our dead kin and our king's resting place. Then we feast among the stones. It is our custom.'

'You sing very beautifully,' she said, and the Law-Speaker smiled.

The blind old man made a speech at the mouth of the tomb, to all the assembled *Felaki*, and Kynwulf sacrificed a red-and-black cockerel to the *gandir* of that ancient place, spattering the stone entrance with its blood.

As the sun sank in the west, the *Felaki* blood-warriors went to the top of the grassy mound and built a fire in the centre of the stones, and prepared to feast and drink and sing the night away. And Bjarki, Valtyr and Leofric went into the tomb with half a dozen male *Felaki* elders.

The oil lamps had been refilled and set in niches in the walls of the tunnel and so their path was well lit all the way into the heart of the hill.

Bjarki saw that the Throne of Arnheimer had been brought up the hill from the village and had been carried into the chamber and set at the rear of the tomb, in front of the stone coffin. He noted with a glow of joy that the treasures still lay in dusty piles, undisturbed, but magnificent, and that the bones of Angangtyr were once more sealed in their sarcophagus.

The Law-Speaker told Bjarki to sit in the huge throne, then he uttered a rather long and dull prayer, calling on the gods to witness this matter, and anointed his forehead with a small pot of the cockerel's warm blood. The blind old man drew an equal-sided triangle in gore on Bjarki's forehead, telling him that it was the sign of those beloved of the Bear.

Bjarki could not help but see Valtyr's crooked smile of recognition in the flame-lit darkness. Then the Law-Speaker, helped by one of his elders, placed the golden helmet-crown of Angantyr on his head and, fumbling only slightly, put the sheathed Loki Sword into his right hand.

The silver wire handle felt warm to the touch. Warm with *seithr*.

'Will you stay this whole night beside the bones of your ancestor – with the bones of your previous incarnation in life?' Leofric asked him.

'I will,' said Bjarki.

'And will you, by the powers gathered in this ancient place and the essence of the man whose tomb this is, become one with Angantyr, and become our king, become king of the Goths, in blood, body and spirit?'

'I will,' said Bjarki.

'Then the great god Sol, who dies each night and is reborn each and every morn, will rouse you with his warmth,' said Leofric, 'and you shall emerge then, a new man, into the dawning of a new golden age of light.'

Someone blew three mighty blasts on a goat horn trumpet, deafening in that enclosed space. The Law-Speaker bent and began to shuffle away, and Valtyr winked at him before he turned away. And there they left him.

As they retreated slowly down the narrow tunnel, they extinguished all the oil lamps in the passage until the darkness claimed Bjarki entirely.

-

'So,' said a deep, dark voice, a long, long while later, 'I see that you are come into your rightful inheritance at last... *your highness.*'

Bjarki opened his eyes. He was in the woods, a great, dark, endless forest of oak, ash and elm that stretched for ever in all directions. He knew exactly where he was: in the First Forest. He saw with no surprise at all that the She-Bear was sitting a few feet away. What *was* a shock was that she was eating a very large, yellow, dripping honeycomb. A fat chain still connected the beast to the enormous trunk of the Irminsul – but not a chain of ice or of iron. The links between the beast's collar and the One Tree were brown, knobbly and seemed to be covered with a kind of bark – a chain of wood.

'I suppose I owe you thanks for that episode in the great hall, *gandr*,' Bjarki said stiffly. 'I did not know you still had control over my body.'

'I do not. Your old witch's magic still constrains me. Am I not still chained here like the lowest of thralls to this, the Mother of Trees?'

'Yet you have managed to find yourself a juicy honeycomb.'

'You don't understand even now, man-child,' said the Bear. 'All this is a dream, a vision. This honeycomb is not real. It fell from the sky and landed at my feet. The One Tree is not real. And I am not as you see me.'

'Yet you made me speak those words to the Law-Speaker. You made me lie to him, and falsely claim that I was the heir of Angantyr.'

'*You* wanted to make that royal claim. *You* told yourself that I was controlling you – but I was not. You truly wanted to lie, but part of you would not allow yourself to do so. So you passed responsibility to me.'

'I… I said all those things? Truly it was not you?'

'They came from your throat, did they not? Formed by your mouth. Besides, what you said was no lie. All the things you claimed are true.'

'What?'

'Listen to me, man-child, I am older than you can imagine, older than the hills and rivers. I have made my home in many great warriors over the centuries – as I have in you… and in your royal ancestor, too.'

'What are you saying?'

The She-Bear laughed, a wet, hot, stewy kind of sound.

'How can I be more plain? Angantyr was my man-child – I was his *gandr*; just as I am yours. His royal blood runs hot in your veins. Did you think I would not recognise its scent? I have known it since we first met.'

Bjarki was too astonished to speak. He stared at the hulking beast.

'But… but I am not *royal*. I do not feel like a *king*. And… and Valtyr paid a hefty sum in silver to the Law-Speaker to fix his verdict.'

The *gandr* laughed again. 'Your friend may have paid him silver. But he bought nothing. The blind one was happy to take the coin because – why not? But his decision was already made. He knew you were the true heir of the king! Then you asserted the claim before us all.'

'But I didn't… I didn't really…'

'You may believe, if you wish, that I controlled your voice. And I shall accept your heartfelt thanks for my help, if you now offer it to me.'

Bjarki gathered his wits. 'If I had not stated my royal claim then, in the great hall – whether it be true or false…'

'It is true.'

'…then I and all my friends would have been killed – executed as thieves. So, yes, I do offer you my thanks for whatever part you played.'

'Thanks are all very well,' said the Bear, 'but what is my reward?'

'If I were to grant you a reward, *gandr*, what should it be?'

'You know what I desire, man-child. My freedom.'

'That I cannot give you. I do not know how to achieve it.'

'You do. Think hard, heir of Angantyr; think, king of the Goths.'

Bjarki frowned. 'What do you want me to think about?'

'What is in your hand, man-child. Look down!'

Bjarki looked at his right hand. The Loki Sword was grasped in his fist. He slowly drew the blade from its leather covering. Unsheathed, the sword seemed to glow with a silvery light. The steel was fine work, he saw, with faint ripples in the metal that seemed to swirl and move as he twisted the blade in the green forest light. A sword fashioned by the Dwarf-Master Dwalin, a blade owned by the god Loki that could cut through anything.

'Cut the chain, man-child, and free me from this bondage!'

Bjarki hesitated.

'You do not trust me,' said the Bear. 'Even after the many times I have preserved you in the fray, given you my great strength. Then listen to me now: we *gandir* are creatures of honour, just like men. We are not the same as you, but our promise is as binding. Now I say this to you…'

The Bear seemed to take in an enormous breath, and Bjarki braced himself for a storm of noise. But the *gandr* let her air out long and slow. 'Free me,' the Bear whispered. 'And I shall make you a mighty oath.'

'What oath?'

'I swear that I shall come to you in time of need, if you call me, and lend you my strength, my ferocity, my power. Furthermore, I shall never again seek to make you my plaything; I shall come at

231

your word, and go at the same. I shall serve you, man-child, and ask you nothing in return.'

'That *is* a mighty oath,' said Bjarki. 'On what do you swear?'

'I swear this on the life of my cub, my beloved child. He is the most precious thing in my world. If I break my oath to you, may my own cub, the young creature you call Garm, perish.'

'You have lived a thousand years – what is the life of one young wild animal to you – *gandr*? By your long reckoning of life, Garm will have lived his span and be rot and dust in the merest blink of an eye.'

'You are blind, man-child, and deaf. Did my cub not speak – at the battle on the ridge a year ago – did you not hear him? You chained him and he broke free and slew your foemen beside you. Can you not see it?'

'Garm is a *gandr*, too,' said Bjarki, wonderingly.

'Now you understand. The cub is of my flesh – and *also* my spirit!'

'And you swear to serve me on the life of your *gandr* child?'

'I do, man-child. With all my heart, I do.'

'So be it,' said Bjarki, and he swung the Loki Sword – and easily sliced through the wooden chain as if it were a fine strand of spider's silk.

–

The light crept slowly along the tunnel, banishing the darkness, inch by inch, as the sun rose above the hills in the east. Until the first faint rays touched the deep-sleeping face of Bjarki Blood-hand, new king of the Goths, as he sat, slumped in the Throne of Arnheimer, his rightful place.

Bjarki woke, dazzled and surprised by bright sunshine in such a deep chamber in the earth. He covered his eyes and peered through his fingers. In full daylight, the chamber was a great deal dirtier than he had remembered it. But the mounds of gold and silver, the gilded armour, the baubles and all the piled jewels of the hoard sparkled with a new energy.

Bjarki got to his feet and, straightening the helmet-crown, and gripping the sheathed sword in his left hand, he began to stumble down the narrow corridor towards the sun. When he emerged blinking into the full glory of dawn, the first person he saw was Tor. Standing with her back to him, shading her eyes and looking east into the hot white glare.

'My *gandr* came, sis,' he said. 'In the night, we spoke a long time. And made a pact between us. I don't think she will plague me any more.'

'I am happy for you,' she replied. 'But right now we have more urgent matters to consider.'

She pointed at a low range of humped hillocks half a dozen miles away, and a line of horsemen slowly emerging from a wood. There were scores of them. Many hundreds even, riding in a double line. All dressed in dark clothing and heading towards the hill of the ancient troll circle.

'Black Cloaks,' said Tor. 'Our old friend Brandt is coming for us.'

Chapter Twenty-three

'You deserve death more than any man'

Tor covertly watched Bjarki out of the side of her eye, as her half-brother looked out under his shading hand at the advancing Black Cloaks. There was something different about him: he seemed taller, bigger somehow, more *real*, in a strange way, after his night alone with the bones of old Angantyr; the gold-rimmed helmet-crown on his head seemed to suit him.

Could he in reality be the descendant of the king of the Goths – the true heir of Angantyr? No, that was absurd. If that were true, then she had an equal claim, although of course women didn't count for as much when it came to inheriting thrones and gaining hoards of treasure. What was a king anyway but a big warrior in a shiny helmet? Someone who everyone else was obliged to bow and scrape before. Someone who was obeyed. What was a queen, for that matter? The woman who stood beside a king.

'So, your highness, what are we going to do about *them*?' she said, gesturing towards the oncoming *Scholares* cavalry.

'Go and fetch Valtyr and Kynwulf, and Leofric the Law-Speaker – bring them here. I need to speak with them all.'

And Tor found herself rushing to obey his royal command without a second thought. A few moments later, she stood with Bjarki, Valtyr and Kynwulf on the grassy slope outside the entrance to the ancient tomb.

'The Law-Speaker is at his house in the village,' said Valtyr. 'He grew tired during the festivities last night and had to be taken to his bed.'

'Do you think they will attack us?' said Kynwulf. 'Why? What reason could these Frankish riders have to make war on the *Felaki*?'

Bjarki looked at him. 'They seek to steal the treasures of Angantyr from his tomb. Their Captain Brandt wishes to acquire the Loki Sword for his master the king of Francia. They seek to possess all that is yours.'

'The treasures, and that sword you now hold, they all belong to you, Highness, to do with what you will. Will you give them to the Franks?'

'I will not.'

'We have warded them for a long time on behalf of your great ancestor, and held them in trust for you. We shall fight these powerful foreigners now, if you ask it of us, to ward the treasures a little longer.'

'If we must fight, then this is the place,' said Bjarki, pointing at the stones on the hill above him. 'Better here than in the village. Is there a place you could take the weak, the children, the old; some hiding place?'

Kynwulf chuckled. 'This is not the first time enemies have menaced the *Felaki*, your highness. There are deep caves in the hills north of here, ready stocked with food and water. I will ask the Law-Speaker to lead a group of those who cannot fight up there. The rest will arm themselves and come to the hill. We'll stand by your side and see off the foreigners.'

He bowed to Bjarki, then bounded down the hill towards the village.

The Black Cloaks were still a few miles off, but it was clear by now that they were heading straight for the hill on which the troll stones stood.

Valtyr said quietly: 'Listen to me, Bjarki. We don't have to fight them. There are pack horses at the back of the hill. They brought up the food and drink for the celebration last night. You heard the *Felaki* War Chief, the treasures are yours – to do with as you will. We have a little time. We could load all the treasure on the horses and make a run for it.'

Bjarki ignored him, still looking out at the advancing enemy.

'It's the wisest thing to do,' said Tor. 'We have the treasure and the sword in our hands, and a good hour before the Black Cloaks reach here. If we go due north, very fast, with the pack horses, we could lose the enemy in the mountains. Or you could order the *Felaki* to make a fine valiant last stand, here, to delay them, which would give us time to...'

'You are quite right, sis,' said Bjarki. 'It is the wisest thing to do. The clever thing. You should do it. Take Valtyr and Inge, and Halvar and Rangvar, too, if they wish to go with you, and make a run for the Harvath Mountains. I'll give you two chests of silver coin and a few of the jewels and some other baubles. But you must leave here as quickly as you can.'

'And what about the sword?' said Valtyr. 'I need the Loki Sword.'

'The blade of Angantyr is mine,' said Bjarki bluntly. He looked hard at Valtyr. 'And the Loki Sword will remain with me until the very end.'

Tor stared at her brother. 'You're going to fight them? There are two hundred or more Black Cloaks coming this way and we have... what? Forty warriors – most of them old men. You'll get yourself killed, oaf.'

'Nevertheless, I shall remain here.'

'Bjarki,' said Valtyr, 'this is madness. There is admirable courage and there is pig-headed stupidity – and you know well which one this is.'

Bjarki rounded on him: 'These people have chosen me to be their *king*. Me! It doesn't matter that it may be a lie; that maybe I am *not* the true heir of Angantyr, nor does it matter that you bribed the Law-Speaker with silver to favour us. It doesn't even matter that we came here to steal their treasure. They have elected me their king. They have *chosen* me. I will not return that compliment, that great *honour*, by robbing them while their backs are turned; leaving them to the mercy of Brandt and his men.'

Tor felt her face flush with shame. She looked at her boots.

'But *you* must both go,' said Bjarki, 'bring the pack horses and load them with treasure. Go, and with my blessing – perhaps we shall meet again in this life, if I live; more likely we'll meet in the Hall of the Slain.'

'Fuck you, oaf!' said Tor. 'Fuck you for a mind-twisting, pig-headed, ox-stubborn bastard. If you're staying, I'm staying, Valtyr's staying, Inge's staying. We're all fucking staying to die here beside you.'

Bjarki grinned at her. 'Cheer up, sis, it's only a battle against the best troops of Francia, in which they outnumber us about five to one.'

She reached up, pulled Bjarki's big head down towards her, and tugged at his thick beard. 'Who wants to live for ever, eh?' she said.

–

They burned the village. From inside the troll ring, when she found the time to look, Tor could see the thick columns of smoke coming from behind the shoulder of the hill, where they knew the village to be. She could see dozens of black-cloaked riders, some with burning torches, galloping about down by the river in the valley. But she could also just see, beyond the valley, on the far hillside above it, the last of the *Felaki* villagers, tiny figures, with their goods in carts and herd animals driven before them, disappearing into the folds of the foothills of the Western Harvaths, happily unmolested by the loot-hungry Black Cloaks below.

'I am sorry we brought this destruction upon you,' she heard Bjarki saying to Kynwulf, who had returned from his mission just an hour earlier. The old warrior shrugged: 'It is not the first time our enemies have come here and burned the *Felaki* village. It happens once every few generations. Usually, it is the Avars. But we have had Moravians come over the mountains, too, to burn our houses and steal our sheep. This is the first time the Franks have done it. But we always rebuild. It kills the lice and drives out the rats. We shall endure here, Highness. Do not fret.'

The Black Cloaks had taken up their positions just out of bowshot, perhaps three hundred paces away, in small companies, scattered all the way round the oval-shaped hill with its ring of troll stones. *Sensible*, Tor thought. *They cut us off from escape but do not yet risk themselves.*

Brandt was a better leader than she had suspected. They made no attempt to communicate with the warriors at the summit, the six Northern travellers and forty-five warriors of the *Felaki*, of greatly varying ages.

These eager descendants of the Companions in the ring were kitted out with rusty mail coats, or old-fashioned leather chest-and-back armour, and round lime-wood shields – painted with fantastical beasts, and lightning bolts – and helms adorned with spikes of iron. They had swords, axes, daggers and spears, too, and a surprising number of rather odd-looking bows, along with a hay cart filled with sheaves of arrows, which had been dragged up to the summit of the hill by a pair of loud, protesting oxen.

They had food aplenty: sheep and goat carcasses, and barrels of ale and mead and bags of twice-baked bread, which was hard and light but could be revived into a pleasant-tasting sop by dipping it in a cup of ale.

There were round cheeses and bundles of fresh green stuff, and onions, herbs and mushrooms, in long strings, and slabs of fatty bacon. With fifty or so folk on the top of the hill, inside the troll ring, with all the weapons, kit and stores, there wasn't a great deal of room to move freely.

Tor had set herself the task of making a proper defensive palisade along the circular row of the stones, using the wooden carts and wagons that had brought up all the food and drink and the spare *Felaki* war gear, to fill the yard-wide gaps between the granite boulders of the troll circle.

Valtyr, for some strange reason, was digging a large circular pit in the centre of the ring, with the help of three big muddy *Felaki* warriors and Inge, who was in charge of the rations and cooking. Tor thought they might be constructing a pit in which to roast one of the oxen – and she found her mouth filling with water at the thought, but she was not certain.

She used the heavy clay that Valtyr's team dug out of their pit to fill hundreds of small, empty linen bread bags and used them to weigh down and strengthen the make-shift wooden barricades she was constructing between the stones with bits of carts and spare shields. Bjarki – or the king, as everybody now called him – had divided his warriors into three equal-sized groups. Halvar had been given all the archers to command, a group of a dozen men and four tough-looking women who were agreed to be more than usually accomplished with their short, recurved horn and sinew bows – weapons that seemed more Avar than Goth, to Tor's mind.

As she wedged a damp, clay-packed sack into a gap between the top of an upright wheelbarrow and a lichen-covered troll stone, she overheard Halvar once again patiently explaining the commands he would issue for nocking a shaft, drawing the string and loosing the arrow at the foe.

Rangvar, meanwhile, had been given command of the 'Stoppers', a reserve company of seventeen of the biggest, strongest warriors, whose task it would be to fill or 'stop' any gaps that the Franks managed to make in the perimeter. Their task was also to kill any Black Cloaks that managed to leap their horses over the stones and break into the stone ring.

She could see Bjarki with the rest of the *Felaki*, demonstrating the move that would be most effective against a leaping horse coming in to the troll ring over their heads. A quick crouch under a sheltering shield, combined with sharp upwards thrust of a spear or sword that would eviscerate the animal as it passed over the warrior's head. With the horse mortally wounded, the Stoppers should then be able to deal with its rider.

When the sun was just a hand's breadth above the western horizon, the dying light a weird pinky grey, and shadows were stretching across the turf, Captain Brandt, accompanied by two Black Cloak officers, and the priest Clovis, trotted their horses up the slope and stopped thirty yards from the ring of stone and the make-shift wood and clay-bag barricade.

One of the officers carried a large blank flag, made from a grubby linen sheet, and Bjarki had ordered the warriors on the perimeter to stand down, loose no shafts, and acknowledge the ancient symbol of parlay.

'What a sweet little play-fortress you have up here!' said Brandt. 'It's a child's notion of a *castrum* and made with sticks, stones and mud.'

'Could we skip all the usual nonsense, Brandt, and get to the point. We are having a feast up here tonight – we have a nice plump ox already roasting, the ale barrels have been breached, and I think we would all appreciate a little brevity, if it's not too much to ask. There is still a lot to do, before we can take our ease. You've come up here to make some sort of terrible threats, yes? Death, mutilation, and so on. And a promise to spare our lives if we render up the treasures of Angantyr – and so forth?'

'Er, no,' said Brandt, after only a small pause. 'Ah… um, I came to get a look at your funny little fort – and to tell you that I'm going to come up here with my men soon… and butcher every last one of you.'

'All right – now we've got that straight. Was there anything else?'

'After we have taken our vengeance on you in this life,' shouted Clovis, the priest, his face twisted in rage, 'your pagan souls will burn in the fiery pit for eternity! So shall all the enemies of Karolus be served!'

'Be quiet now, Father,' hissed Brandt.

'Yes, shut up, Clovis,' called down Bjarki. 'This is a battlefield, or it soon will be, and real warriors are talking. So hold your weasel tongue.'

Brandt glared up at Bjarki, he seemed about to turn his horse and go back down the hill but then he thought better of it.

'Men of the *Felaki* tribe – do you know what manner of man stands in your midst, that lump who claims falsely to be the heir of Angantyr?'

There was no reply from the ring of stones above.

'He is no more than a murderous bumpkin – with a bad temper. He is a liar, a trickster and a fool – no king reborn, I can assure you of that!'

'You call me murderer – yet you tried to have me killed, in Asa's Landing, with an arrow,' shouted Bjarki. 'And, in the Silesian *gord*, you hired men to waylay me in the street. Your hands are as bloody as mine!'

Brandt smiled nastily at him, and shrugged indifferently.

'I know you were behind those cowardly attacks,' said Bjarki. 'But what I don't understand is why you were so determined to seek my death. What is the death of one warrior to the Franks? I have some renown, it is true, but it would not have made any difference to the sale of the amber and the funding of the rebellion. Nor would it make a jot of difference to the realm of Francia, in any way I can see. Why did you want me dead?'

'You deserve death more than any man I have met,' replied Brandt.

'Why? What have I done to injure you? I was always your friend.'

'Not me. Yoni. You slaughtered her, you carved her into bloody meat… I saw her body after the battle – yes, I was there, I was not kept in the fortress of Buraburg with a sore foot – and by ill-luck I did not have the chance to face you, one on one, in the battle line. But I saw what you did to my lovely Yoni, what you did to that sweet girl…' Brandt had gone red in the face and Bjarki realised he was actually weeping at the memory. 'She looked as if she had been… savaged by a pack of mad dogs…' Brandt gave a wet sniff. 'I loved her, I truly loved her, and yet she would not have me. She said she loved *you* – and only you. You, the monster who ripped her apart. That is why you deserve to die, beast-man! That is why I tried to kill you on the road and why I will surely end you in this bleak place, give you the death you so richly merit, unless…'

Brandt mastered himself with a visible effort.

'Unless?' said Bjarki. 'Unless what?'

Brandt straightened his spine. 'I serve Bishop Livinus, and the King of Francia faithfully. And my sacred Christian duty outweighs my own personal desire – a vast, burning lust – for revenge. And so I will spare you, on my word of honour, I will spare you, Bjarki, and your pathetic little gang of old men and ragged children, if you do one thing in return.'

'What would that be?' Bjarki sounded genuinely curious.

'Give me the Loki Sword, put it in my hand, and I'll spare you all.'

Bjarki put his right hand on the hilt of the Loki Sword, which was hanging from his belt. He felt the warmth of its *seithr* in his fingers. He smiled coldly down at the Black Cloak officer on the slope below him.

'If you want my sword, come up here and try to take it!'

Chapter Twenty-four

A strangely clumsy affair

When darkness fell they set up skull lanterns on each of the ancient stones, looking down blindly at the grassy slope below, like the faces of demons. They painted them all with fresh ox blood and wreathed them in flowers and leaves, as if it were for some pleasant summer festival of joy.

The effect was profound. It had been Valtyr's idea, of course: they had taken some of the more recent skulls from the tomb beneath their feet, Kynwulf had made the choices, picking this skull and that from the side chambers, the ones who had been notable warriors, putting the lit oil lamps inside the bony cavities to shine eerily through the big eye holes.

'This is their land, and their ancient fortress,' Kynwulf said. 'They defended it in life – and if they could fight now they would surely defend it in death!' Yet he flatly refused to allow Valtyr to use Angantyr's skull.

'Let the old king rest,' he said. 'A living king will lead us now.'

Walking round the whole perimeter in the darkness, Bjarki thought the skull lamps gave the place a suitably ghastly look. As he stared up at the flickering eye-lights, and the glistening red-painted domes, and the wilting flowers, even though he'd helped create them, he felt the fine hairs rise all over his skin at the sight of their glowing, long-dead faces.

They also dug simple horse-traps into the slopes on all side, foot-deep holes, camouflaged with loose twigs and leaves, that would snap a charging animal's leg with ease. Bjarki hated them but knew their value.

They kept a good watch, too. Ten men on sentry duty, all round the barricade's perimeter, the sentries alternating with their comrades all through the night, taking turns to eat platters of hot, bloody roasted ox, and sink cups of strong ale and sleep a few hours, if they were able to.

All knew this night might be their last night in the Middle-Realm.

Bjarki spent a little time with Kynwulf, arranging the dispositions of the *Felaki*, and trying to put heart into the old man on the eve of battle.

'The Black Cloaks are here because we came here,' he said to the old warrior. 'I am ashamed that we brought Death to your door. But we *can* beat them, my friend, we will see them off, if we fight well enough.'

'Do not trouble yourself, Highness. The old ones had a saying which they claimed came from the lips of Odin himself: "Fear not Death, for the hour of your doom has been set by the Fate-Spinners. There's no escaping it." We all live or die, according to our fates. All we can do is die well!'

Later Bjarki and Tor sat together outside the troll circle in the middle watch, facing southwards, watching the scatter of tiny red sparks that marked the different Frank campfires in the darkness, and listening to the dirge-like Christian singing. There was a cold wind and a growing mist in the valley below and both drew their cloaks tight around their shoulders.

'If you could be anywhere in the world now, brother, where would you choose to be? If some *seithr* could carry you there in a wink…'

Bjarki thought for a while.

'I would like to try another one of those steam baths in the *gord*,' he said. 'But without two big Silesians trying to murder me afterwards.'

'Come on, oaf, try harder. You could be taken to Miklagard, the vast and glittering Greek city by the sea, or to mighty Rome, where their fat Pope lives in a place in hoggish Christian splendour. Where would you go, Bjarki – if you could go anywhere, anywhere in the Middle-Realm?'

'I don't know either of those places. And I'm sure I would not like living among so many strangers. But if I had to go somewhere… well, I really liked the *gord* – most of the time. I'd like one day to meet the Duke of Polans – I told you I met his man Goran in the bath-house, didn't I?'

'You told me. You are not really still hankering after that perfect homestead in the picture, are you? The little boat and happy pig?'

'No. Maybe. I don't know. I feel I am *meant* to be right here, right now, with these people, who have chosen me to lead them. I want to be here, with them, with *you*. Even though we have to fight, and maybe die.'

Tor said nothing for a long time.

'What about you?' said Bjarki. 'Where would you wish to be?'

'I would like to be at home, with Ulli and Inge and my lovely boy Garm. And you, too. I'd like to be back in Norrland, at my own hearth.'

Valtyr plumped down beside them. In the flickering light of the skull lamps, Bjarki saw that his face was covered in several streaks of grey-white clay. His hands were filthy, too, nails encrusted with the same dirt.

'So what are we discussing here this fine night?' the old man said.

'I was saying how nice it would be to have a steam-bath,' said Bjarki. 'Looks like you might wish the same. You could surely use one.'

He nodded at the old man's dirty hands. Tor gave a great cough of a laugh.

'It may have escaped your notice, Bjarki,' said Valtyr, 'but there is not a great deal of running water up here on this bone-dry hillock. Plenty of ale and a few casks of mead. But not much washing water. If I wanted to get clean I'd have to go to the river in the valley, and I heard a rumour that there is a bunch of big, nasty Franks down there who would love to cut me into little pieces. So I'll stay nice and dirty for tonight, thank you.'

'We are surrounded, sure,' said Tor. 'And horribly outnumbered.'

'Hmm, apart from that, how do we feel about things this evening?' Valtyr was looking between the two siblings, at one face, then the other.

Bjarki said: 'Tor wants to go back home to Norrland.'

'I didn't say that. It was just a game, a wistful imagining. I'll fight.'

'I think in truth we would all like to go home,' said Valtyr. 'We have the Loki Sword; we have Angantyr's treasure beneath our feet...'

'I'm not discussing this, Valtyr. Go, if you want to. I am staying!'

'Calm down, Bjarki. We won't get out of here without a fight. Not now. I'm just thinking ahead. Doing a little planning for our future.'

'It's so sweet that you think we have a future, old man,' said Tor.

—

The Black Cloaks' attack, when it came, erupted out of the veils of mists a little after dawn. It was a strangely clumsy affair. Two *cunei* of about fifty horsemen each came straight up the hill from the Frankish camp to the south at the trot. They paused fifty paces away, and shouted their war cries, and brandished their swords and javelins in a warlike manner, and when Halvar lined up his archers and began dropping lethal shafts on their heads, they charged directly at the stones on the summit of the hill.

Bjarki and his people were ready for them. They stood in grim pairs behind the grey stones and in the wood and mud-filled gaps in between, shields high, spears cocked, and braced themselves for the onslaught.

As the enemy cavalry charged, Halvar's men busily showered them with arrows, loosing flat or even slightly downhill, directly into their grim helmeted faces, and the tough little Svear and his small company emptied nearly a score of saddles by their valiant efforts. A couple of riders fell victim to the horse-traps, too, their beasts plunging their hooves into the pits and snapping their own fetlocks, tumbling their riders on to the turf.

Yet the Franks were quickly up at the barricade, riding along the line and hurling their javelins down into the mass of *Felaki* warriors behind the uneven wall, skewering soft bodies, battering the lime-wood shields, steel points screeching off helms and sometimes pinning unfortunate men like insects to the ground with the great force of the javelin throw.

The enemy cavalry curled forwards like a great black wave, crashing against the line of battle, and moving away sideways along it in a tide of shouting men and mounts, screams and yells and the clashing rip of steel. When a Black Cloak rider had flung his only javelin into the boiling mass along the wall, he drew his long sword and sliced and slashed at the faces below, dealing out terrible wounds, before galloping away down the hill.

The barricade held firm. Just. Bjarki, still wearing the splendid golden helm-crown, fought with young squint-eyed Gisli as his shield-partner, both warriors oath-bound to protect the other, in the very centre of the line, as the Black Cloak wave crashed up against them. Amidst the battering, the bellowing and the bloodshed, Bjarki heard the younger man loudly call on Tiw to witness his great deeds as he lunged forwards with his spear and took a galloping Black Cloak right in the pit of his stomach.

The combined force was colossal, as the charging horseman, his belly protected with iron scales, met the tip of Gisli's fast-striking spear. The blade ripped right through the Frank's fine armour, punching into his torso, then hit something – the man's spine or perhaps the high back of his Frankish cavalry saddle. The heavy spear snapped in two, and was instantly snatched from Gisli's hands, spinning away across the barricade.

The screaming Frank, now slipping bloodily from his horse's back, slashed at Gisli with his sword as he fell, and Bjarki easily caught the blow on the iron rim of his shield. He exchanged a grin with his squint-eyed shield-mate. As Gisli drew his sword, Bjarki saw an object shimmer in the corner of his eye and swung up his shield in time to intercept another assault, another javelin, hurled this time from just two yards away. The point *tocked* right through his lime-wood, leather-faced shield, the steel tip ending up, terrifyingly, mere inches from Bjarki's left eye.

All along the southern barricade the battle raged and roared. The crush of dismounted Black Cloaks was now thick against the *Felaki* line, and beyond them the dark horsemen showered javelins on their heads, or, finding a gap, spurred in and leaned forwards to hack down with swords.

Bjarki's shield with its embedded javelin was now too unwieldy to use and he hurled it from his left arm, skimming it at a long black horse-face with a white blaze. The rim of the shield hit the animal's nose, and it shied and reared, partially dislodging its rider. Bjarki jabbed up with his spear, flickering fast, and drove the blade into the flailing man's armpit.

There were even more unhorsed Black Cloaks battling at the curved line of the stones – in a corner of his mind Bjarki knew they must have come up on foot behind the cavalry vanguard; now even more screaming, clean-shaven faces under helmets and swords were hammering at the thin line of *Felaki* shield-men. And the horsemen, too, were far from beaten.

Some were still pounding up the slope, spurring in for a second assault on the wood-and-stone barricade, others were spreading around the sides of the circle, menacing both the flanks. Yet the doughty *Felaki* hammered back at the Franks with equal ferocity. A surging scrum of men and mounts, pain and steel and bloody death. Something large and black loomed over Bjarki's head. He flinched, and heard Gisli give a massive shout, his sword lunging straight up, the blade catching the soft belly of the horse as it leapt over the shoulder-high stones.

The steel sunk in easily and the very momentum of the horse passing over their heads eviscerated the poor flying beast from breastbone to balls. The stallion screamed and thumped down in a slippery wash of guts and dark blood. The Black Cloak, kicked free of the stirrups, tumbled and rolled off his dying mount, rose unsteadily and was about to pull out his long sword when Rangvar's axe spilt his helmeted skull into two halves.

The wounded stallion was down and kicking out wildly in its awful death agonies, surrounded by the enormous red puddle of its own insides.

Bjarki turned to congratulate Gisli and saw the grinning lad, looking the wrong way, take a mighty sword hack to the back of his neck from a Frank who was reaching over the barricade to strike him. Bjarki reached out, lunged and drove his spear-tip into the foe's open mouth, crunching through teeth, flesh, a helmet flap, to spray red gore out of the other side.

Another Black Cloak was now in the very act of climbing the barricade, about to leap down on the other side, both his swords drawn, when Bjarki punched him left-handed in the belly. A big, looping blow, with all the power of his meaty left shoulder behind it. The punch caught the man in mid-air, knocked him back against a troll stone, and left him winded, gasping like a landed fish, to the torn turf inside the circle.

Bjarki stepped forwards and finished him with a simple stamp of his boot to his exposed throat, crushing his windpipe. Then, at almost the same time, he slashed his spear blade at another foe climbing over the nearest stone, forcing him to fall backwards to land on the other side. He snatched a look down at Gisli, the boy's head was half severed, the neck at a horrible angle. But the warrior appeared to be smiling, even in death.

He reached down and picked up Gisli's shield, hefted his bloody spear again and went forwards to the gore-spattered barricade – which was now strangely empty of foes. The crush had suddenly dissolved. The pressure lifted. The Black Cloaks were milling around, a good fifty or more on horse and foot, about twenty paces away from the line of stones. Reluctant. An officer in a black plume was shouting at them, exhorting them to attack the line once more. But the hillside was stacked with their dead and wounded, slathered in blood, and Bjarki heard the screaming of the wounded for the first time. A horrible, heart-piercing, endless refrain.

He turned his head to look at the interior of the stone ring and saw a scene of bloody horror there, too. A dozen of his men or more were down, bleeding or still. Some warriors were sitting with their back to the stones, slumped, utterly exhausted. But Halvar's archers were still shooting, only nine of them now, but their shafts still whipped and whizzed over the southern part of the barricade, slamming into havering Black Cloaks and their horses. Bjarki caught Tor's eye; she was standing beside the rangy form of Rangvar and his band of Stoppers, who had not yet been called to take part in the fight. She looked back at him – and simply shrugged.

Then he looked beyond her, and saw a thick bar of utter blackness.

And the second attack, the real assault, boiled over the *north* side of the troll circle in a clattering thunder of horses and dark, crouched riders.

Chapter Twenty-five

A sweet jolt of fury

Tor heard Bjarki's shout of alarm and whirled in surprise. For an instant, the world seemed to be filled with flying horses. They were pouring over the stone-and-wood barricade from the north side in a flood of darkness, she shouted a warning to Rangvar, hefted shield and spear, ran forwards.

A Black Cloak cavalryman cleared their defences with alarming ease, and pounded towards her. His long lance aimed at her head. She could feel the earth thrumming under her running boots. She stopped and braced herself. The rider leapt over the fire-pit in which they had cooked the huge ox the night before, and seemed to be hanging over her. As the horse was still in the air, she caught sight of Valtyr and Inge, hugged tight together, crouched low in the deep fire-pit right under the steel-shod hooves, with Valtyr holding a round shield protectively over their heads.

The horse and rider landed on the far side with a clatter and thump. Just yards away. Still heading for Tor. Singling her out for slaughter.

At the very last instant before disaster, Tor quickly sidestepped, spoiling the *Scholares'* line of attack, and thrust her own spear deep into the turf between the horse's front legs, tripping the animal, snapping the spear, the charging mass tumbling forwards like a boulder towards her.

The big black animal sprawled sideways and she caught a huge kick from a powerful flailing back leg on her shield, which bowled her over backwards. By the time she had got to her feet, shaken loose her half-split lime-wood shield, and pulled out her sword, the Black Cloak was on her.

He hacked at her left and she parried awkwardly, across her body, and counter-swung at his right side, but he stopped the blow with a clang of his own short sword. She saw he was grinning at her, taunting her, showing his tiny grey teeth. Creeping forwards, the long sword twitching in his right hand, short one in the left. She grinned right back at him; showing her own fangs. He sliced at her head, she ducked and lunged forwards, using the power of her legs. He jumped back and swung wildly with the short sword, missed, and she closed again, flicked away the tip of his short blade and stabbed with her own sword, lightning fast. In, out, the sword coming back glistening. He screamed, collapsed, dropped both swords, hands clutching at the fork between his legs, now pissing blood.

She felt the raw, sweet jolt of battle-fury run all through her body; she pulled out the seax from its sheath across her loins and, blades in both hands, she threw herself into the line of struggling, shouting, jostling men, Black Cloak and Stoppers, beyond the big fire-pit on the north side of the stone circle. She hacked across the back of a battling Frank, making him arch in pain, then buried her seax in another man's kidneys.

Beside her Rangvar was roaring like a lion, swinging and slaying Franks left and right with sweeps of his long Dane axe. The *Felaki* were showing their mettle, too, like their heroic Companion forefathers. Kynwulf, the War Chief, was doing great destruction with his spear, taking hard blows on his shield, and lunging with the pole-arm, jabbing in, slicing faces, ripping flesh, dropping one man after the other and moving ever forwards, pushing the enemy back towards the stone walls.

A willow-thin boy called Oddvin was duelling with a Black Cloak, axe and seax against the Franks' two swords. The youth was getting the worst of it, but at the last moment, his axe smacked into the Christian's wrist and the soldier lost his hand, falling to the turf in gushing agony.

Oddvin glided in and plugged the seax into the side of his neck.

Halvar was in the midst of it, too, drawing and loosing, plucking another shaft from his waist-bag, drawing and loosing. The range was so short that some arrows passed straight through the bodies of his victims.

Yet more of the mounted *Scholares* were pouring over the northern defences. The whole stone circle now was filled with wrestling men, tripping over corpses, blood-maddened horses, kicking, screaming and neighing, men sliced and hacked, at each other, stumbled, tripped and died. Rangvar eviscerated one horse with a swipe of his axe; Tor trod on the neck of a Frank, a fallen man, his opened belly glistening, and the fellow snapped at her, teeth bloody. She pulled her foot quickly away.

She looked over her shoulder, saw Bjarki, rallying the remaining defenders on the south wall, stripping it of all spears; charging forwards.

With a dozen men only, Bjarki, spear couched, shield high, ran and slammed into the battle around the fire-pit. He was shouting: 'Push them back! Back! Back! Back! Push them all *out*!' His spear flickering out, again and again, to kill and maim the foe, mounted and unhorsed. The gore-speckled *Felaki* were bellowing: 'Ang-an-tyr... Ang-an-tyr!'

The Companions were coalescing into tight groups, three or four men, and surging forwards together in tight packs, sweeping the now disorganised Black Cloaks backwards. This was clearly something the *Felaki* had been trained to do. The unhurt horses began to whinny and panic, unnerved by their fellow beasts' pain-filled cries, the threat to the herd overwhelming their equine senses. The *Felaki* regrouped, still bellowing their war cry, and charged again, shoving the foe back and back, spears picking, shields ramming, forcing the enemy hard up against the northern barricade, the line of stones, mud and wooden shields that they had swept over so majestically, so effortlessly, a short while earlier.

'Out! Out! Out!' yelled Bjarki, stabbing at a scowling Black Cloak rider above him, ripping open his smooth cheek. The man struck back hard with his long sword; Bjarki took the blow on his shield and smashed the iron rim into the horse's jaw. The horse reared and unseated its rider.

'Push them out! Out! Out!' Bjarki stamped forwards, his red-tipped spear licking out like a long serpent's tongue. The crush of struggling Black Cloaks was tight against the northern barricade now; three men deep, hard pressed folk, many of them wounded; horses mad with fear.

Tor slipped forwards and took her place beside Bjarki on his right side, his spear side. She had no shield but she stopped a sword strike at Bjarki with her seax, and hammered a sword blow at the yelling Black Cloak, clanging off his iron helm and forcing him to sway backwards.

The man tripped over the corpse of a dead horse, and a *Felaki* thrust a spear into his ribs as he floundered on his back. Another foe, a big man, a black-plumed officer, hacked at her and she had to block wildly with crossed blades, seax and sword. Bjarki swivelled his hips right, lunged and skewered him with his spear. Rangvar was beside her now, on her right, mumbling filthy curses. She saw that he had blood streaked all the way down his left flank. But it did not seem to hamper him. He swung his axe, cracking into a *Scholares* shield, swung again; decapitated the man.

They were grinding forwards, and Tor saw an arrow-struck rider spur back and ride out of the crush, leap his maddened horse over the stones.

The *Felaki* were still screaming: 'Ang-an-tyr... Ang-an-tyr!'

A skinny Black Cloak hurled himself at Bjarki from the left; her brother took the man's full weight on his shield, then hurled him off, throwing him to the right. Tor stepped out and plunged her seax into his groin, then ripped up into his stomach as he sprawled on the wet ground.

And just like that, it was over.

The last of the horsemen were hopping their exhausted mounts over the battered barricade; dismounted Black Cloaks were now scrambling over the wall and streaming down the hillside. Tor turned, dreading that she would see another black wave coming in over the south side, but all she could see was corpses and gore and the wounded, groaning in agony, men piled everywhere, only a score of their own folk still up on their feet.

The *Felaki* threw themselves on the wounded Black Cloaks, all those who had been unable to run from the stone circle, sitting astride their chests and ripping open their throats without a drop of mercy, then tossing limp bodies over the barricade, to roll slowly down the hillside.

Tor sat down hard on the bloody turf, the air whooshing out of her lungs. She let the twin blades drop from her clenched hands. She looked down at her stained fingers and saw they were trembling wildly, like someone with a bad fever. She bunched them into fists. But found she was drawing in great ragged, painful breaths, one after the other, and realised that she was on the edge of exploding into hot, shameful tears.

She jerked her head up, took command of her feelings, and looked for Bjarki – he was whole, thank the gods, horribly blood-splashed and still gripping his gory spear. Standing beside old Kynwulf, who was also apparently unhurt, and who was pointing over the barricade to the north at something she could not see from her seated position. And looking impossibly regal, with the shiny helmet-crown on his big, blond head.

—

A little while later, as the sun was nearing its zenith, Brandt came up the northern slope on foot, under another white grubby flag, with Clovis the priest and another Black Cloak officer walking respectfully beside him.

Tor had mastered herself, eaten a piece of rye bread and a slice of ham, drunk down three cups of ale and bound up a shallow cut on her left wrist. She was standing beside Bjarki on the north wall, watching the man she had once thought dashing and handsome as he strolled up the slope with the big flag flapping tauntingly above his head. She wondered where he had been during the battle.

Hiding, probably. She had seen no sign of him in the bloody crush, nor directing the events from afar. And this noon-tide he seemed to be clean and refreshed, unmarked by battle.

There was a part of her that longed to leap over the barricade and charge down the slope, blades drawn, and slaughter the smug bastard and his men – but she knew it would be suicide, and worse, Bjarki would be upset by her breach of the proper protocols. So she contented herself with hacking loudly and spitting a fat wad of phlegm in his general direction.

'That's close enough,' said Bjarki, when the Black Cloak captain was twenty yards away.

'I've come up here to talk about the surrender,' said Brandt.

'However much you beg, I will not accept your surrender today,' replied Bjarki. 'I mean to put you down for good, you filthy traitor.'

'Not *my* surrender – idiot! Yours.'

Bjarki grinned at him, leaning casually with one arm on a troll stone.

'Oh, I see. You were trying to make a joke,' said Brandt. 'An old jest, not even a funny one. Perhaps this will wipe the grin off your face.'

He made a hand gesture and the Black Cloak officer came forwards. He was holding a big, cloth-wrapped parcel in his hands. The Frankish officer shook the cloth and a round object fell out of the folds and rolled out at his feet. It was the severed head of a very old, wispy haired man. The milky opaque eyes seemed to stare accusingly up at the barricades.

'My men found him and all his raggedy women and children hiding in a cave on the north side of the valley. He claimed he was the Law-Speaker of the *Felaki*. Perhaps he was. He's rotting carrion-flesh now.'

Tor could hear Kynwulf growling low in his throat, like a furious animal. She put a hand on his arm to restrain him but he threw her off.

'We killed all of them – eventually – the men, women and even the children,' said Brandt, as if he were discussing a cull of a herd of sheep, 'and although they were stubborn, particularly this cheeky old goat,' here Brandt gave the head a kick and it began to roll slowly down the hill, 'we had fun with them, and they told us everything they knew… in the end.'

Kynwulf was actually vibrating with rage. He seemed to be on the verge of flinging himself over the barricade and charging the trio of foes.

Bjarki turned to the War Chief. 'Go, now, and see to the wounded.'

'I'm going to gut that dog; I'm going to dig his fucking heart out.'

'Yes, and I'll help. But not now. Kynwulf, this is an order. As your king, I command it. See to the wounded. I'll parley with this creature.'

And to Tor's surprise, after giving Brandt one last volcanic stare, Kynwulf turned his back and stumped back into the middle of the troll ring, where the wounded were laid out, being tended by Valtyr and Inge.

'So, you're the monster now, eh?' said Bjarki coolly. 'A killer of old men, women and children – that's what you want us to understand?'

'You miss the point, fool. I know the treasures of Angantyr and the Loki Sword are hidden somewhere around here – and that these *Felaki* savages are their guardians, and have been for centuries. I thought the hoard might be in those caves where the people were hidden. But now I know better. I now know that the treasures are up there with you, and that handful of cripples you have left. And that's why you won't budge from your toy fortress. I came to tell you I'm coming up there for them today.'

He doesn't know about the tomb! The thought struck Tor like a slap.

'So what was all the talk of surrender?'

'Come down from there now, leave your weapons behind, your possessions and the treasure inside the ring – including the Loki Sword – and I will allow you all to walk away. I am still offering you your lives.'

Bjarki laughed. 'We are happy where we are, monster,' he said. 'And, as I said before, if you want the sword, come up here and get it.'

'You want to die?' Brandt looked genuinely surprised. 'I still have a hundred fresh men under my command, you have, what? A dozen? And I have already sent word up the River Donau that I have the Loki Sword within my grasp. The garrison at Carnuntum will send me another *scara*, or two, or even three – I could have a thousand troops here within two days. All I have to do is sit tight and keep you trapped in that stupid little child's fort and wait. Then we will simply swamp you with our numbers. Or you could give up now and walk away. There is no need to die here.'

Tor felt a sudden pang in her heart. She knew deep down that this Christian bastard was not to be trusted, and that if they left the protection of the troll ring, they would be at his mercy. And that Bjarki was right to reject his offer. But still, she did not want to die. She wanted to go home, sit by her fire, pet Garm, make peace with the Norrland jarl... and live.

She silently cursed herself for her pathetic weakness. Bjarki showed not a shred of fear, he was resolute. She must behave likewise. If this was her day to perish, if this was when her thread was fated to be cut, so be it.

Who wants to live for ever? Today, I do.

'I'd be obliged if you'd send up your people in small groups, just a score or so at a time,' said Bjarki. 'Or in dozens. That will make it much more convenient for us to slaughter them. Or is that too much to ask?'

'You trying to be funny again?' Brandt seemed on the edge of fury.

'Just practical,' said Bjarki.

The priest spoke for the first time: 'The Lord God Almighty will strike you down with a furious anger. Do not mock the hosts of the Lord for He shall have his rightful vengeance upon you. Your doom beckons.'

'So I have recently been told,' said Bjarki. 'Well, if that is all...'

Chapter Twenty-six

'Crack open my poor eyes'

As he watched the three Black Cloaks walk down the north slope towards the valley, still wreathed with smoke from the destruction of the village, Bjarki became aware that Valtyr was beside him and tugging his sleeve.

'Rangvar wishes to speak to you; he does not have much time left.'

He, Valtyr and Tor walked slowly and painfully over to the rows and rows of blood-spattered wounded. Tor said: 'What was all that about them coming at us in scores, oaf? Where you trying to make him angry?'

'Yes, but more than that. I want them to do the opposite of what I told them. I want them to make one big final attack with all their troops. I want them all to be together. Not spread out, not scattered over the field.'

'Why?' said Valtyr.

But Bjarki did not answer. He crouched down on the turf beside the still form of Rangvar. The big warrior had been stripped of his mail coat and his underclothes and someone had bandaged the great hole in his left side, a javelin strike, or perhaps a sword blow. He was deathly pale, his naked flesh seeming almost a pale blue. The bandages around his barrel chest were heavy and sodden with his blood. He was one of perhaps two dozen wounded and dead men who were lying in the torn grass in the middle of the troll ring, while Inge, shaky but determined, flitted between them offering words of comfort and sips from a big flask of strong mead.

259

'H… highness,' whispered Rangvar, his voice faint from agony.

'We have travelled a hard road together, Rangvar, I think you must now call me *friend*,' said Bjarki, taking his blood-wet hand in his own.

'Friend… aye,' breathed Rangvar. 'Friend. I shall call you that now… although it was not always so.'

The dying man slowly reached up his right hand and tapped his big, battered nose with his index finger. 'No… we were not always…'

Then his hand fell away.

'Forgive me for that knock, Rangvar,' said Bjarki, gripping his hand tightly. 'I was angry and you…'

'Ah, pssht… That was nothing. We are men… of war. Hard men. Proper men. It was a little tickle, a playful bump, no more…'

Bjarki said nothing. Rangvar's eyes were fixed on the sky – the great blue empty sky, with a fat disc of buttercup sun peeking through fleecy clouds giving the promise of the warm afternoon to come. For some folk.

'I see them,' Rangvar said. 'Up there. I see them. They are coming for me. The Wingèd Ones. I've been chosen by Odin's shield-maidens.'

Tor felt a shudder of dread – she looked in the sky searching for the shapes of the Valkyrie, galloping down on their flying steeds to take the soul of this dying warrior up to the Hall of the Slain. But she saw nothing but a pair of black crows, flapping high above across the blue.

'You need not ask forgiveness for this,' said Rangvar, tapping his nose again, his voice oddly stronger now, almost forceful. 'But I must beg yours. I hated you then. And when you were acclaimed as a king, as great Angantyr reborn, I was jealous, and hated you anew in my heart.'

'Hush now, that is not important now,' said Bjarki. 'You must rest, and try to conserve your strength. You might yet live to fight again…'

'Let us have no falsehood between us at the end,' said Rangvar. 'I'm done. I'm passing from the Middle-Realm, let me say my piece...'

Bjarki said nothing; tears were running down his bearded cheeks.

'I did not believe that you were... Angantyr the king reborn,' said Rangvar, '...until I saw you fight beside me today, in your golden helm but now, I know... I believe. You are truly Angantyr, you are truly the king of the Goths returned to us. I am a Geat from Gothenburg, as you know... a Goth. And with my dying breath I say this: you are my king.'

'And you are my friend, Rangvar, and you fought like a hero this day. I saw you. Odin saw you – the approach of the Wingèd Ones is proof that you are worthy. I'll see you again, Rangvar, my friend, if I prove to be as fortunate as you, we'll feast in Odin's Hall together, perhaps soon.'

'I'll save you a place on the benches, Highness...' said Rangvar. And he died.

—

Bjarki spent much of that afternoon with the wounded *Felaki* – and there were so many of them. The two assaults by the Black Cloaks had taken a terrible toll on his little company. A dozen *Felaki* were already dead and cold and a similar number looked unlikely to see the next dawn, which left only twenty-three warriors, counting Bjarki, Tor and Halvar, who were either only lightly wounded or unhurt and still able to fight again.

Bjarki went to each of the injured men in turn, sitting with them quietly, praising their courage, assuring the dying ones that their deeds had been seen by the All-Father and they would be rewarded in Valhalla. He changed their bandages, helped Valtyr to sew up cuts and slashes, held their heads while he gave them sips of mead, or ale mixed with powdered henbane from Valtyr's last remaining stores of that drug, for their agony.

He then gathered up the helmets from the dead and set them on the skulls on each of the troll stones. The lamps had long been extinguished but the helmets topping the blood-spattered domes, with spears propped alongside them, served to give the impression to an enemy at a reasonable distance that he commanded a larger defending force than he truly did.

He gazed south down the slopes and saw that the Black Cloak lines were quiet, the horses were tethered and hobbled and grazing placidly, the smoke from a score of campfires drifted over the fields, and dozens of enemies wandered as if they had not a care in the world. More of them were sitting beside their fires, cooking, drinking. Some Franks were even sleeping. A handful of sentries on the perimeter of the site gazed back up at him. He had a mad urge to wave at them. He knew there were more troops stationed on the north side, too, but this was where they had made their main camp. They were not as concentrated as he would have liked them to be, but it would have to do, he supposed. Indeed, it would do.

There was a large black tent in the centre of their settlement, with a pair of sentries outside, the roost of that traitorous bastard Brandt and his priest Clovis, he guessed. But he caught no glimpse of the villain himself.

'Bastard's probably having a nice long nap,' he muttered.

In the late afternoon, Tor brought him some rye bread and two thick slices of cold roast oxen, and a big flask of ale. Valtyr wandered over too.

He sat down to eat his meal and felt a wave cold sorrow sweep over him. 'So, your highness, what exactly is our plan now?' said his sister.

Bjarki looked at her. 'I don't think they are going to come at us again today,' he said slowly. 'We gave them a pretty good mauling. And now they look as if they have settled in to wait for reinforcements. It's the sensible thing to do. They have, what? – a hundred effectives – no more.'

'It is the wise thing to do – looking out from their eyes,' said Valtyr. 'Why kill any more of your own troops than you need to?

If another Black Cloak *scara* were to come up from Carnuntum – or three more of them – they could attack us from four sides and simply roll right over us.'

'Assuming he was telling the truth about his reinforcements,' said Tor, 'and that is a big assumption, now we know about Brandt's lies.'

Bjarki slowly chewed his bread and meat – and said nothing.

'So, come on, oaf, you obviously have an idea – tell us what it is.'

Bjarki chewed his mouthful and swallowed it. He took a swig of ale.

'You ever seen a brown marsh frog take a fly in the air?' he said.

'What? What are you dribbling on about now?' Tor said crossly.

'It's all in the legs,' said Bjarki. 'And the speed of the frog's lunge.'

'I've seen it,' said Valtyr, then he nodded, as understanding dawned.

Bjarki nodded back at him. 'The frog sits very still and quiet, and you might mistake him for a muddy rock. You might think he'd never move again. Then when the insect is in range, he makes a powerful and unexpected spring, a huge leap, and chomps that fly right out of the air.'

'Oh,' said Tor. 'Oh, yes, indeed. I see. So that is your plan, is it?'

–

Bjarki gathered all the fit *Felaki* in the centre of the troll stones ring. He had polished his gold helmet-crown, so that it now shone brilliantly in the late afternoon sunshine, he had washed his face and combed his hair and beard; he had put on his mail hauberk, and his long black bearskin cloak hung from his shoulders. He carried the Loki Sword, sheathed in his left hand. And a long spear in his right. His seax hung horizontally across his loins. A big round shield was slung over his broad back. The fighting men all stared at their king expectantly, with more than a little awe as well.

Away in the west the sun was finally setting, a bloody scarlet, pink and grey wash of colour amid the streaks and furrows of rumpled cloud.

'Down there stands the Dark Warrior – as prophesied by the Seven Sages of the Plain. He waits there with his henchmen, his dark servants.'

Bjarki waved generally at the southern slope below the troll ring.

'He hunted down your wives,' Bjarki said, into a stony silence.

'He and his men slew your children.' The looks from all around him were savage. 'They murdered the Law-Speaker. And our comrades here.'

There was a rumble of raw anger from the circle of fighting folk.

'Now, I say – now, is the time to take our revenge on them!'

The cheers echoed round the summit of the troll-ring hill and beyond. The warriors brandished weapons, shook them fiercely in the air.

'So, let us now go there, and do that.' And Bjarki abruptly plumped down on the soft turf, arranged himself cross-legged, and closed his eyes.

Valtyr came over to stand beside him; put a hand on his shoulder. 'You are resolved to do this, son?' he said. 'You dare to wield Tyrfingr?'

Bjarki nodded, eyes still tight shut.

'And the curse – that the man who wields it shall taste of Death?'

Bjarki opened his eyes and looked up at the old man standing above him, his lean shadow impossibly long in the fading light.

'These are my people,' he said. 'They chose me as their leader, they acclaimed me their king and, whether it is true or not that I am indeed Angantyr's heir, I *accepted* that honour. I *chose* to lead them. So I must use everything in my hand to defeat their foes – *all and any* of the powers at my disposal. In days of old, the king was the servant of his people. And, if the time came, he was fully prepared to sacrifice himself for them. That is what they did for their tribe. That's what my granny did for me. That is the bargain that kings make with those they rule over. They are given honour in life – but must be prepared to sacrifice that life, too.'

Valtyr gripped his shoulder. 'You look like a king; you sound like a king; and now you behave like a king. I am so proud of you, Bjarki. The fisher-boy from little Bago makes his end on a battlefield – as a king.'

'Don't forget,' said Bjarki, and he cracked the smallest of smiles, 'the legend promises victory to the man who wields the Loki Sword in battle. So let us have victory over our foes, whatever the consequences!'

Valtyr nodded sadly. 'I salute you, son. May the Bear guard you!'

Bjarki put the blade across his thighs, closed his eyes and began to hum. The humming was a simple four-note tune, rhythmic, hypnotic. An ancient melody, glowing with familiarity, that vibrated deep in his throat.

–

Bjarki found himself in dreamlike emptiness once more. Not snow fields or thick forest this time but in a velvet realm of absolute blackness. He could see nothing, hear nothing, he felt neither heat nor cold. Nothing.

'Mochta – are you there? It is I, Bjarki Bloodhand. I summon you.'

There was no reply to his words, not even an echo. They sounded muffled, deadened, as if he were speaking into a woollen sack, or talking face down into a pillow. He felt the first chill of a growing apprehension.

'Mother of Bears – are you there? Speak to me. I command it.'

Nothing.

Bjarki found that his heart was beating fast; he had great difficulty breathing, as if he were choking. Had he been tricked by his *gandr*? Had the She–Bear cheated him? He had merrily cut the chain that bound her in the dream world, with barely a second thought. And had she abandoned or forgotten her promise? Did the *gandir* even respect oaths, as men did?

He opened his eyes. And saw Tor and Valtyr and some *Felaki* gathered nearby, watching. Inge, he saw, was stringing a *Felaki* war bow.

'She's not there,' he said to Tor. 'There is nothing there at all.'

'You said you made some sort of pact with the Bear,' said Tor.

'I know what I *said*, sis.' His words came out angrily. 'But *she* does not choose to honour it. She has taken me for a fool and abandoned me.'

'Fuck her – we don't need a *gandr*,' said Tor. 'We'll do this alone.'

'Try again,' said Valtyr. 'Hum the summoning. Go back in there.'

Bjarki closed his eyes. He hummed. He felt the vibration rising from deep in his chest, and let it sing through his body, growing louder, more potent. Then, slowly, he sank back into that pitch-black world once more.

'Mochta – Mother of Bear, come to me. I summon you,' he intoned.

There was no sound except his own dead words in the soft darkness.

He waited, then repeated his words. Still nothing, no sound at all.

He clenched both his hands in frustration and, in the other world, he felt the blade of the Loki Sword through its thick leather sheath. In the black realm, he drew the blade. A flame of pure, shining light that pushed back the dark in all directions. He was in a cave, a huge stony chamber in a mountainside. He could feel the rugged black rock wall all around him, under his haunches, behind his back and above his golden crowned head.

266

'Mochta – Mother of Bears. I summon you, by right of the oath you swore to me. Show yourself, or be known a liar and oath-breaker by all.'

'Who dares to disturb my slumbers?' said a deep, rich voice.

And, by the light of the flaming sword, Bjarki could make out a huge, dark mounded shape a few yards from him. Which shifted a little.

'I dare it,' he said, holding the sword aloft. 'I, Bjarki Blood-hand, son of Hildar, Fire Born and king of the Goths, dare it – and furthermore I demand your aid, *gandr*. I command your obedience with the power of the sacred oath you swore to me – in the name of your only living cub.'

'I am sleeping now. Come back another time,' rumbled the Bear.

'Wake and obey – or I shall cut you in two with this magical blade! I will end you in an instant, *gandr*. I shall slice the paws from your limbs and your head from your body. That shall be the price of your treachery.'

'Very well, man-child. No need to shout at me like a skald. No need for your threats. And put that blinding sword away. I hear you, and I will, naturally, honour my oath to you. Let me crack open my poor eyes first.'

Chapter Twenty-seven

Rage at the heavens

Before Tor's eyes, she saw the very moment when the *gandr* came into her brother's heart. His face, normally a fine, reddish hue, quickly began to grow darker, more purple, his teeth began to chew on themselves, and the muscles of his cheeks writhed like a nest of exposed winter snakes. She could see his huge chest rising and falling under the mail he wore, and he gave the impression of hovering just above the ground on which he sat.

And all the while the drone of his humming filled the air.

'We shall all go down there – together,' she said to the gathered warriors. 'Every man and woman who can run and lift a blade. We shall make our charge upon the Franks – and take our revenge for all the hurts we have suffered at their hands. Furthermore – we shall have *victory*!'

The warriors cheered, and Tor had to hold up a hand to stop them. 'Our most pressing task, however, upon this field of battle is to ward the person of the king. As your brave ancestors, the Royal Companions, always did for Angantyr, so shall we for his heir. Our Fire Born king, filled with the spirit of the Bear, means to strike deep into the heart of their camp and slay their leader. We must ward his flanks and help him in his task.'

She saw the handful of surviving warriors nod and rumble their assent. Valtyr, she saw, had found himself a spear and a shield. The old man looked a little ridiculous, with his skinny white shanks showing beneath his dirty robe, the hem of which was tucked into his belt so he could run more easily, but his lined, one-eyed face was set and resolute.

Inge, too, was now fully girded for battle, with a mail shirt, a sheaf of arrows in a wicker container tied to her waist, and a *Felaki*-style recurved bow held in her left hand. Halvar stood beside her, also with his bow in hand, and a quiver of arrows at his belt, and two other male *Felaki* archers, who were all that had survived the terrible cavalry onslaughts.

'You four archers must remain close to Bjarki,' she said, 'and try to pick off any Black Cloaks who attempt to get in behind him.'

She thought for a moment. 'Stay close – but not too close. He does not know friend from foe when the *gandr*-madness has possessed him.'

She turned to look at her brother, who was now rising effortlessly to his feet. His eyes were wide open, but seemed black as swamp-pitch in the centre, and veined in red around the edge of the white. He was still humming. And the sword – the Loki Sword – was unsheathed in his hand.

This was the first time she had seen its naked steel. It shone as if freshly polished. It might be a blade forged hundreds of years ago, she thought, but it was still a fearsome weapon, with or without any magic.

Every eye in the troll-stone ring was on Bjarki, who had the gleaming sword raised in one hand and the shield aloft in the other. His mouth was working, chewing madly, a creamy froth forming on his lips.

Tor put a hand on Halvar's shoulder.

'We have not always been good comrades,' she said. 'But ward my brother well this day, keep him safe, and I shall be for ever in your debt.'

'I'll watch over him,' the archer said, grinning. 'I'll watch over you, too, girl. And hold you to your word if we both live to see another dawn.'

Before Tor could reply, she heard a bloodcurdling roar behind, and turned to see Bjarki with his helm-crowned head thrown back, screaming rage at the heavens. Then he charged – and all on the hill went with him.

Bjarki leapt over the barricade of mud, sticks, shields and stones in a single bound, and he hurtled down the hill towards the foe. The *Felaki* and his friends were slower getting past the obstacles – but not by much.

They were not much more than a score of fighters but they all streamed down the slope in a tight, howling, pack, heading straight for the Black Cloak camping ground. The *Felaki* screaming: 'Ang-an-tyr… Ang-an-tyr!' as they charged, while Bjarki had fallen silent, and was racing ahead of the pack, with his lofted sword now seeming to glow blood-red in the dying light of day. Tor was roughly in the middle of the swarm, toting shield and spear, with Halvar gliding along on her left flank and Inge close by on the right – and she knew that Valtyr was stumbling along disjointedly on his skinny white legs only a few paces behind her.

Now they were only two hundred yards from the enemy horse lines. And she heard the trumpets of the Black Cloaks sounding the alarm, and saw the first unit of troops, half a *cunei* at least, who had been tonight's sentries, forming up to block their path. These *Scholares* were the best troops in Francia, perhaps in the whole Middle-Realm. And they could not be easily caught napping – even by this most unorthodox of attacks.

A hundred paces away now, and the dismounted Black Cloaks had formed a fine, solid wall, a double line of troopers, forty of them, shields locked, helmeted heads tucked in tight, bristling with steel spear points.

And Bjarki was charging heedlessly towards the centre of them.

Seventy paces away now.

'Archers,' yelled Tor. 'Archers halt. Thin their middle, thin it now.'

She skidded to a stop and was glad to see Halvar and Inge, too, halt beside her; the two *Felaki* bowmen, as well. All panting from the sprint.

They drew out arrows, nocked, pulled back the string and loosed at the solid line of Black Cloaks, aiming for the very centre of the shield wall. One of the *Felaki* shot too long, his shaft sailing high over the heads of the enemy. The other *Felaki* shot wide, his arrow smacking into the shield of the man on the centre-left of the line. But Halvar drew, loosed, and shot true, as did young Inge. Their twin arrows hissed lethally into the centre of the wall, causing a ripple of displacement, as a Frank fell back.

'The centre; target only the very centre of the wall,' yelled Tor.

All four archers plucked up a second arrow, and loosed again.

And struck. Just a shaved heartbeat before Bjarki's huge charging form smashed into the middle of the thick line of dark-clad enemy troops.

The light scatter of arrows did little damage to the Franks – one man killed, perhaps, another wounded in the shoulder – and the experienced troops were quick to coalesce again, closing their ranks instinctively. But the shower of lethal shafts gave them just enough pause for Bjarki to get his hurtling huge body into the middle of the shield wall, bullock left and right, and begin laying about himself madly with the shining Loki Sword.

And whether it was indeed magic, or just a fine blade wielded by an immensely strong, battle-crazed warrior, the Loki Sword seemed to cut through shield, helm and armour, flesh and bone with almost absurd ease.

As Bjarki shoved the Franks backwards with his shield, and sliced and hacked at limbs and faces with his sword, an ever-widening gap was created in the previously tight-knit line of Black Cloaks, and the rest of the *Felaki* blood-warriors piled in behind him, screaming their war cry, opening up the hole the *berserkr* had made in the shield wall, and ripping the formation open. They shredded it, dismembered it, and split it apart.

In half a dozen heartbeats, the shield wall was utterly destroyed, the appalled Black Cloaks reeling back on all sides. Bjarki was still roaring and stamping, hacking and stomping, and slaughtering any man within range of his blade, any man who had the courage to stand before him. The *Felaki* were hard on his heels, howling, shoving the terrified Franks in all directions, their bloody spears flickering out to rip away Christian lives.

Tor's four bowmen, still fifty yards away, loosed two more volleys, and then two more, after which they all ran down eagerly to join the fray.

'Ward the king, guard the heir of Angantyr!' Tor yelled as she ran.

A group of three Black Cloaks on foot saw Tor and her comrades coming at them fast, shouted a challenge, and stood to bar their path. And, while he was *still running* – to Tor's astonishment – Halvar plucked a shaft, nocked and loosed and sunk it into the leading Black Cloak's eye.

Tor took a dizzy, pounding chop on her shield from the second man, threw the sword off its painted leather face and buried her own in the man's belly. He made a whooshing sound like a punctured pig's bladder and collapsed. The third Frank took to his heels – and simply ran away.

Bjarki was running, still, screaming, now slathered in gore, and a dozen *Felaki* were with him, yelling, 'Ang-an-tyr!' over and over again.

It was clear the Rekkr was heading towards the black tent – yes, and there, throwing open the flap and striding out, Tor spotted Brandt – looking rested and, curse him, more handsome than ever, the raven wing of hair flopping over his brow, as if freshly washed. Bjarki howled at him like a frenzied dog, abruptly changed direction, and began to bound towards the dark captain, whirling his red-glistening sword as he charged.

There was a mighty thunder of hooves, an earth-shaking, pounding clatter, and before Bjarki could even get within a dozen yards of Brandt, a score or more black-clad cavalry surged round from behind the black tent and crashed straight into the Fire Born warrior's massive form, bowling him over like a kicked ball of rags, the iron-shod hooves of the horses knocking him this way and that. The Black Cloak riders, thundering over his jerking body, jabbed down hard with their wicked javelins at Bjarki's rolling, thrashing body, plunging their sharp steel into his moving flesh.

They reined in, turned, and rode back over her brother again.

Tor shouted, 'No, no!' And lost sight of her brother in the dust.

A huge Black Cloak officer on foot popped up right in front of Tor and she was obliged to exchange a series of cuts with this snarling foe, his plume nodding like a fighting cock's wattle – before Inge put a yard of arrow through the man's chest from a dozen paces and ended the bout.

When Tor looked again towards the black tent, she saw half a dozen *Felaki* swarming over the riders, leaping up at the men in their saddles, hauling them down to earth, where they savaged them with swords and knives. Other *Felaki* were duelling with the mounted men, lunging up at them with long spears, or cowering beneath hacking sword and the pawing hooves of their well-trained horses. There was no sign of Bjarki at all.

The fight had drawn all the Black Cloaks – scores of them – towards the command tent; they boiled round like wasps from a well slapped hive.

Tor saw Valtyr inside the cloud of foes. The old man stepped nimbly right, hopped left, and skewered a Black Cloak with his spear. A *Felaki* came hurrying to his aid, then another, and Black Cloaks were suddenly all being hurled aside. Yet there were more of them, ever more Franks, every moment there seemed to be a dozen more of the Christians joining the scrum in front of the black tent. Two *Scholares* rushed Tor at the same time, one from either side, and she had to fight for her life, shield going one way, her sword parrying desperately another. An elbow caught her in the side of the face, just under her eye, and she nearly went down. Instead, she rolled under the left-hand man's cut, came up and severed his sword arm with a sweep of her own blade. She got her shield up to stop a crunching blow from his comrade, which did knock her to her knees.

The Frank hammered down, again and again, at her lime-wood protector, sharp splinters of wood flying off, kicked out by the chopping steel, she heard a loud crack and the whole wooden construction split into two parts. She shook the wreckage half-off her forearm, and hurled it at her furious attacker, followed it in, and jabbed her sword under his chin.

He goggled at her in surprise, tried to speak but all that came out was a horrible, bubbling froth. She ignored his pain, shouldering roughly past the dying man, and sprinted towards the tent. She saw *Felaki* falling here and there to Black Cloak blades – all around her friends were dying. There was no cohesion. The *Felaki* were widely scattered, outnumbered. Each one dying as best he could, even as the red daylight died with them.

There were pine torches now alight – dozens of them – lit perhaps by zealous Black Cloak servants. And the squeal of Frankish trumpets called in more and more of the black-clad foe to the cauldron of battle. She could hear screams and howls of combat out in the growing darkness, the foul, oily stench of battle was thick in her nostrils, and the moaning of the wounded soured her belly. Kynwulf was nearby, only a dozen yards away, surrounded by four dismounted Black Cloaks, who all smashed at the grizzled warrior in a brief clashing exchange. The War Chief killed one man, then another. She ran to his side and dispatched a third. Between them they chopped down the last Black Cloak and paused, panting wildly.

She saw the priest, Clovis, a sword limp in his white hand, standing by the entrance to the tent, directing the swarming Franks to surround and cut down the remaining *Felaki*. There were few enough of them left alive.

Where was Bjarki? Where was her big bad Rekkr brother?

She saw Halvar, a dozen yards away, draw and drop a passing Black Cloak rider. She called: 'Kill the priest, Halvar! There, get that bastard!'

She pointed urgently at the entrance to the tent. The stocky archer clearly heard her; and he already had another arrow nocked to his string. He looked in the direction she was pointing, then turned back towards her – a grin lighting his face. He said nothing, drew back the cord and loosed.

She saw the shaft flicking towards her, as she was turning her body to pull out her seax, and felt the arrow whisper past her right shoulder. A horrible, gargling scream erupted from behind her and she turned and saw a Black Cloak, one pace behind, with Halvar's shaft buried in his throat.

Tor lifted a hand in thanks to Halvar and shouted: 'Where's Bjarki?' But the archer merely shook his head, and plucked another arrow from his quiver. There was no sign of her brother anywhere on this bloody, turf-torn hell-scape. He was gone, disappeared – dead, no doubt. That truth struck her like a mule-kick to the heart. The *Felaki* were almost all down. Kynwulf was stumbling about somewhere to her left, exhausted, limping, his face all bloody. Inge stood two yards away, a shaft nocked, aimed at nothing but turf, her small body trembling uncontrollably with her battle terror. They had failed. Bjarki's plan had failed. Her brother was dead. He had wielded the Loki Sword and, as the ancient curse foretold, he had tasted Death.

'Back,' she said. 'Inge, to me – we must get back inside the troll ring!'

Chapter Twenty-eight

'You may not die!'

Bjarki felt as fast as a hunting falcon, as strong as a mountain, lighter than air, blood pulsed through his veins like liquid fire. He heard a voice in his head, a high, harsh, chittering, squeaking voice, the battle voice of his *gandr*, so very different from the deep, oak-hard tones of the She-Bear.

She was calling to him: 'Come then, man-child, you summoned me, and I am here, let us now go down the hill and open up all those juicy meat bags. It's been too long, far too long. Let the slaughter commence.'

He stood straight, taller than a tree, threw back his head, and roared at the dying day. Then, oblivious of his friends and comrades gathered around him, he began to sprint, leaping the nearest troll stone effortlessly, round shield in one hand, naked Loki Sword in the other. He ran eagerly down the grassy slope towards the Frankish encampment, heedless of the pack of twenty screaming *Felaki* warriors all bounding in his wake.

The meat bags were forming up in some kind of barrier in front of him – a shield wall filled with forty mortal men. He looked right into their fearful hearts; he smelled their terror. He howled once, a short, sharp noise, more of a bark, in truth, and threw his body into the line of foes.

He shield-barged one fellow out of his path and then he was inside the wall, punching blade into belly and thigh, jabbing, ripping, slicing, making the sweet juice spray in red rainbows with every beat of his own engorged heart. He took wounds, but paid them no mind, a jab of pain, a counterstrike and a foe lay dead, ripped open by the Loki Sword's *seithr*.

He burst through the far side of the wall and fixed his burning eyes on the campaign tent, a cave of black cloth, the den of his hated enemy. He bounced towards it, growling, snuffling, easily swatting importunate Black Cloaks out of his path, slicing them down, hurling them far away from him. He saw the tall, dark-clad traitor emerge from the tent – once a comrade, now a dirty turncoat – and stare at him, horror in his blue eyes. The slender priest was beside him. He would open them both up, quick-smart, and savour the colour of their guts. Bjarki giggled, sniggered, he wiped the wet blood from his chin with his mailed forearm, and advanced on both men at a brisk run. The tall man, the bad man, the friend-turned foeman, flicked the black hair out his eyes, and opened his mouth to...

A vast pounding and a galloping, then a tidal wave of horseflesh struck the Rekkr and bowled him over, rolling, tumbling, spinning him this way and that. The surging horsemen were over him, all around, their plunging spears pricking and prodding, poking and cutting into his flesh.

He felt the bite of their steel. He felt his blood leaking from a dozen piercings, a dribbling, now an oozing, even a gushing from his skin. He felt an ice blade sink into the meaty haunch of his left leg, and a sliver of steel invade his right shoulder; his big, mailed left arm was pricked, once, twice, the tight iron links torn apart. The stinging spears now tormented him; the hooves knocked him here and there, an iron-shod blow sliced his forehead, cutting deep, and he was blinded by a wash of fluid. The gold helm was knocked from his head and skittered into the forest of fetlocks.

He felt all his power, his warmth, all his red, raw, wondrous joy leaking from his punctured, battered body. He rose, a mighty effort, a heroic feat even; he lifted his blind, bare, bloody head and planted his two feet, striking out indiscriminately at the half-seen whirl of horse and man. He felt the Loki Sword connect, and cut deep, but felt another horse-warrior's spear pierce him through the side, into his belly; then a blow at his right knee, a horse barged him from behind – down he went again.

He was dying, he knew it. He curled into a ball on the torn turf, the cruel blades still biting at his broad back, the hooves still kicking his broken bones. He smelled the bile, shit and piss of war. His own. He could taste stink and rot, filth on his tongue. The taste of Death. He had wielded the Loki Sword and slain his foes, slain so many, but now…

'You may *not* die,' said a dark voice, speaking from inside him. 'I shall not allow it. If you die, I must myself find another man-child. And I do not care to do so. Stand tall, my doughty Fire Born warrior, and stop your childish weeping, cease this pathetic self-pity. Stand up and fight!'

Bjarki felt a dark infusion of raw, feral spirit fill his entire body. Like a draught of rich meaty soup, too hot to drink, but pouring into his empty belly nonetheless. It felt like a vast, expanding bubble of rage, beginning in his scalded gut and growing, growing, until the tips of his toes and fingers were filled with a white heat and power he had never felt before.

He jumped to his feet. He had lost his shield somewhere on the field but the Loki Sword was tightly grasped in his blood-sticky right hand. He pulled the seax from its sheath with his left, and like a blurring wind of destruction he hurled himself at the Black Cloaks, the men on foot and those still a-horse. His arms moved in swift arcs and curves, lines of red death in the darkness. He felt he was flying, soaring; weightless but expanding; filling the battlefield; he possessed the space around him like a bolt of undischarged lightning. A Rekkr's raw potential for carnage unlimited by drab reality.

He battered and sliced at his swarming enemies, roaring, raging, howling, shedding power in all directions, dealing death to all who came in range of his steel. The horsemen skittered away, their mounts spooked, terrified, the men in the saddle sickened or cowed, and Bjarki Bloodhand found himself three yards from the entrance to the tent, the bad man's cloth den, staring at his enemy, his own body a blood-soaked bundle of indomitable will – a glistening blade in each of his gore-clotted hands.

–

Brandt stared at the vast gory apparition crouched before him in the flickering light of the pine torches, and he could scarcely believe his eyes. Darkness had come and with it this vision of hell on earth straight from the pages of the holy book of *Revelation*, this mounded, soggy, crouching beast-man, this diabolical monster, dripping with his own fluids, but still snarling, growling and slavering like a huge, cornered quarry of the hunt.

He found he was mumbling 'Ave Maria' under his breath, over and over, as he drew his own blades, the long and the short, and took a stance.

A movement to his left, that cowardly priest Clovis, turning tail and sprinting away into the safety of darkness. Other human shapes, servants, his troopers, also slipping quietly away. This bloody creature before him had ripped their flesh, crushed their bones and drained all their courage. The Black Cloak captain seemed to be all alone in the night, alone with this thing, this unnatural demon-possessed perversion of the pagan North.

He scanned the torn and bloody field and saw only the dead and dying everywhere; no enemies, but no allies either – just a Black Cloak trooper now crawling towards him, mouthing something, and Brandt saw with disgust that the man had no left leg. Where were his troops? They couldn't *all* have fallen. They must be scattered, pursuing the beaten foe.

He would attend to this matter himself – it was only that big, doltish peasant-boy Bjarki under all the gore and rags and growls, and the fellow had already been wounded a dozen times. He would dispatch this pagan lunatic, and swiftly, cut him down without mercy, then round up all his far-flung *Scholares* and return some decent Christian order to the camp.

Brandt took up the first position, right leg forwards, left foot at an angle; short sword in front, long blade cocked behind to strike or defend.

Bjarki seemed to be slumping, like a blown-up pig's bladder slowly losing its air to a leak. He took a stumbling step forwards, snarled softly.

Brandt struck. He jabbed at the madman's eyes with the short blade in his left hand – an obvious feint – but poor, blundering Bjarki flinched out of the path of this false blow. Brandt pivoted in smoothly, turned and hacked with the long sword, a lightning-fast cut to the side of the foe's head or his neck. And Bjarki, now off balance, staggering, weak from loss of blood, parried with his iron seax, clumsily and too late. The sword-strike deviated from the original path, pushed down by contact with the seax, now angled lower. But it still bit home. The blade did not sever the madman's head at his neck, but it thumped horribly into Bjarki's left shoulder, and Brandt felt it slice through the sodden bearskin, through his torn mail, his linen shirt, and cut into the humped muscles above the arm.

The bellow of pain that Bjarki emitted shook the very earth beneath their feet. This fresh wound, even after so many taken, seemed to give the Rekkr a jolt of renewed strength, and just as Brandt was withdrawing his blade from the wound, in one long agonising slice, the Rekkr struck. Bjarki slashed across his own body with the Loki Sword at the bloody length of shining steel that was even now slipping out of the suck of his shoulder flesh. Tyrfingr crunched straight through Brandt's tempered steel Frankish blade, as if it were no more than a stick of frail kindling.

Brandt looked down in astonishment at the shattered stump of the sword in his right hand. Then up at the *berserkr*, who was now advancing on him like a rumbling mountain avalanche. He got in a half-decent block with his short sword, stopping a vicious seax swipe, and, as a counter blow, he jammed the snapped off sword blade into Bjarki's left side. But nothing could stop the Rekkr's furious onslaught. Brandt just had time to whisper a single word

– *Jesu!* – before Bjarki's whirling, jabbing, filth-encrusted blades caught in his flesh and ripped all the life from his body.

–

Bjarki stared down at the corpse of Brandt lying before him. He swayed slightly, and felt the familiar sudden deflation of spirit, as the *gandr* quit his heart and went back to the Spirit-Realm, the familiar hideous sick, oily sensation in his belly, the emptiness of soul, the scalding shame and partial memory glimpses of the terrible things that he had done when the Beast was in possession of him. Yet this man, this bloody, shattered, partly dismembered fellow, had richly deserved his death. He had pretended friendship to the crew only to betray them to their enemies, and bring down ruin upon them all.

Perhaps there had been some justice here.

Bjarki looked about him in a daze. He could see figures moving around in the darkness, slinking Black Cloaks, maybe a *Felaki* or two, half-illuminated by wavering pine torches that someone had bizarrely lit. None seemed to pose a direct threat to him. He could see old Boden lying in a half-circle of Black Cloak corpses, his sword still clenched in his hands. And another dead *Felaki* over there whose name he was not sure of – Thorfin, it might be. He wondered whether Tor or Valtyr yet lived.

It seemed unlikely. Bjarki could feel his vision fading, a vast black pressing weight on both his shoulders. Perhaps he would be with them all again soon. He shambled away from the torchlit tent, his boot squelching with gore at every stumbling step, the darkness was rising all around him, not just the darkness of night but the blackness at the ending of the world.

He staggered on a few steps, and a few more, one more pace, until he found himself alone, surrounded only by the pitch-black noisy night. Then he summoned up his very last shreds of courage and strength and, raising the bloody Loki Sword high in the air, he called out: 'Odin! Hear me, Great One. See the destruction I have wrought, All-Father, with the powers you granted me. Witness the death of your Fire Born. Now send the Wingèd Ones to carry me from this field up to your Hall of the Slain.'

His knees gave out and he collapsed in a heap on the dark turf.

–

The She-Bear was with him, Bjarki knew that much. She seemed to have somehow removed all his clothes and armour and was licking his body, soothing the many cuts, punctures and slashes with a strong, warm tongue. It hurt a great deal and he felt very cold inside but it was also soothing. He thought he was in her black cave in the Spirit-Realm but he could not open his eyes to see. 'Don't,' he mumbled. 'Don't trouble yourself. No need. The Wingèd Ones will come and make all well again.'

'You're not dead yet, oaf,' said the She-Bear, using the voice of his sister Tor, for some odd reason. 'Rest now and we'll get you out of here.'

He sank gratefully back beneath the smooth, shiny skin of sleep.

He surfaced again to find the starry sky above him. It was still very cold but now he was wrapped in many cloths and blankets. He could hear the whinny of horses nearby, the chink of metal and whispering voices, and someone gave him a sip of mead with something bitter mixed into it.

And he slept again.

Now he was climbing, or being dragged upwards, to be exact. He seemed to be strapped into a kind of sling, a contraption made from a couple of blankets and two spears, and he was being dragged by a pony up a steep and stony incline. He called out: 'Where am I?' And was immediately hushed. He felt a small hand on his mouth and a whisper right in his ear. 'Keep silent, oaf; lie still, we're not out the woods yet.'

Sleep, a long, long sleep, and waking to bright sunlight and sound and movement all around and a mouthful of broth and more of the bitter tasting mead. And then down again into blackness. He was moving again, rocking in his blanket-sling, the soft sound of clopping hooves in his ears.

The dreams came – horrible dreams of pain and fear, the cold sweat-slime covering his whole battered and itching body. He shivered. He felt consumed with flames, then plunged into an icy stream. His old master, the fisherman Thialfi, who had ruled his life when he was growing up on the island of Bago, scolded him, his gnarled finger wagging in his face.

'Good for nothing,' the old man said. 'Useless lump of stupidity.'

He saw the faces of the *Felaki* around him – all of them dead, he knew that now. He saw Gisli, Boden and Thorfin, and the Law-Speaker, too. 'We died for you, Highness,' the Law-Speaker said. His body was absent, only his disembodied head spoke to Bjarki. 'We died so that you could call yourself a king. We sacrificed ourselves for you, Highness.'

The She-Bear was there: 'Do not forget what I have done for you,' she said. 'I gave you strength, I brought you back to life. Do not forget.'

Yoni was beside him now: 'Why Bjarki, why did you kill me? I only wanted to love you. I did love you – yet you killed me.' Bjarki tried to explain but his mouth was sealed shut, like a healed wound, and he could not create a single sound. Yoni's violet eyes bored piteously into his.

'If in doubt, go north,' said his father Hildar. Bjarki could see him standing beside his sling, his gore-slathered body hacked and gashed all over, his left arm half-severed. Were they travelling north – how so?

'You did this to me, you and your sister,' Hildar said, his broken jaw flapping loose. 'Yet I loved you both. That was my crime: to love my children. What is the crime the gods hate the most? Father-slaying. Yes!'

Then darkness and light and colours – and pain, all the way down his spine. His limbs aching, his belly a-fire. His right thigh humming, too.

Images from all the slaughter yards: all the battles he had fought, the gore, the ripping of flesh, the terrible, terrible screaming of his victims.

Valtyr's face looking into his. The old man's face was drawn and pale, his cold hand was lifting up Bjarki's eyelids. Inge was there, too. He heard Tor saying: 'Just leave him alone. He'll either live – or he won't.'

Then he was awake. A high place, the air fresh and cold, despite the sunshine. Mountains. Grass, wildflowers – snowy peaks in the distance.

'Where are we?' whispered Bjarki.

'The Western Harvaths. We've come right through the passes.'

It was Tor, her faced bruised, one eye nearly closed and a rainbow of colours, but it was his sister. Alive. She held out a gently steaming mug.

She supported his head and helped him take a sip: hot ale and honey.

'Where are we going?' Bjarki said, his voice strange in his own ears and thick from lack of use.

'We are heading north, oaf,' she replied. 'We're going home.'

Chapter Twenty-nine

A trail of blood

Tor kept one keen eye on her brother as he stumbled along beside her. It was his first day of walking on his own after two weeks of being dragged, mostly unconscious, over the Harvath Mountains, in a travois rigged up with a thick blanket and two spears, behind an exhausted pony.

It was only mid-morning, they had been marching for not much more than an hour, but already she knew that he needed to rest. She was beginning to regret their decision to slaughter the poor horse and eat its carcass. But the animal had become badly lame on the northern slopes of the Western Harvaths – they had worked it too hard, that was the truth, dragging Bjarki's bulk was no easy task to start with, and they had also laden it with their belongings, too – and the choice had been to stay and hope the miserable creature healed itself after a few days of rest, or to eat well for the first time in many hard-travelling days and proceed on foot.

They were not sure if they were being followed or not. There had definitely been some Black Cloak pursuit in the first few days of their flight but, as they got higher into the hills and further from the River Donau they saw no more of the Franks. Nevertheless, Tor had argued that it was better to be safe than sorry. And that had sealed the animal's fate.

Bjarki had benefitted from some good red meat, too, Tor told herself. He needed something substantial to replace all the blood he had leaked over the rough tracks through the mountains. If they were being followed, it would not have been hard to follow the trail of blood drips and the twin furrows of the travois. So they had made something of a celebration of the animal's demise, feasting round a small bonfire in a small, secluded valley, and telling Bjarki how he had been discovered by Inge, who had stumbled over him in the dark, then hauled up the hill by Tor and Valtyr.

'You went back up to the troll ring?' he said in astonishment.

'It seemed the safest place to go. We lit the skull lamps again, and spent the whole night up there. Kynwulf made it back up there with us; and Oddvin, too. That is all of the *Felaki* who lived. Halvar crept in too over the barricade after midnight. The surviving Black Cloaks – and there weren't that many of them – never even came close to us. They could have slaughtered us. But they didn't. Too tired – or just plain scared.'

'Leaderless, too,' Bjarki muttered. 'How did you get out of there?'

'By tunnelling!' said Valtyr. He had an air of smugness in his tone.

He began to explain. 'When I was digging the pit to cook the oxen the night before the battle I found I had dug so far down that I was scraping solid stone. When I delved further I found that they were the ceiling stones, those great big slabs, remember, that formed the roof of Angantyr's tomb. So when we got you up to the troll ring after the fight, I spent the night digging up one of those slabs. At dawn, we went down into the tomb. Getting you in there was a bit of a trial, but we managed.'

Tor said: 'We spent the whole of the next day in the tomb, and we could hear Franks moving outside on the hillside, talking, searching, but the entrance was hidden by the willow tree and they never found it. Oh, by the way, Brandt's reinforcements arrived. He wasn't lying. Two more fresh *scarae*, we think. So there was nothing to do but run for the hills.'

'They were looking for you, Bjarki,' Valtyr said. 'Frightened you might return to slaughter them all. The Beast-man, they called you...'

'We waited till dusk,' interrupted Tor, 'and then we crept out of the tomb. Inge had managed to find a cavalry pony loose on the hillside, and we made up the travois and headed north into the Harvath Mountains...'

–

They rested by a small stream at noon and ate the last of the cold roasted horse. Bjarki immediately fell asleep after the meal, and Tor was reluctant to wake him, even as the sunny afternoon gently slipped away. With Valtyr, she unwrapped all the bandages and looked at his wounds, which were slowly beginning to heal, although that morning's stroll had opened up the deep cut on his thigh, and he was now bleeding copiously.

'How fares the king?' said Kynwulf. Tor could see slender Oddvin, peering at her round the grizzled old War Chief's shoulder. She clicked her tongue. 'We'll camp here,' she said, turning, allowing no discussion.

So they did. Inge went out into the woods with her bow and killed a pair of hares and a rock dove, and they stewed them all together in a pot with some wild garlic roots for their supper. And in the morning, Valtyr tightly bound up Bjarki's wounds once more and they set off again, with the Rekkr using two spears as walking staves. Even unencumbered – Tor, Valtyr, Inge, Halvar, Kynwulf and Oddvin carried all their heavy bags, boxes and baggage between them – Bjarki was struggling to keep up with them. They were down in the marshy flatlands now, with the mountains far behind them to the south. By mid-morning, they came to a river that Valtyr claimed was the Oder. It had a well-worn, muddy track beside it.

'We are not far from the Amber Road,' he said. 'If we follow this bank north and west, we will come to the Silesian *gord*, in a day or so. There we may be able to find a trading ship to take us all the way home.'

Tor nodded distractedly; she was looking at Bjarki, who while still just about standing upright and leaning heavily on his spears, had his head down, eyes closed, and was swaying like a sapling in a high wind.

'Sit down, oaf, before you fall down.'

Tor walked over to Valtyr. 'We're not being chased by the Black Cloaks,' she said quietly. 'I'm sure of that. There is no hurry. And I think if we go any further we might finish off Bjarki. So, if you want to go, go. Take Inge, if you like. We'll stay here with the big oaf and tend to him.'

Valtyr glanced at Bjarki, who was now slumped on the grass by the river, and snoring softly. He said: 'I think it would be best if we...'

But Tor never heard his words of wisdom. There was a rumble of hooves and two score of horsemen rode out of the woods behind them. Small men on ponies, with leather armour, lances and felt-and-fur hats.

Polans.

-

There was no question of fighting. Nevertheless Tor drew her seax, and Inge had an arrow on the string in an instant. Halvar nocked a shaft too, and Kynwulf and Oddvin, the last of the Companions, took up positions standing over Bjarki's sleeping form. The Polans were shouting in their own language, and Valtyr was saying something urgently back to them.

'Put away your blades, all of you,' he said. 'Let's be very calm.'

The Polans surrounded them, their lances pulled back and poised to strike. Valtyr kept repeating over and over something about the *druzyna* of the Silesian *gord*, Lord Piast, claiming friendship and promising gifts.

Which certainly saved their lives.

The Polans did not molest them; they did not even take away their weapons or riffle through their pile of belongings. Instead, they doubled them up on their mounts, all seven of the company climbing up behind a Polans warrior. Inge – who was looking in amazement from face to face as their captors spoke to each other

– swung up behind a young warrior, and gripped him tight round the waist. Two pack horses bore their bulky baggage without complaint. Bjarki, unconscious, was more of a problem. They soon found a solution: lashing him to the saddle of the largest pony, with a powerful Polans behind keeping him upright as they rode.

Mercifully, the journey did not take long. Valtyr, for once, had been mistaken about where in the Middle-Realm they were, and they rode fast. By nightfall, they were back in the great hall of the *gord*, where Bjarki had been judged by the *druzyna* for the killing of the two Slav assassins.

Bjarki was still out cold, and Tor was worried about him. After they had been ferried across the wide river to the island fortress, they carried him into the great hall and laid him out on a bench at the side of that big space. Twice Tor found herself leaning in close to his face to check that Bjarki was still breathing. She sat beside him, with the five others all in a line on the benches, waiting to be granted an audience with the *druzyna*.

The aristocratic lord of the *gord* was in no hurry to see them, it seemed. But they were given soup, bread, cheese and ale and after they had eaten, they rested contentedly on the benches – grateful to be warm and safe – and watching the ebb and flow of the great hall. The space was busier than the last time they had been here, Tor thought – was that only a few weeks ago? It seemed like a lifetime. Now there seemed to be many more bold young warriors strutting about, too, trying to look tough, along with several well-to-do older merchants and their wives, and all manner of craftsmen, farmers and slaves with thick iron collars round their necks.

As Tor watched, a pair of older women in gaudy red kerchiefs and aprons came out of a curtained-off section of the hall with a tray and went over to the wedge-hearth on the corner where a cauldron hung over coals.

They filled up four clay beakers with hot soup from the cauldron there and went over to the square sacred pillar on the far side of the hall, where they placed a beaker and a thin slice of mutton on a piece of bread in front of each carved face on the plinth, then both women chanted a quick blessing, and one rang a tinkly little handbell – presumably to summon the four gods from the Spirit-Realm to their feast in this one.

Tor was entranced – she had never seen a ritual quite like it. And then found herself rather shocked, as half a dozen noisy hounds, most of them brown, flat-faced brutes, attracted by the little bell, came barrelling over in a pack and wolfed down the bread and meat, one of them knocking over a beaker of hot soup with his snub-nose and lapping up the spilled contents.

'The *druznya* and his honoured guest will see you now,' said a new voice in the Svear tongue, his accent that of a native. And she looked up to see a handsome, long-haired man in fine clothes smiling down at her.

'Who are you?' she said.

'My name is Goran, and I serve Leszko, the Duke of Polans – who is now waiting to meet you. I have already made the acquaintance – twice – of your big sleeping friend there.' He peered at Bjarki, stretched out on the bench, unconscious. 'Now he does not look healthy at all,' he said.

'He needs a good healer – if you have such a thing in this place.'

'We have several skilled healers here,' said Goran. 'I'll ask the duke's personal *lekarz* – a learned man – to take a look at your friend.'

Goran turned away and issued a stream of orders to several slaves and stewards, and a pair of big men with iron collars round their thick necks came and gently lifted an oblivious Bjarki and carried him away.

'Piast the Wise and his honoured guest, my lord, Duke Leszko, invite you to join them in the *druznya*'s private chamber,' said Goran.

So Tor, with one final backwards glance at the door that Bjarki had been carried through, followed Goran to the side of the hall, through a thick leather curtain and into a small cosy room, warmed by a brazier, and filled with a number of tables, chairs and stout three-legged stools.

Two elderly men were sitting side by side, separated by a small table on which were two fine glazed pottery cups and a large jug of something.

Valtyr stepped forwards from their group and bowed low before the very thin white-haired man on the right.

'Lord Piast,' he said, 'what a great honour to see you again!'

Piast gave him a haughty stare down his long nose. He sniffed. 'You Northern vagabonds are back, I see,' he said.

'Indeed,' said Valtyr, 'and bearing fine gifts for your excellency.'

Piast sat up a little straighter as Valtyr rummaged in the large linen sack that he was carrying. Then, to Tor's amazement, he pulled out a splendid war axe from the inside, a fine weapon with a shining double blade and a ridged horn handle embedded with tiny milky pearls. He took a wood casket out of the sack too, and held both items out in his hands.

'If I might approach, your excellency...' Valtyr said. And Piast beckoned him forwards. Valtyr kneeled before the Silesian prince and opened the casket: it was filled to the brim with fat, blood-red rubies.

'A trifling tribute for our munificent host,' said Valtyr, laying them before the *druznya*, whose face was now the very picture of delight.

Piast the Wise took the axe reverentially. 'I heard a rumour that some Svear warriors had found the tomb of Angantyr, king of the Goths – and battled an army of Franks for possession of its treasure – is it true?'

'It is true but, alas, we could not carry all the treasures away with us,' said Valtyr. 'The victory was ours but the field was left to the Franks and their black-cloaked legions – and those same treasures by now will be surely adorning the halls of their Christian king in the city of Aachen. But we managed to carry off a few items – as fitting tribute for a prince.'

Tor looked away. She was a poor liar, and did not wish to spoil Valtyr's game. Her eyes fell on the second man – a little younger, a little larger, a warrior by his bearing. He was not looking at her; he was glaring at Inge, who was beside Tor, and she in turn was staring back at this lord.

'You have brought the fabled Axe of Angantyr as a gift for me!' said Piast the Wise. 'And a casket of his royal jewels. That is generous of you, Far-Traveller – though I have no doubt you expect something in…'

The other lord said something harsh in his own Slav tongue. Then almost angrily snapped something else to his Svear bondsman Goran.

'My lord asks me to translate his words,' the long-haired man said in Norse. 'Just now he asked, "Who are these dirty, raggedy supplicants?"'

'Oh, but where are my manners!' said Piast. 'My lord and master, Leszko, Duke of Polans, ruler of this whole region, allow me to present to you Valtyr Far-Traveller, and Tor Hildarsdottir, and… and their friends.'

Goran translated for his duke.

Leszko grunted something. He pointed a thick forefinger directly at Inge. And Goran said: 'What is your name, girl?'

'Inge,' she whispered. 'My name is Inge.'

There was a brief exchange between Goran and the duke.

'What is you real name?' Goran said.

Inge had to think for a heartbeat. 'My name used to be – Czeslawa.'

The duke said something explosive, loud. And he rose to his feet.

Inge said, tentatively: 'Grandpa? Are… are you my grand-father?'

And, as one, the old warrior and the young maiden rose to their feet and rushed at each other, folding each other into a warm, loving embrace.

Chapter Thirty

'Push the fat bastard overboard!'

Bjarki had always been a fast healer, but perhaps now he was getting old, or his wounds this time had been more severe than ever before, for, even six weeks after the Battle of the Troll Stones, he was still as weak as a newborn kitten and his whole battered body ached almost continually.

The Duke of Polans' healer had shaken his head in sheer disbelief, after closely examining Bjarki from head to toe; then he had washed, stitched, salved and re-bandaged all his various hurts – and confined him to a bed in a room next to the pantry in the *druznya*'s palace for a month.

That had been irksome to Bjarki. Summer was in full bloom outside his tiny shuttered window; in the noisy Silesian *gord*, the markets were thronged with a variety of folk, traders from all over the Middle-Realm who came and did their lucrative business there and ate and drank and made merry, and Bjarki had to lie there and endure the pain of his healing and the isolation of his cot, while listening to their merriment.

He wasn't entirely alone – although the healer protested loudly, he was visited every morning by Inge and Valtyr, who cheerfully gave him the news of the day, and in the evenings by Tor, who was growing increasingly bored and restless herself and wished more than anything to resume the journey home to Norrland.

'I went to that steam-bath place this afternoon, oaf,' she told him one day. 'Didn't like it. All the other women in there stared at me – at my scars and burns – and tittered with each other

293

behind their hands. If I had been armed, I would probably have… Anyway, I thought it was horrible. The smell was bad, too. It was like being inside a giant's sweaty armpit.'

Bjarki just smiled weakly at her but he said nothing.

Kynwulf and Oddvin, both fully armed, had posted themselves outside his door from the very first day, although there seemed to be no danger at all – thanks to Valtyr's lavish gifts – of the Silesians attempting to harm him. After a week or so, Kynwulf came to see him one afternoon.

'Highness,' the old warrior said, 'if you are strong enough, and if it isn't inconvenient, I should humbly like to enquire about your plans…'

'My plans?' said Bjarki stupidly. He had been very deeply asleep when the grizzled old Companion had entered the sick room.

'Yes, sire, what do you plan to do now? We are sworn to serve you, of course, but we – Oddvin and I – would like to know whether you mean to return to the *Felaki* lands, to our village. Because… if not… we both hope to… well, Oddvin and I wish to see if any of our folk still survive.'

'You want to go back there?' With an effort Bjarki dragged himself upright in his bed. He felt something tear, hot blood began to seep, but he ignored it. He summoned all his wits. 'Of course, you wish to go home.'

'With your permission, Highness. Those Franks will not stay in our valley for ever, they will probably have gone back to Francia by now, and there may be some of our people, some of our women and children, a few who escaped, who were not slaughtered by the foe. We left in such a hurry – rightly so, since our first duty is to you, Highness, but we would like to go and see what can be saved. The village has been destroyed before, but we always rebuild. If you chose to rule over us there – us and whoever yet lives – you would be given all the honour due your blood…'

'Kynwulf, you, Oddvin and the rest of the *Felaki* have served me well. I shall be for ever in your debt. But your people have suffered more than enough in service to me. I shall not soon return to that valley and your village. I'm headed to *my* home. So I release you from your vows.'

Kynwulf knelt at his bedside, there were tears running down his withered cheeks. 'Our traditional vow as Companions is until Death and beyond. We can never be released from it – it is our honour, and none of us would choose to live without honour. But… if you will permit us a leave of absence, a few months, perhaps a year or two, Oddvin and I will travel back over the high Harvaths and see what can be salvaged from our burnt-out homeland. We have lived in the *Felaki* village under the troll-ring hill for many generations, and with Odin's blessing, perhaps we may live there again. If you are agreed, if you will permit it, we shall indeed take our leave of you, Highness – but know this: should you ever call us, should you need our help, the *Felaki* will surely answer the call. Until we meet again, heir of Angantyr, king of the Goths. In this life, or the next!'

As the old warrior left the room, and closed the door softly behind him, Bjarki felt something else tear inside him. This time inside his heart.

A few days later, Inge and Valtyr had news to relate. 'The duke is allowing us to use one of his ships to go north,' Valtyr said. 'One of his men, a sea captain, will sail us all the way home. He's in the Austmarr now but has been summoned. It will take him some weeks to get here.'

'That will give you time to rest and heal up before we get home,' said Inge, who'd brought a posy of wildflowers to brighten his chamber.

'You're coming with us?' said Bjarki. 'I thought that now you have discovered you are the granddaughter of a duke, you would be too fancy to live in the backwoods with the likes of us, too dainty for thrall's work.'

He was only half-joking.

'Oh, Tor has already released me from my thrall state,' she said. 'Grandpa insisted; it was a condition of him giving us his ship. And

Tor made Valtyr give me this!' Inge pointed at her neck where a fine necklace of silver and blue gemstones sparked. 'These are called sapphires, Bjarki, are they not beautiful? But I don't want to stay here in this noisy, muggy, treeless place, and I don't want to live in Grandpa's palace in Poznan either. I want to be the fanciest girl in all Norrland. I want to see our boy Garm again. And Grandpa has agreed that I may come stay a while with you and Tor, so long as I have Sambor come along to look after me.'

Sambor – this was Inge's new servant and bodyguard, a solid, short-legged, extremely powerful man, almost spherical in shape, with a bald, egg-smooth head; a man who spoke no Norse or Svear at all and seemed to have very little to say even in his own tongue. Bjarki knew that Tor already disliked and distrusted the big man. Bjarki himself had nothing against the fellow but found his brooding presence a little disconcerting.

'Are you *sure* you don't want to stay with your family?'

'I told you, Bjarki – you *are* my family, you and Tor and Garm.'

–

The ship had duly arrived and Bjarki's month of bed rest was over, and he and Valtyr, Tor, Halvar and Inge had boarded the *knarr* or trading vessel, with Sambor waddling up the gangplank board ahead of his little charge and looking suspiciously about for enemies or potential dangers.

As Bjarki was passing down the centre of the ship to take his place – there would be no need for rowing since the ship had a large blue-and-white striped woollen sail, and plenty of strong Slav crew members, and they were heading downstream, with the strong current, all the way to where the Oder debouched into the Austmarr – he caught his foot on a sea chest and stumbled. He reached out to grab Inge's shoulder to steady himself, gripping her hard – and, in a split instant, Sambor was right up in his face, long knife in hand, growling at him like a mastiff.

Bjarki had been quite taken aback – and he was still so weak that if Sambor *had* intended to knife him it would have been all over in a flash.

It took Inge a good deal of wheedling, in her only half-remembered Polans tongue, to get Sambor to calm down, and put away his dagger.

Valtyr thought the situation was hilarious, and collapsed into a fit of giggles. A little while later, once they had shoved off and waved goodbye to the Silesian *gord* and were spinning downstream, Tor came to sit beside Bjarki and said very quietly to him: 'How about we wait till we get to the open sea, completely out of sight of land, and together we just shove that big fat Slav bastard over the side of the ship?'

In truth, Bjarki slept for most of the week that it took to reach the coast, curled up in the bilges in his now tattered bearskin – Tor had washed all the blood from it and sewn up the worst of the rents, but it was a long way from its former, furry glory. He woke and ate and slept again.

In the evenings, at camp on the riverbank, he and Tor occasionally did some of their old battle practices, slowly rehearsing the usual cuts and blocks of the sword, and sparring gently with shield and spear. But Bjarki soon grew tired and had to sit down. Nevertheless, while he was far away from his former health and fitness, he was, very slowly, growing stronger.

They spent one night drinking deeply, all together with some of the Slav crew, in a shabby little town at the mouth of the Oder called Wolin, and Valtyr told them rather owlishly that they were now in the heartlands of the Wendish tribes, which Bjarki already knew, since he had long been listening to the conversations round him in the ale-house in that tongue.

'On that side of the river lie the lands of the Obodrites,' Valtyr slurred, flapping a hand generally west. 'Remember them? Those were the bastards who attacked the Eastphalians when their backs were turned. Those traitors; those *fuckers*… ensured that Widukind lost half his army.'

'We were there, Valtyr,' said Bjarki soothingly. He rarely saw the old man this drunk. But it was not unknown, and their journey had been a particularly brutal one. So many good friends had perished along the way.

From a certain perspective it was Valtyr's fault so many had died. From another viewpoint, Bjarki himself was responsible for a good deal of the carnage among their friends – most of his loyal *Felaki* followers were dead. And he blamed himself for it. He had insisted on staying on at the troll-stone ring to fight the Black Cloaks. He could easily have fled.

But what would have happened to the *Felaki* tribe if he had run away? Brandt would not have spared them – would he? No, they'd all have been slaughtered by the Franks either way. And Valtyr's liquid answer to the guilt he was feeling suddenly seemed like a more sensible option than before. So he drained his full cup and poured himself another.

He remembered then something Kynwulf had said to him on the eve of the battle: '"Fear not Death, for the hour of your doom is set by the Fate-Spinners and there is no escaping it." We all live or die, according to our fates. All we can do is die well!' And many of the *Felaki* had done.

It did not make him feel all that much better. But it helped a little.

'And Rerik – you were in Rerik, weren't you?' Valtyr stared up at Bjarki blearily. 'If you sailed west for two days you – *hic* – you would reach Rerik. You could go and – *hic* – see your friends... those *fuckers*!

'Alternativ... alternatively, you could sail east for three or four days and you would be back at Truso. With the greedy amber-selling *fuckers*! Greedy merchant fuckers. And that great big *fucker* whatsisname – Asa!'

Valtyr considered this knowledge for a moment, sloshing more ale inaccurately into his cup. Bjarki figured that either he or, more likely Sambor, would have to carry the old man back to the ship in a little while.

'What was that you father used to say – Bjarki Bloodhand, pay attention, I am ask… I'm asking something. What di' your father say?'

Bjarki frowned at the drink-sodden old fool. Then, he remembered.

'Old Hildar used to say: when in doubt, go north! It was his creed, you might say. When in doubt, go north. He said it to me several times.'

'Thass… that's a good… creed. We should do that. Go north!'

–

The duke's shipmaster had agreed to take them to Gavle – the small port on the eastern coast of Svealand that was only half a day's walk south from Bearstead, their home – but, as they slid through the narrow jaws of the inlet that opened out into a wide, placid bay, with the ship quays in its gullet, Bjarki could not but help feel trepidation. He and Tor were outlaws – so decreed by Starki, new Jarl of Norrland, only a few months ago.

They could be killed outright, by anyone, without penalty – yet it seemed unlikely that anyone would rush to tangle with Bjarki, imposing as he was, even only half-healed, and Tor, who was armed to the teeth, as usual, and Sambor, glowering at all the unfamiliar sights like a cave troll.

With the ship safely moored at a jetty, and disembarking down the gangplank, Bjarki could see the jarl's hall, the largest building in the settlement, and the smoke of hearth fires seeping from the wind-eyes at the nearest gable end. Beyond the hall was the forest, an endless sea of dark pine. There were a few warriors slouching around in the town, and some trappers in from the woods to trade their furs, a few thralls humping cargo in the quays. But no one seemed to pay the new arrivals any mind.

'We could avoid this whole matter and just go home,' said Bjarki.

'No,' Tor replied, hitching her heavy pack higher up her back. 'We must face it – grasp this nettle. Else we'll never be able to sleep sound.'

Bidding farewell to the shipmaster, and thanking him, the six of them began to walk towards the jarl's hall on the mud-slick pine planks that made up the only street of Gavle, Tor taking the lead, then Bjarki, Inge, Halvar, Sambor, and Valtyr bringing up the rear, leaning on a staff.

As they approached the hall, they began to be noticed by the people they passed. There were now whispers: '...That's the redhead who slew Hafnar the Silent, cut his head clean off, when he tried to violate her...'

Halvar was back in his home town, and from time to time he greeted people he knew in the street. 'Any free man or woman of Gavle has the right to enter the great hall,' he said, 'and demand an audience with the jarl. There is nothing they can do to stop you walking in there.' Bjarki was uneasy in this – he felt weak and unprepared for a conflict. But Tor was perfectly calm and confident. 'Then that's what we'll do,' she said.

The lone guard on the door of the hall, a young fellow with a sad, wispy blond moustache, took one look at the heavily armed travellers, and darted inside to announce them. So when Tor pushed back the leather curtain that kept out draughts, and stepped inside to the smoky interior, every eye in the place was already on her. And Bjarki, Inge, Halvar, Sambor and Valtyr shuffled in behind her.

It was a good-sized building as befitted a great jarl, the elderly Svear monarch's representative in this northernmost part of his realm. The hall had a traditional dais at the northern end where the young jarl, Starki, was sitting with his counsellors. They had been discussing great affairs of state, no doubt, and drinking from horns set in stands on the long table in front of them. Now all of them were staring at the new arrivals.

The young fellow with the wispy moustaches came out from a back room of the hall with half a dozen sleepy-looking warriors behind him, and they too gawped at the newcomers. But no one made a hostile move.

There were a few benches and tables in the body of the hall, on either side of the long central hearth, but they were largely empty. A few female thralls were moving about, some carrying bundles of goods. A pretty woman in a blue embroidered dress sat at a loom in the far corner, working the clacking machinery. Five warriors were gathered on the rush-strewn floor beyond the hearth throwing knucklebones on a blanket. They looked up curiously at the six people who had entered the hall.

It was the middle of the afternoon, and no great feast was taking place, just the jarl and his household going about their normal business.

As Tor and the others walked further into the hall, Jarl Starki eyed them from his seat, made a vague gesture of welcome, and said: 'Who are you, strangers? Name yourselves if you now seek an audience with your jarl.'

'I know at least one of them,' said a voice, and a figure stepped from the shadows at the back of the hall. 'That is Tor Hildarsdottir – she is the one who murdered my father. I guess the big one is her brother Bjarki.'

A flat silence fell over the whole space like a curse at these words. The thralls gawped. The knucklebone players slowly stood up. The older drinkers on the dais put their horns into the silver stands in front of them.

The man who had spoken was Rorik, but a different Rorik from the amused stripling who had so admired her pigs at Bearstead. He was far better dressed now: a fine green silk tunic trimmed with sable, and a rich red cloak, leather lined, clasped with gold, which fell to his ankles. He had a good sword at his waist, too, with silver gleaming at the hilt. And a fine leather pouch. He was a substantial man, then, Tor thought. No longer a boy. The death of a parent sometimes made adults of children.

'You are the outlaws of Bearstead?' said Jarl Starki, surprise in his voice. 'What are you doing *here*? Have you come to pay for your crime? Do you welcome the sentence of death I've passed? What do you want?'

'We have come for justice,' said Tor.

'That is the same thing,' said Rorik. 'You people are vile murderers – you attacked and killed my poor father – and you deserve to die.'

'You, Starki – you are the new jarl, yes?' said Tor. 'And the jarl is the representative of the king in Uppsala. You stand in the king's place.'

'I do,' said Starki. He looked confused more than anything else. Not fearful, not angry. 'But what would a woman know of jarls and kings?'

The five dice-playing warriors had come forwards and were fingering their hilts, unsure whether to draw. The warriors at the back of the hall had spears out, as if to surround the newcomers.

Sambor growled at them all.

'I know a king is honour-bound to dispense fair justice and protect his people,' said Tor. 'Or he is no rightful king. His local representative – the jarl – therefore must be similarly bound.'

'You say Harald Fox-Beard is no rightful king?' Starki frowned.

'No. We stand here before *you* demanding justice. All we ask is that you let us speak, and then you may pass judgement in the king's name.'

Starki sat back in his chair. 'Speak then, woman. Say your piece. But be in no doubt that I may still have you all hanged for your crimes.'

Tor strode towards the table. 'First there's a matter which I wish to quickly resolve,' she said. There was a general uneasy stirring among all the surrounding *hird* warriors. But Starki lifted one hand to calm them all.

Tor reached into her jerkin and pulled out a fist-sized leather bag, which she slammed on the table in front of Starki. It made a metallic chinking noise, and as the untied sack hit the wood a few bright coins spilled out.

'This is tribute,' she said. 'That is five marks of good silver, given freely to you, jarl, as payment from a free steading-holder in your lands.'

The jarl's eyes widened, then fixed on the coins: Frankish *deniers*.

'Your champion, the captain of your *hird*, a man called Hafnar the Silent, came to my steading in the early spring,' said Tor. 'He came well armed and with five of his henchmen and he demanded money from me. He asked for five marks in silver as tribute – and he demanded it in your name. But I did not possess that sum then and, furthermore, I felt that the man was attempting to cheat me. I had, after all, paid your late father Viggo the White a large sum in exchange for permission to build my hall at Bearstead. I sent this Hafnar away with a flea in his ear. I insulted him. Which I now regret. But insult was given and he and his men crept back to my steading in the dawn to try and kill me. Instead, I killed him.'

Jarl Starki frowned down at her. 'You admit the killing, then.'

'I do. But I do not count that as a wrongful killing. He attacked my home. I still do not know if Hafnar the Silent was speaking with your voice or not – I suspect not. Either way, jarl, I offer the sum he demanded to you, today, freely and without any reservation or condition,' Tor said, 'so that you may understand that I wish to live in peace and amity with you, in your northern fiefdom, under your lawful authority. But also so that whatever happens now, no one may say that I do not pay my debts.'

'You have made a good beginning to your plea, Tor Hildarsdottir,' said Starki, 'but there is still the matter of Hafnar's murder to unpick.'

His eyes kept returning to the spilled sack of coins on the table. One of his older, heavily bearded counsellors reached forwards to pick up one of the coins, but before he could touch it, Starki slapped his hand away.

'This evil woman slew my father,' grated Rorik, eyes sparkling with fury. 'Words cannot change that. And I shall have my vengeance on her.'

'And I will offer you a chance to take your vengeance,' said Tor. 'But there is another way, too, to settle this matter. I will offer you *weregild* for your father, a fair price to be determined by the jarl. I killed Hafnar – I admit it – and I must take the blame. But my brother Bjarki was not there at the time. Neither will I allow anyone else to be punished for what I did. I take responsibility for his death. Now you must choose, Rorik, which would you have – vengeance or a payment for your grief?'

'Hold fast,' said the jarl. 'You say Hafnar attacked you at your steading, after claiming he was collecting tribute in my name. This is not the tale I was told by you Rorik Hafnarsson. Your story was quite different.'

'She lies,' said Rorik, throwing up his chin and putting his hand on his silver hilt. 'My father and I and some of the other *hird* men were lost in the northern forest after a long hunting trip, and we came to a remote steading seeking help. And before we knew it, this brutal woman and her fellow criminals were shooting arrows at us from the steading's outbuildings. Their warriors were everywhere. We were driven off by their ferocity but Hafnar, brave Hafnar fell and Arnulf, his friend, too, was slain by these cowardly murderers. On my oath as your *hird* captain, I hereby swear to this truth.'

'Why would we do something like that?' said Tor. 'Why would we brutally attack some poor lost travellers in the forest? Why?'

'For the silver in my father's purse,' said Rorik. 'He was a rich man.' Too late, Tor remembered that they had indeed taken the purses from the two dead men. The spoils of war, she had called it at the time.

'You lie, Rorik. Your father and his men attacked us first.'

'Jarl Starki – I appeal to you. Who will you believe – me, your oath-sworn *hird* captain; or this unnatural mannish girl, who admits she is a killer. I beseech you, jarl, have them bound and I'll execute your justice.'

'Ah…' said Starki.

'My father served you well,' said Rorik. 'And I have served you, too, Jarl Starki. Is this how you repay my father's loyalty – and my own?'

Starki looked very troubled, Tor thought; the young jarl was being pulled one way by loyalty to his own people, and another by a strong sense of what was just and fair. It was the time to make her final move.

'It does not matter who you believe is telling the truth, Jarl Starki,' she said. And the lord of Norrland now gazed at her in astonishment.

'I killed his father Hafnar the Silent – I make no denial of this. He attacked me and I killed him. Rorik, son of Hafnar, has sworn vengeance in public against us for the slaying of his father. He declared a blood feud again us. We *must* fight. We *must* allow the gods to determine our fates.'

The silence in the hall was total; not a cough, not a rustle of cloth.

'So I challenge you to a *holmgang*, Rorik Hafnarsson – with the ghost of your father watching – and may the gods of battle decide our fate. Odin hates a liar – the All-Father will judge who lives and who dies. In the hazel square, you may try to take your vengeance. Do you accept?

Tor stared into Rorik's eyes as she said the words. And saw his fear.

Chapter Thirty-one

Too angry to breathe

A sad surprise greeted them when they finally returned to Bearstead as the last rays of the sun were filling the western sky with a rosy wash. The corpse of Ulli, their old friend, was hanging from the limb of a pine tree just outside the hall's bare courtyard. He had been dangling there for many weeks by the look of it, probably since they'd fled from Bearstead.

Birds had got at his eyes and lips and something large had eaten one of his legs. Tor hoped that it had not been Garm who had consumed part of their friend. But despite these depredations, the rope around his neck had been stout, and the rotting cadaver still swung gently in the breeze.

Tor stood as close as she could bear and looked up at his swollen, greenish-black face. He was scarcely recognisable as the man who had worked, lived and slept beside them at Bearstead for so many months. It looked as if he had been disembowelled too, by a sword or a seax, before he was hanged, which she supposed would have made his end quicker.

'Rorik did this,' said Bjarki, looking up at the body. 'He could not get his hands on us, so he took his revenge on our poor dear friend.'

Tor said nothing. She was so angry she could barely breathe.

'Still, you will pay him out handsomely for this tomorrow,' he said.

The *holmgang* was to take place the next day at noon on the strand beside the river that flowed through Gavle. Rorik had had no choice – if he wished to keep his honour. He had grudgingly agreed the time and the place and the choice of weapons, axe and then sword, with two shields each. Jarl Starki's men were the marshals who would mark out the square and make sure there was no cheating, no hidden knives in boots or belts.

'I'm going to make it a slow death,' Tor hissed, through her teeth, 'very, very slow. Or I might cripple him, blind him – then let him live.'

Bjarki shuddered. He knew she could do it. Indeed, she *would* do it.

He was hungry, he realised, and wondered if Inge had managed to get the cold hearth fire started. They had purchased a good deal of fresh food, including half a pig, in Gavle's market before they left to walk the six miles home, and some sacks of good strong ale, too. Money was not likely to be a problem for them any time soon. Perhaps not ever again.

Before they had left the tomb of Angantyr, Valtyr had packed several stout bags and boxes with coins, jewels and other treasures. They had had a whole night in the tomb to choose the best of them, and the easiest to transport. What the old man had said to Piast the Wise had been indeed partly true. They had not been able to take the whole hoard, and doubtless the Franks had found the entrance eventually. But they had left the troll-ring hill with a considerable fortune in coin and bullion and jewels and other precious materials. And Valtyr was prepared to hand almost all the treasure to Bjarki and Tor – in exchange for only one item.

The Loki Sword.

Bjarki had flatly refused. 'That sword is mine,' he said. But Valtyr had set his mind to persuading him on the long journey home, nibbling at his resolve, which was weak as his battered body, wheedling mercilessly.

'Think what the Loki Sword could mean to the Saxons,' he said, often. 'Think how many Northern lives the blade could save. Think how grateful Widukind would be. The Loki Sword could transform the whole course of the Saxon war in our favour.'

Finally, one dawn, as the coast of Svearland was coming into view, Bjarki found he had had enough.

He had taken the sheathed Loki Sword out of its woollen wrappings and handed it over to Valtyr. 'Just promise me, old man, that you will never mention this old sword or Widukind or the Saxon struggle again.'

Valtyr had remained behind in Gavle after the successful audience with the jarl, waving them off when Bjarki, Tor, Inge and Sambor began to walk home. Halvar had stayed with him. The archer had a chestful of silver coin and jewels under one strong arm, and said that he planned to have a drink or two and then look up a young widow of his acquaintance in Gavle. 'You shall always have a place with us at Bearstead,' Tor said.

Valtyr told Bjarki he wanted to speak to a horse-dealer and make arrangements for his journey south, all the way south to the Dane-Mark, where he would present Widukind with the magical blade. Bjarki scowled at the old man for breaking his word so soon, but made no complaint. Valtyr had promised he would remain in Gavle for the *holmgang*, to cheer Tor's victory. 'There can be no doubt about the outcome,' he said.

–

Before she bedded down in the musty smelling hall at Bearstead, feeling oddly uncomfortable to be home at long last, Tor went out for a walk in the fringes of the woods near the steading. She was looking for Garm. She returned at moonrise, tired, blank-faced and utterly miserable.

'Are you worried about the *holmgang* tomorrow?' Bjarki asked her.

'That? No, not at all. I haven't even thought about it. He is not much more than a beardless child. I could slaughter him with one hand tied.'

'You don't want to be too confident, Tor. That's very dangerous.'

'Do you really think he could beat me, oaf?'

Bjarki thought about it for a moment. 'No. I don't. But be careful.'

'I will.'

'So what is it then?' Bjarki peered into her pale, drawn features.

She did not reply for a while. Then, unexpectedly, she said: 'Do you think that wild animals can ever feel love?'

Bjarki rocked back on his stool, very surprised by her question. 'Love?' he said. 'Animals?'

'We love them. Do they love us back? Or are we just food-givers?'

Before he could answer that tricky question the door to the hall burst open and Valtyr stepped into the room. He was grinning like a monkey.

'Do you want some good news?' he said.

Bjarki nodded and shoved a stool towards him with his foot.

'Sit down and tell us your good news,' he said. 'There's some roast pork left, and some greens, too, if you want them. Sit here by the hearth!'

Valtyr reached out and stole the large ale cup from Bjarki's hand. Then he drained the contents in one huge, gulping swallow.

'Come on, spit it out,' said Tor.

Valtyr smacked his lips. 'Good ale,' he said. 'Got any more?'

Tor just glared at him.

'All right,' the old man said. 'The good news is this…' He pretended to cough, and whispered 'Dry… throat… can't…'

Bjarki impatiently slopped out some ale and went to find a fresh cup.

Tor got up and said menacingly: 'I'm going to count to three…'

Valtyr said quickly: 'Rorik has fled. He stole that five marks in Frankish *denier* from the jarl's coffers – his own *hird* men were charged with guarding it – he also stole one of the jarl's best horses, and fled to no-one-knows-where. There'll be no *holmgang;* you don't need to fight!'

Valtyr's news was greeted by Tor with a long, stony silence. Bjarki returned and sat down beside her, and filled his own cup from the ale jug.

'Did you not hear me?' said Valtyr. 'Rorik has proved himself a *nithing*. You have your victory. And you need not risk your life. The jarl sends his congratulations and asks if you would pay him a visit tomorrow, anyway. He is minded to offer you the now vacant post of captain of his *hird*!'

Valtyr looked between his two silent friends, and over at Inge who was approaching and bringing him a steaming platter, heaped with food.

'What? What is the matter with you all?'

'I *wanted* to fight him,' said Tor. 'He killed our Ulli. I intended to slaughter the bastard. I wanted to rip him from gizzard to gullet and back again. Now, if I want that joy, I must track him to the end of the world.'

'Well, I think it's good news,' said Valtyr, a little sulkily. 'And I think we should celebrate your victory anyway. Pass over that ale jug!'

Epilogue

A debt redeemed

They did celebrate, at least Valtyr did, and Bjarki joined him for a while, drinking cup for cup. But Tor was strangely out of sorts and went to bed early, and Inge and Sambor followed her example soon afterwards and retired into the darkness at the back of the hall, where Inge kept her bed.

Bjarki wrapped himself in his tattered bearskin, and bedded down beside the banked coals of the hearth. Valtyr was telling a long story, a tale of gods and heroes, of battles and bloodshed, when Bjarki fell asleep.

He awoke in the half-light of dawn, with a painfully full bladder, and stumbled out of the hall to the latrine trench by the empty pigs' enclosure.

With an indecent amount of pleasure, he was releasing his usual thick stream, when a deep voice spoke to him from within his own heart.

'Can you hear me, man-child? Can you hear my voice?'

'I hear you,' Bjarki said. He finished his piss and tucked himself away. 'What do you want with me, Mochta? There is no battle to fight.'

'Not for you, perhaps,' said the She-Bear.

'Then why are you speaking to me, *gandr*?'

'I saved you, do you remember that? I saved you from the black-garbed horsemen. When you were dead, I pulled you back to the fight.'

'I remember. And I thank you. You kept your solemn oath.'

'I don't want – or need – your feeble words of thanks, man-child.'

'What do you want then?'

'I want you to recognise your debt to me. I saved you, plucked you from the sharp claws of Death. I wish you to acknowledge that truth.'

'I freed you from the chain. You made an oath to me – you promised to give me your strength and ferocity in battle when I demanded it.'

'And I did. I gave you my strength. And more. Much more. When you were dead, I gave you life again. Do you not acknowledge *that* gift?'

'I do, *gandr*. I do and, as I say, I am grateful. I am in your debt.'

'I am glad that you should say that, man-child.'

'Why?'

'I want you to do something for me. To redeem your debt to me.'

No one else was awake in the hall. Valtyr was snoring like a hero, the big ale jug cuddled in his left arm, a rivulet of drool spilling from his open mouth. Bjarki found his boots, and a cleanish tunic, and put them on, and clasped his ragged bearskin cloak around his shoulders. The day was already warm, although it was just past dawn, and the thick fur was a little too heavy for a fine summer's day – but he felt it was appropriate.

He slung on his seax and found a spear for a staff since his half-healed thigh was still stiff and painful. He chewed a crust of bread and a piece of the pale hard cheese that they had bought in Gavle, and washed it down with a swig of ale from one of last night's half-full cups. Before he walked out of the door, he broke a large chunk off the round of cheese and stowed it safely in his belt-pouch.

'Where am I going?' he asked, as he stepped out into the sunlight.

'I will guide your feet,' his *gandr* said. 'Trust me.'

Bjarki walked for most of the morning. It was a beautiful day in high summer and the forest around him was alive with the calls of birds and the furtive scurry of squirrels. He felt impossibly light of heart to be alone and walking easily, surrounded by all the sweet sounds and familiar smells of the Norrland pine forest. He felt that he was truly home at last.

But, of course, he was not truly alone.

'Where are you taking me?' he asked the dark occupant of his heart.

'West, man-child, towards the mountains. Keep the sun on your left.'

They walked a little while longer, and Bjarki began to see the signs of recent human activity. The trees had been cleared in large sections of the virgin forest and a road, a wide, muddy track, had been cut through the wilderness, with the signs of drag marks and hooves where the felled timber had been hauled away by heavy ox teams. He saw the remains of a campfire, and the remains of a butchered deer, hung in a tree. Evidently someone had been hunting successfully in this part of the forest recently.

'Hurry, man-child, for he is growing very weak now!'

Bjarki broke into a jog, and with the increase in pace, his wounded thigh began to pain him more. But he endured it and trotted onwards.

'Hurry!' the *gandr* said.

They came to a clearing in the forest. A dozen trees had been cut down and dragged away and in the centre of the space was the circular mouth of a wide black hole. Bjarki approached it with some trepidation.

He stood in the lip and peered inside. It was a hunter's trap – a deep dark pit, deeper than a tall man, once covered with cut foliage, to disguise it, and there was something large and black at the bottom. It moved a little. Then it mewled, as if in great pain and sorrow.

Bjarki said wonderingly: 'Garm? Is that really you, boy?'

The bear at the bottom of the pit looked up at the sound of his voice. His triangular face was lean, the eyes glowing red-yellow in the darkness.

The young bear gave a sort of woofing cough, a low, feeble sound.

A new voice sounded in Bjarki's head. It whispered: '*Help me!*'

So, as carefully as he could, Bjarki got on his belly and lowered himself over the edge and down into the pit. There was not a great deal of room in there with a huge young bear, but the animal seemed pleased to see him, excited even, licking his face, lovingly pressing its furry body against the human's. Bjarki stroked Garm's back, feeling his terrible thinness, the sagging looseness of his fur and the big, hard bones easily detectable beneath. There was something wrong with his right back leg, Bjarki felt, it was grossly swollen and there was an odd lump where the limb met the pelvis. Dislocated by the fall, he thought. He wondered how long Garm had been alone in this dark chasm – a month? Perhaps two. In constant pain, starving, crying for help that never came. The bear seemed to have no fat on his body at all, as if he'd emerged from his winter sleep.

The floor of the pit was marshy and wet under his boots, and he could make out deep scratch marks, furrows, in the soft earth of the wall.

'We'll get you out of here, boy,' he said, stroking the animal's soft muzzle. He reached into his pouch and pulled out the lump of cheese. As he fed it piece by piece to the young bear, he could see, even in the dim light, streaks of grey in the black fur of his face. 'But I don't know if I can lift you, Garm. I don't think I can get you up to the top on my own.'

'You do not have to do it *on your own*,' said the deep, dark voice.

Bjarki nodded. 'Give me enough strength to get your child out of the pit, *gandr*, and carry him back to Bearstead,' he said. 'That's all I need.'

Then he added: 'And fear not, Mother of Bears, your cub shall live. When he's safely home, I know that Tor will take very good care of him.'

'I shall not forget this,' said the *gandr*. 'Your gift of life to my child.'

And Bjarki simply nodded, closed his eyes, and began to hum.

Historical Note

The idea for Valtyr's rousing campfire tale of the battle between the Goths and the Huns – as well as large chunks of the plot of *The Loki Sword* – came from reading an essay by Christopher Tolkien (son of J. R. R. and a fine Norse scholar in his own right) in the University College London *Saga-Book of the Viking Society* (Vol. XIV, 1953–57).

This legendary battle is recounted in the *Hervarar Saga*, one of the oldest pieces of heroic poetry in the Norse language, according to Tolkien, which tells of how Hlodr (Hlod in my novel), the bastard son of King Heidrekr by his Hunnish mistress, started a war to recover his Gothic inheritance from his half-brother Angantyr. At a great battle, probably somewhere on the Hungarian plain, there was colossal carnage so that 'the rivers were choked and rose from their beds and the valleys were filled with dead men and horses' and Angantyr slew Hlodr with his father's blade Tyrfingr.

No one is sure *when* this battle took place – sometime between the fourth and fifth centuries AD, and most likely after the death of Attila in 453, since the great Hun warlord is not mentioned in the poem – nor *where* exactly it happened. Scholars have suggested a bewildering variety of sites stretching from Orleans to Kiev but the poem says it took place in the shadow of the Harvath Mountains – which Tolkien says are the Carpathian range that curls around the north and east of the Hungarian plain. The poem also references a 'holy grave' of an ancient Goth king, which I appropriated as the tomb of Angantyr. The troll circle on a hill is purely a figment of my imagination.

Because historians are unsure about *any* facts surrounding this famous battle, it exists like so many other Dark Age heroes and conflicts in the vague, fuzzy gap between myth and history. And thus gave me the freedom to invent my own version of the legend, tailored to the needs of my novel. Likewise, the tale of the god Loki and the Dwarf-Master and the giant bird Vithnofnir is my own, although Vithnofnir, a cockerel that sits atop the World Tree, is an established character in the mythology.

It would be absurd to compare myself to the immortal J. R. R. Tolkien, yet it would be equally silly to pretend that I have not been influenced by his superb works. I loved reading *Lord of the Rings* and *The Hobbit* when I was young, and more recently I have watched and rewatched the six Hollywood movies. The storytelling, the sweep of the action, the impossibly brave heroes and despicable villains, have all coloured my novels in one form or another for many years. But this time I took a leaf straight from J. R. R. Tolkien's tomes and pilfered the Norse legends directly, mixed them up, added my two heroes and turned them into my own original epic saga.

I further combined these mythical Norse elements with fragments of real history, since this novel is designed to sit in the historical fiction shelves of a bookshop, including the Amber Road, a millennia-old trade route for fossilised pine resin, which ran and still runs from the coast of the Baltic to the Mediterranean, and the friction between Charlemagne's Franks and the Avar Khaganate beyond the bend of the mighty Danube (Donau). Carnuntum, too, near Vienna, remained a thriving market long after the Romans and their galleys had left. The *Wave Serpent* is modelled on several Norse vessels preserved in modern facilities, including the incredible Gokstad ship in the Viking Ship Museum in Oslo, the pictures of which I have drooled over online but which I have not yet had the chance to see in the flesh.

The rebellion by Hrodgaud, Duke of Friuli, in the spring of 776, was a disaster. Charlemagne (Karolus in my novels) was forewarned of the rising, crossed the Alps and swiftly crushed the Lombard forces. By Easter, Charlemagne had installed a new

Frankish duke to rule the region. There is no evidence that the Amber Road was used to bring funds down to the rebels from the North, although it seemed plausible to me.

This cocktail of 'real' Norse mythology, genuine history and imagination led to the birth of *The Loki Sword*. And, to be honest, I'm rather proud of my confection. I can only hope that you've enjoyed reading it as much as I've enjoyed researching it.

Acknowledgements

There are many people that I would like to thank for their help in creating *The Loki Sword*, apart from the shades of J. R. R. and Christopher Tolkien. My editor Craig Lye at Canelo has been brilliant at his job in keeping my story on the straight and narrow, as has his excellent copy-editor Miranda Ward. My agent Ian Drury, and the rest of the gang at Sheil Land Associates, have also been massively helpful, with Ian offering his sage advice from time to time, as well as tireless encouragement. Lastly, I'd like to thank my darling wife, Mary, who has kept the show on the road in our household, marshalling the kids, running several small businesses, and keeping our lives ticking over smoothly. She has given me the time and space to bang away at my computer in the garden-office coming up with new sagas for the twenty-first century.

Angus Donald
Tonbridge, May 2022